ON OTHER SHORES

ON OTHER SHORES

NELSON MCKEEBY

4 Horsemen
Publications, Inc.

Published By: 4 Horsemen Publications, Inc.

4 Horsemen Publications, Inc.
PO Box 417
Sylva, NC 28779
4horsemenpublications.com
info@4horsemenpublications.com

Cover & Illustration by CD Corrigan
Typesetting by Autumn Skye
Edited by Charles Miano

Library of Congress Control Number: 2023946708

Paperback ISBN-13: 979-8-8232-0335-7
Hardcover ISBN-13: 979-8-8232-0338-8
Audiobook ISBN-13: 979-8-8232-0336-4
Ebook ISBN-13: 979-8-8232-0337-1

Dedication

For Janis and Steve, who raised me,
and for my Pumpkin, who keeps the cats happy.

V5

Contents

Chapter I

The Gelding Rack

The Dominar of Cycus met his Chief Justicar, Abrams Taffez, outside his dungeon's torture chamber. The Justicar was gray, thin as a dockside waif, showing the effects of the cancer that was eating his insides, the exact opposite of his Dominar. He had two insulated wooden mugs filled with amber Jalosie tea, one of which he handed to his Dominar. The Dominar took the hot beverage, drinking it deep, savoring the expensive, rare tea's soft and complex flavors. It was a shock to his tired system; he took down the balance of the liquid in a second deep draw with satisfaction.

Letting the stimulant spread over his system, he handed the empty cup to one of his Life Guards and said, "Colonel Taffez, report your success."

Taffez sipped his own tea, then said with a bow of his head, "Dominar, my spies reported to me five days ago that the Princess had married a man of low character, a navy officer by the name of Javier al-Rasheed. Major Standish was approached by my second, and she reported that after observing the couple, she confirmed that the princess was not only married but pregnant. My soldiers were able to capture the rake as he visited the Princess last night. He claimed he was seeking your blessing for the marriage."

The Dominar looked at Taffez's uniform. It hung loosely on his body like a poorly made peasant's chiton, one of the white cotton smocks that were favored by the poor. His fingers were stained from smoking sijars, no doubt to reduce the pain of his disease, while his eyes protruded from his skull like terrible hollow lights lit in the marshes in the depths of winter. The man had the marrow-colored skin of someone from the center of the island; however, his beard and hair were a sickly platinum white. Like his uniform, his skin seemed draped on a skeleton with no muscle mass or fat to fill it out. The Dominar imagined he could gather it up like a scruff with enough flesh left over to make a second man altogether.

Still, the Dominar thought, Taffez had recognized the threat that a lover finding his daughter represented, used his spies to root it out, and then wisely chose Major Standish to handle that problem. Now all that remained was to deal with the fallout. It had been a hard week. "I spoke yesterday with Major Standish. Is she inside with the scoundrel?"

Taffez looked uncomfortable. "She is inside, but so are the priests-counselors."

"The gods blast that. How did those sanctimonious head-bobbers end up here?" The Dominar screamed, spluttering incoherently. Turning to his guards, he said, "Stay outside," then barged into the chamber.

It obviously had not gone as he planned. Three priests nervously spoke to each other while standing over the supine form of his daughter's new spouse. Three dungeon masters were clustered into a darkened corner of the chamber, seeming to shrink from the arrival of the Dominar. Major Angela Standish, the renowned Justicar Armsman of the Dominar's guards, the youngest person to be named major since the Dominion was formed, was looking on with a bored expression. She had her hand on her chin as if considering its dimensions was a more pressing matter than a naked man chained to the torture frame.

It was, after all, the naked man taking up the center of the room that truly commanded attention, even if the people standing around the torture rack were trying to look anywhere but at the doomed sailor. Only Standish seemed nonchalant in the presence of the cause of all the Dominar's anger. She lowered her hand, using it to sweep the restrained figure as if she were selling a tuna to a fishmonger. "Meet Javier al-Rasheed, famous explorer and popular clothes horse of your court, all smiles and tilted cockades at parties," Standish said. "He is a worthless sot, a gambler, and while rumored to be a brilliant naval commander, his drunken escapades are the sole cause of his popularity. He does, however, wear his custom-fitted naval uniform well and has caught the eyes of many men and women of the court because of it."

The Dominar stepped in and approached his daughter's defiler. The torture masters had stripped him of his court finery and trussed him into a metal contraption that exposed all of his most sensitive areas to their detailed mechanical visitations. A pleasant selection of sharp and brutal torture instruments was lined up on a table, all made of enough metal to send a truly religious person screaming for the safety of a stone cave. "Dominar," the fettered al-Rasheed said, "I would genuflect but in the circumstances am prevented from showing honors." He tilted his head and smiled, like being strapped naked into a wooden cage was an everyday occurrence.

Standish slapped his head. "Remain silent, Captain."

The Dominar looked angrily at Standish. "How did the priests get here?" He levered his gaze to the three religious figures. Having priests act as lawyers and government officials was an old Kemeyan practice, predating the days of Dominion, but it was a custom Abelard had wished his father had left in the homeland when he invaded Cycus.

The head priest stepped forward, saying, "May it please your worship, but we have the gods to vouchsafe our movements and place us where we should be. You may not put a man to death who wears the colors of the court without the consent of the pantheon. And in the case of Captain al-Rasheed, there are other issues at hand that must be considered. If you understand me, but financial issues that your daughter brings to the table, so to speak."

"Insufferable!" Abelard yelled, causing the head priest to step backward in fear, but then he said, "Explain what you mean, Priest?"

"A moment please, your worship," the high priest replied as he fell in among the other priests to discuss the matter.

Standish stepped close to the Dominar. Abelard has known her since she was chosen as his daughter's companion, a young orphan from the outer court. The woman was loyal and fearsome, but this mistake had the Dominar steaming in anger, reconsidering her value.

"A word, Dominar," she said.

"Later," he commanded. Let his wrath test her loyalty, he thought.

The priest cleared his throat, turning away from the rest of his coterie. Abelard looked at him, then said, "Proceed."

The priest was dressed in a cowl with dark makeup around his eyes, the feathered staff of his office in his left hand, and a golden sheaf of earcorn around his neck. He bowed deeply and said, "Your worship. I fear we cannot come to a unanimous consensus on this matter. We feel the majority of the readings are in your favor, yet we also fear the law will not permit you to take this man's life." He then bowed again, adding, "My compatriots have views that will further allude to the findings of this issue. And again, perhaps the gods are moved by matters of coin."

The second priest bowed deep as if his words were a weight on his tongue, then stepped forward. "The augury does not completely support your position, yet it is not all negative. To your benefit, al-Rasheed has not offered guild and his family has no seigniorage, giving you great leeway in your response. If he had been of the old families of the Guisarmes, or a Kemeyani noble, your possible actions would be circumscribed. Also, he is sworn to service and is of a rank that he must be considered titled, if not landed. Added to this, your daughter, as part of the great family with her descent to the Nabeels and also to the rulers of Canus Cragia, and thus entailed into the chain of rule, is technically not a citizen of the realm who may take any mate she chooses; however, the entailment of her money and her future seat as 'heir proved' means she cannot be ignored in her choice. This man, Javier al-Rasheed, could be gelded and hanged by fiat, but I cannot say for a certain fact that the act would be accepted by the Commons or by the Great Bank, and it would anger the Auditors, meaning you may lose your right to the money now backing your government, held in honor and placed there by your esteemed father Nawaz I, the Conqueror."

All eyes then turned to the third priest, one named Domingus bar Calad, a rare Bryonian from the mountain people, few of which offered service to the Dominar or his father. They all knew he had no care for the Dominar's threats and would speak in a way that hewed closely to the truth. "The real issue is not sanctity, or rank, or the commons. It is her dowry and her progeny. When the child she is rumored to carry is born, she becomes 'am alshaeb' or mother-of-the-people. Your father, my Dominar, for reasons not known to me, chose to invest your firstborn with the fortune of his hand and hew the family line through her—it is part of the Cycus 'dustari that settled the war and made the leading families of the Guisarme's our allies. The Youseffi, Cinci, and others may press for you to kill this upstart, and indeed, we have discussed your daughter's fate upon the day she births an heir, yet many other families hew closely to the old agreement. Your daughter Nazira is heir-in-fact. You are merely the keeper until she hands you an heir. The theory was you would remain as trustee through Nazira's majority and birth of her first child. When this happens, no matter his status, Nazira becomes heir protector, this al-Rasheed becomes heir-consort, and all three become legally untouchable, at least by you, my worship. Killing him now will cause its own issues in the Commons and with the Bankers. And I will mention the money as well in a second, but your father wrote good law, and many families consider that law sacrosanct."

"My daughter chose a man of no honor, a drunkard, skate, and baboon," the Dominar said.

"That hurts, my Dominar. I am a hero, after all," Al-Rasheed said from his truss, earning another slap to his head from Standish.

The Dominar turned and pulled the head priest off his feet with his powerful hands, throttling the man and causing him to urinate down his cassock. "I am Dominar Abelard 'Arba'a 'Aashar,' King of the Cyclonidees, Lord of Cycus, Admiral of the Camellia Fleet. My daughter is a vessel created to carry for me the wrongfully taken money my father, robbed from me to the chagrin of the gods! I care not one jot about your stammering. He dies, she dies, as long as the heir lives and the dowry is legally invested, nothing else matters. It is for the good of the Great Dominion!"

He stood, holding the struggling priest face-to-face with him, ready to choke his life out when Priest Domingus placed a hand on his shoulder. "Then there is the rumor of the entail."

The Dominar was fifty years, hale of body, and strong of spirit. He was wearing a handsome sateen sherwani of clean white, with the pink flowers of his house printed on it around his family crest. He twitched with the touch of the priest, standing motionless for a few seconds, a swaying statue dressed in a thousand coins of finery, then tossed the young priest to the ground. He turned to a table of torture instruments, grabbing for a tool. When he spun around, his hands held a flensing knife. It had a clean metal sheen that caused it to reflect the light of the burning braziers. "The testicles first, I think!" he yelled. Then he stopped and looked at the priest. "What entail?"

"We are yet in possession of the facts, but your daughter has done more than marry this rake. She has, apparently, taken a loan on her dower property. A sizable loan."

Abelard looked at Domingus. Then he looked at the senior dungeon master standing in the darkness, hidden by the flickering of the torches lighting the room. The dungeon master nodded, putting his index finger by his nose. Abelard let out a scream and slashed the knife he was holding through the air.

Despite the threat of death and horrible dismemberment, Javier looked as if he was relaxing in a recliner at an officer's club, waiting for tea and sweet crackers. His bright green eyes glanced in turn at each person in the chamber, seeming to drink in their visages like they were some form of mobile statuary produced for his visual approval. Even as the Dominar waved the flensing knife through the air, Javier did not seem to be concerned.

The Dominar turned to the silent warrior who was standing by his side. "Major Standish," the Dominar said, "You are so young, yet in my mind, you are the realm's greatest warrior, and I have chosen you to be the protector of Princess Nazira, the stone mace inside of my Dominion's velvet gloves. Where I direct my ire, your wrath follows with deadly practice."

"My Dominar," she said in her harsh, gravelly voice, a voice that silenced the murmurs in the room immediately.

Dominar Abelard reached out to the tall woman, his nose breathing fire like he was an enraged bull. His anger though, was mitigated by his own respect for the warrior's prowess. "Speak, Standish," he barked.

Standish motioned for the doorway where they could speak quietly. They both moved away from the others, huddling in a tête-à-tête. "My Dominar, the entail they speak of is a loan taken out by your daughter on her dower wealth. They are not brave enough to say it, but if you kill this man, it could collapse the Dominion if not done right. You know we discussed the alternative way yesterday?"

"The pirate crew." Dominar Abelard said. He lifted his cap, revealing the horrible dent in his skull that had occurred when she was a child. It made him self-conscious, but when he was angry, it throbbed angrily and was hot. He rubbed it for a second, then returned his cap to its place.

Standish waited for her Dominar to finish, then replied in a low voice into his ear. "I have paid one of the torturers to see it done. A simple word from you and your troublesome nobody finds a shallow grave on the beach. Your daughter will have her child, live long enough to prove the line of descent, then you can bury her next to her so-called husband."

The Dominar stared at a flickering brazier and its acrid light. "Damn my father to the crossroads of the depths for not giving me the fiscals. Damn his eyes. You are tasked, Standish; get it done."

Major Standish turned, walked back to Javier, and asked in her deep voice, "My Dominar, as much as looking on this man naked in a gelding chair is amusing, may I ask you a serious question?" Her voice was like one cast on a marionette, devoid of honest intonation.

The Dominar stepped back into the light. "You may speak." His voice was exaggerated as if he was saying the lines in a play. He looked at the major, his daughter's companion since her mother left. Standish was as tall as most men, as fair-haired as a Westerner, and as a sign of foolishness or bravery, wore a complete set of brigantines tinted red without even an effort at propitiation. On her right hip was a talwar, on the left, a jambiy. Around her shoulder was a flex of cartridges for a large firelock, the weapon being kept slung across her back, ready to use. The sheer number of weapons she had on her person made her look like an armory wall done in a crimson scale motif.

"I learned from my arms master," Standish said with a sweep of her hand, "on the day you are scheduled to geld the goat, if you discover it can busk and sing, that nothing is lost by delaying the operation in hopes of discovering the value of that talent."

There were several moments of silence. One of the dungeon masters, a man named al-Cinci, farted loudly in the corner, receiving a punch from his partner, a dour, muscular man who had taken the position of lead dungeon master from his executed father. The priests tried to remain silent, but their nervousness caused them to shift back and forth, making their protective fetish charms tinkle like small bells. Only Standish was silent, moving not a muscle as her Dominar ran his thumbnail up the back of the knife with an odd frisson of atonal noise.

The Dominar looked over al-Rasheed's exposed nudity one last time and said, "The priests can take a day to find unanimity over the issue of what to do with this troublesome whore."

Standish nodded. "My Dominar, a deed done that need not be done today, can be delayed for the next day. You cannot un-ring the bell though. The goat may yet busk for your benefit," she said. Her face said that she felt none of this was true, speaking more for the audience than her liege.

"To the Tower with him then. Tomorrow I will ponder his gelding for his crimes once the priests rule with certainty." The Dominar stared intently for a minute at the captive, then left the dungeon room followed by the priests.

Standish waved to the trio of the dungeon masters, summoning them over to her, telling them, "Captian al-Rasheed is to be taken to the Firthing Tower and turned over to Warden-Superior Beaumois." She stopped for a second and looked at the taller of the three dungeon masters. "You are Petrov's son?" She asked.

The man was broad-shouldered, yet stooped. He had huge muscular arms and a simian look to his stance. He was marked from an encounter with the pox in his youth and had wild hair that had not seen a comb or a bath in three years. He wore a leather worker's apron with a set of cotton ruggles, none of which were in good repair. "I am the son of Petrov," the dungeon master said. His hands were clenched, signs of a wellspring of rage running through the man, but otherwise his manner was surprisingly controlled. He opened his mouth with exaggerated calm, carefully stating, "It is said you were the last face my father saw."

The man next to Petrovson, al-Cinci, smiled, trying to lighten the mood, "Hey, not so serious, Major Standish. Who does not have a few skeletons if we fling open doors? I mean, we have all served as our parents did, have we not? Petrovson is just doing a job, no? We can bend an arm tomorrow if you wish. We have some nice ale, no?"

Standish turned to the man, "Who is your father? What skeletons do you have in these dark closets? You are of the kith al-Cinci, a powerful group, no?"

"My father is Abd al-Cinci, perhaps you know him, he runs the flower garden as did his father," the nervous dungeon master replied.

"I do not know him," Standish said. She looked at the third dungeon master, who stood silently, dismissing her as well, though she had known her almost from the first day of her adoption. It was that way growing up in the palace. You knew everyone.

Standish turned back to Petrovson. "It is evocative that a man who begged for a position held by his father, when that father had done so much wrong, told the Butler he was not made in the image of his fore-kin, should change his name to an honorific of that said man, no?"

"I serve the Dominar," he said through clenched teeth. "I am proud to be Petrovson."

"Just know you are in my vision," Standish said, putting her hand on her talwar. "You should have taken a less evil name, Petrov d'Cycus." She reached over and brushed some faint dirt speck from his costume. "Fart, and the breeze will betray you to me, *Petrovson*."

"No, that was me farting," al-Cinci said with a self-conscious laugh. His comment was ignored.

"You are in my vision as well, Major." Petrovson replied.

Standish nodded, then turned to the woman in the shadows and said, "You know what I want from you?" She nodded without saying anything.

Standish took one more look at the three dungeon masters, the two ragged men and the woman in the shadows, daring them to release any funny japes. When none were forthcoming, while radiating menace, she turned, leaving the dungeon by the same exit as the Dominar.

Chapter II

A Farewell to Love

Major Angela Standish had been busy since dawn and would see another dawn before she slept. Her lover had set her to a mad plan; like the idea or not, she was committed. People and resources were moving across the capital of Cycus, accomplishing tasks that made her dizzy to contemplate.

She left the torture chamber, climbing a set of stairs off the main vestibule that led to a transverse wall with a hollow walk path. The pathway was built from one of the older curtains, which let her walk under cover of darkness until it joined the southern mercer. This path was wider and better illuminated, though rarely traveled at night. Unless you played as a child in the old castle, you would never know that there was a steep path leading from the mercer down to a grotto where clear water rushed in from an old water pipe. It used to be the castle's water supply but was supplemented when the town was expanded to increase the amount of water that would flow in from the tall mountains to the south. The green, clear water filled half the room, creating a perfect place for two girls, young lovers, to meet where the adults would not discover their hidden tryst.

Sitting on a large rock they called "the couch," Princess Nazira smiled when she saw Standish. Behind her was Oban Bey, the old eunuch that had raised them to adulthood. Standish walked up, hugged Bey, then turned and tried to hug Nazira, who backed away.

"You know that part of our life is over Angela Standish," the Princess said. She was thin, with olive skin, dark flashing eyes, an intense gaze, and black shiny hair. She wore a dark chattel dress, bound to allow freedom of movement, and a scarf.

Standish stood in front of Nazira, looking at her with longing. "Your father plans to kill you. You will die the second he gets his heir and the entailed fortune. You should not have made the deal with the bank. We could have fled."

Nazira stood, her natural anger breaking through her reserve. "I told you, my friend, Standish, how this game had to be played, that marrying al-Rasheed would be key to my salvation."

"The man is hardly worth the spit in my mouth," Standish replied, clenching her fists.

Nazira walked over and placed her hand on Standish. "He is worth more than you can imagine."

"He is a worthless drunk whose only accomplishment is bedding you!" Standish yelled, her face red in anger. In these rages, she wanted to hit something, anything, to make the pain go away, but she could not give in to the anger. It had to be held inside.

"You are jealous, not seeing the potential he holds. I am not a farmer who marries anyone she wants and grows sweet turnips while my spouse weaves basket hats. He creates an heir, and he will secure my future." Nazira turned, walking to the mere. "You are still of use to me, and not just for the warmth you brought my cold childhood. My child may not be yours of seed, that was never to be by nature. Yet, you have an important role. I am sending you to deliver my message of faith in Javier, to see that he returns a great captain, not a drunken fool."

"What about the other one, the one who follows him?" Standish said.

Nazira nodded. "The one called Devious. Forget his shadow, pretend you do not see it. There is more there than meets the eye."

Oban Bey stood forward, "My princess, that is not to be discussed."

Nazira ignored him. "I am tasking you to be the major of the Marines on the ship I am acquiring and to gather the people who I will need. My new husband will be of great benefit if you can keep him in check. Protect him from his kinder and more sinister impulses."

"You are sending me into exile?" Standish said, tears in her eyes.

Nazira continued to look at the green surface of the clear water. "You are my reserves, Angela, the people who my father will not know are in play. When he finds I have leveraged the money in this scheme, he will not be able to move until you return. You have connections with the Navy. I need you to send money and treasure back on Navy ships so that I can use them to keep my father off balance. When I return from *Remarker*, I will be confined to the Tower resulting in a complete lack of freedom of movement. My father's loyalists will support him, while mine will walk with great care to avoid being hanged from spikes."

Major Standish said, "I will do all you ask, Princess."

"It will be a morning of betrayals, no?"

Nazira felt her stomach and wondered if that was a clever thing … or a mistake.

CHAPTER III

Riddles of the House of Fire

The Dominar, Standish, and the Priests left the realm of darkness, the dungeons that Petrovson considered his birthright. Al-Cinci walked around the supine Javier and said to Petrovson, "Plain as the flame on a candle tip it is." He slapped the prisoner on the belly. "Obvious, is it not?" He turned to the woman in the shadow. "I bet you noticed the fishing pole that lured out the royal fish?"

Petrovson ignored his companion as he prepared the shackles to transport their prisoner.

"It is not like an onion hidden in a stew, is it?" Al-Cinci bumped his fellow dungeon master with his shoulder. "I mean, why would a princess choose this lowborn? Seeing him in the gelding rack exposes the obvious!"

Petrovson stopped working for a second, shook his head, and then started leading out a hemp painter, checking it for strength.

Al-Cinci whistled loudly. "I mean, maybe the Dominar has no perspective on such things, but Major Standish has to appreciate the weight of evidence as to why the daughter of a monarch would hang with a scoundrel like this."

Finally, Petrovson could take no more. "Lister al-Cinci, what in the doors of the firelands are you entertaining yourself about?"

Al-Cinci laughed. "My friend Petrovson, you cannot possibly not notice that Captain al-Rasheed is carrying an absolutely huge sidearm, now can you? I mean, I have seen them pass in the baths, where some were entertaining in length and girth, but this one could block traffic on the Circum-Valus!"

Petrovson clenched his hands in rage again, letting his nails dig into his palms. "If you do not shut up, I will show you what my father's brass pineapples are used for. Now get ready to move the prisoner." He turned to the woman in the shadows, telling her, "You handle the doors while we walk this sot to his reward.

Al-Cinci began to remove the prisoner from the arm and leg locks of the gelding chair. Once free, he methodically dressed him in the shackles Petrovson had prepared. Thus secured, he said, "How do those shackles feel, al-Rasheed? Ready for walks?"

Javier replied, "Can I have some water, please?"

Lister al-Cinci picked up a water thief (usually referred to as a "thief") from the side table, which was normally used to drip scalding liquids on prisoners, filling it with acrid water from a bucket that had long grown rancid with algae. When the thief was full, he brought it over to Javier, letting him have a good half-liter of the foul liquid. He wanted to see if the prisoner would complain; he did not. Javier drank the scummy water as if it was rain from the brows of the gods, nodding thanks when the last drop passed his lips.

With the thief empty, al-Cinci threw the copper device down onto the tool's table, saying, "It is a cool night, Captain, do not get too cold."

The third dungeon master, Gullen, picked up a load of wood and was watching the process of getting the doomed sailor ready for his last walk.

Javier, limbs now in manacles, was pulled from the gelding rack, blindfolded, dressed in a rough jute front cloak that could be fastened to him without taking off his irons, and had heavy wooden clogs placed on his feet. He was then bound on top of the manacles with hempen rope, the left-over line arranged to form a leash to drag him along with. He did not struggle in the process and said not a word, keeping a serene look on his face, as if this binding was some form of meditation. The feeling of calm seemed to disturb al-Cinci, while it made Petrovson cross.

His eyes blindfolded, Javier was led away from the dungeon, helped down a set of stairs, and then out a creaky doorway to an open area where he could smell the sea air. After a few minutes on a rough path, they stopped in front of a large portal that groaned as it opened. Petrovson told someone, probably a guard, "Prisoner transfer to the Firthing Tower." After a few minutes, they passed through the gates into an area where he could hear and smell the city.

The Firthing Tower was the tallest structure in the castle complex, isolated from the main fortification, normally reached by a narrow path up the side of a cliff; however, this was not the route they took. At about where the pathway should turn up the cliffside, Javier was led to the left down a set of stairs that were familiar to him; they led to the city. The cobbles became rougher and larger under his feet as the pathway became less steep. The sounds of dissipation indicated that it was nighttime in Cycus City, with revelers going to jai alai, plays, bars, or recitations. They did not stay on the main road. Instead, they took an immediate right-hand turn into one of the twisty backways through, by the smell of it, Jazar Mintaq, where the butchers plied their trade. The district, Javier remembered, had runnels running down the middle of the street, which carried offal to the sewers by the north wall. The smell of the district was distinct though, because of its coppery death odor. It was also the first thing that had cut Petrovson's own odor.

They stopped him at another doorway, a thick one with a lock and metal hinges by the sound of it as it swung open, then helped him navigate a steep winding set of stairs to a second door, which let out onto a place with sand underfoot and the roar of waves on rocks. The dungeon masters walked Javier a few hundred meters, then had him sit on a large round rock, which was wet from rain or surf. He could hear the wind, the surf, and the sounds of the night around him once the clatter of his clogs was no longer distracting him.

The roar of the surf did not cover up the noise of al-Cinci starting to make a fire. The dungeon master cracked driftwood, cursing as he tried to get the wet tinder to strike a light. After a few minutes, Javier could hear the soft crackle of the blaze catching. It was a smokey fire, apparently quite large, since Javier could feel its heat on his face. It seemed a major effort to start a fire on the wet beach, and hardly worth it. Javier reflected that captives did not get to dictate logical thinking to captors who were intellectually not really all present.

"Is that the best fire you can make? It is not big enough to warm myself from, yet it blocks my view of Ferris to tell time by," Petrovson said in a bitter voice.

Al-Cinci replied, "Since when do you know where Ferris is, anyway? Stop bitching. If you want a better fire, get better wood like Gullen did."

"Gullen was an idiot to carry three logs from the dungeon for a fire we do not need," Petrovson grouched.

Something metal went on the fire, pinging as it heated. They must have brought a teakettle or other supplies, as Javier heard water being poured into what sounded like a copper brewer. Plus, he could hear the low rumble of boiling.

A second load of wood landed in sand, causing Petrovson to ask, "What do you have for us to drink, Lister, if you are all set to have that damn fire?"

"Twelve grams of Black Junebug," al-Cinci said as if this was an absolute luxury.

"God's fire burn you for a piker," Petrovson complained bitterly. "Did you piss in the pot as well?" He sounded as if he was kicking sand like a schoolchild. "If you went through the work for a fire to have tea, why the fuck make it swill?"

"A person who complains on tea that is offered should offer it themselves," Lister said, misquoting the proverb.

Petrovson must have kicked sand at the fire this time—a sign of his temper—because embers exploded in an audible spray around them. "You ever think that the upper class uses tea to control us?" Lister said in a distant, maundering way.

Javier heard a rock fly through the air then clatter around in the distance.

Petrovson raged. "You are really lowborn, Lister. I mean, you could be the punchline of a bad joke. Gullen! Quit gathering wood. There is too much already."

Lister laughed a weak, almost scared laugh. "If you think I am a bad joke, there is no reason to drink the tea! I mean really, you have us out here on the cold damn beach. Seems like you would appreciate my work. Have you ever been down in the middle of the day, feel like the world is not going to let you live much longer, and then a cup of tea with a friend makes it all better?"

"Crap," Petrovson said. "You are like a stage show of yourself, Lister. Too stupid to know he is stupid. First, you are not my friend. Second, you make tea every time there is work to be done."

"You lot make a lot of noise." It was a third voice, a new voice, coming from the direction of the cliff. A voice that Javier knew.

Petrovson asked, "Who else is out on a night like tonight?" More sand kicked. "You are early, but that is all for the good." There were motion sounds Javier could not make out, as well as shuffling in the sand.

"Take his blindfold off," the woman said to the three dungeon masters. Javier squinted as the blind and gag came away from his face, blinking and looking into the flickering firelight to see Daniella, the accountant-enforcer of the Red Hand Gang.

Petrovson threw the blindfold into the sand, pointing at Javier. "I give you your quarry."

Daniella walked over, picked up Javier's face, her hands under his chin, as if checking on the quality of salt beef. "Why the fire?" Daniella asked.

"Tea," Lister al-Cinci said. "I am making some for all of us. Would you like a tin?"

Daniella looked at Lister like he was a bug. "I do not take tea from metal, you heathen, and neither should you."

Maybe it was time to say something, Javier thought. "Good evening, Daniella, my friend of the Red Hand Gang. Strange to meet you here, is it not?" He then looked at Petrovson and al-Cinci, giving a friendly nod to the third dungeon master, Gullen.

"You could have called on me in a more normal manner at a more normal time."

"Do not get devious with me, Javier. I know your tricks. You owe a lot of money. The boss is planning to have some good times with you unless I can find some manner to collect your debt." Daniella said. She removed her silk gloves, then folded them over her messing belt. "Seriously al-Rasheed, a slick man like you with the connections you have, could pay off a gambling debt twenty times over if you wanted. Instead, you make me hire this idiot Petrovson to snatch your worthless self from the damn torture chambers of the Dominar."

Lister al-Cinci interjected, "You know those torture chambers do not get used as much as you think. People think the Dominar does a hundred a week, but some weeks it is only two or three. Petrovson's father probably did ten times, and sent even more to, well, the island."

Petrovson backhanded Lister, telling him, "Enough of this!" Subsequently inquiring, "Do you want the merchandise Daniella, or do we take him back to the Firthing Tower for the Dominar to play with?"

Javier tried to recline a bit but caught himself as he almost slipped off the rock into the sand. "Sounds like I will be expensive, Daniella. Why not drop this, then come see me when the Dominar kicks me loose? I question why you are meeting me here around a fire with this lot at all. Seems like the work for a dark corner, not a beach party."

Daniella looked struck by this. "Javier, you are speaking rationally." She drew a firelock handlock from under her robes, a big Carver Dragoon Rolling Block, cocking it. With exaggerated care, she pointed it at Petrovson and questioned, "Let me ask you, why the blazes are you standing here making tea by that huge fire?"

There was silence, then another voice came from the night. "I have no idea why these defectives built a fire, but it led us right to you!" Javier looked as Harmond Karr stepped from the darkness with two thugs. The night was growing crowded with his lenders; Karr was an unlikely addition, although Javier owed him a lot.

Daniella turned her handlock toward Karr, asking, "Who are you?"

"Javier al-Rasheed owes me money, therefore, I am here to take him with me!" He had a short pike in his hand; one of his bullies had a shotgun cocked, ready to fire.

Daniella waved her handlock in frustration. "No, I mean literally, 'Who are you?' The 'Boss' owns all of this man's debts from all the bookmakers in the Dominion. I have literally never heard of you in my life."

Javier said, "I am sorry Daniella. You are correct that at this point you have acquired all of my debt, or at least the Master of the Red Hand has ... the one you work for. However, gambling debts are not the only debts I owe. This is Harmond Karr, the man from whom I rent, living in his very well-cared-for and pleasant seaside apartments. He is indeed owed quite a lot by me, having likely found out the Dominar canceled my half-pay when I was captured." Javier looked at the group for a second. "Harmond is a surprise though because I never would have thought of him as the type to recover a debt through thuggery."

Harmond walked over to Daniella and Javier, close to the fire, saying, "You owe too much silver, Javier. It was ok when your half-pay account was paying on the note, but when the notes go dark with so much left to pay, even a timid man may be forced to unusual circumstances."

Daniella pointed her handlock back at Petrovson. "You damn well sold him twice? To this landlord and me as well?"

Petrovson, who had a saw-bladed knife in his hand, replied, "I only took money from you, Daniella, to clear my gambling debt. I have no idea how this Karr item showed up here. How did you show up here?" he asked, turning to Karr.

Harmond Karr was dressed in the same black cowl and jony hat that he wore when he skulked around pretending to fix the bungalows he ran. He said, "We were waiting for you to take him out of the dungeons to one of the towers. When you went for the beach gate, it was good enough for us. We did not pay off anyone. What do you take me for, a criminal?"

Daniella rubbed her head with her handlock. "Gore, come out of the shadows."

Javier knew the man, Gore, who Daniella called from his place of quiet watch. Al-Rayiys Maqrid Almal, known as the Master of the Red Hand, "the Boss," or simply al-Maqrid, employed the most fearsome fighter in the Dominion, a man known simply as Gore, as his enforcer. He liked to pound people with a giant wooden peg-driver when he was in a good mood. In a poor mood, he could be very creative in his violence. "Thank you, Daniella. Is there tea?" the huge man asked.

Javier yelled to Gore, "Hey there, Gore, is the family safe?"

Gore stopped. "Hello Javier, yes, they are quite well. Your gift last year was welcomed."

"When a child is sick, there is always call for a whip around with the hat, you know," Javier replied.

Gore nodded his giant head, "Sorry 'bout this all, Javier. I promise to do only what is needed."

"What do you think they will need?" Javier asked.

Gore thought for a bit, then said, "I think the Red Hand wanted to pull your lungs out to watch you breathe with them on the outside. I truly am sorry, Mr. al-Rasheed. I am not sure how to make this painless."

"You have to put food on the table, Gore. No one blames you," Javier replied.

Daniella screamed at the top of her lungs. "Gore, quit talking to the idiot boy. He will be screaming soon because you will make him scream, you dumb turtle!"

"Can I wish him a happy marriage?" Gore asked.

Daniella replied, "The hells, no, you may not." She then turned to Javier. "Come to that, is it true you married the Dominar's only daughter?"

Javier hung his head. "Yes, I certainly did, his eldest daughter in the line of secession, at least. How do you think the Dominar's dungeon masters have me in their hands? It is not like Petrovson is a sliver on his old father, no?"

Petrovson yelled, "Shut up!"

"Silence Petrovson, you are not a sliver on your dad. Al-Rasheed is absolutely right. He is my prisoner now." Daniella said, turning back to Javier. "Is marrying the Princess a scam? Will it bring in cash to pay your debts?" Daniella asked.

Javier shook his head slowly. "Sorry Danny, I did it for love. There is no money to be had. The Dominar locked up her money long before I informed him of our wedding, at least what money she has. I do not think her dowry or inheritance is hers to spend. Not that I would touch it to pay off Maqrid."

"Then there is no way out of this for you," she said. She looked about the beach. "Personally, I thought you were smarter than to corner yourself in a marriage. It is not like you seeded her."

Silence filled the beach.

"God's Flash, Javier al-Rasheed, the dapper breaker of hearts, hero of the voyage of the *Constellar*, seeded the Dominar's daughter!" Daniella laughed.

"You should see what he did it with," al-Cinci added. "Talk about plowing a field good."

Petrovson slapped al-Cinci again and said, "Enough talk. Time to take your prize, Daniella."

Harmond Karr stepped forward, growling, "You seem to forget me."

Javier added, "And the fire."

Daniella looked at the fire, then asked, "Why the fire again?"

Gore said hopefully, "Tea?"

Then, from the darkness of the water, came a new voice. "A sack of silver to al-Cinci to start it, then guide my boat to this shore." Captain Naseer al-Dinni, commander of the pirate-trader *Remarker*, called the "Jinn of the High Seas," stepped into the light. Four men followed him, all pirates trying to carry themselves with sinister intent, although they stopped a little short on seeing.

Gore on the beach, his hulking shadow cast by the fire making him seem twenty meters tall.

The newcomer swaggered up, confronting Daniella. "I have claim on the marriage and bed of Nazira, daughter of Dominar Abelard 'Arba'a 'Aashar,' won fair in a contest with her uncle Abram. I thus have rights to take this man who has falsely wed her, to punish him for his presumptions on my property." The pirate had a wicked falchion in his hand, while his men had a mixture of firelocks and glaives, held with threatening intent, their silver metal glinting in the firelight.

Daniella looked angry with the newcomer. "Women of the Dominion have the rights of the constitution. You cannot force her to wed because of a gambling debt. You also cannot simply take the prize of the Red Hand without a by-your-leave from Maqrid."

Naseer laughed, "Ahh, Daniella, you pimp and accountant to a pimp. Are any of the men and women you sell for services protected by this constitution? You can explain in person to the Red Hand how little I care for his bluster."

Harmand Karr, a brawler in the best of times but perhaps naïve as to the power of the people he faced, asked, "Three claims on Javier al-Rasheed, yet one indivisible man?" He looked like a kid trying to get in line for school rations when the rest of the school bullies were determined to have him out.

"There are four claims so far," Javier said. "The Dominar is not happy with my wedding to his daughter, so he claims me for gelding."

Gullen, the quiet dungeon master, her stocky figure hidden by a cloak to keep people from seeing her scars, made a meek interjection. "The Dominar hired me to kill him, Petrovson." She gulped, then said, "The Dominar lied that he was letting you have al-Rasheed. He instructed me to kill you myself here on the beach, then I was supposed to geld him."

Al-Cinci piped in, "I do not think the Dominar really wanted Javier nutted. He is not one to waste a freak of nature like you have."

"Shut up al-Cinci, and you also Gullen, or whoever your name is. Untie the man, give him over, and you can have your silver." Naseer said. "I will not be left last of four in this transaction."

Petrovson was shaking his head, looking at his partners al-Cinci and Gullen. "You sold me out?"

"It was good money," Lister al-Cinci said.

Gullen added, "The Dominar wanted it to be an accident."

"You really screwed this up," Petrovson said. "One dim-witted playboy with four people to claim his ass.

"Five people claim the prize." Standing in the firelight was a dark man with a deep voice, with the face of a ghoul, painted on or real, and protruding teeth that were unfortunate as well as fear-inspiring. The man was a feared rumor or a bad joke around the palace, the sinister man with enameled nails, makeup, and a tall, dry demeanor. "Lister al-Cinci and Petrov Petrovson, how dare you take the Dominar's captive from him? Daniella, you and I have crossed blades before, although you did not know it. Do you really want to face me?"

Daniella laughed. "I was wondering if you would come to the party, Devious. I am happy to have met you at last. It would have been boring just dealing with Naseer and his idiotic followers."

Naseer said, "You keep your mouth shut, slut. I will have dealings with you shortly, you and your moronic bodyguard."

Javier said, "I think, Devious, that there is a certain lack of care for your ominous presence."

Devious bowed. "Indeed, but I suppose you warned them about the fire, so what can you do?"

"How did you know I would warn them about the fire?" Javier asked.

"It is your character to do this, Javier. It's very annoying." Devious spoke as if with a labored voice.

"Enough of this! I own Javier al-Rasheed! I have two hundred at my back if I call out to my ship!" Naseer yelled.

Devious nodded to Javier, leaned back on the rock, saying, "In fact, you have 186 who are by now drunk and besotted in the city, four crew at your back who wish they were, and six crew on your ship who, if they surrendered, are cast adrift on a launch, pulling for shore. It turns out your first officer was very happy when a message came from you with a chest of silver to allow the entire crew liberty in Cycus City."

Javier said approvingly, "Very clever, Devious."

"It was Nazira, really. I am but a puppet in her hand," he replied.

Daniella laughed, saying, "If that is true, then even now my footpads are coming here to inform me, Naseer. There will soon be a new master of your ship." She waved into the darkness, stating, "I have seventy and four loyal knives at my side." She turned to Devious. "This little game you played will not save you though. The Maqrid will have Javier, no matter what you play at. I will have you as well."

Devious made a tsking sound. "Daniella de Tomei al Fortuna, I must correct your misconception. Your so-called army of footpads even now have broken into a naval store's warehouse, which they were informed of by a note you sent them. Sorry, Princess Nazira sent them in your name—to be accurate. They are currently carrying these stores to lighters for transport to the *Remarker*. They expect, and will, in fact, receive, a chest of silver in return for your stunningly well-thought-out plan. The Princess is most happy for your assistance."

"My guess is the bully boys I gathered are the ones moving the stolen supplies?" Harmond Karr asked with fatal finality. "Is that how you repay the debt for my rent?"

Javier raised his shoulders, looking bashful. "I am just a passenger."

Devious smiled. "Mr. Karr, you are very perceptive. If I had my hat, I would tip it to honor you." He put his hand on his head, then said, "I do have my hat," and tilted it.

Devious stooped, picked up Javier's discarded leather bindings, then ran them through his fingers. "By the time any of you can leave this beach and collect your followers, this will be finished. Naseer, I was able, when I discovered your ship anchored in the roadstead yesterday, to conceal its presence. If I had not done this, the Camellia Navy would have killed you. It is very foolish to assume you could brazenly moor on the roads of a Dominar whose daughter you threatened to kidnap. Your ship is taken, but your crew all live and can escape in the confusion I have caused." Addressing Javier, he stated, "Plus, you do have a chest of silver to allow you to escape."

"Thank you, uh, Devious," Javier said.

Devious nodded. "As for you, Daniella, Javier al-Rasheed still owes his debt. You are richer by a chest of silver each. I have provided young Javier a way to earn a living, thus the ability to pay you back."

"All of this fancy double talk means nothing! I will kill you!" Naseer yelled.

"Naseer." Javier tried to get the pirate's attention. The man who was calling himself Devious was obviously "working the room," and he had not come unprepared.

Naseer pulled a salwa from his sash, waving the shiny blade in the air. "Say your last words, Javier, say them now so that I can run you through before any of these idiots can save you."

"You forgot the fire again," Javier said.

Naseer looked nonplussed. He turned, looking at the fire that was, with the added lumber, growing even larger. Daniella and Harmond joined him, wondering at the greenish color and strange smoke coming from the conflagration. "Looking at the fire buys you only a minute of life, and was surely a sad ploy from a dead man," Naseer said.

Javier was grabbed by "Devious" who pulled him down, diving for safety behind the rock they were leaning against.

As he rolled into the sand, he heard Daniella say, "No, he is right, there is green smoke coming from the logs."

Then a massive, ear-shattering explosion shook the beach. Devious sat up and waved, which caused two black-masked fighters to rush in from the darkness and grab Javier, getting him to his feet. Before they could cover him with a canvas yard, he saw Naseer with his left arm off at the elbow, looking confused. Daniella was blown back on fire, but Gore, always loyal, was putting the flame out on her with his hands. One of Hammond's men had a tea kettle embedded in his chest, while Hammond was busy trying to save the life of his other bullyboy who was broken by the explosion. All four of the pirates were rolling on the ground, covered in flames.

Head covered by the tarp, Javier was rushed down to the surf and dumped into a pinnace. He removed the head covering as soon as he settled into the boat, seeing that the beach was a mass of light as rockets and flares flashed across it. From the darkness came a score of people dressed in red sailor's frocks, who took control of the pinnace. Devious and Javier watched the fireworks for a bit.

Javier looked at the man, "You are not Devious. Who are you?"

"I am a friend of Oban's," he said.

"My wife's servant? Oban the Eunuch?" Javier asked.

"Mr. al-Rasheed, perhaps the questions can wait until you are away?" The man said, wiping away makeup and pulling out false teeth. "Your wife is on the *Remarker*." He waved as the red jacketed crew launched the boat, aimed at a mysterious liner moored in the roadstead.

Chapter IV

The King of Crabs

When they broke into the open water, the boat's officer made a little genuflection to Javier, just a tilt of the head, telling him, "Mr. al-Rasheed, you should thank your wife for this rescue. Most of the details are hers. We are the new crew of your new merchant ship, the *Remarker*. We have been assigned to carry you to the ship and keep you from trouble." He did not offer a hand but turned to look straight out to sea. In the distance, the dark shape of a large liner stood tall against the stars.

"Will you follow my orders, or my wife's?" Javier asked.

"Your wife's naturally, Mr. al-Rasheed, until the ship is ready to leave harbor. Then you, of course. You will be captain then," he said.

Javier looked back at the carnage on the beach. There was still chaos, fires, and screams filling the night. Then Javier noticed that the real Devious, his long-time friend and not an imposter hired by his wife, had snuck onto the launch and was sitting next to him. "Do not feel sad for the people in that explosion. You know how hard life is. Do you think your wit would have gotten you out of there?"

Javier shook his head. "Devious, your machinations worry me. Someday you may go too far." Javier said.

Devious laughed silently. "I have lived through horrors you would never survive. It is what the world intended for me. Now I exist merely to protect you, to see you find your way. In some sense, my life is attached to yours. It is a job I accept." He then looked back at the approaching ship in the roadstead.

Javier nodded. One of the pinnace crew turned and handed Javier a flask cup. He drank from it, finding it to have a simple Junebug tea, hot from the vacuum container. The tea warmed him down to the core; while bitter and unyielding, it woke him from his stupor.

As the pinnace sculled out to the roadstead where the *Remarker* swung at anchor, the night became calm and quiet; the chaos dropping away with distance in the night. When they pulled up to the liner, a gang net was lowered, allowing Javier to climb on board. When he reached the top of the net, he came face-to-face with Angela Standish's ironic smile, the smile that said she knew way more about the world than he did. She gave way as he swarmed over the railing, allowing him to see an even more surprising face—his wife, Nazira al-Youseffi muta-Rasheed. It was like all the tension of the past days had broken free and he was released from care. He rushed at her, grabbing her up in his arms. She accepted a certain amount of this affection, then pushed him away. "There is little time. I was able to make many arrangements, unhappily they are imperfect even now."

Javier asked, "What are these arrangements? How have you done all this?" He looked, seeing Devious on deck, standing quietly in the shadows. "Who was the imposter, Devious?"

"The man is a friend of my warder, Oban, my dear. A dear friend who agreed to play a role in the drama we faced tonight." Nazira answered. She took out a package from her bodice, then handed it over to him. It was a bundle of documents, some clutched in waterproofs, others loose in a ship's notebook. He looked down at the bundle, identifying one as a ship's lading, another as the start of a ship's log. There were newly written papers for the former pirate ship *Remarker*, now taken into trade as a tea merchant, Javier's warrant as captain of the newly minted trader, an accounting book with bank drafts for a hefty amount of silver to continue fitting the ship in order to enter trade with, and a pair of sheafs sealed in wax with a note that said, "open when the first when *Remarker* reaches Acanthia Minor, deliver the second to the Moderator of that island."

Javier looked up from the documents, searching Nazira's eyes. How had his life partner, newly wed, arranged all of this? Was this the work of fat Oban? If so, did she know of "the island," and of who Oban's friends likely were? He could not see any horror lurking inside Nazira's eyes, making him believe she could not possibly know what tools he wielded, nor the source of her servant's connections to make this all happen. Javier ended up standing dumb for quite some time, knowledge racing in circles like a rat on a circus wheel, forced to run forever without a way to leave.

Standish said sarcastically over her shoulder, "See Nazira, what a stable genius your husband is, finger on the pulse of the world. Now you are making him a captain?"

Men and women were moving around on the deck of the ship, carrying supplies to the hold, pulling personal possessions of the previous crew for a raft that would be heading back to the city docks, and preparing the rigging to warp away from the roadstead. Javier, who had spent years at sea as a child, plus more years on ships as a Navy officer, felt his skin crawl at the disorganized dance of moving people. There was no one in charge, just people realizing things had to be done and going to do them, often out of order of how they should be completed. Nazira looked at Angela Standish, asking, "Angela, can you prepare to have my launch cast away for the castle docks? I want to talk with my husband in the Master's cabin."

Standish looked at Nazira for a second, then at Javier, making little effort to hide her disdain. She struggled herself with indecision, then turned, stalking to where a party was preparing to set an oared launch off the port side, shaping its way to the castle docks by the reading of its springer flags that were just visible over the side of the *Remarker*.

The *Remarker* was a four-masted hardwood vessel, worn looking and fane from hard use, yet sturdy of construction and strong of trim. It had two deep holds, each with a geared nodding winch, a center deck house that had the galley and ship's fire, a forward platform deck called the forecastle, and a quarterdeck aft. The quarterdeck was topped by the helm and kept safe in a cockpit with a protected shooting station, a generous set of communicator's lockers, and a vantage on top of the cockpit before the aft mast that could serve as an observation point for a Master to see around the entire ship. The quarterdeck structure itself housed access to the command berths, the aft gangway from the well deck up to the top deck, and down into the bowels of the ship. The layout left nothing to be desired in terms of living space or practical arrangement.

Nazira led Javier to the command berths past a newly hired marine guard and a few members of the cadre preparing the ship for a warp. She touched one by the shoulder, saying, "Tea for both of us." The woman nodded, gave a salute, and left through the well deck hatch.

The berths themselves were quite large, an office that could be slept in rather than a bunk with room for an office. The *Remarker* was renowned for its power and size, constructed as a liner and a cargo hauler, and later fitted out for piracy. It was a ship that could defeat frigates and outrun capital ships. Her roomy size was born out in the command berths, where the captain's cabin, officer's wardroom, and senior officer's cabin sat side-by-side on the aft of the ship's quarterdeck. The ship's office and the second officer's cabin were on the port side, with the ship's locker, sully room, and the officer's head on the starboard, all at the deck line of the well deck.

The center space of the command cabins included a weather-safe chart table that converted into a space for officer meals, a pair of offset compasses, a rack of navigation tools, and numerous red leather chairs clinked to the decks to allow crew to participate in meetings. Nazira walked Javier to one of those chairs and said, "Sit down, my love. I want you to be happy; however, this may not make you smile. Still, you must listen to me."

Javier sat down, his head spinning. "My dear, how have you done all this?"

"Growing up the daughter of a Dominar, people overlook you and your qualities. They see you only as an extension of the power of your father, not as a power yourself. I know you love me. Still, you do not know me and my quality. You know a person who you met at court whose sole responsibility was to support her father while looking charming in a fine dress. You fell in love with the real me, because that was who you were, a man ignorant of the currents of the palace, a fish who was not aware of the water in the pond you swam in. I have considerable wealth that I cannot spend until I am married to a person who can, to quote the law, 'see to the continuity of the Dominar's line.' I married you after you proved fit for the task, although many have argued this is not the case. My father then entailed that wealth, arguing you were no good, just a fortune hunter. It is time I broke with my father. I am now with child, thus my person is safe from harm. However, he is keeping me from money I own, as well as from my rightful powers of court."

"I do not know what to say," Javier replied, sandbagged. "I will fight the Dominar if that is what you wish. I have no love for him. My loyalty is to the crown he wears, not to the man."

Nazira laughed. She had a wonderful, deep, basso voice. Further, despite being a tiny wisp of a woman, she had surprisingly big hips and wide shoulders. Her head carried an immense main of blue-black hair. Her amber eyes were disturbing. She turned, looked at Javier, spearing him with her intense gaze, and crossed her arms as was her wont, forming a dark-haired pyramid with her body.

"Do you want my money, Javier?" she asked.

Javier recoiled a step. "Hell no, my wife. How could you say that?"

"What about power? You could, if you knew your worth, throw down the Dominar and take his place!" she exclaimed. "Your issues, and do not argue these, might even be a benefit."

"My dearest, what causes you to say these things to me?" Javier asked.

Nazira walked over to the charting table, then pulled a compass from a clip. "Why are these clipped to the table?"

Shocked by the line of questioning, Javier said, "In storms, they will fly around and injure people if not restrained."

"What is this?" she asked, pulling out a long wooden measuring stick with a slide running down it.

"A computing protractor with a rotating point. We use it to determine course when using tolan maps," Javier answered.

Nazira smiled. "Everyone who my father spoke to said the same thing. You are a brilliant leader, a powerful commander of men and women, a gifted sailor, and utterly incorruptible when it comes to your duties at sea. Yet, there is something broken in you, many said. They said you were two people who could not be welded into one. That you lacked guile with money. You were someone who would be just as happy on a beach with a pot of stew on a driftwood fire as taking real power. They said you would probably make a nation of crabs and be its king, never once realizing you could grab real power by simply leaving the beach."

Javier looked wounded. "Have I offended you, dear?"

Nazira laughed, again sketching the pyramid with her legs and body that seemed to make her as if cast by stone. "These are not insults, dear. They are compliments. I proposed to you because your guile is safely locked away, your thirst for power is easily diverted, and you want nothing if not for adventure. If I had married any of the men my father bade me to marry, then I would have no protector, just another cretin who would do for me as my father did for my mother. We have created a baby between us that will soon enter this world, which was the right thing to do. I am satisfied with you as my spouse and father of the dynasty whose children the electorate will favor."

She walked behind Javier, placing a hand on his shoulder. "My father plans to have me killed. You have saved me without realizing it. Now I must save you. Through my own hand, I have set this dance of shapes in motion. We will either see ourselves to position or power, or we will our-selves to doom."

Javier grasped her hand. "I do not know what to say." He looked at his wife, then stumbled a little before he could bring out the next words. "Come with me then. Let us flee."

"Others have said that to me, not so long ago." Nazira smiled. Her dark eyes, long dark hair, and the impish lips that had attracted him to her were all there; however, there was also an iron behind her eyes that he had not been smart enough to see. She had played dice with some of the most dangerous people in the Kingdom, defeating them in a game they did not even know they were playing.

Nazira touched his forehead, saying, "You are to take this ship which I have leveraged the fortune stolen from me to make me a new fortune. I have tasked you to speak with one person, a person who neither of us has ever met, but who is the only person in the universe who may feel they own all to my dynasty. Additionally, turn hard work and your real talents of navigation and ease of character into a hold full of silver! Come back then, come back so we may face my father and his misdeeds together."

Javier looked up at her. "I must stay to protect you."

Nazira laughed. "You must do no such thing, gallant. You will lose your balls, then my father will kill me, knowing that another man might be more effective. No, my darling husband, you must do as I say if you truly love me."

Javier hugged her while wiping a tear from his eye. He then escorted her wordlessly onto deck. He stood next to Devious as Nazira said goodbye to Standish, watching her launch pull for the castle docks. Devious was but a shadow of himself tonight, seeming to keep to the shadows to avoid being seen by the crew.

"You certainly spread your cheeks this time, and the ramming will commence."

Javier shook his head. "You are always so negative, Devious. I can sense this is the making of me."

"Does making you include having your balls cut off and hung around your neck? No matter what they say, there is no growing them back," he said. "Or you might end up on the island. Have you considered this?"

Javier shook his head. "I know the island as well as you do. I know that it no longer does what it once did. Let the lost stay lost, man."

Devious snuffed. "That is a good way to have the lost show up on your doorstep wishing dinner and a sniff of tea."

Angela Standish approached Javier, stopped in front of him, standing ramrod straight at attention, although she could not remove the disdain she carried on her face. She was a large woman, perhaps 185 centimeters tall and massing 90 kilograms, a bulldog of a woman with a ship's cut hair. She ignored Devious, addressing Javier, "I am your new Major of Marines, Captain al-Rasheed."

Javier said, "You should get to know my Quartermaine, Sederick Devious."

Angela pretended like she did not see Devious, replying, "Nonetheless, Captain, we are ready to warp for our first alien shore."

Javier nodded, then closed his eyes. He thought for a second over his wife's plans, her hasty departure. This was her test of his mettle. For him, success was for his wife and child. "I want this circus cleaned up, Standish. Bend sail in thirty. Have whoever is navigating take us out of this roadstead and over the horizon before dawn!" He looked out on the ship. It was indeed a sorry sight. They had not enough crew and were poorly ballasted. Her sails were threadbare, her lines slack and unbraided in places. The deck was in need of soapstone, the paint was rough and blistered, and in some places, the planks had twisted. However, the ship had character. It stood tall in its decrepitude. Some would say she was a thousand planks floating in close proximity, but Javier felt her soul, knowing this was the ship he had always wanted.

As dawn creased the sky with shards of light, Javier found a package of tea in the disorganized mess of supplies that still cluttered the deck. His crew was ill-trained and unknown to him. Further, he had no destination, with no clear idea of how he would make this all work. He watched the Coxswain fumble the wheel while the Navigator cursed over the tolan sights, while he occupied his hand with brewing the tea over a paraffin lamp.

When he was finished, he sipped the results, then audibly groaned. The tea was bitter and hard to stomach. One of the armsmen, who had been called as a newly minted marine, set his firelock down and asked, "May I have some tea, Captain?"

Javier drank another draught, then warned, "It is Junebug." The soldier shrugged. "Bad tea is better than no tea."

Chapter V

Stranded on the Shores of Eternity

Javier al-Rasheed handed the sexton to his navigator. "Fix your computer paper to the desk. Make sure you have a fountain pen that functions with ink in it. Then take your sextant and choose the brightest star in the sky. That will almost always be Ferris at night, the sun during the day. Point the sextant at the horizon, then clamp to release the telltale arm. Swing the telltale until your star on the right side is matching on the left side of your optic. If you have a tight sight, you can swing the sextant back and forth with the star remaining in place. Write that on your programming form, then take a shoot from your compass, then enter that as well. Go to the tolan book to convert your programming to latitude. Finally, write the estimated time down so you can get your longitude."

Rabia Ibn Saludi was the Lead Navigator. Like many aspects of the *Remarker*'s first cruise as a trader, she was not really the Navigator, just a surveyor who had answered

Nazira's call for crew on a merchant ship. Her grasp of math was wonderful, but she was slow in making sights and had no skill, at least yet, for the rapid estimations needed to serve as the Navigator of an open sea ship. She was, though, a wonderful department head for the deck crew, turning a trio of shallow water launch drivers into coxswains in only a few days' time. Still, unless she could become a better Navigator, then the entire ship would depend on Javier's own skills in this area.

He turned to the teapot which served the cockpit in clear weather, unlocking it from its holder in order to pour himself a portion of Junebug. The acrid, pettish, tannic brew was unpleasant to drink, yet it was growing on him. Besides, bad tea was better than no tea, as the Marines said. He had taken to simmering it with willow bark and spruce, with the result being a jolting infusion that caused his tongue to recoil into his mouth with fear each time he applied the cup to his lips. He imagined his stomach preparing to receive the hot splash of horrid liquid like soldiers ready to take fire from an implacable enemy, actually feeling the organ contracting in pain as the hot liquid splashed down his throat, assaulting his body with the aggressive elan of a barbarian invader.

He could get used to Junebug, just as a prisoner got used to torture, even reveling in his ability to survive the experience.

While Rabia repeated the sights he had assigned her, Javier locked the teapot back into the frame, then walked over to the coxswain. "How are you holding up, Leopold?"

"Twelve on and twelve off. I can keep this up, I think," he replied. Javier preferred a parade of eight schedule, but that would have to wait until they hired more crew. logbook He turned and looked at the weather station next to the wheel, growing concerned. He pulled the to check what the readings had been earlier in the day. "Bit worried about this," he said.

"What sir?" Leopold asked.

"We have lost ten millimeters of mercury in about one hour and the wind cups show we have a following wind up five since dusk. It means we are in for a storm." Javier said. He stepped up to the wheel. "Go down and get a meal and some sleep. If you see Mr. Devious or Ms. Standish, send them up." Javier then looked over at the Navigator. "Lieutenant Saludi, lock up your station and go down as well."

Javier looked nervously at the weather gauge while he guided the wheel. The helm responded with a sluggish, almost crepuscular reply, something he had not realized. The ship was large, the helm ropes were old and stretched, plus the rudder was not digging into the sea as well as it should. There was water shipping over the side as the seas grew, the spray reaching the top crew.

"So Captain, how is the ship handling?" It was tall, sallow Devious, looking a bit odd out of his fine clothing, instead dressed in an officer's uniform two sizes too small.

The stars, which had earlier been brilliant in the sky, were starting to disappear into the cloud cover. "We have a crew of forty-one on a ship that needs at least three times that number. We are running with an empty cargo hold, and the weather gauge is dropping."

"I assume, sir, the weather gauge is significant?" Devious asked blandly, catching himself as a wave struck the ship.

"It is a storm gradient—looked as pressure in the air. The faster it falls, the bigger the storm. On a tolan course like we are on now between land chains, we have no coast to run to for shelter." The wind cups took that moment to change their timbre, spinning up faster in response to the gusting gale.

"The ship certainly has a crescendo of sounds that one may wonder at their significance," Devious said.

Javier looked past Devious to a sailor huddled in the corner of the cockpit. "Wake the crew, everyone but the people I sent down. Get everyone into the sheets to slack sail to one quarter. That will keep us digging in. We only have two people aloft on the watch. When this thing hits, no one will be safe up there. Once the sheets are in, get a meal cooking, tea for everyone, then start the lot of them at calking if we can do it. Have someone explain waste lines to the new fish. I do not want anyone over the side when this gets nasty."

Devious laughed a bitter laugh. "Shouldn't this be the duty of the Senior Officer to make these arrangements?"

"Hire me a Senior Officer and you can put your suit back on." Javier replied.

"When was the last time you did less than two jobs on any ship you signed? We will get more crew. You just have to sail us through this storm to get them."

Javier laughed. "I can find crew on an island of goatherds."

A few minutes later, the Sailing Master, Alia D'casio, was on deck. "Captain, how would you wish the sails to fair?"

Javier looked to the sheets with a heavy heart. Damn dangerous to reef on the edge of a storm for an experienced crew. The deck was a long way down; the chance of mistakes was high. He glanced over at the Sailing Master. D'casio was young, maybe twenty and one. She had come from the fishing fleet where she was a sailmaker, where she had some time aloft, but not much. Calling her a Sailing Master was simply not fair to her considering what was coming. In a crew of forty, she had two people who had been aloft before this voyage. She needed forty in the sheets for a rapid evolution.

"Take your two able hands and give them the two main masts. Tell them 'down and dirty.' That means they will rig stay lines while a crew on the deck will heave to, one sail at a time. Quarter sail means we are flying only a quarter of our possible cloth but divided across at least three masts so that we do not become unstable. That way, the helm will still respond, keeping us on a clean heading." At that moment, a wave came in on the transversal, causing the ship to fall off the line of the wind. Javier corrected starboard, yawing *Remarker* into the sea to keep her steady and underway.

"Yes, Captain," she said. On a liner like *Remarker*, as Javier explained to Devious, there should be forty hands for the sails. In an emergency, all forty would be aloft, the sails taking less than thirty minutes to reef if all went well. Using crew on the deck to heave the sails through block and pulley is not the ideal way to handle reefing, but it would save time at the cost of sloppy handling that could rip the sheets. D'casio turned to catch crew as they came on deck, but Javier grabbed her shoulder for a second. Into her ear, he said, "Safety lines for all. Tell your Ables that if I see a swan aloft, I will shoot them off the sheet-yard with my own hands, understand?"

D'casio nodded, then went down the ascent to catch crew to send them to their places in the well deck. Javier watched her move on the heaving deck, impressed with her sea legs. Unlike many of the crew, she was not seasick or turned about. He could detect that D'casio was scared though, as the ship depended on skills she did not really have, which was weighing on her just like it was causing gloom among other crew positions.

Javier watched D'casio take charge below, happy with the results. He caught her attention from the quarterdeck, then yelled, "You do what you can do. Each word out of your mouth today is coming from my lungs. No one will second-guess you. Tomorrow, when we have survived this storm, we will discuss without rancor how to do better. Today, whatever you do, whatever happens, is good enough. Understand?"

She replied to Javier with a nod, then continued to push and prod the crew, yelling out, "We are going to reef. I want quarter sails in thirty!"

Quarter sails in thirty would be a challenge for a complete and experienced crew, but Javier approved of the aspiration, even if it was impossible. Likely they would end up cutting sheets.

Major Standish came up the gangway, then climbed the quarterdeck ascent. "Storm?" she asked ironically.

"No thanks, have one already," Javier replied. He looked at the barometer. "Two or three hours until we are in its teeth, but we do not have the Staff to skirt it. If I change course off the tolan, we may simply be beating our way into it."

"Tolan?" she asked.

"A course from one roadstead to another along a given compass bearing following a prevalent wind and current. We lit out of the Kingdom with no real destination, so I simply chose the cleanest tolan in the book, Cycus-Roads to the Cape of Darts. Twelve days at sea given good winds. At the Cape, we can get the ship refitted and look for more crew. O-Town, the capital, has several outfitters present," Javier answered. "Alas, once the storm really bites, we have to simply steer to save the ship, which means we could end up anywhere on the map!"

"Cannot be helped I guess," Standish said, grasping a stanchion to remain standing as the ship caught a rogue wave.

Javier looked at the crew struggling to reef the sheets. "How is the morale of the crew?"

Standish looked at her captain. "Three people I figure for trouble. The rest, I am surprised at how well they are taking this sudden departure."

"Three people?" Javier knew that a wounded ship in need of repairs was dangerous; however, nothing was more dangerous than a crew member who decided mutiny was a better answer than pulling together for shore.

"Hiring was my job, therefore, it is my responsibility," she said. "I can always call crew overboard if one of them steps out of line."

Javier shook his head. A crazed crew person on a ship in the teeth of a storm was not something that was humorous, yet Standish did not seem worried by the prospect. A wave again hit on the transverse, so he had to fight her back into the wind. Javier looked to the sheets. The first of the big sails were coming in sloppy, well beyond any aid now. He noted his fight with the waves and wind had caused the ship to fall off compass. Just then, another wave caught them on the starboard, so he gave the helm more correction to bring her back against the unbalanced forces pushing her through the sea. The wind was starting to fall too, meaning he had to abandon any pretense of keeping the tolan any longer. "You and Nazira did well, very well. Three laggards in forty is amazing. Someday I will have to ask how you and my wife brought it all together."

"Best ask her," came a terse reply from the marine major. He looked at her, noting she was losing her legs in the waves.

"I see something!" came a scream from the watch aloft. Javier thought of screaming back for the watcher to give a proper reply, then, on second thought, realized this would just end up being a long conversation shouted through a gale of wind.

"Take the wheel," he said.

Standish did, looking dubious. He had finally found a way to shake her laggard bravery by having to risk the ship and all the souls on board to do it.

"The wheel is backward. If you see us fall to port, correct to port. Right now, if you are within forty-five degrees of true, you are winning the fight." Javier yelled. He pointed to the wind gauge. "See that thing with the arrow and the cups? Keep the arrow to the foreend. You won't be able to, but we can handle forty-five degrees to either side. More than that, we could breach, you would lose the rudder, then we would all be dead!"

Standish nodded, drilling her eyes on the wind compass and the cups.

Javier ran through the confusion of the sail reefing to the forward center mast to swarm up it, knowing that he was violating his own rules about staying connected to a painter line. He could sense the eyes of the crew in the well deck on him as made a leap for a crossover at the bottom yard, then monkeyed up the first hemp stay to the crow's nest. The sailor in the nest was not more than fifteen, scared as hell, his eyes wide with fear. Javier clipped a painter on his safety belt, admonishing, "A proper report is the quarter the sighting was made, distance, and nature of the sight."

"I need permission to throw up, sir," the boy said in a warbling tone.

"Use your hat, then scale it over leeward. I will buy you a new one," Javier said, pulling his range, finding glasses to his eyes while grasping the mast with his legs. Leaning out as far as he could, he caught sight of a fire on the water burning on a confused mass of wood rafts, and what looked like half a ship. He was staring at it as a white apprentice's hat flung past him, caught the wind, starting to sketch an unlikely trajectory overboard. He looked at the rating, knowing the boy would not be able to get out of the mast. "What is your name?"

The boy was now crying, covered in sick, almost bent double. "Just 'Mouse,' sir. Sometimes 'the Mouse.'"

"Your parents named you 'Mouse,' did they?" Javier asked, trying to take the lad's mind off his obvious terror.

"No parents, sir. Just what they called me under the pier. The gang, you know," the lad said.

"How did you get hired on?" Javier screamed as the wind again took up.

Mouse shrugged. "No one hired me. I just followed some of the jacks who said there was food in it if I ran their bunks."

While they were talking, Javier formed a rope seat from a painter, then another. He struggled into the first seat, then started to rope the other onto Mouse. The tackle box fixed to the nest had tension clips, line serpentines, plus a really impressive amount of other gear. Javier built Mouse a full cinch and hooked it into the rope seat, then through his own harness. The young apprentice finally noticed that he was almost completely helpless in a rope harness attached to Javier, but bravely nodded, gulping down his terror.

"What are you doing, Captain?" he asked.

"Do you know what running a Jack's bunk means?" Javier asked.

"Cleaning it?" the boy responded.

"When we are down, you go to the major. Tell her you were brought on to run jack bunks. Tell her the truth, or else I will find out." Javier said, then leaped out and around the watch nest, dragging Mouse behind him.

The moment of truth in any rappel that lacked belay was when the weight bit into the harness. Screw the loop through the hardware, a person would end up hanging in midair locked into the line. Fail to make the bite run right, that same person would simply plummet to the deck, bashing their brains out. If they did it in a way that allowed them to see cross lines and other deadly obstructions ... it meant they would be falling face first in the descent, a scary way to rappel.

The good point of any rappel from the yards is that it would leave a few seconds to worry one way or another. From Javier's point of view, he took a breath, leaped into space, saw the deck rushing at his face, checked, landed on his feet, then took a new breath. Once on the deck, dozens of hands helped pull the kid from his seat on the captain's back. Those crew who were not recovering the terrified Mouse were staring at their captain, mouths gaping, eyes wide with wonder, as if he was a shanty wizard who had just summoned a hedgehog at a child's birthday party.

"Keep working on the sheets, get the kid down below! Prepare rescue stations. We have a foundering craft ahead of us!" Javier ordered in a loud voice.

The Sailing Master yelled, "You heard the captain! Even gangs in the sheets, odd gangs at the railings until we hear better! Be ready for other orders!"

"Navigator and Coxswain to the helm, with my apologies," Javier added.

On the quarterdeck riser, he gathered Standish, the Coxswain, Sailing Master, Steward, a sailor named Hujja el-Nawaz, who was acting as a runner, and the Navigator. Devious remained but hid in the shadows, listening. They were all dressing in woolens and oilcloth as he spoke, draping themselves in rescue belts, painters, and chains of d-rings. "Listen close!" he yelled because the storm was truly closing in, the wind past gale into a blasting scream of angry air. "I scoped a broken, frigate-sized ship foundered in the waves, surrounded by a dozen or more rafts that looked to be sea dwellers—Sea Folk. Major, direct traffic on the deck. Forward hold for Sea Folk, after-hold for survivors of the frigate. El-Nawaz, nets to the side, four crew on one winch. I am going over in that net to see if we can scoop up survivors from the wreckage. Coxswain and Navigator, I want you to try to keep us on a tack that protects those people in our lee. I know you will fall off. Just port back to keep us port side to them if at all possible. I want wind and seas to the starboard. Sailing Master, two people only, keep reefing sails. If you have to cut sails, drop them to deck then roll them into a hold, even if you have to drop them on top of survivors. Steward, fires lit, one crew plus you to brew tea and get some sort of hot food produced, as much as you can. I do not care what it is. When things become too bad, we clear decks, batten the cargo doors and the gangway hatches, then only two people on the helm, myself and one volunteer on thirty-minute shifts. Understand?" His yelled commands were barely breaking the howl of the storm; however, the entire crew seemed to react at one.

El-Nawaz chose the forward winch to swing out port. It was a clever contraption operated by four crew, two of which controlled the geared line which fed to a cargo net, one who controlled the swing of the winch arm, and one who was the eyes of the crane sitting aloft yelling orders. Javier monkey-climbed into the net made from thick hemp lines, then tied a painter off with a set of d-rings to allow him mobility but protect him from a long fall. He marveled as the *Remarker* heeled to the Coxswain's steering into the heavy following sea, making her come around smartly for the wreckage while losing way at the same time. It was possibly luck; Javier noted it as a place to complement the scared sailor's helm performance when this was over.

He could hear Standish yelling orders, keeping the deck moving, while the Navigator called out fixes for the rest of the crew. Other crew were in the sheets, yelling to each other to balance the reefing, while others were attaching then throwing the side nets over, and running out line to belay climbers with.

The net began to swing over the side, allowing Javier to clearly see the catastrophe unfolding in front of him. Somehow, in all this open sea, a nimble frigate had penetrated through the middle of a cluster of rafts belonging to a Sea Folk colony. Faced with a storm, Sea Folk rely on their ability to reconfigure their rafts to avoid the worst of the weather, often beating to the storm shadow of an island in the worst seasons. It was rare for them to land in a tolan route since they were vulnerable to piracy and shy by nature.

Further, a frigate was just too damn maneuverable at speed to hit an assembly of rafts by accident. With all their sails standing, they could almost cut circles around a liner like the *Remarker*, and the *Remarker* was very agile for a large ship.

As he swung out over the water, he could see dozens, maybe more, people clinging to both wrecks, with more in the water, bobbing up and down in three-meter swells. He looked over his shoulder and yelled, "Do not be scared to dunk me, cheat low!" He had lines, painters, and clips dropped over himself, enough to drag him to the bottom if he came loose, but was himself protected by the safety line whose parting strength was higher than the parting weight of his own body.

The ship tacked twice to keep away, then struck the outer rafts that were already underwater. Suddenly, Javier dropped into the water. Hands reached for him, and he grabbed back, pulling them into the net. A small boy came in, followed by two men, then a small family group. Others grabbed the nets on the side of the ship where his crew were themselves hanging over the side, tossing out painters attached to wooden rings for desperate people to grab. As the survivors scrambled into his net, he tied them off as best as he could with clips and painters, yet one man fell into the sea. He dove after him, but the man was lost, so Javier had to swarm up his safety line back into the net.

The net swung back onto the deck where a multitude of hands helped him loose the wet, broken survivors, then send them down into the cargo hold. More were coming over the sides. Then the Coxswain hauled to a port tack. The ship groaned as the waves struck its side with wild determination to roll the poorly ballasted liner over. The winch crew, though, was handy with their controls, as Javier felt himself lifted off the deck as the last survivor was dumped to the ground without ceremony from the net.

This tack had them almost bumping the broken frigate, where men and women clung to its hull, as well as to an overturned pinnace in the waves. The net dropped and more survivors reached for succor. This time Javier hooked the pinnace through its fore-end eyebolt, then was able to get the chain into a clamp, a desperate attempt to use it to get a larger group of survivors out of the water. The winch could handle the mass of the boat easily—it was designed to launch a fully loaded cargo lighter. The men clinging to it were then able to clamber up the boat across its benches, easier than trying to catch the net as it swung by. The winch, though, was slow to lift, its gearing biting down on the weight, making it hard going for the crew, who had to engage its highest gearing to move the mass. As the ship passed the broken frigate, Javier grabbed one of the sailors in the net, yelling, "Get anyone who can help to right this damn boat on our deck so I can swing out again!"

The man, although terrified, was enough of a trained sailor to understand what he needed to do. They needed hands to recover the pinnace, or else they would have to drop it, meaning the men and women clinging to it would fall into the sea, having then to make their way to the side nets. Javier threw a rigged line to the crew on the pinnace as they swung inboard, relieved when most took it, while using another line to swing to the deck, then taking charge of the heavy ship's boat. When it was in place, and the survivors in his net had swarmed on board the *Remarker*, he cut the pinnace free of the lands to let the winch crew bring him back over the wreckage on their next pass.

The seas went to four meters, then five as they worked, with the sheer size of the waves ending any chance to rescue people who were not clinging to wreckage. They tried though, coming around ten times, all hands bending to the rescue with a fierce will. After an hour, no more survivors could be found, and the *Remarker* was in danger of foundering if she again came abaft the wind gage. Javier gave it ten more minutes without seeing a survivor, after which he called the winch crew to bring it back aboard. When the winch stopped inboard, Javier removed his safety painter, falling right from the winch to the deck, where he then collapsed, exhausted like the rest of his crew.

He came to a few minutes later, dragged into the protection of the quarterdeck's cockpit with Standish kneeling by him. "Clear the deck!" Javier yelled.

Standish nodded, stating, "We separated the two crews, frigate crew to the aft hold, Sea Folk to the forward hold, as you ordered. The two groups were fighting even as we were rescuing them."

"Dog the connecting doors, make sure they do not get to wander the ship. Let them have their own holds, none of our people in there to become hostages. Tell them we are poorly ballasted, cannot have them wandering around. Also, hand out firelocks to reliable crew," Javier said. "Now off the deck, this storm has many hours yet, and it will be bad. Fires out. Everyone who can, should shelter. Only one volunteer up with me at a time. Your only responsibility is to make sure none of the people we rescued go for us."

Standish nodded. "As ordered, sir."

The storm swell rose over the hours to nine meters; the winds topped 60kph. Fishers survived worse storms but in strong ships with experienced crew. There was no way to keep way on the tolan as the compass quit making sense an hour into the worst of the storm. With no way to cast a knotted line, Javier had to pay attention to the water gavel, which was unable to cope with the shifting currents, instead steering by the wind gage. He had a quarter sail lofted; unfortunately, to achieve this, nine sheets had been cut free and sent below. He did not know if they had enough line to rehang the downed sails once the storm was over. Further, the ship showed signs that her poor repair could see her suffer a catastrophic failure.

As he fought to keep *Remarker* steady into the wind while dealing with her tendency to breach as transverse waves crashed upon her, Javier thought of all the elements that could end their voyage. The liner had 44 frames driven to a centerline keel, with an H-frame at the level of the main deck. She could lose two or three frames and stay afloat; however, one frame cracking tended to break the transverse, putting fresh stress on the next frame. A ship could lose all the frames in series in a matter of minutes, coming apart like a box of matchwood. He hoped *Remarker* was built better than this.

Javier noted that the ship was unbalanced from leaking into the lower spaces, and this was causing her to hog excessively, which could break the keel if it developed enough. The four masts were no longer under great strain due to their reefed sails, but if one was cracked, if the line stays gave way, or if the crossarms created enough tension to sever the top of the mast, it would add more stress to the wooden hull, which could then collapse under the stress.

Javier thought again. The question was: How well put together was this old liner after years of neglect? Additionally, did some ship-fitter at some point in the ship's life substitute ash in some hidden joist or joiner when oak was called for? His original brief look at the frames showed they were made from the best ironwood, an amazingly expensive lumber. Further, many of the thwarts and decking were live oak, perhaps the best dense wood that could serve a large ship in the form of planking. He worried that shipworm and gutter rot might have infected the planking in some place that could not be inspected underway, as well as if the tar seating for the masts was decayed where they butted wood. They did not have the time to find out; the lack of knowledge could kill them.

Remarker was his now. Its strength, its integrity, was all that protected his 41 crew members from death. Maybe seven score survivors shivered below deck which also depended on the performance of his ship. On the sole question of if she would hold together.

She did.

When the storm abated, Javier ordered that the Coxswain steer a general western course with the sail she had in hopes of seeing land. Then he went to sleep for a day.

He woke to a breakfast of murgoo and a pot of Junebug simmered with spruce water. The sailor acting as the Steward seemed relieved to be working below deck, as the ship still rocked quite a bit. Devious was sitting by his bunk. "Quite the storm," he said. Javier did not answer, instead applying his efforts to eating and drinking. "I feel like your lack of small talk indicates that our issues are in the past."

Javier shook his head. "The weather turned around through the compass several times during the rescue, then I had to climb out of the storm's influence by taking its wind's spin-ward. Now there is a lot of guesswork as to where we are."

Devious said, "You told me you could find out where you were from the stars and the sun?"

"I can, if we make landfall, find our approximate location. Then I can either shape a course for an island with visual cues that let me find it, or I can gamble on creating an untested tolan, then shooting a warp."

"Why are these choices causing you to be glum?" Devious asked.

"Time, food, and water. We have a lot of people on the ship now. They all have to be fed and given water. If I cannot really get a tolan together, then we may be fighting the currents and the winds, which will take a long time. We might not find an island with water or food. If we drifted into the northern Extents, storms like the one we just went through will become more common, and the temperature hotter as the year progresses. I have never done this sort of navigating before. Neither has the Navigator, for that matter. I could become sick, which would cut our skills in the cockpit by eight parts in ten," Javier said.

"You should gather the key crew and explain," Devious said.

"Al-Vohra!" Javier yelled, and a crew person showed up. "My compliments, the major and the Navigator to the war room. Ask the major for five Marines, and you will stay as runner."

"Yes, sir," the apprentice said.

Javier took ten minutes to recover from his ordeals, then entered the wardroom, rested, if not carefree. He recognized the Navigator and the Charts Keeper first. "Rabia, you and Kwame are who we have to create enough celestial data to run a program and either shape us home or to even write our own warp. We may have to do this at sea, so I want both of you plotting as much as you can so that I can work on the programming. You are going to make mistakes with your sight, but I have found the more mistakes you make, the more they tend to average into useful data. Take a sun sight right now, then tell me the time it would be in Cycus based on that sight, then continue from there. Have the Coxswain steer steady eastward."

He turned to Standish, "Have your Marines on the by, then bring me the leader of each group of castaways in my office. When they arrive, I want you in the room to listen in." Standish nodded, setting about her task.

Javier put on his best uniform and arranged for Devious to be present for his insider knowledge of Halo politics, while keeping Standish for her aura of professional menace. The marines arrived first with the captain of the frigate to his office. The man was from Emporia, with shocking orange hair and skin where the freckles had combined into a general tone of red on a round face with piercing green eyes. He came into Javier's office with no ceremony, looking on his rescuer with scaled eyes. After a minute of silence, he said, "I am Commodore Manuel Tarkington of the warship

Repulse. Are you aware of the requirements of honor when addressing a superior officer, Commander?"

Javier smiled. "Have a seat, Commodore. I will let you have a copy of the Tea Merchant's Diplomatic Manual. However, you are, in fact, a guest on my ship through rescue. As the captain of the ship who is now sheltering your men and women, the genuflections you are demanding, in fact, belong to me. In spite of that, I accept that they are a bother, simply asking you remain polite."

"If you dishonor me, your king will have your head," Tarkington said.

"He wants my balls already, so your threat is, how should I say, less than persuasive," Javier stated with a laugh. "Do you know what vessel this is?"

"No, other than you are wearing rank from the minor kingdom of Cycus," Tarkington said dismissively. "I have seen the name on a map. So far to the edge of the Halo that it is almost part of the Extents. I am not impressed."

Javier pulled a paper written by Devious, who had in the past shown an ability to get people to talk. "Your frigate, the *Repulse*, rammed the raft community of the Sea Folk as they traversed the sea on the tolan between Cycus Roads and the Cape of Darts. Now, Sea Folk are known to frequent this area; however, you are quite a distance from Emporia or your own trade lanes. Begs the question, why the ramming?"

Tarkington waved in the air. "Not that this is your business, but we were in hot pursuit following up on their encroachment of our fishing rights." Devious laughed silently from the back of the room. The laugh seemed to shake Tarkington.

"Major," Javier said, "take the Commodore to the stateroom we have prepared for him. Mr. Tarkington, I am assigning you a crew person should you wish to wander the decks, at least until we can figure this all out."

When he left, Javier looked at Devious, who came up out of the shadow. "I spoke to the crew. They have been at sea for 91 days, only locating the Sea Folk four days ago. Even the next senior surviving officer is unaware of why they rammed the Sea Folk." He seemed puzzled. "Now you get the other side ... if you want."

Javier picked up his steel teacup, then leaned back. The brew was good Shanty. It opened your eyes without making you jitter like most sailor's tea did. After a minute of thought, he said, "Bring the opposite side in if we have to consider castaways as being on sides."

The man who entered was thin and tall like Devious. The sun had burned his skin black, while his hair was straw gold. He wore only slacks despite the nip in the air, his skin tattooed in red ink across his body. He also was rather pompous, seeming to expect some form of genuflection from Javier as the Commodore had. When it was not forthcoming, he seated himself, saying, "Name's Mayor Fleet of the Star Band."

"I am Captain Javier al-Rasheed. You can call me Javier. I am curious, why are you in open sea during storm season? I understood your folk wisely anchor in the lees of islands to obtain the protection of Storm Shadow, as well as stay in the calmer regions of the Halo."

"We were chasing a bank of heriots looking to get a good head on winter food supply. When a clear opportunity comes, you take it," he said in a brittle voice.

Javier looked the man in the face. "Then how do you come into conflict with a foreign frigate?"

"My people and I have never been to the waters of Emporia, nor met the Commodore of that frigate before," replied Mayor Fleet.

Javier stared at him, causing the mayor to shift in his seat. "You will have an officer's cabin and will be free to walk the decks with an escort. I would advise, nay insist, that you and the Commodore of the Emporia ship not interact unless I am present. Further, I expect that you will keep order in your deck spaces until we find succor. Thank you for your time."

The mayor stood and left. Once he was gone, Major Standish said, "How odd, they are both lying, I believe." Javier looked into the dark corner where Devious stood silently, nodding. Something was definitely going on.

Despite the mystery, Javier could not spend more time on the castaways. He had 181 souls on board. He had a damaged ship with 40,000 liters of water and 10,000 kilograms of foodstuffs. That water and food had been planned for 41 crew; it would last only 50 days now. Worse, they had no idea where they were. Whatever solution he came up with had to occur before the food and water sources began to run out.

Later that day Javier had the charts out, shooting sights, and contemplating his dead reckoning notes. The Navigator was with him, learning the trade as much as helping him. "The problem with the Halo is that it is completely possible to plot a rhumb that will cause you to either miss all the known lands, or worse perhaps, get you becalmed in one of the eddy spirals. Once you leave a tolan, if a storm pushes you around, you can set your latitude, but your longitude becomes guesswork."

"Why not head north or south?" Rabia asked.

"We are too far rim-ward for that to work," he said. Javier pulled out a map from a roller. "The Halo is a circle, roughly. All of the islands we call home are inside of this circle. Interestingly enough, there are currents that are fair constant, plus winds that are usually blowing in a predictable direction, which together allow us to travel efficiently along some routes better than others. Leaving the Halo for the Extents means you leave the predictable sea routes where sailing is no longer easy. There are no clear tolans that we can follow to the outer islands. For example, the Noothens, here on the eastern seas, cannot be reached by an easy rhumb. You have to plot a changing course series to account for changing winds and tides. Any mistake in shaping your course means you can be cast into the deep sea and die. If we were blown from our tolan into deep sea, getting our way back to the Halo may be impossible, at least with the water we have."

"What about the birds?" came a little voice from behind them. Mouse looked far better now that he was no longer frozen in fear on a crow's nest. He was wearing a fresh canvas uniform, his face filled with a smile that showed his perfect white teeth.

Javier turned, asking, "What birds?"

"There," Mouse said, pointing into the air.

Javier squinted into the blue sky, then, unconvinced, grabbed his range finder and peered out into the distance. Scanning for several minutes, he almost gave up the search, but finally saw them. "Flare Cormorants. Mouse, get my book in my cabin that has a big bird on the cover." Javier marveled at the birds in flight, their wings spread wide, their circling pattern, how they would dive for the sea then return to the air like missiles thrown by an angry god.

The Navigator had a scope as well, also trying to see them. "Hard to see. Why are birds important?" she asked.

Javier answered, "They live in colonies on land." Mouse returned with the book, putting it on, then opening it on the navigation desk. Javier flipped through it until he found the page on Flare Cormorants. Reading, he quoted: "Navigators can use different animals to predict where landfall is. Flare Cormorants can fly a thousand kilometers as individuals, but hunting chiffons like to see land." Explaining, he told them, "Up there in the sky, they see farther than we do hugging the sea. When they fly out, they can see their home even if it is beyond the horizon from us. That group is twenty-five kilometers from land at most."

The Navigator looked skeptical. "What if their home is five rocks in the middle of the sea?"

"It is not in their nature to nest on small rock outcroppings in the sea. They flock in colonies of tens of thousands of birds. The Flares like cliffs on the lee of large islands. They drink fresh water, making nests from tree matter clutching rock. You see, they are just like us. One cormorant is a fluke. Fifty, are getting food to take back home. Home is always some place that has a cliff, fresh water, and trees. In other words, an island." Javier said excitedly. "Coxswain, bring us about by a quarter west. Mouse, get four people aloft for me. Tell the major we are possibly in sight of land."

The birds stayed in sight, giving Javier stomach cramps. They were supposed to hunt close to their islands, yet they could be hundreds of kilometers away if food was scarce. Further, they could fly so much faster than *Remarker* could chase them. Mouse kept them in sight, while Javier steered almost completely by the boy's keen eye, tacking across the wind with his limited sail strength. Finally, the cry came from the watch aloft, "Land away forward quarter!" Javier swarmed the line to the forward nest, looking out, confirming they had found a large island possessing a cliff filled with birds snugged against freshwater falls. The island was quite large, verdant, and green, with a sandy beach. A perfect port to call home in their dire need.

Hours later, they were in anchor off a beach on the lee of the island. The mayor of the Sea Folk and the Commodore of the Emporians were standing with Javier, as far apart as the quarterdeck would allow, each with an able sailor keeping careful watch. A dozen others stood on the quarterdeck trading the glasses and the range finder back and forth, taking long looks at the sandy shore. When he was sure to be heard, he said, "I am putting a crew ashore to look over the resources of the island. If the water is clean, if no one who might object to our harborage here lives on this land, and if there is sufficient material for us to repair the ship, then we will be staying on this island awhile. At least long enough to cast out, prepare food, fill out the water casks, plus figure out a plan to get us back to the Halo safely."

Mouse, of all people, raised his hand like a pupil in a finishing school. Javier nodded at him. "Does this island exist on a map?" he asked.

Javier replied, "No, we do not even know if humans have ever stepped onto these shores."

"Humans have been everywhere, they just forget," Devious said from his place behind Javier.

Ten people took the launch to the beach. Javier, Major Standish, Benji Sloan the Steward, Yulen Fix from the Sea Folk, Robbi Van Guerster from the *Repulse*, plus five ordinary sailors from the *Remarker* crew dressed in red jerseys and white sailor's pants. Javier tasked two sailors to construct a fire on the beach and watch the launch while he led the rest of the group into the forest with him.

The forest was filled with large oaks, spruce, and alder; it was also alive with animals. There were game paths that indicated larger animals existed, plus a number of bogs teeming with life. When they pushed through a glade, hundreds of crabs carrying borrowed conch shells would explode outward in a chitinous stampede that took minutes to calm. Deeper into the glade, a second canopy of parasol plants protected colonies of flutter-byes while gauzy chiffons sat alight thousands of mayapples and mock ferns. Fat black squirrels and flocks of gray quail kept a cautious distance from the group.

Van Guerster stopped at a fair-sized blood oak. "If this island was on the trade routes, it could make a rich living just from selectively cutting these oaks. There must be a thousand of them in this tract alone. This one is easily 50 stere. Not many wood-producing islands could make this claim in the core."

Javier stepped up to touch the ancient blood oak. It was old; its core would be close to ironwood. It also had the height and mass to form twenty frame segments, each of which could be warped into whatever shape a wood founder wanted.

There were also many small game trails on the island, cutting through the oak lowlands, breaking the understory of fiddle ferns and gumdrop plants. The trails round their way through peeper bogs and breaks cluttered with dark green bracken, dripping with the nearly constant rain from the upper stories of the forest. Bright red and orange birds occasionally flew low over the group, each making a clicking sound like someone tapping a set of steel-toed clogs on a wooden floor. The birds were occasionally chased by cat-like lemurs who would ambush their quarry from tufts of leaves. When not chasing the birds, the lemurs would cluster and stare with big eyes at the traders.

The main trail turned around a wet bog, then passed through a wetland that had hundreds of snails with colorful shells. The snails looked like the conchs that roamed the beach just offshore. Occasionally, the huge, beautiful shells would not contain a snail at all, but a soft, clawless crab with huge eyes.

When the party had navigated the small bog, they came to a river that was crossed by a sturdy stone bridge. The major pulled her firelock over her shoulder, then carefully walked forward. "Unless there is a new type of carpenter wasp, I believe we have found this island is already owned by someone."

Sloan drew his falling block, but Javier shook his head. "Leave it pouched unless they come screaming out of the woods. Notice anything about the bridge?"

That drew general attention to the condition of the structure. The bridge was two meters wide, twenty meters long, and spanned a deep riven with a trickle of water flowing down it. It was made from wood, covered in vegetation, and its parallels were, in some places, missing. Javier said, "Lazy group to let a fine bridge go to seed. Cross it with care now."

The bridge held as they crossed it. The trail became a lost road that was cobbled under the debris of fallen forest leaves. Slowly, they followed the road as it climbed through switchbacks until they were above the cliffside where the cormorants nested. They found a plateau on the edge of a line of higher mountains, each mountain maybe 2,000 meters tall at their highest point.

The road became an eerie boulevard as it crested the main plateau, where dozens, perhaps hundreds, of ruined human-made structures sat. As the group walked, it became obvious that this was a sizable city, as big or bigger than Cycus, which could have housed tens of thousands of souls. Large fields for crops or animal penning were surrounded by fieldstone walls, with some of the fields having grain towers and even occasional bits of farm technology.

Cordairs for mulch pits were scattered around the fields, some of which had the red cockades of fallow keena growing from the fertilizer mounds. There were orchards that, while crazy without maintenance, still showed fruit-bearing trees, quinces and paw paws, olives and derinos, enough in one field alone to feed five hundred people if properly tended and harvested.

Each plateau formed a dozen small sangers for agriculture. Dry waterbeds flowed across each one. They were blocked by tumbles and empty of water, but when they were flowing the land would have looked like a water-fed heaven. The builders did not, apparently, believe in straight channels, instead carving constantly curving streams lined with rocks that gleamed blue in the sunlight.

The road up the mountain ended in a large plateau built into a plaza of stone with a large dry lake and dozens of small waterways, each crossed by small bridges of stone. While designed to allow movement of agricultural products from the lower plateaus, it also seemed simply like a place where people could wander and rest. Broken and tumbled statues, smashed arbors, and indestructible fire pits that had been filled with scree started to give the merchants a sense of what had happened here. The land was destroyed by some sort of violence hundreds of years ago.

At the far end of the final plateau was a set of shallow stairs that climbed forty meters further up the mountainside. As the only way forward they climbed them, arriving at the gates to a huge city, perhaps the size of the capital of Cycus, all in ruins. It had no defensive wall unlike most cities of the Halo, instead being a compact mass of masonry and brick construction three meters above the street level, as well as three meters below. In places, they could see where the city dwellers had fit their roofs into the stone using square-planed wooden beams. The party could imagine the former inhabitants preferred their dwellings, shops, and stores to have a ground floor, a flat top that could be lived on, with a basement, saving space in the crowded city. Burned beams remained exposed in some places to attest to the original form of the buildings, as well as the cause of its demise. Disaster had struck; the city looked to have fallen in a day.

Inspecting a structure, they found it was made of an internal course of stone and an external course of red brick, with a layer of scree between the two. The scree alternated between broken shells, sand, and clay from amphorae or other pottery. Even burned, the walls retained their shape and dignity. It seemed almost like they could be built again if a person could simply find the wood and put it into place properly.

The first body they found was lying in the street, clearly killed at a time when no one was left afterward to claim them. No one had tried to rob the body, to bury it, to mourn it, or to in any way disturb it since it had fallen. It was now a skeleton with only clothing and armor to keep it connected in a recognizable form. On inspecting it, they found it was a warrior, dressed in excessive bronze armor, carrying a spear that was pristine even after years of exposure, although time had dulled its edge, while a patina of green showed it was no longer shined nor cared for. The helm the warrior wore had been caved in with considerable force, showing that the creature, man or woman, had fallen when someone had struck them with great force.

"Volcano or storm, disease or God's Flare, it is the hands of the barbarian that carried us away in the night." Yulen Fix sang an ancient song.

"What is that?" Javier asked.

"It is The Song of Lost Galatia. A fable of a great land destroyed by a barbarian horde. Many of the Sea Folk like to believe we are the descendants of that land." Fix stood still, hat in his hand, looking at the corpse.

Javier nodded, turning to one of his crew. "Mr. Sloan, break out your flags and signal the ship with this message: 'Making camp at location of abandoned city, arrange for delegation from Sea Folk and frigate ashore.'" Sloan pulled off his pack, assembling the flags.

"Major Standish, take the crew except for one rating and Mr. Van Guerster back to the beach. We will be landing all survivors ashore to allow us to work on the *Remarker*. I will be down tomorrow at noon, but I suggest you consider the resources we have discovered and discuss what a complete overhaul of *Remarker* will need to complete." He then walked to a single rating, looking around with awe at the ruins. "Can you build a camp?"

The young woman was named Catella Stern, a member of the Stern clan that lived inland from the capital at Cycus. It was likely a Stern, not a wealthy family, had learned to live rough and could handle a camp when called on. "Stern, we need a fire, water, tents set up, and all that before dark. Can you do this?"

"Yes, Captain," she replied. She stood dazed for a second, then realized the question was also a request, beginning to remove gear from the packs of the people heading back to the beach.

The group heading back to the beach dropped most of their gear. After finding water in the sizable stream that followed the mountain's edge to the cliff, they turned to follow the boulevard down to the landing beach, silent in their contemplation of the city they had discovered together. With Stern making food, Mr. Van Guerster and Javier were left alone to wander together in the ruins.

Van Guerster had softer, paler hair than was normal for a person who was Emporia born. He was also taller than the others from the frigate. He wore the ship's gold and green uniform with careful fare despite not having had access to a sea chest. There was care in how he tied his cravat, his rank and medals were aligned in a regular order, and he carried his officer's sidearm, a small sword, strapped to his belt in a way that kept him from having to fiddle with it as he walked. He had a tricorn hat with the name of his ship represented by two silver letters, plus he had chosen a utilitarian set of field gear to carry with him. It included a Carver Dragoon firelock with five rounds for it on his holster, his messing kit, two leather and percha canteens, a set of range finders of commercial make, and a pouch with his navigation tools. Altogether, he was a tidy and squared-away officer no matter what service he was from.

Javier had chosen him, who was formerly the third officer of the Emporia warship, because he appeared cool and in charge of himself, but betrayed a worried look of uncomfortable secrets, like secrets he was tasked to carry yet did not care to know. Javier motioned him over so they could talk in the ruins and take notes, which made him look more serious and more worried.

As they walked Javier said, "How random that you and I should end up alone with lots of time to talk."

Van Guerster replied, "Not random at all, sir. You arranged it, Captain al-Rasheed."

"I suppose I have. Your captain is playing at something, and I cannot believe his officers are happy with the results—half your crew dead, the rest castaways a long way from home and family," Javier replied with a laconic wave. "Did your Senior and Second Officers approve of haring across the Halo after, what exactly?"

"I am a loyal officer of Emporia," Van Guerster said. It was a statement that did not answer the question but was evocative of the man's troubled mind. Clearly, Van Guerster was not a man who gambled much. He was exactly as he appeared, a middle-ranking officer in over his head, worried about the actions of a captain who had literally driven them to the end of the world.

Javier clapped the man on the back. "What does 'van' mean in your name? I must say it seems an honorific. Is it your hometown?"

"I am from Guerster, a small island outbound from Emporia. We grew up speaking a tongue called Daeglish, where the word 'Van' means 'to come from.' All of our youth must leave the island to work for Emporia. If we work ten years, we can return to our homes. The 'van' reminds us of where our true home is."

"My own people of the south and east Halo do the same thing with our names." Javier smiled at the shared experience.

Guerster stopped, asking, "So you are from a place called Rasheed?"

"No," Javier laughed. "The Rasheed is my clan. We hunt fish off the shores of Cycus, so my clan is the Rasheed, and they call me al-Rasheed after my clan. I could be al-Rabaan d'*Remarker* which would mean sailor on that ship. In some documents my wife's patronymic is added, so I could be d'Cycus or even d'Cyclontensus, if you use my island or the cape on which the Rasheed live."

Guerster nodded, explaining, "The Emporians are named after the people whose land they work. Tarkington is technically a Lord Maine because he is the second son of the Great Tarkington of Baylis Faire, a region that grows grapes and has oyster pens." He thought for a second, then said, "You cannot walk thirty feet without your shadow crossing a Tarkington in those lands. The Commodore wants all the officers to use his name, but I cannot forget my home island that easily."

Javier looked at the fire growing in the distance, seeing that it was almost noon. "The rating may have food for us. Perhaps we should shape a course back to our camp."

They turned to walk back, but after a few moments of silence, Javier said, "You were rescued by a private trade ship. If you can tell me that you won't harm my ship and that your Commodore is following the mandates of his command, then I will accept your statement, making my inquiries on the matter finished."

The fire was made from osage wood, giving the air a spicy smell. They sat down, the rating handing them bowls of battata stew with a savory fish base and local greens. Somehow, the young sailor of the Stern clan had reproduced Cycus hobo stew in all of its savory glory. She produced a bowl for herself, then moved away to leave the officers to their inexplicable chatter.

Only there was no chatter, there was silence. Javier turned to Van Guerster, eating his stew with slow, measured tastes, and looked into his blank face. "Good enough," he said, and Van Guerster turned away.

The next day Javier had to put aside his worries about the mystery of the frigate and the Sea People because repairing the ship became the immediate priority. A top-to-bottom inspection showed she was solid, but there were hundreds of poorly planed boards, dozens of patches of peeling paint, plus maybe a thousand items on the rip list which could cause issues if they faced a storm when they attempted to return to the Halo.

The *Remarker* was hauled into shallow water, a rough cofferdam built while she was propped by timbers, allowing her to have the warped and stove planks along her base replaced and re-calked. With four carpenters, a sail and rope maker, a metalsmith, plus plenty of crew who had experience with agriculture, hunting, and fishing, repair proved easier than sailing her. It was a huge amount of work, but there were plenty of hands, more than a yard would have, with the raw materials close at hand.

A bank of placer of raw iron was found which, with charcoal from the trees and a clay blast furnace built, the raw iron gave way to carbon steel, which was then formed into fittings. When copper and tin were found, brass fittings were replaced as well, while scrap from the ship was removed and formed back into ingots to be used again some other time. Waste was almost nonexistent.

Dead trees proved to be more useful than live ones. Many were old, fifty years or older, standing without decay all that time. All were gravel oaks, a cold-tolerant tree similar to the prized warm-land live oak, seasoned when forest creatures had stripped their bark bare for food. Hundreds were found, often standing in a cluster of stunted scions thrown off in the last years of the old trees' growth. With no top branches or leaves to cut, with their sap long since dry, they did not have to be fast-seasoned. Instead, they were cut down, dragged to the beach, laid in the sun, then formed into planking using the *Remarker*'s large saws and planes from its tool chests.

The Sea People's matron, Versa Fleet, came to visit the *Remarker* camp after the ship was hauled up into its cofferdam. She brought Yulen Fix, who was their supply master, who carried a bowl of green leaves. Standish and Javier took seats at the camp table that had been placed under a canvas tarp to allow the process of celestial discovery to continue in hopes of figuring out accurately where they were, so they could shape a tolan to the Halo. Fix busied himself making something from the green plant matter while Fleet sat to talk with the *Remarker* officers.

"I understand you are working to shape a tolan?" Fleet asked, her gaze peering into the eyes of Javier like a schoolmaster.

"It would be ideal," Javier said. "Once we know where we are, we have a better chance of getting back than otherwise, but without a proved tolan, this island will never be part of the Halo.

It will become a backwater like the Extents, where only the most sturdy will risk their ships to go."

"How is a tolan proved?" she asked.

Javier laughed. "Well, by sailing it without dying. A tolan accounts for currents and prevailing winds. In the Halo, most islands can eventually be warped to by following tolans. Sometimes you have to take a rather circuitous route. Two islands may be a hundred miles apart but require a three-tolan route that sketches nearly eight hundred miles, which is why some trade is done by drakes rather than liners like *Remarker*. It is easier to shape a course across the current while ignoring the winds if, otherwise, you must warp a complex route to your destination. However, it is just possible this island may have a combination of currents and winds which allow it to both be reached and to reach the Halo. By that definition, it is part of the Halo and not an Extent."

"How terribly complicated, Captain. My people do not go in for any of those complications. The rafts float, we follow where our rafts go," she said.

Javier looked at her with a keen eye; she returned the look. She had just told a bold lie to a sailor who knew better and was daring him to call her on it. Of course, the Sea Folk liked to drift, even though they did have the means to move their communities on their own. They just found tolan sailing useless. The world was not designed for the convenience of the Sea Folk, and when storm season arose, they could make amazing efforts with sea anchors and wafted sails to shape a course for safe harbors.

"So, Matron Fleet—your arrival in the path of both storm and tolan was the happenstance of currents and the chance of the longshore?" It sounded ludicrous asking it that way, which is what Javier intended.

Yulen Fix returned with a pot of tea. He carefully poured out four portions of the hot liquid, then sat down. After a minute of silence, he indicated the brew and said, "Please try our tea."

Standish looked nonplussed. "I did not imagine we had rescued tea, only men and women."

"And yet, I offer you tea," Fix said.

Standish looked at the clay cup she had been provided. The Sea Folk had started to fire pottery from clay-banks. Some of it was quite good despite the people having never had red clay before. The cup was fitted with a cozy of woven field oat straw. In it was a soft-looking tea that had been strained through a woven screen of jute. She took the cup in hand, drinking deeply, perhaps to show she did not fear poison; however, her eyes betrayed a different emotion. Joy. "It is fine green tea!"

Javier looked at Fix, asking, "How did you come about this tea? Everyone knows green tea does not ship worth a damn."

Fix chortled in joy, an almost teenage expression of happiness. "It grows on our island! Wild, it is very high quality despite having gone to seed. You could call it unique. We are looking at how to ferment it for travel while keeping that wonderful taste."

Javier looked at the cup, finally bringing it to his lips. If Junebug tea had an opposite, this was this. The green tea was subtle, slightly smokey like Breget, without any bitter taste at all. Despite the tea's quality, he put the cup down after one taste, saying, "You speak of this island as yours."

Fix said, "I am sure this is the island of our ancestors. Why should we not claim it again?"

Matron Fleet looked troubled. Javier carefully replied, "My crew and I have no claim to a land such as this, nor can we say our ancestors lived here. So of course, your claim would be better than any we could put forward, even if we wished to do so. I wonder though, if the troubles with the frigate crew may get in the way of your ideas of claim and colonization."

The Matron looked Javier in the eye, telling him, "There are no troubles with the frigate crew. None that you need interfere with anyway. I do ask this. Not every person in our community wants to quit the sea for this amazing land. I ask that they be allowed to work passage for you until they can be let to another raft-town of the Sea People, or if they prefer, perhaps to find a home with you." The Matron picked up her tea to blow on the cup to cool it.

Javier only needed a second to think on it. "If a person wants to sign as crew and are of sound mind, body, spirit, and soul, then they may be a crew until we reach a port in which they wish to leave our employ. They will not work passage but ship's shares. Of a person wanting to deadhead, I will be happy to carry them a year and a day, leaving them at a port where they can seek the Sea People, or with Sea People if I find them." He picked up the cup of tea, then held it aloft. "Your people are fine hands as artisans, there is no doubt we can trade with you in times to come, although I warn you, if the frigate crew makes the same claims to the island, I cannot be the judge and jury."

The Matron nodded. "I think this is well settled then. As long as you do not interfere with our claim and let us work out our issues with the people of Emporia, we have no complaints with you."

Later that day, Javier discovered that the Commodore had loudly forbidden his people to work on repairing the *Remarker*, taking the tack that they were prisoners, and therefore could not be set to work; however, his influence among his crew seemed to be slipping. With silver to pay, Javier paid both his crew bonus money, the survivors fixed fees for work. The ship repair went fast with the three competing groups seeking to outdo the others. Soon, Javier was paying competitive bonuses for most labor done in a day.

Javier was with Devious inspecting a new planking set in the hull of the *Remarker* while considering the efforts to careen the rest of the bottom when Tarkington approached with two of his Marines, each carrying clubs made from forest logs.

"Al-Rasheed, I must protest your high-handed use of my people!" he yelled, drawing attention from the entire beach.

Devious reached into his officer's jacket, but Javier shook his head. Whatever his Quartermaine and lawyer had concealed, there would not help them solve this issue without violence. "Walk with me, Commodore." He left the two Marines glaring at Devious, who simply looked at his manicured and painted nails as if they were of more immediate concern than the two enormous fighters.

Once away from the ship and prying ears, Javier said, "State your complaint in logical language. I am not going to keep changing your diapers for your insane comments."

The Commodore grew intensely angry. "You are using for labor captives from my ship as if they were slaves."

Javier laughed. "Commodore, you have no ship. Your men and women are castaways, not captives. Technically, by the Merchant's Code, I can require they provide labor in exchange for rescue and succor as long as they can leave the ship when we reach safe harbor."

"The codes of my navy..." Tarkington tried to interject.

Javier interrupted him brusquely, "...Are meaningless. If you want to convince without violence sailors formerly of the *Repulse* that it is in their best interest to sit in your called 'naval headquarters and molder,' then you may try, however I may also reduce their rations and confine them to the hold of the *Remarker* as dangers to good order. Do not mistake me that I will. On that subject, why did you ram the Sea People in the first place? Is it not time for you to tell me the truth about that?"

Tarkington became unhinged by the accusation, clenching his fist and dancing a tattoo in palpable anger. "I will duel you per the codes of the rulers of Emporia. I will kill you where you stand!"

Javier was startled at the arrival of Major Standish, who had a small firelock in her hand. "Tarkington, some night if you threaten my captain, I will kidnap you as you sleep, then spend a month killing you. Do you understand my threat?"

"Standish!" Javier yelled.

"Sorry, Captain, if this one suddenly goes missing, he will not be found in one piece." She turned to him. "Your balls go first."

Tarkington turned pale. "Will you let this being talk to me like this?"

"Tarkington, I will handle my people. She will be punished. Now take your sorry ass back to your camp before I turn my back on my major." He watched as the man nearly exploded in hyperventilation, then turned and left for his camp, while yelling for his Marines to follow.

Major Standish asked, "My punishment, Captain?"

Javier looked at his major. "You make the tea for the next three days at mess." She nodded, then turned away.

After a week, the crew and survivors, with time on their hands, started exploring, with the destroyed village giving up treasure to treasure seekers. After Javier discovered that the sailors from the former *Repulse* and the Sea Folk had been fighting around the village, he developed a hard and fast rule. All treasure hunters would refrain from destroying the ruins further. They would work in groups of three, a crewman from the *Remarker*, a Sea Folk, and a survivor from the *Repulse*. Then all treasure would be pooled, with one item being selected at a time from the pool until it was dispersed. He also arranged for his own crew to retain more of the spoils they found. By contract, one coin in ten realized by crew freelancing was paid to him, while four coins in ten went to his wife. To encourage the crew of the *Remarker* and reward them for their efforts, he cut his own share in half, putting the value accrued into the ship's crew fund. Five coins in a hundred shared between 41 crew was a nice reward.

A major improvement in their lives came from finding that the island was teeming with shallow water conches.

It turned out that the long-dead islanders of these islands loved conch above all other foods. The city was filled with conch art. There were shell ornaments and piles of shells discarded behind long-defunct food stalls. They crushed up conches and used the coquina in their farms for fertilizer, as well as between the walls of their houses as scree for insulation. Conchs formed mortise for their roads, and cement from broken shell pieces was used as wall art.

Javier was fascinated when the first book was found. Able Sailor al-Bindi brought Yulen Fix of the sea people by with the first volume that was discovered. The tome had pyrographed leather covers and contained deep tan mashed wood fiber pages inked with brown soot ink. Fix handed him the book, saying, "This is a gift for you."

"Such a beautiful gift," Javier said, looking at the book. He examined the pages, realizing it was unreadable. The words were in the script of the Halo, but not in a legible language. The book was illustrated; every third page had a conch on it, displaying its anatomical parts, cutting the conch for cooking, using the shell for ornaments, and other aspects of the care and treatment of related single-shell creatures.

"It is more than a gift. It is an admission." Fix reached into a pouch, pulling out several more books. "The people of this island wrote these books, then hid them in caves when the end came near. My crew has been finding them. They prove, though, that the People of the Sea are not from this island."

"How do you know?" Javier asked. Fix handed him a second book which had no illustrations, written in the same confusing language use the script of the Halo.

"The Chanters of the Sea Folk tell stories of a hundred families leaving the shores of a great island. When we come together, different Sea Folk villages share these stories. All of these stories agree that literacy is not, was not, and never has been one of our arts," Fix replied.

Javier processed for a second. "Then this is not your lost homeland?"

"It is," he said. "Just not the real homeland. This will be, if the dame and myself have anything to do with it, a new place of home for the Sea People. However, it was not the long-lost island that our people left."

"Rachel," Javier said to a sailor standing for his orders, "bring us a pot of tea from the fire."

Sailor al-Bindi nodded, putting her hand to her cap in salute. Yulen watched as she went to the fire. Once she was away, he pulled three more books from a sack he was carrying, placing them on the camp table. Javier nodded to the chair across from him to reinforce his offer of a seat. He scooped the new books up, amazed at their condition. "I wish I could read them. Can you imagine what they would say?" he pondered aloud.

Yulen smiled as the tea arrived, taking a sip. "They say nothing of the Sea Folk, for the books were not written by us, as the ruins were not created by our people. It is a convenient story, nothing more. Still, I am giving the books to you."

"Why give me the books?" Javier asked.

Yulen shrugged theatrically. "The Sea Folk do not do well when we dip our toes into the worlds of the great islands. We live hard lives, our rafts founder, our people die on the waves of the Halo. Our mayor holds incredible grief at how many died in this latest accident, as do most of us. That is why I must speak to you now. The truth is owed to you, and the mayor, he will not give it, or perhaps does not know it."

Javier sat up. "You want something in exchange for the truth?"

"I do." Yulen nodded, taking a cup of tea offered by the sailor. "I am told you know where we have landed. Where this island is?"

Javier pulled a small worksheet from one of the books he had been reading. "I have a theorem that would allow us to rough a tolan line to the Cape of Darts. This island is not easy to reach ... if my sights and surmises prove correct. There is no land seaward, and to your lee is no route that will naturally allow a drifter to reach land. Do you understand my meaning in this?"

"It means that if a ship follows a tolan, or shapes a rhumb without a tolan, and they miss the island, they would be bound for open sea ... and death," he replied. "Your tolan, though, will make us one with the Halo, rather than an Extent."

"Quite so," Javier said. "If my tolan works, at least there will be a way for a skilled navigator to reach the island. It will never be an easy course to bend, but traders can bend it if they know the secrets."

"Do not publish the tolan," Yulen said, pleadingly.

"You will not be easy to find, even for Sea Folk, if you stay on this island, as you claim you want to do," Javier said gravely.

"Wonderful," Yulen threw up his hands. "If all Sea Folk are travelers, then we have found the way home. This home. The story of this being a Sea Folk land, a place where our relatives just a few generations gone were driven from, I will make this the true story. The books prove it is otherwise, so you can take the books with you. We do not speak the language that they were written in. The Sea Folk do not write, not a scrap, not a jot. That is Islander magic, not ours. Erase the books, then this land is ours in our minds. Never publish the tolan, so we will be left to our own and legend. As you say, this island is remote, hard to reach, on no maps, told in no sea stories. Do you not see the beauty of being a retiring people who finally reach the other shore?"

Javier looked at the intense man. "You will be stranded on the shores of eternity."

Yulen shrugged. "Five generations past, someone found this island. They had spears of copper, swords of iron, and they massacred the people who called this land home. I do not feel that isolation is a penance. I see it as a gift."

"I will keep the tolan my secret for you. I ask only that we can visit you. Is that possible?" Javier asked.

"It would be a useful thing, because you may run across other bands of us in your travels. If you bring any of them that are tired of the way of the seas to our shore, we will reward you. If you are willing to trade with us, we will see that as a blessing. On the honor you claim of your ancestors, no more than you though. We will not allow other ships to land men and women we do not know." To emphasize his comment, he slid a cluster of small muslin bags over the table. "This island has wild tea plants, spicy cardoon, sea lily, merlin goats with great tufted fur, plus bloodroot and giant coreopsis for orange dye that is more brilliant than I have ever seen. It has a long shore sweet plant that drips with an oil that smells so sweet that perfumers would fight their mothers to get a dozen grams. It has giant aloes, cold mountain agave, summer sloe, castor root, and baybex burl wood. For the past weeks, as you fixed your ship, we have worked to learn what is on this island. It turns out that it is a cornucopia. Yet if we reveal this wealth to more than you, there could be a stampede to this shore, the land would be wrested from us."

Javier nodded. "If this is a land of treasure, then you will have to either fight for it or be removed from it. The

Merchant's Code prevents this. However, the next people to land will not automatically be merchants. I feel you are right to conceal your location."

"Then I must pay you for my debt in keeping this tolan from the annals. A year ago and more, we came upon a man clinging to life on a raft made of mahogany. We were anchored in grounds we fish at that are not close to any travel ways, so his presence was a mystery. The mayor bravely steered a cockle to the dying sailor's side. From the vantage of my raft, I could see them speak, and the mayor take a small item from the man, who seemed to fade into death even as succor was at hand. Then we did an odd thing, or I say the Mayor had us do an odd thing that caused loud arguments with our matron and puzzled the rest of us. A vessel from Emporia, seeking this very sailor who died in our arms, collected his body from us not too many days later. The mayor tore three pages from what turned out to be a book, then asked a mate on the ship to write a message on their back. The mayor told me no more of this. When we sighted the frigate that would ram us with evil intent, he grew imperious, yelling at them, in a way that is not our custom, with demands of silver bound in chests and fine food from their larder. I can only surmise he was trying to sell the book to this Commodore who we have both met."

A sip of tea fortified the Sea Folk leader's senses. "We were separated by currents and a storm, yet the captain grew fearful, driving us across the channel in the wrong season, where the frigate destroyed our community at the edge of a great storm."

He looked solemnly at Javier, then said, "He holds the secret close, but our mayor is visiting the Commodore tonight. He wants recompense. I fear he will find a grave."

Javier took some paper, wrote a note, then wrapped it around the muslin bags. "Rachel!" he yelled, and the crew person arrived with a bounce in her step. She was holding a castle crab which had found a home in a conch shell. Javier admired the clever animal for a minute, then said, "My compliments to the major, present this message and these bags to her person immediately."

The rating saluted, then looked at the crab. Javier added, "If you can figure out how to keep the clever thing alive without cruelty, you may take it with you."

It was late at night when Javier was woken by Devious, dressed all in black, with a black cassock fitted for him as well. He shrugged into the garment, armed himself, then allowed his Quartermaine to lead him into the forest.

Devious was a hole in the darkness, a shadow that never seemed to be trying for stealth, never hid behind a tree or moved faster than a walk, yet was silent and almost impossible to follow. Javier tried to be quiet but was aware that even his most carefully vetted breath was shatteringly loud compared to Devious. There were no words spoken, no breaks taken. He walked unerringly to where he wanted to go, then stopped Javier with a silent hand.

In front of them were two men, candles lit on the ground between them, talking in low, urgent growls. Commodore Manuel Tarkington and Mayor Fleet stood close to each other, fists clenched. Their words could not be followed, but there was anger in their stance.

Suddenly Tarkington lashed out with a knife, slitting Fleet's throat, who grabbed his neck, then fell to the forest floor, dead in an instant. Tarkington cleaned his knife on Fleet's jersey, then said, "You can come out of the woods, Mr. al-Rasheed. You make enough noise to disturb a veldbeast from mating."

Devious made a sign with his hand, crossing his neck with his finger, which Javier downvoted with a shake of his head. Instead, he stepped away from Devious into the light of the two candles. "I know why you did that," Javier said in a casual tone, watching as the gush of blood from the poor mayor's neck slowed to an oozing trickle staining the forest floor.

Tarkington drew a firelock, cocked it, and aimed it at Javier. "So the mayor told you of the contents of my logbook. You will, of course, have to die, and I will be taking your ship."

"Rather extreme," Javier said.

Tarkington waved the handlock in the air. "Thirty-and-three of my crew want to stay on this blighted island. More of them want to ship with you, turn traitor to our nation for the life of a merchant! However, there is a treasure here. With your ship, I can bring it to market, plus buy my way out of this mess."

Javier advanced a few steps, stopping when Tarkington pointed the firelock at his stomach. "There is treasure here, but not what you think," he said.

"Of course, we see differently, but 61 Sea Folk will fetch 20,000 grams of silver at the Ardmore slave market. Further, like you, I have now figured the tolan to this island. Did you think me an idiot? None of my crew can figure a rhumb without me, and I reckon that idiot of a Navigator you employ is equally useless, so with you dead, there is only one captain left." Tarkington laughed like some stage villain from a Halo play.

"I would rather have God Flash destroy my ship, stranding my crew, than let you step foot on its deck again," Javier said, leaning against a tree.

"What you want does not matter. Only you and the dead mayor know the secrets in my logbook, and you will take it to the grave." Tarkington raised his handlock to sight down its barrel. There was an explosion of smoke and flames, followed by him falling to the ground, grasping his neck with the look of a wild animal. He kicked a few times, then settled down into death next to his victim.

From out of the flame and smoke, Robbi Van Guerster stepped, throwing a case from his firelock, replacing it with a fresh round. "I hope I did not pepper you with powder, Captain al-Rasheed."

Javier looked at the pair of dead men with a bit of bile in his mouth. "No, I am fine. How come you to be here?"

Robbi Van Guerster replied, "It was time to end this. The Commodore's death will cause trouble back in Emporia. It had to be done though."

Javier repeated, "It had to be done." He walked to the body of Tarkington, removed three pages of scap from his pocket, then moved to the Mayor, whose pocket gave up a leather-bound logbook. He looked at Van Guerster, asking him, "Have you read these?"

The survivor from the *Repulse* shook his head. "No. We made port, where those pages were waiting for us. They drove the Commodore mad once he read them. He was obsessed that his log had been read, and that he was being blackmailed. Now I guess the secret will come out, whatever it is."

Javier picked up one of the spilled candles, resetting it in its brass holder. Then he used it to light the leather-bound logbook and the three pages ripped from it on fire. "Commodore Tarkington made one mistake through this. No matter how venal the mayor was, he could not read. Neither can any people of the Sea. He wanted to sink their community, to kill or enslave its members, to hide a secret they did not have."

The burning paper danced in the darkness, creating a red light and a smudge of foul smoke. Javier watched it, shadows playing across the wooded clearing, and said, "If any of your people want, I will return them to the Halo and pay for their passage home. They can also stay here or join my crew, as they see fit. The three of us, though, have seen a miracle. A powerful beast with three heads and the sounds of a thunderstorm in its stomach attacked the mayor as he searched for food on this barren island. The commodore, who had befriended him when both ships collided in a storm, futilely came to his aid as the beast killed them both.

We arrived too late to save the friends, who stood their ground bravely to the end."

Van Guerster nodded with an odd look on his face. "Three of us?" He asked.

Javier said, "I would never come out here without Devious to watch my back."

"As you say, sir," Van Guerster replied.

CHAPTER VI

A Halo for a Sailor's Head

The *Remarker* was trim and playful in the waves, its hold filled with goods from the lands of the Cape of Darts, a crew compliment now 90 strong—not complete but learning every day how to drive the great ship forward, with a port just seven days away, the promise of a proper landfall at a trade port with all of its wild culture and business opportunities.

Javier had hopes of sending the letter he was writing his wife, having it sent from the next Sublime Port. He began taking his relaxation, glancing at books from the island now named "Faraway" while writing his missive by the light of paraffin lamps and sipping horrible Junebug tea infused with spruce.

Dear Nazira

    I hope this missive finds you well. By now you will have heard of the discovery of Faraway Island, and our experiences with the Sea People and the crew of the Repulse. With this letter, I want to speak of more mundane things, of life on a merchant ship warping passage between two ports, as we are doing when I write this.

    We found land at the Cape of Darts after a harsh passage from Faraway. The dangers of the passage are so extreme that no further traders save ourselves will likely ever want to seek her barren shores again. I would advise you to inform our mutual backers that Faraway is a dry hole, which we will visit occasionally merely to supply the islanders with essentials. It is ethical and good practice for us to keep the island and its people out of our conversations.

    As for the Repulse and its late captain: I am taking the sword and personal effects of Commodore Tarkington to hand to the next ship of Emporia I find, along with the story of his heroics in helping save the Sea Folk not once, but twice, when he gave his life fighting the horrible 'Red Beast of Faraway.' While that beast is confirmed to live in certain caves on the leading edge of the island, it can be avoided simply by not wandering the forests of that land at night, but is so horrible that Tarkington's bravery cannot be understated. I can attest that my own sight of the creature was life-changing, and I will go to my grave remembering the being's great fangs, snarling breath of fire, and the wings which it could deploy to make great leaps. The Sea Folk of Faraway are braver than me to share an island with such a beast, which looks like a large Drake with an added pair of hands and wings of an even greater width.

As for life on a ship, I can say that an unusual event happened that caused me to have cross words with the crew two days out from Faraway. There were two men that we took on with our first draft of sailors at Cycus who were, in some ways, not adopting the spirit of the ship that I expected. They were both Navy-trained and used to being lead jacks who applied their power to maltreat the weaker of the apprentice crew, something that's called tossing or rousting. I was considering how to deal with them when their general clumsy nature and the hand of the gods intervened.

The first one, a caper from the northern shore named Buskus, was before all eyes swanning in the sheets, casting about with no painter to suspend his fall. I was not on deck to see, being asleep in my cabin, and my cadre were scattered around the ship, none being present for the incident. The man was though, being observed by the crew of three gangs, all of which were less than amused at his insults and antics. Suddenly a yell from the deck roused me, and I broke from my sleep dressed only in my bedclothes with a talwar in my hands, where I found Buskus, his brains bashed in, having fallen from the sheets when the foot line he was standing on came atwain from the halyards. Observing the mess of what was the man's intellect I took to the crew over the twitching body of the unfortunate Buskus and told them that his death was only on his head, but that from now on no one would swan, lest they take fire from my own firelock in response. They were rather quiet about this and not too amused, but it had to be said.

I also took the opportunity to inform the crew, which included the partner in many evil deeds to Buskus looking on, a man named Cosh, that we were not a naval ship but a merchant, and that our behavior was not that of a pack of jackals ready to fight at an instant. Our least man or woman was as important as our greatest, and that the behavior, how we made the lives of our crew-mates easier or harder, would earn marks not just in the captain's book, but in the book the gods keep that measure our souls. Everyone knew I spoke of the behavior of Buskus, who was a bullyrock, and not in any good manner.

I intended to have Cosh in for a discussion, to see if I could save his soul, but I did not move fast enough. When a crew person dies, there is a period of contrition where the crew drinks a libation of palm rum from one of the casks we store in the sully maine, and they hold a ceremony of memory. In such a ceremony, the crew takes the personal possessions of the dead and buys them with pure silver. Then, as captain, I close out their crew account and more silver is put forward, representing their bonuses and pay to date. Then the crew fashions a box with no lid, and into that box goes the silver, the dead crew person's hat, any personal writings they had left unsent, a lock of the dead person's hair, and sometimes small gifts. The box will be given to the family of the crew person if they can be found, or after three years is opened and used for a final day of remembrance.

It was the palm rum, and perhaps grief, although the crew deny the man had access to such an emotion, that cost Cosh his life. Each imbibing member of the crew was given 50 milliliters of the palm rum in a tot cup. In that passage, the books showed 74 souls, half drinkers. 2.7 liters were consumed from a cask that had 10 liters in it. Yet when the cask was measured prior to being sealed and returned to the sully maine, it showed under six liters.

Normally, this pilferage is expected. You unseal 10 liters of rum, and you expect to have heavy tots, seconds, and drinks snuck by the crew who guarded it. However, two bits of evidence show this may not be the case. Cosh, drinking his rum, became intoxicated in a very sloppy way, as if he had 500 milliliters rather than 50. In fact, one would suppose he had taken other chemicals, as he was almost as bad as a person who had been at the poppies. Second, it was noted that he was gone to the head several times more than others in the group. The absences were, in fact, noticeable. Finally, he was ordered gone from the group due to his behavior and left in an angry, incoherent huff.

It was three hours later that the equation added up, when we found Cosh face down in the after-port head, the circle of the defecation stool forming a halo around his noggin, his neck broken in his attempt to purge himself in the small closest. Now, any man or woman, my dear, has felt the difficulty of using a head during high seas, and since Cosh had high seas in the form of his own, unsteady legs, it was not a big mystery that in tending to himself over that gaping hole into the sea he had met his fate by breaking his neck, and the missing rum merely served to confirm the story on how Cosh died.

Rather than holding a second ceremony, I just had the one we were already involved in extended, more rum distributed, and the belongings of the second member of our crew to die prepared for his kinfolk should they ever be found. The previous lecture may have been more effective because it signaled that behavior mattered and that poor behavior saw the gods' hands in its punishment.

The main issue I personally have: how random the gods make death! Two men, hale and healthy, push the gods once too often with acts of hubris, and they pay for their play with their very lives. After the ceremony the crew not directly needed to guide the ship to safe harbor gathered on deck, and I read to them from the Heshuan the dirge of the dead, after which we sang the drive-shanty "Teamaine Traders Lost at Sea," and put our dead to rest behind us.

On the nature of the crew, I must say the stories I told you of life in the navy do not apply on a tea merchant, at least one that I am master of. The sea can be cruel, and the crews of fishers and fire ships are called on to terrible pur-pose when each wave break may be their last, but somehow they tend to turn this fear in on themselves, and under a weak master they can rot under bright sun or dark stormy night, taking on their fellows like dog-jackals hunting a weak pack member on the side of Igalemath Mountain.

On my ship though, at least I hope, this tendency to bully and bocob each other has been limited, and the crew is tied together by more noble thoughts. Take Samson ibn Machias. Samson cannot tie knots, he is slow, he cannot climb, and he seems to live in a fog, so I assigned him to simply clean the heads. There are six on the ship, which is five more than a fisher has, and left without cleaning they become foul, leaving the crew to do their business in buckets rather than put up with the stench of a defecation stool closed in a small closet.

Despite the seemingly low level of this work, Samson does not complain. He takes in the heads and each day spends hours seeing the lot are clean. Soon I find he is using old tea leaves with spent tallow and oil of almond to create a soap, while he cozens his own ration of vinegar as a cleaning sot, and he has developed a way of making the heads sweet smelling even if not tended for a day or so. The able jacks are completely put off by the lad because they have spent weeks trying to teach him a turn-in-four knot and he is completely useless at it, yet left alone he invents a concoction to make heads smell sweet. They swear the gods did him a good turn and now are more polite to him because they believe he is touched magically.

Then Eddy Sandals, a top crew we were able to sign on from the old Repulse gang, gets an idea and suddenly all of our wasted tea, rancid almond oil, and sadly, much-desired vinegar has gone into a huge billy-pot and everyone is helping Samson dry, cut, and wrap his bars, storing them in their own dunnage. It has become a ship's industry far past the needs of the ship, with plans to sell the product in ports that we stop in.

My policy on crew trades that I announced on the first day out was that, so long as they do not steal or smuggle, each sailor may carry on small package trade in their own dunnage. This policy became important as they found treasures of ancient armor, weapons, and jewelry at Faraway, but I did not expect the head-soap, as they called it, to become a product of trade or of considerable profit. And my crew thus taught me a lesson on loading the ship and the value of having each crew person available to apply their creative impulses to problem solving. They ended up selling out of their soap and making a tidy personal profit.

Now, Nazira, I must defend myself and say that when I took on cargo, there was not much choice as we left Faraway. The best product I had was the tea of Faraway, which is world-class and amazing to taste, and I hoped twenty barrels of it would set us up to at least break even in this disaster-filled initial part of our journey. And when we heaved into the roadstead at the Cape of Darts, there were five big company merchant liners standing tall and ready to trade with us, which is rare for that port. However, when I showed their tea masters the tea, they declined. It turns out, unless a tea has been tasted and reported on, and that report distributed to the grandmasters, and that report then further sent to the masters, then it does not really exist. They can only sell it as junk tea. They advised me to find an apprentice tea master and help them write a monograph to establish the new tea as a brand.

Yet it was the cultural objects that first sold well. Each object I wrote an account of where it was found and what it likely meant and signed it. Then Devious did the same, and we placed them on deck to be looked over. We thought that a spear might fetch a few silvers, a breastplate twenty silvers, for the sheer novelty. So we set out bidding forms and turned to other tasks.

The breastplate from the first dead warrior we found sold for ten times what a new breastplate would. All of the items made money, so the crew pulled their own cache of the treasures of Faraway out and they made even more, as our own treasures were already bid on and distributed.

It turns out the captains were buying the treasures to make their own wardrooms look worldly and well-traveled. By providing a signed page telling the providence of the item, a lost treasure of an ancient island of the Extents, I had provided a sea story to the captain who purchased the treasure, and the story was what made the item desirable and expensive.

However, my dear Nazira, this was not the greatest surprise, nor did it bring the most money. It was the cleaning soap that made us a fortune in our first port.

As I understand the story, the Mouse and Sampson, along with Eddy Sandals and a group of other crew, sculled over to a trader and offered to clean their heads. They cleaned them and sold twenty bars of the soap, plus were given all the oil of almond, tea scraps, vinegar, and palm rum they could carry away. They added palm rum into the ingredients to make it seem this was how they made the soap, which was clever. However, I had to confiscate the intoxicant for fear of what it would do to the ship if consumed in quantity.

Not all of the crew's ideas sold. Conch shells were amazing in size and color, and none were purchased by any merchant. A crew member who had taken on as a pet a crab that lived in a conch was offered a sum for it, but the creature was very much a mascot for the ship and the only mascot that could live in the presence of the ship's cats who were murderous beasts but who learned to avoid the armored and fast-moving crab and his pincher claws. However, like I lauded earlier in this missive, my own trade sense proved faulty and that of the crew accurate, and they were responsible for us breaking even on the first leg of our journey.

On to another subject. One thing you and I spoke of was the diet of the fisher and of the sailor. This diet is often limited to simply what will not go rancid on a ship set to sea for fifty days that can affordably feed a crew of a hundred. Ships in place where many people want to find employment, or where through impressment such as navy ships use, the crew are unwilling guests, the food can be quite vile, and even cause significant health issues. A poor ship will carry only biscuit, which is grain flour baked four times to be desert dry and rock hard, and salted meat of the cheapest form. It will keep man and woman alive for weeks, but over a period of months teeth are lost and joints swell from the poor quality of the fare.

Merchants work differently if they are successful, as we seem to be. First, the crew are volunteers and can leave a ship each time she warps into a new roadstead. We received good crew, crew that will be missed, from several merchants, not all of which were poorly run. It is the nature of the merchant trade that its members are gamblers, always looking to trade up to a better ship. There is no way to stop them from leaving. So the food has to be better than what fishers or soldiers eat.

This does not mean the food is always good. When the better supplies are eaten, in the end, we sup on crackers cooked in oil, that being the last thing on the ship that remains edible but the least likely thing to be eaten. When I say edible, biscuit is consumable only in the most narrow and generous sense of the word. A crew can understand this, as long as it does not happen often, and even be nostalgic for the deprivation, but a captain that does not pay attention to the food the crew eats will soon have no crew, unless that crew is retained by lash and sword.

As we warp free from the Cape of Darts to Genvis Gate and our first sublime port, we will have ten days at sea, maybe more if the winds do not give us their expected cooperation. We carry, though, enough food for seventy and five days. Twenty days are biscuit and vegetable oil, our emergency supplies should we find travel interrupted, but our main food is what landfall provides, and it provided well at the Cape of Darts.

Each soul on Remarker who is not a member of the cadre lives and works in a gang, of which eventually we will have eight on the ship. The gang forms a mess and is issued by contract one ration per person per day. Thus, a ration is the amount of food needed to keep one sailor healthy and hale for one day, while an issue is twenty rations per day per gang. A mess of twenty crew gets a ration of around 25 kilograms each day. On this voyage, each mess was given two kilos of dry keena, a kilo of rice, a kilo of barley, two kilos of yellow beans, a kilo of dried and salted meat, a kilo of lentils, two liters of olive oil, four kilos of wheat berries, six-kilos of salted fish, two-kilo of pumpkin, a kilo of sour cabbage, a kilo of dried tomatoes, a kilo of ghee. Added to this is 200 grams of Junebug tea, 20 grams of salt, and a liter of brewed fish sauce, soy sauce, or some other condiment. From this, the crew will decide how to make three or four meals for their score of members, assisted by the Steward, who schedules use of the stove and galley.

The food a gang serves itself is so important that it causes transfers from one gang to another. While we cannot have every coxswain on one gang, we do have people who do not eat meat on one gang, and they trade their meat ration with the other gangs. Some gangs prefer keena over wheat, and some like one bean over another, and will work to acquire more of one ration product than another. All have access to the galley space and its fires, but they routinely take turns using it to allow more complex cooking to occur. They also indulge in buying and maintaining their own spices for the good of the group.

Each gang is amazing in their competition to eat better than other gangs, and they will sometimes cook for each other as part of this never-ending contest. In addition, from the captain's purse, I pay for one meal each week for each of the eight gangs, called the Captain's Service. I try to attend as many as I can, but they always salute with a filled glass of tea the ship and the cadre even if I cannot.

Bread making is a favorite pastime of the crew, but with results that vary wildly in quality. The crew, though, have a secret I am not allowed to know about, and that is bad batches of bread are as beloved as those whose loaves stand tall and warm for each gang's stomach. This is because each bad batch of bread ends up feeding a secret shipboard operation of beer brewing.

Standish allowed me to taste some of the brew, and it is not bad.

However, that got me wondering how the crew was able to make bread on even our large ship. My eyes, I assumed, fell on each inch of the ship on a regular basis. I discussed it quietly with Devious and he agreed to quietly discover the details of the process and share them with me. We agreed, though, that as long as behavior was not affected, the secret brew operation was the right of the crew and none of the cadre's business.

Which brings me to the problem I face, and that is sugar. While better than half the crew is of a religious or personal preference against the drinking of spirits or consuming poppy, the other half is willing to indulge, and some take that indulgence past any clearly rational process. Those few create issues of safety and good order past all other problems on the ship. Spirits turn the men and women into thugs.

The ship carries a product known as palm rum. This is a rather harsh drink made from the nut of the palm tree that is not just fermented but then distilled until it is useful as a medical therapy. It is quite toxic in my opinion, and I have no idea why one would willingly let it pass their lips, but some people adore it. However, we carry no means to produce this product on the ship. The palm rum we do carry is locked up.

Many foods though can produce various beers, and this beer is not much of a worry as I have said. One would need to consume quite a lot to get intoxicated in an extreme manner. But if sugar is around, some sailors will use this to boost the demons of the drink. It is not as strong as palm rum, but it is many times stronger than the sully beer they produce in secret and which we turn a blind eye to. So of all things, the various forms of sugar, which include honey, cane, maple, birch, and keena sugar, are all doled out from their own locked containers, and those containers are checked on a regular basis for adulteration and theft. Missing sugar is the fear of the crew because the cadre, Marines, and myself have to turn the ship upside-down, not looking for the sugar, but for the distillation installation and the fire, which can burn down the ship, burning somewhere below the decks. I have not had this happen ... yet, but have been advised to expect that even the best crew occasionally has an outbreak of sugar thieving.

My worry is that the normal punishment is to lock the miscreant up in a lazaretto with as much poppy as they can drink and let them see their way to the gods in a hazy stupor. The preference is to simply drop them at the next port and let them be someone else's problem. However, I have been told I have too light a hand, and some crimes need harsh punishment to keep the crew itself happy.

As for the issue of finding new crew. Getting crew has been hot and cold, at least to this point. The Cape of Darts had a lot of stevedores who wanted work due to the barbarity of their employers, but while hard-working, they lack skills and experience and will need time to train. I had my eyes on several able sailors on the liner Sun of the South, but their captain told me quite forcefully that he would not part with one crew person. I recruited four from the Vane's Surprise at the Cape of Darts but most of the recruits came on without reference. I let Devious and Standish give them the once over, and they seem to have the measure of it, although we have to work hard training the new fish.

The problem with a large liner compared to a fisher is that we need a lot of people. To be nimble, you need men and women in the sheets changing the configuration of your sails. To convince casual piracy and attacks, you want a strong marine detachment, and they need to be handy boat operators, good with firelock and talwar, skilled at handling the larger serpents and adders we carry for throwing deck-penetrating shot, and big men and women in general to hold a bayonet line in the face of civil threat. To keep from having to pay high costs in port, you need carpenters, metalsmiths, sailmakers and menders, cargo hands, and a few divers. Plus, you want enough helm and navigation crew to keep a steady watch at sea. It is not a mistake that the average four-masted liner like us carries more than eight-score crew and cadre.

Plus, I have found much to be fond of with a diverse and mentally active crew. They save me from having to be the person who always has an idea, the center of attention on the ship. Let me share with why I love the crew you gifted to me with. The bread making is not fake, just to cover beer brewing, and the crew loves the bread they make, but it turns out that the Steward maintains the ship's only yeast culture, which is called "the monster," primarily to bake bread for the cadre's use. I never thought about how we have bread on many nights, or why the Steward apologized that he could no longer make us loaves at Faraway. It turns out maintaining the so called "monster" is a great deal of work, and it can be called on as food itself. Once gone, the Steward has to trade with another ship for a new monster and feed it until it can be divided for bread making.

However, letting the crew use this monster for their own bread is good for its health. The monster is a living being made up of flour and yeast, and dividing it keeps the creature from going too sour. On land, apparently, they do not have this problem because monsters are of a different character, not having to live on a ship. But a seaborne monster is a special creature and one which brooks little deviance from its desires for heat, water, or flour.

The Steward though, does not have time to make bread for the crew, but is not opposed to them making their own bread, as long as they do not waste the wheat berries that bread requires. The results, though, in the hands of amateur bakers, can be so variable as to create inedible masses if it is baked, so the Steward will not allow it in the ovens, and the crew need to find other uses for it.

Calling the dough mass "beer bread," the crew now turn to a man who works the cargo as an able sailor, Winston al-Luis, who you will remember was the clever dock worker who you hired as a strong back for the cargo. Turns out the man is also a brewer, as he has an amazing brewing operation hidden in a tiny corner of the after-hold. He has concealed the device to use heat from the ship's blacksmith furnace, with him on one side of the draw, and the blacksmith on the other, all protected from firing the ship by firebricks and sand-filled tin strakes. Apparently, he found the arrangement when exploring the hold, and when we rebuilt the ship, he did much to improve it using firebricks taken from the dead city on Faraway. He used scrap copper from the island and made his brewery that much more effective, while the brew he makes is dispensed into empty vinegar bottles.

In keeping with the illusion, Standish made it be known that Winston could keep his operation as long as he does not serve drunks, does not charge excessive fees for using what is in essence ship's resources, and that the captain never finds out.

Which is hard because our crew, in some ways, lacks all guile. They would not last ten minutes in the cutthroat world of a fisher. During a toast of the captain just before I started this missive to you, the Mouse, of all people, handed me a vinegar bottle filled with beer for the toast. Everyone looked at me to see if the secret was out, but I laughed and said, "Mouse, I am a sour man, but not this sour. Tea for me, not vinegar."

Anywise, I enclose this letter in an envelope to send on at the first possible minute. I hope to see you and our new child and rejoice in our love.

Yours Truly,

دي‌شر

Chapter VII

Hands Filled with Silver, Hearts Filled with Gold

Buskus carried me onto the *Remarker* in a sack, to wait on him and his mate, or so he said, then left me stifling in that canvas bag for hours. I grew scared at my kidnapping because where I was from, under the dock at Cycus City, my fellows dreaded the day some adult would come and grab you. The next time you would be seen, your tortured body would return to the docks, floating on the tide, eaten by the crabs.

I expected that the two bullies who had grabbed me would be the next who would put hands on my bag. In fact, when it opened, and I was dumped on the deck, it was a marine named Suelimon dressed in a resplendent red uniform who asked, "How did you get on board?"

Buskus came running up. "Here now, Suel, you keep hands off the bum boy."

Suelimon got close to Buskus, asking, "Why do you think you can pull this sort of caper and not end up on the end of a knotted rope?"

More sailors were starting to crowd in, with one pointing out, "Move this along or the cadre will find out."

"Buskus, you damn fool," another said. "No way the captain and Standish allow you to keep a seraglio on the ship."

"What is going on?" came a questioning yell from the gangway to the well deck. Right away, hands grabbed me and I was spirited away by a sailor. From then on, I can say my life changed.

You see, while the sailors who kidnapped me were intent on ill use, the rest of the crew were not willing to allow this on their deck. As we were at sea, there was no other way to have me than to make me a member of the crew. That is the story I will tell now to you.

At first, I thought this might be an illusion, a dream I would wake from, the men who had me come aboard seeing me eventually to a grisly death, but a ship does not really work that way. Of course, that was the life I had known, so had nothing to compare.

My first memories were hiding. I lived under the great lengths of wood that stretched along the shore and out into the harbor, where boats lashed their wooden walls to the structure of the piers. I was not alone under the docks, hundreds of others my age and older could be said to form a community there. It was a place with neither succor nor warmth. Evil men and women hunted us by day, while we hunted each other by night. You learned to follow the biggest person and do favors for them. You learned that this ruler of the docks would last for months, killing younger, weaker kids, until at last a group of his lieutenants would turn on him or her, then strangle them in their sleep. Then there would be chaos until all of them were dead when you ultimately found yourself following another big kid. It was the limits of the world; I did my best to survive.

The ship I assumed worked the same way, however I soon found that the crew did not want me dead. I was not to be a passion toy for a bully sailor. The marine Suelimon took me to a woman named Ms. Crestwell, an old, able sailor of thirty-and-three years who oozed sagacity and wisdom. She was sitting on the forecastle, a place she called the "swan deck", with a length of rope she called a "painter," tying knots. "They called you Mouse," she said, tying a complex knot in the painter.

"I was called that," I replied.

"Mouse, the captain will be furious if he hears about how you arrived on the ship. The man is a bit … off. All captains are eccentric, but al-Rasheed is a hard man one minute, a soft one the next. That leaves the crew one choice with you, at least until we know his moods better." I was fascinated by the woman's hands, how fast she made a knot, then loosened it, like the rope was water, her hands magical water-thieves. "We are going to have you signed on as a sailor apprentice, which means you will have work on the ship." She then coughed into her hand, then continued, "If Buskus or his mate try to do you harm, you come to me. You will be working in my gang, understand?"

I did not understand, however I soon learned what it meant to be on a crew.

The hands took charge of me after that, assuring me I was never to be bothered again. I understand that on weaker boats driven by weaker crew, there can be horrors for the juniors, but on a strong ship crewed by persons whose iron backs drive this world of wood through the universe of water, how the lowest is treated is a measure of how the highest will fare. The senior sailors, called Able Hands or "Ables," with names like al-Bindi, Sloan, Crestwell, Castons, and al-Luis, took me in charge. They took responsibility over me, saw me shaken down and fitted out as an apprentice sailor, with all the rights of any other to food, work, and space to sleep. None of them required I kill anyone or steal anything. It turned out that it was to the crew's advantage to see me taken in charge and fitted out.

See what I mean by slang? When you take something or someone in charge, it means you are responsible in the eyes of the other crew for making that thing or person work in the manner it should. Shaking down means you get yourself straight and ready to work for the benefit of the ship. Fitting out means you acquire the tools needed to be a sailor. What it practically means is that you have people who want you to find your place, willing to expend their labor and time in making it happen.

Ms. Crestwell then did something amazing. She took me to a room called the crew locker, then began handing me items of clothing. It may amaze people who know me today, but my first possession ever was a uniform, which the crew calls a "rig." Ms. Crestwell took my breechclout, discarding it. She let me keep my moth-eaten wubby only with a promise I would keep it as a memory item. Then she gave me the clothing of an apprentice sailor to fit out with. That meant a pair of sturdy, yet soft, hand-sewn short pants called breeches; a set of white canvas pants that gripped the waist almost up to the nipples and reached down to the shoes below called shanties; a blue and white striped cotton shirt that was worn tucked into the shanties; a red short jacket with the name of the ship sewn over the pocket; an oilcloth long coat; a wool sweater; and a brimmed hat of blue woolen-felt, also fixed with the name of the ship. They had me sign my mark on a piece of paper while informing me I owed 39 silver pennies to the ship's locker.

This scared me, but Ms. Crestwell, an old hand working the tops, said this was not a real worry. The debt meant that if I jumped ship immediately, the captain could get me back. The tradition was a year and a day after signing, the captain would clear the debt, with the uniform being my pay if the ship failed to profit, or if I was stranded on another shore. For many of the crew, their uniform rig was not important. They came aboard with better, only purchasing what they needed to conform with the ship's regulations. Despite that knowledge, I felt grand in my new rig. I loved the entire ensemble immediately, even learning how to sew just so I could keep it in the finest condition. Later, I would invest frugally in new rig clothing, as well as a fine canvas sea bag to carry on my shoulder when I took to the shore. I looked right and nautical, very proud of this elevation of my circumstances. If the captain had thrown me to a sandy beach in the furthest Extent, my uniform would have made every second of the adventure to this point worth any pains I suffered.

Let me tell you about the rig some more because I am not sure many people who hear this will understand what it meant to me and how important every piece was to my comfort and well-being. The rig was designed to be versatile wear. In the beating hot of a summer solstice day, you could work on deck in breaches and sandals with a bleached-white cotton thawb purchased from the slop chest to hold back the rays of the sun. In wild winter gales, you would put on all of your clothing and waddle like a shore duck wrapped in oilcloth as you did your chores. When we went ashore on a deserted island, your oilcloth was your shelter from the rain. Further, members of your gang would use them collectively to form a fine accommodation for the lot of us, with a pit in the middle to have a fire with blankets from your bunk to keep you warm. I got so I saw my oilcloth as not just a garment, but a tool that could be a temporary home or a device of personal survival. Like many sailors, I stuck a water bottle in each lower pocket, a survival kit with emergency supplies in a hammered tin box into the inner pocket, and a waterproof envelope with my sailing logbook in the pocket under the shoulder. I sewed silver into the lining for emergencies, with a side effect that it allowed it to drape better. Likewise, I placed wire, wooden handles, a small blade, a tin of matches, and other goods in small concealed pouches I sewed in convenient places. Dropped into the sea in a cockle I could, I imagined, reach land hale and whole with what my oilcloth contained.

That first debt of 39 silver was the best money I never spent, as it dressed me warm and fine plus gave me comfort in my health and survival. However, I was worried about the entire concept of this. How could I have less than zero silver?

The Ables laughed, but it was the Quartermaine who finally agreed to explain it all to me.

Let me tell you about the Quartermaine, Devious. People thought he was just the shadow of the captain, some long-running joke that no one got, but I knew him along with his individual and quite unique traits. Unlike the captain, who dresses only in uniform and lets his long hair fall down on his shoulders, Devious dresses as a fancy man with makeup and hair that is held tight in a ponytail in back. He claims the same upbringing and background as the captain, yet comes from his past in a very different way. The captain served in the Navy with considerable honor, while Devious was someone who clutched to the shadows, advancing with the captain in rank and position, while taking a darker route.

The captain was almost gentle in his manner, while Devious was an iron fist in a silk glove.

In my ignorance, my money would have been on the major for being a bullyrock on the ship. Instead, my fellow crew assured me it was the quartermaine who would be the last face you saw if you did the ship wrong, a strange assurance because of his obvious close relation with the captain. People feared Devious.

I liked that the first time I could find him on deck, he was willing to speak to me. Unlike most of the crew who would wait for the captain to return, I soon found Devious an excellent substitute for information.

Seeing him lounging in the cockpit and being legally free of duty at the minute, I gathered my nerve, approaching him. "Commander Devious," I asked, "how can I have less than no silver?"

He laughed. "Come here, Mouse, and let me show you." There was a shock on the faces of the cockpit crew. I ignored their wild stares, going with him to the chart table. From the secure locker, he pulled a big, leather-bound book, then opened it up. It was covered with squiggly lines that people with the knowing of a scribe always dabbed on this. He filed around the leafs, until he reached where he wanted, saying, "This is your account for this voyage, here that account page is your name." He pointed in the book at a bunch of sticks written in soot ink.

alfar

What does it say?" I asked.

"Why, it says Mouse, unless you want to be called something else," he replied. "I can change it, then you would become someone else."

To my knowledge, this was the first time anyone had ever written my name in my life. It gave me a sense of permanence, like my end would not be a pile of bones moldering in the sun. That a piece of me would live past this second. "Mouse is fine," I replied.

"Good. A name is a singular possession that each unique intellect should guard. Now look at this next line." Pointing,

Fn ~039

"The first two letters are the abbreviation for silver—'Fn.' The little symbol means charge against. You may not have heard of the term 'riyadiaat.' It is the art and practice of counting and summation. A very powerful and magical skill with many arcane aspects to study and understand. The next three figures are what we call a quantity, or in the old tongue 'kamiya.' By tradition, when the number is below ninety-and-nine, we write a zero in the first place. Three tens, nine ones, means thirty and nine silver coins. You do not need to find a way to have fewer coins than you have, because it is just in the book. Now look at this line." He again pointed at a new line.

Fn +010

"Silver, but different symbols," I observed.

Devious made a motion with his fist like he was nailing a peg into a board. "Correct, boy. Here is where the captain gave you ten silvers for sighting the birds. Now the next line."

Fn +08^5

"That," he said, "was the pay added to your account for working the Cycus to Faraway passage, including your time on the island. Eight-and-one-half silver pennies. The lines below it represent the Faraway to the Cape of Darts passage, which includes three mils for ship share of cargo sold at the Cape. If you cash out at the next port, we figure all this together, giving you that much silver in your pocket. Of course, if someone had a large sack coming to them, we do not pay that out, they have to get it from Cycus. Normally, we have enough to pay off our hands if they find they can no longer live on a merchant. It is called mustering out … since you are stricken from the muster book. Muster is a word that just means 'to assemble.' We assemble your pay, give it to you, then send you off the ship."

"What if I do not want to leave the ship, sir?" I asked.

"Mouse," Devious said, removing his hat and placing it on the chart table. "This is not a navy ship. The mere fact you are talking to me in the cockpit shows that. A merchant is a band of brothers and sisters who are bound together with the goal of seeing other lands and earning money. As long as you stand tall in front of the mast and do your duty, as long as this ship is commissioned, there will be a mouse hole for you to call home."

The seniors gave me a rank, apprentice sailor, and then they gave me a place to live, a family to live with, plus I was being paid for all the work I was doing. They assigned me to a gang, putting me on what they called the wagon wheel.

How do I describe what it is like in a crew gang? All the sailors on the ship except the Steward and the Blacksmith are assigned to one of eight gangs. I am on 3/gang. That means we awaken a half hour before the seventh hour of the day to work our duty shift from the beginning of the seventh hour to the end of the ninth hour, at which time we have three hours of "off" time. Then we work again starting at the beginning of the 13th hour, until the end of the 15th hour, then have another three "off" hours. Finally, we stand a three-hour watch, which means taking to the sheet yards or walking the deck of the ship, making sure nothing is amiss with the world. The watch is done at the end of the 21st hour of the day, at which time we return to sleep, starting our workday again the next day at the seventh hour of the new day. In total, we work nine hours, have six hours of "off" time during the workday, plus nine hours to sleep each day. Each of the eight gangs has the same routine, just starting at a different hour of the day.

Does that sound easy? It isn't, really, but it also is not onerous. It is a long day because even when you are off, you are on. We eat three meals a day, one at each "off" shift and one during the watch. However, someone in your gang has to do the cooking, so each gang member will be working in the galley every three days. When you are not in the galley, you have to spend your "off" time sewing your clothing, cleaning your bunk, washing and airing linens, and any other necessary tasks. Plus, if like me at the start, you are illiterate, then Captain al-Rasheed will have someone on the cadre teaching you letters and numbers. After we left the Cape of Darts, a young member of the cadre, Salvador Ligongo, was assigned to teach me ciphers and grammar during my off time. We would work on it an hour a day, while I was expected to spend more hours practicing what I learned.

I want to take a second to talk about reading, writing, and ciphers. Under the dock where I made my first memories, I could not conceive of a thing that might be as useful as these skills. The skills that needed honing were paying attention, having awareness, and reading the mood of people who could hurt you, as their words were meaningless. Watching the water for a change in tide, knowing how to warm yourself in the cold in order not to die like so many you knew, frozen for lack of preparation for a dire night. Fires were a rare treat. You had to know how to find wood, steal flame to light a small fire, concealing it, or you would die. Yet for all of these skills, I never contemplated the utility of reading, writing, and numbers.

The reason I say this is reading and writing were the gateway skills to more knowledge. With math, I could learn navigation. Math and reading allowed a person to learn cargo. Reading made one knowledgeable about the cultures of the islands of Ocean. Math could lead to bookkeeping. It was like a flower unfolding in the morning. How wonderful the petals were as they caught the sun of learning.

I envied the ones who could read when I could not. Some of my gang spend off-time learning navigation, how to communicate using flags and fans, helping the blacksmith or the carpenter out, or working with the cargo team. Their learning gives them hope for promotion so that if the time comes, they can strike for a position with more pay. They see their learning as investments in the future, as tools in a mental tool belt that will lead them to better lives. Therefore, while reading is wonderful in and of itself, it is also a bridge to a new island of experience.

The captain encourages this by offering a few pieces of silver at the end of the month for anyone who is learning a trade. It makes life on the liner busy, with people putting in long days while looking askance at those who are not. I see how the days are not impossible, just well-filled. Would lazing about the deck or swanning on the forecastle be better to pass a day? Certainly, it would be a nice change, however, sea travel would be unendurable boredom if not for work, and learning is the easiest work I have ever done.

As I said, our days are like a wagon wheel, the spokes going round and round, off duty and on, on watch and eating meals, learning and small breaks with friends. I cannot say enough about the meals because the head of my gang, Ms. Crestwell, insists we do more with the rations than boil the lot in a bucket. We have dus, meat pie, scuddy, and liner-stew, along with flat breads with flavored oil. Everything done well, or the culprit is manhandled easily by his or her mates. I have to cook as well as the next jack, so there is no help but to learn the skills. Meats are browned before boiling for taste. You do the same to the keena. When you make bread, you mix your well-ground flour with Monster from the steward, letting it sit through a shift so that it is rising and begging for the oven rack. Leftovers are never heaved over, instead, they become the little meal we fix for watch.

At the time, the tea ration was this horrible stuff that I have only seen the captain enjoy drinking. Luckily, new tea comes with new ports. Let me tell you though, I had never had tea before, unlike most of the crew, but I fell in with it. Handily brewed tea at the first of the day and in middle duty station is just what the gods of the sea ordered to keep a boy's heart hale. There were days when the ship would be rolling hard, making meals hard to cook and eat, let alone digest. I threw up more food for the fishes than I care to admit in genteel company. As long as there was hot tea, the day was not bad with the stomach growl; nothing a lad of my background could not face.

They call leaving one port to go to another on a different island warping. Warping is when the wheel rolls best because when you come to a new port, the wheel slows down, and life goes from home-like comforts to hard work, which is, at least, followed by easy times exploring a new land for opportunity. You see, if a fisher looks for fish, and a soldier on their warship for pirates, we are looking to sell the contents of our hold and find new cargo to buy. To do that, we have to make the locals smile, plus be willing to let our wares go to other traders without getting cheated or taxed into worthlessness. The captain allows us to speculate with our own money—running our own merchant deals as long as we do not run the grift or otherwise bring trouble to the ship.

Our senior able crew, though, let us know that while the captain glad-hands the chinooks, a term for the swans in the sheets, the men and women below deck have to be ready to stand tall. With many of the crew newly caught, the eldest senior told us how it stands when a ship pulls into port. Ms. Crestwell gave us the straight paint in a private talk between the sailors in our gang.

"You lot," she said, "a ship has a reputation to uphold. Our captain is tough as they come if you catch him in the right phase of the moon. We are making more money than I would have bet for our first time before the mast, but it is how we act in port that the reputation of a ship is made. *Remarker* has never been on the circuit. She does not have a syndicate. The liners standing in the road when we warp in will look at us as easy meat because we are new, unknown, untested, and as far as they are concerned, callow." Her face was angular, almost sinister in the light of the paraffin lanterns as we gathered in a cabal in the after-hold, lookouts ready to warn of the pitter patter of cadre feet or the ears of people who had not been invited listening to our lecture on port manners. I would bet that Commander Devious knew every word spoken. Of course, if he shared with his captain then we were not all that secret, although there was a tradition of the crew keeping some issues off the minds and out of the hands of the cadre.

"When we pull into the road and let out our anchor, whoever is in the sheets will want to make note of the bigger ships, the liners. They are the ones who will see us as rivals. The ones with good reputations, they will push us and bully us, but no more than that. It keeps us all sharp. It is the ones who sail just that side of the black line which we must measure and be ready for." She pointed around at all of us. "If you are given liberty as a gang, you go as a gang. You do not start fights, but if one is handed you, right or wrong, your brothers and sisters are who you defend. Juniors, you listen to the senior Ables. If they say back off, you back off. If they say tear them up, I do not want any one of you to leave one of them without blood on their uniforms."

She then took out a cudgel. It was old, gnarled, and bent. "The last sailors of the *Remarker* hid this when they knew they would lose the ship, just so the next sailors could find it. Their honor or dishonor made this stick what it is. We cannot change that yet. When we become a crew, a real crew, and the senior Ables agree, this is burned on the short, and a new one is forged. Until then, we are on borrowed honor. I will tell you though, one thing. When you fight the crew of another liner, you do not tell the seniors of their ship, nor ours if they have kept faith. If our fights spill onto the quarterdeck without good reason, we are dishonoring the ship, therefore, we will never get our own cudgel to carry before us when *Remarker* needs us. Understand?"

I was on deck when we warped into the port at Genvis Gate, seeing ten liners flying proud flags, dwarfing the other boats and ships at harbor. Ms. Crestwell was in the sheets with a lot of the other top crew, yelling the names of the ships to the Second Officer as they were identified.

"The first two are the *Glory* and the *Grace* from the Genvis Combine," came a yell.

A second voice added, "Abaft of them stands the *Stammering Princess* of the Quorna."

Another voice yelled, "I see *Voyage Respite*, *Jaded Vagabond*, and the *Quest Venture* in the next three anchorages!"

"Third row is *Legacy Spice*, the *Fandango*, and the *Prosperity Queen*," came a voice from the forecastle.

"Last in the first slot, third file is the *Fancy*," from the top sheets sounded out.

Next to me, Sloan was writing the names rapidly in a logbook. "Any of them to look out for Mr. Sloan?" I asked.

Sloan looked out at the ships at anchor. "You look out for them all, but *Voyage Respite* is said to be outright pirate, while *Prosperity Queen* is no spring onion herself." He looked back through his glasses, then at me. "You have nothing to worry about though. The captain said you were to be given the freedom of the port, with your gang at your back. You pay attention to Ms. Crestwell, and all will be well."

Into port the *Remarker* slid, the captain dropping the first anchor to aft, overshooting the slot, necessitating crashing down the sails with nearly all of us in the sheets using deck lines to spill their wind, then chucking the front anchor and arresting the line to the aft. The anchor lines were then run into the fore- and aft-capstans, making tight the anchorage with bully force, locking us in granite hard like a steel brick in a wall of iron. Once the after-watch yelled across the boat that the knotted line showed the roadstead had good sand for an anchor hold and that none of our "hooks" were dragging once they bit the sea floor, there was a collective sigh of a portage well accomplished. A snug ship that does not swing gives others in a roadstead the message that we kept things on an even keel and were a good crew. It made us all proud, if not a bit cocky.

Once we were locked in, a launch chugged up to us, a sidewheeler with a crew of prisoners running the wheels to the sounds of a cross whip yelling a loud cadence. The Port Master was some sort of rich lord. He came up in a seat rather than the side nets which his followers had to scramble up. As he and the captain talked, the crew was set to labor opening cargo for inspection and moving crates. Finally, all of the crew were lined up to sign a book carried by one of the entourage, which would allow us ashore when our turn came.

The wheel kept turning, even in port. The captain insisted on a complete watch, with the duty times subject to change to allow us to take a harbor launch ashore. The rules for these excursions were simple; we wore our best, bleach white with starched shanties, striped thawb that was clean and did not smell of sweat, our red *Remarker* jackets, and our blue hats. No weapons, yet our uniform included a rather large jack knife which we all wore with no one complaining. That seemed rather weapon-like to me. A lecture from the major about our behavior, plus a disbursement of silver from the ship's accounts to each of us, finished the preparation.

Eleven people in my gang of twenty who had been granted shore leave climbed on board a taxi, riding in it into the docks. I was jumping in excitement over my first excursion to shore, this first foreign land I would step on, if one discounted poor Faraway Island. The taxi was a sturdy shell with two landsmen called motors, along with a pilot, whose strength at the locks was enough to propel us at a rapid pace through the water. The amazing part for me was how heavy the traffic was of light boats crossing in all possible angles the roadstead, and how handily the taxis slipped through the traffic.

The pilot was a woman in a bright green, baggy single suit, standing at the tiller, yelling and gesturing at other traffic in a strange tongue.

"Menakeitewhaaiakoeeauirotoitekaihenatepuhoikoee mimi ana koe!" she yelled across the waves at a kvetch whose pilot waved two fingers into the air.

Another pilot yelled at her, "E uwha, ka toremi ahau i a koe mo te kapiti kaihe!" while coming close to hitting our taxi.

Sitting in the back, I was amazed at the woman's ability to work the boat. "What did that pilot say?" I asked the woman.

While looking down at me, she said, "He said the sun was beautiful today, and that he hoped my care in seeing you to the dock was rewarded with a fine tip." She then jammed the tiller to port, yelling to an intruding cockle, "Ka tuku koe, kei mau taku hoe ki te wahi e raru ai to kaihe, Chackro!"

Chackro, who must have been the pilot of the cockle, a small shell filled with crab pots, gave the two-fingered salute, pushing his boat away with great sweeps of his single oar.

Ms. Crestwell tapped me on the shoulder to tell me, "Most islands have some sort of port, I am told. Maybe the port is nothing more than a place to drag a boat up to the shore, but if humans live on an island, there is a place to come ashore. This is a Sublime Port though."

She waved across the spread of boats and ships. "The Sublime Port operates docks on many islands, concentrating on running ports that have a lot of trade that do not want the mess of running the port themselves. How it was explained to me by smarter minds than my own is that an island may make a deal to have its docks operated by the Sublime Port, which opens an 'extraterritorial trade community' that is the only place a merchant may sell or buy products on the island. The island and the port split the profits. I know, big words, they seemed intimidating, but it is really just like one person hires another person to run his food stall, then cuts them in on what they make to encourage success. That is important to know. We will not go into the main islands but will spend our time in the port. If we do not behave, more ports other than this one could be closed to us, especially those run by Sublime."

I looked at the looming city that spread up a hillside from the docks. "This is not Genvis Town?" I asked.

Ms. Crestwell shook her head. "The community of Genvis Gate is actually a walled town located on the hill above the roadstead. The island of Genvis has other moorings and harbors that traders and strangers are not welcome in. All trade goes through the Sublime Port and its docks. For us, the Port of Genvis Gate is the only thing of the island of Genvis we will likely see. That is not true in every port. If we had taken too short in the Cape of Darts, the main city of Dartia plus all of the island is open for us to explore, if we had time. Not so at Genvis. This is the only part of the island we will be allowed to visit."

"Why is this?" I asked.

Ms. Crestwell shrugged. "I do not know about Genvis. Not every island is open to every person walking across it as they see fit. When you travel the Halo, you will find hundreds of ways that people decide to organize their affairs. There are many that do not care to be seen and judged. All I know is that Genvis won't let you past the gate of the port."

We arrived at the docks, clattering to a rough stop on a small wooden sub-dock with ladders to the main quay. We scampered off the taxi, making our way to the dispatch desk.

The port seemed to be a nice place to me. However, most people never had to spend a night under the docks as the meatheads hunted for dinner, so my own eyes perhaps see things in a different color than my mates. They seemed to think there was no wonder in being on a new shore, nothing special or unique about the sights or sounds of this new land, while I was fascinated. The first obvious point was that the main docks did not have big ships tied up, as the liners were restricted to the roadstead. Nevertheless, it was busy with the traffic of dozens of lighters, drays, kvetches, day boats, oar jollies, pinnaces, launches, and gigs. It was a mass of humans and the machines they used to move over water, with seemingly little effort to keep order of any sort. Our own taxi pulled in for only a few minutes before leaving the spot to be replaced by another.

At the dispatch stand, Ms. Crestwell began negotiating for a return taxi to avoid wasting precious shore time waiting on the dock for an opening. It gave me a chance to look at the busy docks with wonder. It was like watching a lightning-filled cloud roil in the distance, the billowing majesty, all the moving parts formed into a massive, water-pregnant whole.

I watched as an empty lighter came in, a stout wooden raft with a dozen oars in the water. It slammed into the dock with a bone-shaking force, then immediately started to take on cargo. Once a hundred large bundles of some canvas-wrapped product were stacked precariously into the craft, it left not more than fifteen minutes after its arrival.

Across the docks, stevedores, cranes, and dray carts pulled by oxen all helped shift cargo, each element moving at an amazing speed. The dance of cargo and boats was directed by a woman in a short tower bossing a gang of blue-coated runners. She had a megaphone which she screamed into constantly, the blue-coated runners racing up and down the steps to her tower with wooden boards that were coated with wax. The wax was written on by a wooden stylus that allowed letters and numbers to be seen, since the wax was black and the board underneath was painted white. The scraping away of the black wax made bright white letters. Somehow, this woman, dressed in a long flowing robe and wearing an odd, tall, cockaded hat, was able to keep the entire length of the docks moving with her voice, her acolytes, and a bunch of wooden boards.

I stopped a drayman for a second, asking, "How do you work so fast?"

"It is the nut, boy," he replied as he left me behind.

A cargo inspector in a gilded Jackson coat tarried for a second and expanded on the idea. "Each crew gets a bonus if they break their quota. Once they break their quota, they get a bonus for all cargo moved. They work their ass off to make the day, then they work their ass off to make the bonus." He then left to begin opening cargo containers coming in from a dragoman.

A port, it turned out, is more than a dock. Right off the main way was a length of cargo terminals, large warehouses where produce was moved into and out of locking boxwood cages. On the front of each warehouse was a series of placards that showed who was using that warehouse, where I noted that *Remarker*'s name and sigil was proudly affixed to one of the warehouses. Cargo was brought into and out of those warehouses, some into the islands Genvis and some to be delivered to liners heading for other parts of the Halo. The chaos on the dock extended to this row of buildings.

As my mates sorted our return to the *Remarker*, I saw a group of men and women exiting their own water taxi. They all wore yellow jackets with a pair of letters on it: JV.

I pointed it out to Ms. Crestwell, who said, "*Jaded Vagabond* crew. Note the sigil of their ship, the figure of a green man playing a lute? Learn the symbols of the liners if you can. See that lot in orange?" Ms. Crestwell asked. I looked, seeing a group of sailors getting off a second taxi with orange half jackets that had no name, one a tall man with a plug hat on his head. I nodded.

"That guy in the hat is a cadre. They are off of *Voyage Respite*. When you are on shore with an officer, it means they are here to work, so you give them wide berth. None of us want to bump heads with an officer in tow. That makes it ship's business, which can get bloody if someone does the wrong thing." Ms. Crestwell took the reservation sheet from the dispatcher, then said, "Slop chest, then lunch, then we can do a bar."

There was general agreement. Ms. Crestwell was a handsome woman, with strong muscles and severe face, who was sweet on Rachel al-Bindi, a senior Able for 4/gang. They had known each other in Cycus port apparently, so took the chance to go to sea together. I was told by Kevin Foalix, a helm assistant from 2/Gang, that you could see a man or a woman you liked, as long as you held the same rank and were not on the same gang. It sounded weird to me, but then again, there was no percentage I could see in coursing with a man or a woman when I was not yet steady on my own legs. That got you pretty well dead under the docks if you coursed with someone who had another after them, so it was better to just make people think you did not have a clue what that all meant. Dead meant dead; you always had to remember that.

Ms. Crestwell was the only one of our shore party who had been to this port and was ready to take us around. She knew the places that were fair priced and friendly to sailors from long-range merchants. A slop chest, our first planned stop, is just like one on a merchant, only bigger, with more stuff, more of a store. The second officer handed us all drink money as we left the ship, then handed me 10 silver pieces, besides for my spotting the birds of Faraway, telling me it was my first port so I should have extra to have fun with. Most of our watch had also done well with private trades. They wanted to get comforts for the ship that they had been unable to load in Cycus, Faraway, or from the limited supplies that the Cape of Darts offered.

We started off down the row of warehouses, then turned onto a large boulevard lined with trees and shops, filled with every sort of human that could be imagined.

"What is a slop chest?" my fellow apprentice Pukak asked as he walked.

Ms. Crestwell replied, "When you die, or if you discard clothing or tools, they can be sold in a port to a slop chest, who repairs the stuff, then sells it at good prices. All ships have their own chests, but you really cannot beat a shore-run chest to save some silver getting things you need. There are some that are targeted for the rich clientele like officers, the best ones are run by a sailors' home. The one we are going to is called the Guiding Light. All the money it makes pays for old and disabled sailors who work sewing and fixing the items they sell."

When we arrived at the shop, there was a line of sailors sitting in front of the home, all working on some task. They were making and taring rope, sewing clothing, making handmade sandals, rehooping sea chests, melting candle ends, and sharpening knives. A dozen cats played about their feet, big fur-covered things with giant paws that the sailors called seacats because they loved ship life.

None of the sailors seemed to be whole. They were missing legs, hands, arms, ears, teeth. They had parts of their scalps burned off, eyes hidden by patches, backs bent in unnatural ways, and every other infirmity that mankind could invent. Ms. Crestwell walked up to one who was setting olive oil to cracked leather and tipped her hat. "Hello Felix, what do you know?"

The broken sailor smiled, showing his absolute lack of teeth. "Ms. Crestwell, I saw your 'Amita' yesterday. She said you were in the port."

"That I am. New ship and new crew to fit out. Do you or your fellows need anything?" She asked.

"Give at the Traveler's Temple is enough, Cresty," he replied. Ms. Crestwell saluted him, directing us into the store.

The actual store was a warehouse filled with upended crates into which all sorts of goods had been piled. Sailors wandered the aisles, and there was an old salt sitting a table with a coin box taking trade, donations, and payment for purchases.

I was standing dumbfounded for a second, then Ms. Crestwell called over me and Pukak. Pukak was quite large, a bald mass of tattoos. He had muscles that made him look like a statue, unable to find clothing that matched his size—his legs and arms stuck out oddly from his uniform. Ms. Crestwell motioned to the store, telling us both, "Although we have a wooden sea chest and a basic rig for you, you need to get some clothes to bash around in on deck, or else you will wear out your good uniform. Also, get spare clothing for your rig, except for the jacket. Get a duffel bag, a good wubby, slotted glasses for the sun, deck shoes, a medicine box, a sewing kit, a mess kit, and a kapok floater. Then go to the food section to get some tins of crackers, water bottles good for four liters, and tinned meat. Do not sweat the cost. You won't eat any of the food unless it is an emergency."

I went and picked up all that I was told. Still having my silver, I bought a package of scap. I had an idea of burning some charcoal and using the scap to write on. The whole idea of letters and numbers had been fascinating to me. I thought it looked pretty simple. Symbols made sounds. If you could speak, you could write.

I wandered to where the crippled sailors were working, greeting the one called Felix, "Hello, sir."

"Hello, my fresh fish. It is nice to see such a young face taking to the sea," he replied.

"How were you injured?" I asked.

The entire line of sailors turned and looked at me. He set down his leather conditioning and said, "A great big fish ate me all up."

"Really?" I asked. It seemed plausible given his missing parts and the gashes across his body.

"Truly child. I was a diver of the old *Dustain*. I was in the water to fix the rudder when it swallowed me up. I fought it as best I could, luckily my fellows hauled me in. I was young Ms. Crestwell's mentor, you know." He laughed into the air. I did not know if he was truth-saying or spinning fancy. It seemed, though, that he was serious, simply saving me from the horror of his own inner thoughts.

I considered this, saying, "I have only ten silver that is not spoken for. You all should have it. I promise to have more someday." I pulled the coins from my bag. They made a fist full of silver, an amazing amount of wealth for me. However, I realized that the ship gave me all I needed. What was silver? I had clothing, food, a home that brought me across the great sea to see amazing places. There could be nothing more I would want. At least at this second, I could not think of anything my money could buy better than a little comfort for men who had given their bodies to the people of the Halo, to make sure the merchants' rant and civilization remained intact. I laid the silver into a small wicker basket in front of the men and women, nodded, then went into the store.

My silver gone, I had enough for a drink and, hopefully, a meat pie with the gang. I walked jauntily with them to the docks to lade our purchases for the outbound taxi, locking it in a transit cage where other material was accumulating for our ship. We then hit the streets looking for a place to eat, led by Ms. Crestwell.

The lunch bar she chose was Foulsages, where they served meat pies just as I hoped. Further, Ms. Crestwell said the meat was not rodent. Personally, I thought she was being a bit narrow-minded because the docks I grew up under had rats that made very good eating if you did them savory with goatsbeard and cress, then cooked them spitted on a rail piece. Still, Foulsages did a good pie—I could smell it long before the actual eatery came into sight. They had pig, which they called pork, cow, which they called beef, sheep, which was called mutton, and goose, which was called just goose. There were varieties of each meat—red sauce, brown sauce, bean sauce, hots and milds, you name it. I ordered the beef, which came to me steaming on a wooden plate, bigger than I had any right to expect for five coppers. Another three brought me a liter of what they called "half-ale," which again was more than I could normally drink. Turned out to be weak, so I did not get loopy. Altogether my wants for food were well satisfied, I had a warm and cozy feeling in the universe.

After our meal we sat on the patio, having a ribald time throwing witticism at each other like a shower of arrows fired after a sneak thief. Despite our hilarity, the proprietor seemed happy for our silver, willing to put up with our loud ruckus. He was more than willing to take our silver while keeping us well-plied with ale, although I switched to spruce beer early to save my senses and keep from becoming a nuisance. It did not matter that I was not a big drinker, as more than half of our gang were abstainers. It did not matter, though, as the somber-minded were just as ready to jape and swan as the most liberal consumer of hopped beer or sour ale.

I was laughing at a joke from one of my gang when I noticed none other than Devious walking by us, trying to be stealthy in the crowd of sailors and landsmen crowding the main street. I have good eyes that notice detail well, so it made me curious why he was doing on shore, as I had heard the senior officers were not inclined to roam the docks. Then I noticed the tall man from the *Voyage Respite*, a man with a distinct scar on his face, along with some of his fellow crew skulking after our shipmate. The group was out of uniform, definitely not filling me with ease. Their demeanor was sinister.

"Ms. Crestwell, what business does Commander Devious have on shore?"

"His own, my lad, we do not notice officers ashore," she said through a mouth of mutton pie.

Betina and Jinx were next to me and seemed to follow my gaze. Jinx nudged me, nodding to a group following Devious. We watched the gang off the *Voyage* who were following Devious, just creeping through the crowd with an obvious goal of pernicious skullduggery. Their heads were twisting about like they were hanging on swivel springs. Further, they kept checking under their coats for what were probably concealed coshes or other shillelagh designed to commit outrages on the human body.

I saw Jinx whisper to Ms. Crestwell as I took off my hat and jacket, handing them to Betina. She looked at them, then silently nodded. I went off without waiting to explain why.

The first rule of coursing a target is to make sure you know who that target is. Though they had lost their jackets and hats, there were eight of them in the *Voyage Respite* groups seemingly divided into two groups of three, with their officer and a rather brutish-looking woman walking together. They were a dab hand at stalking, but they were bruisers, which worked to my favor as everyone knows a bullyrock is thinking of the kill as they stalk, rather than considering their own vulnerability. You could, if you lived on the underside of it long enough, get to understand the street, and when you understood it, things would come alive for you.

Take this fine port city. There were soldiers who stood in groups of two, clutching glaives, acting as enforcers, yet were probably quite useless. A glaive may be great at pig-sticking, although no one would bring one to a knife fight in a narrow avenue. The average sailor, though, took notice of the guards, making them bolder, and more willing to carry coin. Probably merchants off liners were out of bounds for the average footpad, so the soldiers were there for comfort, not defense.

I saw behind this façade as I walked. Two children playing with a wheel and a stick bumped into a man and a woman in fine clothing, ending up with something they quickly concealed in their rags. A small thing, no doubt, perhaps the incident would be forgotten—the thing they stole not even accounted for. That was the way to work under the radar, but it was clear that they were part of the local understory. As I stalked, I made note of the children, wondering if they would talk to me.

Then there was the chalk man. No one saw him work. He looked like a duffer from a local boat, carrying a length of wood upon which chalk had been fixed. I saw him chalk the boots of a woman in a uniform of some sort, a navy type, then not four minutes later huskers were trying to get the woman into a bawdy house, telling her she could have two for one, seeing what everyone knew about men from the island of Katar. Yet even as they hustled her, they relieved her of the coins she would need to pay for the experience. Who was Chalk Man? Was he the boss or simply a minion in the crime community? How interesting it would be to busk him out one day and listen to his story.

As I walked, I noted that the eight stalkers from the *Voyage Respite* were made by the underside of the street. They were like a big shark swimming through a cascade of fish, able to kill anything in their path, but if they grew too bold, there were shark hunters swimming the shoals, ready to take them out. They clumped by an opiate den, the sinister elements there coming to the door casually, just by happenstance, or so they wanted it to seem. Yet it was obvious that the *Voyage Respite*'s thuggish crew was being looked at, tested, almost tasted. Were they part of the normal rules that made liner crews off-limits from the worst the street had to offer, or were they losing their immunity by swimming too deep?

I turned around, observing that the *Remarker* crew mates following me were just as inept at navigating the street as the *Voyage Respite* crew. They were twenty-five meters behind me, just ambling along like a bunch of hayseeds newly in from the country. They were not even trying for stealthy and sinister. Instead, eight of them, sans jacket and hat, were walking like bullocks dragging a dray cart. They radiated an aura; I hesitated to think it, of lawful goodness, like some cleric fresh out of the chantry. If they had suddenly started genuflecting and keening an ambrosian tune, I do not think anyone would have been surprised. They were so clean that not even the poppy dens and bawdies were ghosting them. Even the chalk man gave them a clean pass. If the crew of the *Voyage Respite* was a group of sharks, my fellows off the *Remarker* were implacable dolphins riding the wake of a great ship.

There was a sudden rumpus in the crowd ahead of me, the remaining larger groups of *Voyage Respite* crew joining in. I ran up quickly, seeing that someone had scattered a few pennies worth of copper coins onto the cobbles of the boulevard. Most of the stalkers had found better game than following Devious in seeking to be one of the few that came up with copper in their hands. Knowing that my own gang would not stop for copper but would lose me in the crowd, with the chance that I could lose Commander Devious myself if the two still following him slipped away from me, I ducked low making like I was heading for copper, popping into the scrum and back out of it with my hands clutched on one of the *Voyage Respite*'s crew's paper wallet, likely filled with important documents covered in mysterious writing that said to the world he or she existed. It was too big not to be missed. I heard the howl of a navvy and three of her shipmates, who immediately gave chase. I ran as fast as I could, running into the tall cadre from the *Voyage Respite* and his partner, creating a big mess in the street to rival the hunt for copper coins. It was all that I could think of doing.

Ahead of me, I saw a small group of sailors off of another ship. I ran right for them, colliding with the group, causing me to fly like a doll into the air, landing with a thump. As I landed, I dropped the stolen wallet from the *Voyage Respite* crew person at the feet of the group.

"What is this?" The man I hit yelled, his short washed-out hair showing the redness of rage that told me I could be in for a toweling if this did not work. He had a purple jacket with a noble lady looking cross-eyed on the back, off the *Stammering Princess*, I thought.

"I am sorry sir, I was running from that scrum back there," I yelled as loud as I could, drawing the attention of the of the sailors from the *Voyage Respite* from whom I had relieved of their papers.

"Here now," said the woman I had stolen the folder from. "I think you lot have done me foul. That is my folder at your feet. Which of you took it?"

The sailor said, "I did not take your swag, but you lot be careful. I have no respect for a person who drops their colors. You lot give way to the *Stammering Princess* if you are going to go without your jackets."

The *Voyage Respite* thug balled her fists, "Who are you, dog, to tell an officer of the *Voyage Respite* anything? Now bend to the knees, give me my wallet, then you give way!"

The woman from *Stammering Princess* said, "I am a mate from the *Stammering Princess*. You lot have some explaining to do, being out of uniform and all. Further, you can pick up your own wallet and see where to best keep it."

The cadre from *Voyage Respite* scoffed, saying, "I am Commander GoForth of the *Respite*. If you lot do not draw off, I will have you on the hanging yard dancing the sisal two-step before you know what hit you."

The *Stammering Princess* mate said, "Try to bump me in this roadstead and you will find the *Stammering Princess* does not bump worth a damn, clodhopper."

"I was the one who took her wallet," I helpfully interjected. Twenty meters up the boulevard I saw Devious with a pair of figures in dark clothing. They patted his back, then disappeared into the crowd. Devious looked right at me, putting his hand on his nose. It was time for me to make like a crab and race for my hole. I turned to leave, but the *Respite* officer named GoForth grabbed me up in an iron vice grip.

"This one goes with me. Phillip, take my folder." More *Voyage Respite* crew were showing up. One named Phillip grabbed the leather folder. More crew from the *Stammering Princess* were also arriving. The *Voyage Respite* officer GoForth ordered another of her crew, "Bertha, if any of these *Stammering Princess* bastards lift a hand, use your bustard gun to take them down."

The officer's companion drew from under her ship's suit a wide-mouthed shotgun, leveling it at the crew from the *Stammering Princess*.

"GoForth," came a voice from the crowd of passing people. "Your choice of sexual assignations is truly becoming, how might I say, ghadib?" It was Devious, standing like a dancing master, straight as an arrow, with his walking stick pulled apart revealing a ludicrously tiny sword.

GoForth threw me to the cobbles and turned to him, retorting, "Syid Captain, being lectured by a tajdif such as you, if we are showing erudition of the old tongue, is almost as comical as your sword. Is now when you want to meet your gods?"

Devious sniffed, removed a box from his sleeve, then took some sort of medicine into his nostrils. "Acamee al-Bahaari, it is my profound sorrow to have caused the crew of the *Stammering Princess* any trouble. You are not part of this, please withdraw with my apologies. Further extend my salutations to your captain, the great Cook Barrabas of the Brethren-of-the-Quorna. Explain there was no desire to show disrespect."

The *Stammering Princess* mate shook her head. "The Code says the kid pays for the prank by our hand or your captain, clever prank it was. Any talk of taking this child by an officer of *Respite* and drawing down on us with a firelock is beyond the pale and must be answered here and now." She looked at the woman holding the shotgun on her, walking up until its barrel pressed into her chest between her breasts. "What say you *Respite* bullyrock? Pull the damn trigger or off with you."

Sailors of the *Remarker* started showing up, while the street was becoming eerily quiet. Three crews about to draw down on each other to rumble was not unheard of, or even unexpected. However, it happening in public, in the middle of the main street, in view of civilians, was apparently unusual. I was being ignored, so I drew a tiny dagger, concealing it behind me. If the *Respite* woman with the blunderbuss even nodded the wrong way, she would get to meet my little dagger in a place that would make her yelp plenty.

As the tableaux lengthened, other liner crew plus the guards with their halberds began to strengthen the circle. My own mates were shrugging into their jackets while fondling their jack knives. The *Stammering Princess* mate continued to stand with the bell of the firelock pressing against her chest, her chin stuck out, and her fists balled into two hard orbs. Devious said to GoForth, "Do not worry, I hear that the Captain of the *Voyage Respite* has an amazing sense of humor. I doubt he would hang you for starting a gun battle with *Stammering Princess* and *Remarker* here on the street. One understands the man is quite gentle." I could taste the irony dripping from Devious.

No one was even looking at me, so I stood up and carefully stepped back, bumping GoForth on my way out of the circle. She looked angry as a boar, yet she ignored my bump, being fixated on Devious. After a few more seconds, she turned to her crew, motioned them with a nod of her head, then stalked away. You could almost see the steam coming off her head as the crowd parted for her. The gentle hands of my gang touched my back one at a time as if to assure I was still alive. Then Commander Devious took me by the shoulders. "Young man, I feel you owe twelve hours of labor for the crew of the *Stammering Princess*. My suggestion is you work loading cargo on dockside, but if they want you to eat the ass out of a dead possum, you salute them while getting to business."

I saluted, "Yes, sir." I did not let him know I had stolen the wallet back again from GoForth.

Loading cargo for the *Stammering Princess* was hard work, as I had no experience with it, making it a significant education. You see, cargo is not simply a case of tossing bags, crates, and other transport containers into hold. The Supercargo and Quartermaine sit down with the Senior Officer to discuss how the load needs to be balanced, plus the order they expect the cargo to be removed. Then a group of people like me with dull wits and strong backs run the cargo from the lockers in the warehouses to the dock. Along the way, you check for shrinkage, which is stuff getting misplaced or stolen. I looked over at *Remarker*, watching the captain actually riding a pair of crates onto our ship as we moved cargo ourselves. I asked the *Stammering Princess* foreperson why people ride the cranes, to which he replied, "It is done for fragile and expensive cargo. If the captain is dangling on the hook, no one will jerk the line too hard."

Then I got to ride the carryall winch myself. The winch on the dockside was like ours on *Remarker*. One crew person sat aloft to give voice commands, while three crew worked a set of wheels to move the winch pulley up and down, and to swing the arm left to right. The wheels had shifts designed to engage a series of gears to allow the people working the mechanism to control the amount of work each spin of the wheel was able to conduct. I could see how the clever operator moved very heavy loads by being in a low gear where many turns of the wheels only advanced the cable a few inches. Alternatively, you could reel in the cable in just a few turns by setting in high gear. Every few hours, you would stop to use almond or another tree oil to grease the gears. Occasionally a gear would break, in which case you would do something they called clutching, just replacing the gear cog on which the teeth had broken.

The *Stammering Princess* crew were good sorts. They called me thief, telling everyone to check for their wallets. When I stumbled, they all laughed. Yet when we sat to sup, they gave me a bowl of chicken meat, almonds, and barley mush, with as much water as I could drink. It was good cheer. I listened as they each told stories of their shore-side romances, conflicts, and victories. When my penance was done, they slapped me on the back, telling me that I was the first Mouse they had ever seen ride a cog-jenny, to which I replied they were fine lads while telling them that I would return their wallets in the morning.

I returned to the ship on a gig carrying 6/gang back from revelry. When I climbed the side nets, I ran face-to-face with Commander Devious. "Glad you are back boy, how was your work of hard labor?"

"I learned how to pack a hold and how to run a winch!" I replied.

"There was no intention to punish. You did correct in chasing those men who were chasing me. I am happy you do not see your efforts scorned with punishment." Devious said to me.

"How could I, sir? I never would have known what I know now if not for this day, no?" I was actually very happy, I just did not know if this made me look a little foolish.

"Young Mouse, I will have a task for you for as long as we are in port. We have brought four new crew on that, for reasons of my own, must not be seen topside. Come with me to see." He led me to the after-hold, down the hold gangway, to a narrow corridor cut through the accumulating boxes and bags. Someone, it must have been the carpenter, had fitted out a set of crate fronts as doors, creating a room in the cargo crates that resembled a tight bunk room for four people. Devious led me in, then closed the false front. "Ladies and gentlemen, to protect you while we are in port, I am assigning our young Mouse to bring you food and remove your necessary buckets. Mouse, these are castaways from the *Voyage Respite*, Commander GoForth was following me, hoping they were still on shore. They have jumped ship to our crew. Let me introduce Banji Hate, our new gunner; his brother Lobar Hate, our new sergeant; Mina Eversail, our new tea master; and Sunstar Nine, our new Senior Officer."

The lot looked tired and hungry, so I excused myself, went to the Steward, who, since we were in port, had less work to do serving cadre their meals, and asked for four of his best. Sloan, who used to run a shore-side food cart, was as new to the sea as I was, who was kind to us gutter kids, did not even ask why I was making this extraordinary request. He had his food boxes set out, designed so that meals could be carried to the watch aloft, shoveling into them an amazing quantity and variety of provender. He had fresh provisions brought from shore each day while in port, allowing him to dish out steaming mock turtle pie made with beef—since a lot of religious types won't eat turtle; cranberry cobbler steaming hot; real bottled DesJens beer; oven bread, milk-curdled butter, and vinegar slaw from the briner. When he was done, he said, "Been told five rations you would be drawing, yours and four. Best we have, three per day. Let your gang lead know your messing is handled in port."

"Yes, Mr. Sloan, it is appreciated very much." I thanked him. On the jump I ran through crew and cargo, handling back into the hold, then into the hidden bunk room where the food was met with cries of delight.

I sat in the corner watching our new crew digging into their food like it was gold in a mine, while I considered them carefully as any child of the docks would consider a new face. The Hates looked bullyrock, ones you did not fool around with because they would hand out their fist fast and hard to ones who they felt were wronging them. Yet those types were deeply sentimental. A kid under the docks could get a biscuit or some castoff clothing by offering to shine their shoes while not asking for payment. On their racks were their uniforms, the handsome colors of ship Marines, the same as the major wore. A ship like ours needed thirty-and-five Marines who were the scullers, fighters, and all around labor where you needed someone hale to bend their back. I noticed the two uniformed were tagged smartly, one with three chevrons across the chest, the other with a sigil that looked like a boat in the braces. That meant Gunner and Boatswain, the highest ranks that are not cadre.

Sunstar Nine, our new Senior Officer, was a follower of the Sun God. Her head and the brows of her eyes shaved, a gilded torc of gold around her neck. I did not have much truck with religion, only the Caustals would let a child of the docks like me pray in their temple back on Cycus, the rest called dock children soul-lost. The sect that Sunstar followed believed that the God Flash, a provable, observable event triggered by the actions of humankind, or so I am told, was proof that the god of the seas and the earth was, in fact, the sun and that the god's soldiers were the stars and the planets.

When Sunstar said something she thought was spiritual, she would place her right hand on her head, close her eyes, then lift her hand up to the sky like she was removing a hat. Rather than snicker, the other three in the room would give her a second of quiet. It was those seconds of respect that merchant crews gave each other that I loved so much. For all the ribald humor that crews japed about with, real emotion came out when they showed their respect for the feelings of another being. Even the profane and tough Hates stopped to show respect when Sunstar passed a benediction.

The fourth member of the group I was serving in their hiding place was a thin woman with her hair shorn short, wearing a fine suit of wool, her face adorned with glass spectacles, which were seeing devices which were similar to our sunglasses, that instead of having a slit in a wooden pane, the pane was transparent glass sporting an array of smaller glass panes which could be lowered in front of the main pane. She looked forlorn as she ate, so much so that I felt I had to cheer her up. "Master Eversail, what does a tea master do?"

She looked over to me as if she had not known I was present. "We grade as well as guarantee the quality and reputation of tea sold in the Halo. Although I am no master. I mean I did the study to be a master, but I am not really one," she answered.

"Why not?" I asked.

She looked over her plate, then down to the bottle of beer and cubby of tea I had brought her. "The Captain of the *Voyage Respite* took my tea book, my thesis, and all of my writings, then forced me to serve or he would burn them. I applied for master, however, because I am unable to confirm my ranking without those books, I am just a journeyman who has trade rights. I am not a master at all unless I can get my tea books and thesis in order to activate my rank at a port with a grandmaster."

The Hates both growled. "Captain Cagion and his bulldog GoForth are pirates, not true humans," Lobar Hate said, finishing his bottle of DesJens. "Ask me where Acton, our dear brother is. Cast adrift in mid-warp in a cockle with no water and food to die. Where is yon Sunstar's brother? He kicked his last attached to a hempen line pulled aloft over the sea by his best mates. We left our kit behind, our Commons, everything, with her the worst off because she also left a decade of her doodles to the hands of Cagion. Yet, I and mine will not be back. Not to that pirate."

When they finished eating, I took the dishes back, emptied their slops, and thought of them being so much like me when I came aboard: broke, alone, and with no kit. That led me to my bunk where my sea chest was locked up, well protected from even friendly hands. On the island I had found quite a bit of dodger, with the thought that I might keep it until I knew how to trade it, even though I knew that the posh in my pocket was better than the stuff I did not really have much heart for, only a vague idea of larceny. In creeping the city, I had been lucky because when it was time to choose from the pile I had kept my best catches, small shiny things, easy to pocket, easy to trade. I gathered the lot, taking it to Suela Fleet, who had a proven eye for the glitter.

She was standing in the hold, working on a chart which was designed to help her balance the ship along its center, growling. She caught my eyes and asked, "What have you to say for yourself?"

"About what Ms. Fleet?" I asked.

"No-no-no. You heave that Ms. Fleet crap over the gunnels. Fifty crates space you are taking with your odd cargo … yet it masses nothing. Like we are shipping air," she replied.

"Have to ask the captain 'bout that one, Suela. I just work here. I do not order where crates get stacked, though maybe I can make you happy," I responded in my own ingratiating voice.

"How will you do that, jockey of the lowest deck?" she questioned in a rather snide voice.

"By giving you a quarter of the posh taken on a double handful of glitter," I answered.

"You are born under the docks, yes?" she queried.

"So far under I could burrow like a sand crab," I replied.

She looked at the glitter, then asked, "What will you do with all that posh if I get it into those grubby bread-stealing hands of yours?"

"My business is it not, mistress of double deals in the glitter market?" I asked.

She looked troubled, saying concernedly, "If you go to shore with posh to spend, have Ms. Crestwell help you hire a Bandersnatch."

I pretended to know what a Bandersnatch was, even though the truth was a boy from under the docks never had to worry about money because when we get money, we tend to get killed soon after the cold silver of it warms in our hands. Still, I was coming from feeding the castaways when Suela handed me an amazing bag of silver, more posh than I could ever imagine existing. I flat-out goggled.

"Five point two kilograms of posh in clinking form," she told me.

I opened the bag. No slugs or copper orbs were to be seen. It was a mass of larger and smaller trade tokens, all in pure silver. "How in the sun god's mercy Suela?" I asked.

She laughed. "You know most of the jewelry you handed me was gold, correct? Even without the captain's clever certificates, one gram of gold is twenty of silver. Also, silver spends."

Feeling sheepish, I went to Ms. Crestwell, who was washing her rig on the aft riser with the rest of the gang. She looked at me and the silver when I spilled it out, asking incredulously, "Damn, Mouse, what do you want to buy with a sack of silver that size, your own ship? How did you get that much silver?"

I had to admit the truth. "Suela sold some glitter for me. This is what she got. Now I want something, and I need your help."

Ms. Crestwell listened to my plan, then stated the whole gang had to be in on the deal.

The first trick was to lay in a bandersnatch. A bandersnatch was a merchant who would hold money and objects for two parties that did not trust the other, charging a fee in order to ensure that the correct party got the money, and the correct party got the goods. To accomplish this, the first step we took was to carefully carry the silver to "Otagu House and Financial Factors" and hand the old woman who ran the place, Sophi Otagu, all the silver I had in the world, which left me with just as much money as I had the day before, which was as much as I had ever had in my life.

Then I had to find my mark. The crew of the *Voyage Respite* all stood out since they wore orange jackets. However, it turned out they stood out in another way. I had called them sharks before. This was an understatement. Off-ship, the crew of the *Voyage Respite* thought they were quick hands and clever manipulators, yet they were not subtle. They were, in fact, just another gang in a town of gangs, with a little more brutality, a less subtlety. They shook down the town when they were in port, then left before the town could respond. Or so it seemed.

In reality, the town did respond. No amount of money would have caused chalk man to doss down a street rat. The crew of the *Voyage Respite* passing through were not given the same courtesy. I passed silver to him in the early hours of the day. An hour later, I was equipped with amazing intelligence on the *Voyage Respite* crew and their double dealings. I was under no illusions that the chalk man I bribed was loyal—as it turned out there were nine "chalk men" who all worked for a crime boss named Cupra Magna. Since there was no profit in selling me out at that second, the deal worked.

He pointed out the Supercargo of *Voyage Respite* was going through: every prossi and benchmark that money could buy, a lasher who shortchanged his meat puppets when he did not get exactly what he wanted. At the same time, he was nosing around the poppy dens asking who would be interested in buying ship's dross, with part of that dross being the belongings of our new crew.

Best of all, the wayward *Voyage Respite* Supercargo was also selling cargo off books, cheating Cagion and GoForth with a little penny and pence action that showed the man liked to gamble over a pittance, having no respect for the integrity of the ship he hewed to. I watched across a bar for an hour and saw that he cheated at everything, yet was not bright enough to be good at it. No wonder he was a one-man wrecking ball on the street and that the underside hated him. No doubt if he ever showed up without the crew of a pirate behind him, he would be divided into handy pieces to be fed to the crabs.

I paid coins to a fancy girl the Supercargo frequented, a sad thing named Sally Portly, who set me up with the man who was called Fredup. Poor bastard had so much larceny in his heart, I could feel his thoughts as he heard of my desire to buy what he was selling.

He came into the tavern, finding the seat I had left for him. The bar was filled with liner crew, many of which were drinking on my coins handed out by my lead, Ms. Crestwell. He was comfortable because I had chosen a merchant's bar and he did not know me to be a merchant. As he stopped at my table he blinked, nonplussed to face what he thought of as a guttersnipe. "I was under the impression this was a meeting with a person of dealings," he stated flatly.

"My noble sir," I said, promoting him about eight ranks in the social order. "A person of your peerage should understand that a person of dealings does not bend his or her own hand to such acts, instead employing lackeys that match the world where the dealings are conducted. To you, I am a guttersnipe, to my master, I am his hands dressed in the gloves of the Sublime Port, able to cross the wall as I might because I look like I do. Your assumption of my youth is how I have this position of trust."

"How does a guttersnipe bring surety to a dealing with myself, a private citizen making a few trades of the book?" he asked.

I laughed like I did not have a care in the world. "You are, of course, not trading with me. My master, who we will call Mr. Port, has banked silver with a bandersnatch, as well as taken the rental of a cage on the dockside. Product in the cage confirmed by a Mistress Otagu is paid with silver counted into your hand. I never hold a jot of it, nor pass my hands across a brass oboe. The expense for Mistress Otagu being paid by my master, of course."

Fredup threw his hat onto the table and sat. "Then we have a concordance, Mr. Guttersnipe. I am to understand you wish cargo of a very general, yet very targeted nature."

I nodded. "Inland, there are people of wealth who are struck by the fashion of the sea when looking for the trickery that they adorn their walls."

"I have heard of such," Fredup said. That relieved me quite a bit because I had made such fashions up just to have an excuse to ask for what I was going to seek.

"They want," I started, "sea chests with rig, nautical books, maps, and logs. Tools of brass, wood, and percha. While my master can see that a certain amount of this dunnage is less than the kraken-odds, it must be centered on real objects with stories that ring true to the buyer. We call it adding the salt." That was my best sea bluff overheard from a dozen grifters selling a dozen types of gems, that there was salt in every stale cracker. A grifter like Fredup should see my fictional master as his kindred spirit. We wanted to buy salt at salt prices, to make money selling crackers. It made us understandable to him, or so I thought.

"Come with me to the port," he said. We left the bar, turning down the street, where each block someone who I had contracted was standing idly, eyes rather than muscles. I had never had money, even though I knew what it could do. It could buy a scout, a messenger, a dagger, a club, or a ruckus. The stage manager had the street as a stage, all the actors working for pennies if their roles were small. Since standing around looking at the walls was what many did anyway, there was no hard task to purchase this service for a few hours.

I walked with the pirate down to the port, to a set of small lockers, private ones that individual sailors rented for their own off-ship trade. Fredup opened one, saying, "We had a storm. The captain lost his tolan, compass, astrolabe, logbook, rudder-book, and some other stuff from the helm. Plus, we lost six crew, their affects are in the sea-chests. If you do not like this, I can get a few more."

I looked at the books and equipment with wonder. "How did you get away with the captain's own swag?"

"Who looks for what was lost to the sea? When does a captain inspect their own scuppers?" he asked.

I had a vision of Captain al-Rasheed, who was down in the scuppers at least once a week, thinking to myself that this was a lesson on how to be a captain. "The captain's book is worth a kilo of silver," I said. "The rest is nosh."

Fredup faked chagrin. "The lot is sold as a lot. And twenty kilos is the lowest you will get your gutter-stained fingers on even a button from an oil coat."

"Ok, I will double my go for the lot to two kilos. That is two-thousand pennies more than you walked into here with," was my reply to him. I could tell it was too low, but this had to be proper.

"You will be breaking me. I will have to sell my arms to a slaver. Seven is the bottom of the ask here. Be smart," Fredup countered.

I looked at the lot. "I will be whipped at five, so five is as high as it gets."

Fredup complained, "You can go to five and five."

I shook my head. "I only see fifteen profit at five flat, so I have no reason to go any higher."

I could see him convinced this was real, as he was, in essence, selling a load of garbage that he would lose if they warped out, against a fortune in silver that could never be tracked to illicit deeds. Finally, he said, "Five flat in my hand in one hour."

We walked up to Otagu House and Financial Factors, where Fredup handed over the cage check and key. Otago had the key run down to the docks, where it was handed to Ms. Crestwell and my gang to carry to the *Remarker*. When their runner came back confirming it was on the way to where it was supposed to go, Lady Otagu weighed out five kilos of silver, a pile of clinking posh.

Fredup and I left each other's company. When I reached the ship, the deck was filled with hands and silent as death—the crew on deck had stopped working, watching me silently as the cargo crane lowered the sea chests into the after-hold. Word of my trip to shore had reached the hempen telegraph, apparently causing the nature of my experience to become common knowledge.

I ignored the eyes that seemed to click in their sockets despite feeling exposed as I never had in my life, grabbing the crane to ride the chests down into the hold. Once in the hold, I checked the plates on the chests. The Hate's had their chests, as well as their dead brother's, while Sunstar had both her and her dead brother's chest. The teamster's chest was there, as well as a stack of books and folders of scap, all written by her, her entire thesis. Having assured myself of the bulk of the materials, I got a gurney to take the chests to the four new crew mates' hiding place.

When I revealed that their personal goods, all they owned in the world, had been returned to them, the four new recruits to our ship screamed joy while dancing little jigs. When they found their dead relatives' chests, along with the tea notes for the thesis, they became more somber, remembering those who could no longer be there. I ducked out after dragging in the last sea chest in, running face-to-face with Commander Devious, who said, "I have reserved for us the fore lazaretto for a discussion of your role on this ship."

That was scary. The lazaretto is two rooms between the fore-end chain lockers where an unruly or sick crew person could be locked down. I thought for a second that this could be it. How many of the waifs had I grown up with that had gone into the dark with powerful people, never to emerge again? How often had I woken from sleeping in a warm corner to find the body of one of the children beneath the docks laying out strangled for us to find as if our beings were dark messages in a sinister conversation between surf and sea, the sand crabs the secret messengers of doom? I really thought I should not emerge from the dark room.

Commander Devious led me into the lazaretto, lit a paraffin lantern, then closed the hatch behind him. "Mouse," he said, "I want to tell you a story." He motioned for me to sit down, then did the strangest thing. He took out a length of gauzy cloth, then began to rub it between his fingers.

"When a craftsperson makes a blade of the finest carbon steel, they are said to first bring it to an orange-white heat, then do something curious. It is called quenching, which means they rapidly cool the blade in a bath of liquid. An ordinary smith uses hot water, which makes blades that, though strong, are brittle, breaking if abused. The masters, though, have a secret. True masters make a very special oil, one that has all the characteristics they want the blade to have, using that oil in place of water to cool the blade in a flash of fire and smoke. The iron they withdraw from that oil is called steel, which is one of the strongest materials humankind can create with its hands." He stopped, staring at me, a deep serious stare. "You, my dear Mouse, are a gem, an ingot of the finest sky iron found amid a flotsam of bent tin. You were thrown by the gods into the hottest fire, a hell under the docks of Cycus where cast-off children live short, brutal lives. Now you are, for the first time, free to explore your world, yet you have not been quenched. The question I have for you is, do you wish the bath of oil or the bath of water?"

I looked at him, not comprehending his meaning, which I could tell he read this on me. "I do not understand?"

"I think you do, even if it confuses you. You did a dangerous deed today, boy, yet you saw the issue clearly, worked to a purpose that was not a benefit of your own, just to see it play out. That is the route to a bath in water. With a brittleness that you will pay for by breaking. I ask you; do you want to undergo quenching in oil?" Devious said seriously.

"I think I do, Commander Devious," I replied.

"Then I have three things for you to understand and agree to. In the next few days, before we leave port, expect the *Voyage Respite* to take revenge. This revenge is not your fault, thus will not be mentioned. Do not plan your own counter ploy, just hide the anger and remain in the shadows. Second, you are now my notary. Tell your gang leader and the Second Officer this. Finally, half of your duty shifts are now devoted to reading and writing. I will assign you a tutor with more time than the clerk. Got this?" he asked.

I replied, "Yes," then he unlocked the door. It turned out that the *Voyage Respite* would not get its revenge while we were in port. I was not informed what all besides the property of my fellows I had gotten, until several days later while warping to the Carnival Island the captain said to me, "Mouse, it may not be that justice is gotten by your find, however, I am certain some families whose loved ones were lost now know why the sea claimed them. The books included a *Voyage Respite* log of their kills. Not worth money, yet well worth your efforts. I thank you."

Chapter VIII

Throat of an Angry God

Javier squinted into the scope of his master sextant, then made his star sight. He marked the position on the attached two-axis vernier, then slowly turned the course procession wheel until the second star he was shooting came into view of the master register scope. The target scope he set by the fine procession wheel until it was in position of the minute register. Checking his scope one last time, he locked the vernier arm. Turning his lantern to shine on the number wheels, he recorded their information into his programming form, then began to work his location data.

It was when he pulled the algorithm book from the dry storage that he realized he rather liked working a ship in the middle of the night while warping. Away from port, the sky was black and still; the sound of the passage of the sea and the flapping of the sheets regular and calming; and the stars, by their many thousands, twinkling down on you like gentle candles. Keeping the quarterdeck watch meant keeping yourself busy by taking sights, keeping time, and updating the position logs, while listening to the crew aloft and on deck call out minor observations with firm voices. There was something in the mentality of the night that kept people to themselves. The ribaldry on deck was replaced by crew on the forecastle preparing their meal with soft discussions.

Sailors who might be dancing or playing tunes in the early evening had set aside their music for thick throws of wool to wrap around their shoulders, hot mugs of tea to warm their insides, and the light of a single candle to see the faces of their friends. Everyone else tended to work quietly as if the open black sky and all the lights of the stars were a cathedral of light dedicated to the Silent God.

Could there be something in the primeval makeup of the human species that made them respect the night, even on a ship? Could ancient humans, first arrived on the islands, have huddled together for warmth and comfort when darkness fell around them, this habit somehow having been conducted into the very marrow of the human form? Did those ancient humans standing on the edge of the great night fear great cats, auks, drakes, or lizards stalking them in the darkness, thus closing together into respectful circles to defend themselves and their families? It made an odd sense if the human creature had learned in the center of its being to fear animal or god, and this was why, even on a ship, people found it comforting to draw inward, moving quietly through the night. For Javier, the blanket of darkness was a calming thing for the very reason that humans seemed to fear it. Very few people bothered you at night, which let Javier feel he was more in control, that he was in charge of his destiny. It was refreshing to not be needed, to not make constant choices. He loved to process his sights and run the math that ruled the world of navigation, only occasionally using a nearby crew member to bounce ideas off of.

That meant he could work on the codexes. Theoretically, every captain had a responsibility to make maps. In most cases, merchant ships shirked this duty. Maps were hard work, and no one paid money for second-rate maps. Javier, though, enjoyed improving the tolans that allowed commerce to function in the Halo. A tolan was only as good as its data. The more data on winds, currents, sight lines, and weather that a tolan had, the larger the so-called statical universe each warp included, the more reliable it was.

Javier had all of his sights and notes from their confirmed warps carefully noted in his tolan book, their programming pages locked into a leather binder he kept in the waterproof safe. Faraway to the Cape of Darts was the only one not recorded, he had that one safely hidden; however, he had finished comparing their trip from the Cape of Darts to Genvis Gate, from Genvis Gate to Polyu Roads, and from Polyu Roads to the Sugar Islands in front of him. Right now, they were in mid-trip to Codis Aletia via the Shoal of Clams, a two-point warp.

He took a calculator out to begin the math for his latest sight against the location tables. Each sight, when averaged with and checked against the tables in his navigation books, provided a clearer picture of their location. Each programming sheet could be compared to the rest to see how closely the current path matched the predicted path of the tolan. His own data on wind speed and direction, current speed and direction, date and weather on the date in question, all fed his plot to make his next passing on this route fractionally easier. The world's seas lacked mountains, except for when they were above water in the form of islands. There were no trees to use as sighting guides, except when they grew out of an island. The ship moved in a circle about where vision was clear on a good night for ten or fifteen kilometers in every direction. Despite the seas teeming with people, islands, and life, you could go days without seeing anything that could be called permanent.

Javier finished his figures, then put all the books away, also storing his calculator and most of his tools. In the deep dark night, a consideration not normally made became the fodder for a running brain. He was a master of the spaces in between, the places where no one drew a dot on a map and said, "You live here." His math, along with the math of many other traders, created a world that could be comprehended, and that comprehension was a process of understanding the sea was at once very large, but also incredibly small.

If the world was one giant blot of land, there would be no need for traders, Javier thought. The people of the land could simply hand goods to another village, a town could take their products to the next, and trade would inch across the surface of the planet like water spreading from a spill. The sea may seem empty, even though it wasn't. It was this vast quantum of featureless landscape, roiled by waves and torn by wind. That was the real reason for the ties of trade between people, which is why the *Remarker* existed in the first place. To a trader, each stop meant money, or at least the hope of money. The Faraway warp had made many of the crew wealthy beyond their dreams, while the Genvis Gate and Polyu Roads stops had been lucrative in terms of paying back more than the cost of the journey. They had run into a frigate, the *Greensway*, from the Kingdom of Cycus at Polyu Roads, needing silver and willing to pay in letters of credit at 15 percent. For a Cycus based merchant, that meant they were able to offload their accumulated treasure while making money on the deal, assuming they ever made home port again. Their living was made from the land, coupled with meeting the people who called the Halo home. However, it caused Javier serious questions.

The trade was why they were here. However, it turned out to not be as interesting to Javier as he had hoped. It was the emptiness he really craved. Devious could count silver coins, line them up, weigh them, put them in bags, then put the bags in chests, then strap the chests to pallets. Silver was the trade token that made humans push their bodies and risk their lives sailing on a trader. Silver, though, could not feed anyone, could not grow, nor tell a human the time or where on the surface of the sea they were. Silver was, at least to Javier, unless made into a fork or a spoon, largely useless. You could starve on a pile of silver. Disease could rip your body even as you clutched a double handful of coins. Silver meant little on the open sea. A chest of it could not bring you to a safe port, could not steady his hand when he shot a sight, would not make a lookout see better, nor steer a storm around their fragile ship.

Yet silver was the entire reason they ventured from harbor. His people had taken on conch shells at Faraway, beautiful things that had once been home to a massive creature that slowly patrolled the sandy shallows of that island. They then sold them for a silver each to the people of Mount Polyu. The new tea master had graded and written a report on the tea from Faraway. Soon after the merchant Xenia Blossom had traded them two for one for Old Hamp tea, a popular mid-range leaf, now each roadstead they visited, silver came to them through selling chests of the drink to shore-based tea traders, ever desirous of this product. Silver dictated their every move.

Yet the silver was not the point, not really. It fascinated Devious, made Standish a little less sour, gave the crew a marker for personal success and hopes for a future, yet Javier felt that these were all side issues. He realized his own motives were murky on the issue. His drinking and gambling were perhaps caused in part by his complete lack of interest in accumulating wealth. He had little problem forgetting about the coins he was earning or where they ended up because deep inside of himself, it just was not all that important. What he accumulated would not be squandered, as was his personal want, on dissipations, but would be saved to build a life with his wife. He drank Junebug tea, eating sailor's rations cooked by the cadre's steward to save money. He pulled his uniforms from the ship's stores, same as the crew. The money he made was intended for his wife; when she was not present, useless to consider.

So, treasure had meaning, but he had forcefully pushed his own mind to reject it as a measure of what he was about as the captain of this ship. He limited his licentious behavior to buying books, maps, and mathematical instruments in which to feed his mind. He knew he had a problem with cards and dice, and that a dog running a 500 could part him with all of his money. It was like his brain was a spring-in timekeeper, that if there were no hands, he would spin until he broke. Instead, he gave it hands to fidget with, while deep in the center of his being he sought to create order from the chaos that roiled him.

He stopped his figures and looked at the helm, holding the main wheel to course, straight and awake in the cool night air. "We are much more than trader, helm."

The helm replied in a curious voice, "As the captain says."

Javier returned to his numbers. Down deep though, this effort at honest penury was simply the hounds chasing his natural tendencies through some dark woods while he struggled to avoid his addiction. Perhaps it was not really a life goal or anything that was clearly laudable. Perhaps he was building castles made of white clouds in some effort to keep the hurricane back. He was a man that knew he lived in a strange lie. He was a tea merchant who knew the tea was not the point. Javier felt for the first time he had a mission that was not simply to keep his demons in check with elaborate mental games. He was vouchsafed by the gods to connect the world together, to protect civilization, to see that the trade lanes remained open, and that the tiny motes of human life did not die like the embers of a fire that had been scattered by the hands of an angry god. The tea was not the point. It was the excuse to weld society together.

"What do you think on while you staff the wheel, Mr. Davey?" Javier asked the stout lad at the helm.

"I am not sure I understand the captain, sir," Mr. Davey replied.

Javier put down his computer, staring out at the sky, then turned back to the helm as he kept his grip on the main wheel. "You are a fine helmsman. You give the cockpit your best attention. Yet, is there anything else that runs through your mind as you keep to station in the dark of night?"

Mr. Davey frowned. "The guide pip takes a lot of my mind. I think of how you set the course in a straight tack, how the pip has to be kept set on the dead reckoning compass, how it is then up to me to keep the pip where you said to set it."

"And nothing else?" Javier asked.

"That is quite a lot, sir," Mr. Davey replied.

Javier returned to his charting. As he entered information into the computer, writing figures on his programming sheets, it came to him that perhaps he was not as all others were, in that his mind would never stop unless he had a reason. He should say he was here to move the ship, to market tea, to earn money. Yet some aspect of his soul knew that this reason alone would lead to his failure, hands filled with dice, stomach with drink.

Instead, truth or pompous lie, saying to himself he was here to discover, learn, and preserve what he learned for others, put a coat of mail onto his predilection for delicious self-destruction. He was the master of the in-between, an idea so rarified that most did not know it existed. The in-between was what isolated people. Someone had to master it, to see that even if no X marked a map to tell you where you were, the place had meaning that needed to be understood and conquered.

Silver and personal growth were the byproduct of his true meaningful goals of mastering these empty spaces. He would not dwell on his addictions, on the mental issues that haunted him, or on the fight to turn a profit. Instead, he would work on his sights and collected books, even write some himself. There were stories, and there were numbers, each making the world make more sense. Underneath that was the idea that he was a drop of blood in the creature that made human existence possible. That was the salve on his wounded soul.

Javier looked at the sand clock, noting the time was on him for a new sight. He always stored his instruments, never leaving them out, therefore he had to open the storm-proofed secure space to remove them, to lay them out again on the chart table next to his computer and programming sheets. Two sights an hour was his current goal.

He took up his sextant, set it into its clutch, then connected the vernier scale to its mechanical. Then the books came out, each filled with tables, each table filled with arcane numbers that all tried to answer the question, "Where am I now?" Such a simple question, the answer existential in nature, since missing landfall by a mile in a storm could mean death for the entire crew. He pulled out a clean sighting sheet, clipped it onto the chart table, then placed the ink and pen into a holder that would keep them from spilling in all but the worst storm, allowing him to record his clear sky sights in a legible hand.

His first star pair was Ferris against "The Otter," so he turned to the correct table, spinning the course wheels on the sextant to line up the sight to allow him to "coach in" using the fine controls. When he had the first star in a fined-down position, he carefully found the second star of the pair. Ferris split with The Otter soon was properly aligned, so he peered into the scope and checked his sight quality by giving the swing arm its full range of play. The half images of each star remained in constant focus and position. Satisfied, he locked the alpha, then entered the elevation and separation data onto the first line of the new sheet.

Then he looked for Gallego. Gallego was not, contrary to popular opinion, a star that refused to stay still because it was filled with gas. It was instead a planet like Ocean, very large and distant, circling the sun at a different speed. The relationship between it, The Otter, and Ferris could be used against a mathematical formula to tell time. It was not perfect. The mere fact that five people could get five figures from the elevation and separation of Otter and Ferris, tiny dots in the sky, when taking sights from the rocking deck of a ship, meant that time at night was harder to measure than when you could see the sun and had an accurate idea of what day it was. Still, it was a data point, each data point tending to collapse to a middle place where reality lived. He entered his numbers for Gallego, then did the math on one of the programming sheets that had space left for a calculation. The result was a rough location and a time that came close enough to what the tolan stated that Javier did not feel a need to run the sight again. He entered onto the log sheets the estimated wind and sea current, then used the numbers for his logbook and rudder. The programming form then went into the day's sights folder. He then returned the results into the helm's secured dry-locker where they would be safe from weather. The tools, he boxed, then placed into the navigation dry stores.

It was now time to walk the deck. The ship had a hundred-odd souls on board, a quarter on duty, an eighth on watch, the rest sleeping or resting in some manner. There was no time, day or night, that the crew was absent from the deck, but at night, things became quieter and the crew more insular. It was a good time to inspect the ship.

The helm was on the quarterdeck, a riser where the ship was navigated, and also where one mast was positioned. A tour of the ship started with looking over the aft, port, and starboard rails to see that the ship was trim, the rudder was well bitten into the water, that no debris or lines had come loose and were dragging, that no one had attached a follower onto them, a line which could carry some object that would slow their travels. Javier checked the compass, the steer guide, the wind sock, the speed wheel, and that the safety supplies and spare painters were all in their proper places. The deck was starting to shine a bit, so he touched the after-watch stander, instructing him, "Tell the watch patrol to get an idler to give the deck a run-over with a pumice on our next shift."

Then he turned to the sheets. There were four masts numbered from fore to aft, one, two, three, and four, all square sails with three risers. That gave *Remarker* a lot of power, necessary given her construction and her hold spaces.

In addition, *Remarker* carried a jib, a triangular staysail at the far forward edge of the ship.

Although Javier knew the sail configuration that was set, he followed the procedure. Looking at the yeoman's tell-tale board, checking that it reflected the current yardage being flown. He could, if he discovered that the ship was not well trimmed, carrying too much or too little sail, for example, order a change; however, the real goal was to make an officer look to their sheets for fault twice a shift. A missed sail anchor or a drawing sheet could lead to all sorts of mischief if left untended for an entire shift. The inspection was important for a taught ship.

An apprentice sailor tapped him on the shoulder, offering him a cup of tea. There was a constant movement of copper tureens filled with hot water to various crew stations, where they could be locked into service holders that protected them from being lost overboard in hard weather. The tureens were double-walled, wrapped in woolen battens to retain their heat while protecting the person carrying them from scalds. They were designed to be held over one of the ship's fires in the galley firebox, heating the water through the thick base of the carrier. Crew kept tea makers in the various supply cupboards, using either tea from their daily ration, or privately bought tea. Javier had his Junebug, harsh and acidic, which snapped him away from the doldrums of his night mind. The crew knew to make him this from his chest. He thanked the apprentice, then turned to inspect the rest of the ship.

The quarterdeck had two gangway ladders down, one to the well deck, another to the officer's wardroom, and Javier's own office and bunk. He took the ladder to the well deck which ran from forecastle to quarterdeck, had a deckhouse for the galley, cargo holds fore and aft, two winch cranes, a capstan, a gig, two pinnaces, and three cockles stacked into two groups so that the winches could carry over a cockle, a gig, or a pinnace without having to reorder the boats. Under the boats, hard to reach but important to shift odd-sized cargo, were four rafts on stays and sixteen fenders filled with kapock. The well deck was cluttered at best, an obstacle-laden garden of nautical equipment that also served as a workspace for crew. Even in the dark of night, it was being used by the crew for work. Some of the idlers were sewing sheets. They obliged Javier's inspection by turning over the gig by brute force. Clapped inside were four oars, a five-meter canvas, a mast poll wrapped in guys, a cask with forty liters of water, another cask with forty kilograms of cracker, and ten personal kits, all of which were fixed into place by painters and netting. The gig was the captain's launch, but Javier insisted that it be kept prepared as a lifeboat as well. His own father had died in an open boat, and the bodies of him and his mates when recovered so horrified the fishers who found them, they did not allow him to see the remains. All he knew was that his father had left the world thirsty, hungry, and suffering. The fragment of writing that one of them, perhaps his father, had left still haunted him. "Alone in a sea of lights..." No one Javier commanded would die from neglect of the boat they sailed in, not if a cask of water and one biscuit could save them.

Javier then climbed to the foredeck, sometimes called the weather deck, a raised area above the forecastle. The crew mostly lived in the forecastle, their bunks stacked three high on three decks, so the foredeck was where they liked to eat and relax in fair weather. The second capstan and the jibs cluttered the deck, the crew having rigged a gallant sail to form a tent for their comfort. By tradition, a cadre member announced themselves as they climbed onto the foredeck to prevent embarrassing incidents. "Captain on the deck, take your ease," Javier yelled.

It was echoed by the senior member of the crew, "Salute for the captain." It was supposed to mean that the group, off-duty and enjoying their rest or meals, would have saluted, but recognizing that the captain called them to take their ease, they had acknowledged the courtesy and showed respect for leadership.

Thirty of the crew were eating together under the canvas tent, the leading Able sailor being Beef Malley, the new sail-maker. Several were working with copper water kettles to brew tea, while most had their personal cups ready to accept the sacred brew. Although the ship issued plates, the sailors preferred to use large mugs that could hold a liter of water to take in their portions of food, while their tea was had from doubled-walled copper tankards that had a lid held in place by an interrupted screw also sporting a gum lining to prevent spilling. Sailors also affected a leather belt pocket into which their fork, eating sticks, a jackknife, and a fat spoon were carried. You never saw sailors without their utensil pockets on their belts; further, when they wore their oilskins, they were often bulky with water bottles, crew books, personal kits, survival kits, patent medicine, gambling implements, and tidbits of food they called nosh. Their jackets were always sewn in a way so that they contained coins, wire, line, bob-bers, cordage, flints and strikers, little packaged soaps, tough tallow candles, plus all sorts of other odds and ends. Sailors were a superstitious lot. Their oil clothes were their homes should they become separated from the ship. A merchant sailor, it was said, could wash ashore having all the tools they needed to build a new ship on their belt and in their oilcloth. Javier doubted this to be completely accurate, although it was certain that sailors, once the sheen of their first days as an apprentice wore off, tended to carry an amazing amount of kit around with them, physically attached to their bodies through their belts and pockets in their clothing.

"Evening hands," Javier said. "Is the bill of fare to your liking tonight?"

Beef tilted his cup to show it was a stew of some sort. "Barrel of dried abalones came undone. The Supercargo had the Steward cook a plate for each gang. Personally, I do not know what the posh see in it, but any change is a good one I say."

Javier replied, "I had some of the abalone, and agree. Our last port did not have as much for cargo as we might have liked, so we took on preserved foodstuffs in hopes of at least meeting our costs. Some were poorly packed, so like as not, we will be eating that for a number of days."

"Well and good, sir. Course no sense of grumble on the tastes of the posh and all, just different I guess," he said, shoveling in a spoon of the stew they had concocted of the surprise rations.

"Sighting starboard rear quarter on the horizon!" came a yell from the watch aloft.

"If you would forgive me," Javier said to his sailors.

The aft watch crow's nest of the foremast was fifteen meters into the sheets. Javier loved to monkey climb the mast, but in an effort to display safety to his crew, he crabbed a painter onto his belt, using the mast stays to climb. In the nest there were two watch standers, one with glasses peering into the darkness. Javier followed his lead for direction, putting his own range finders to his eyes. When he saw the object that had sparked the attention of the watch stander, he made a new report himself, yelling down to the helm station, "Log sighting, starboard rear quarter, fire on the horizon. Estimate is twenty kilometers and receding."

He took down his glasses and said, "Good sight, lad. Nothing we can do anything about, it will be below the horizon in five minutes, but we could have missed it all together."

"How do you know how far the light is?" the watch stander asked.

"Fair question you ask. Ocean is a big ball. Here in the sheets, you can see all around you, yet the planet falls away. At twenty kilometers, a ship or an island is just above the horizon. At twenty-five kilometers, it has slipped below." Javier demonstrated with his fist.

The second watcher asked, "My glasses have a crease in them. Can I fix that?"

Javier accepted the glasses, putting them to his eye. It was not the glasses. There was a line across the horizon. "Malediction," he breathed to himself. He handed over the glasses, then placed his better-quality range finders to his eye. It was a damn crease in the surface of the sea, a line across the horizon. He used the range finder's binocular setting, turning the knob until both right and left side of the optic showed clear and the line was continuous. Scant 19 kilometers. The damn crease was big to be seen so far away, and it stretched across the horizon.

The two watch standers in the nest looked at him with white faces. A captain who cries mercy to the gods is bound to scare the crew. He yelled to the Coxswain in the cockpit, "General quarters all hands rig for capsizing!" That made them even more scared.

Grabbing the first watch person Javier laid eyes on, he instructed them with a fake voice of total control. If he had allowed his real voice out, it would have been a screech of fear. "Five minutes to take in all sail except the mains, top first, and work down. All hands aloft to help. Scale down and get people into the sheets, now!" The scared rating complied, yelling the commands into the night as he slid down from one gallant stay to the next, landing on the deck running for the forecastle crew doss.

Javier looked at the second watch stander. "You keep your sights on that damn thing, letting it catch you up here—it will be moving quicker than you think. Down you come when I yell for you to get under hatch. Understand?"

The watch stander nodded.

Javier scaled down the mast, safety-be-damned, landing in the helm station in a controlled fall. He grabbed hold of a startled rating who was serving as Coxswain. "No time to change crews. You are going to ride this damn ship over the edge of the world." Round, scared eyes, probably reflecting Javier's own, stared back at him, the rater's head nodding.

The Senior Officer, Commander Nine, and the Second Officer, Commander Van Guerster, arrived sodden with sleep to the helm just a minute after general quarters. Javier composed himself. "Nine, get the deck double dogged and the crew below in five minutes. Then report to me here with painters and kapok for the entire helm crew. Van Guerster, all fires out and scaled over the side. Oil lamps doused. All crew to take up position braced for collision below deck. Once the sails are in, no one is to be on deck aside from the crew in the cockpit. Don't forget to make sure the watch gets under cover."

Javier heard his orders repeated. He looked over the fantail to starboard on the quarter, not yet seeing the line, knowing he would soon. Mr. Devious was suddenly, as if by magic, standing by him. "My Captain has stirred up a hornet's nest," he observed.

"You will need to go below, Mr. Devious. Out there is a ripper wave, a wall of water. In storms, you can get hit by huge waves, but this wave comes from nowhere, looking innocent as hell.

Only it has enough force to bowl us under if we do not intersect it at the right angle," Javier said. "Four minutes to get below."

"Good luck, sir," Devious said.

"Luck to you, Devious," Javier replied, always marveling at how Devious could come and go with such stealth. He wished that he could hand the duty of running the ship to him; however, he had long ago discovered that Devious had no head for the sea nor heart for maneuvering a ship in distress. There was no doubt in his mind that Devious had as much knowledge of the sea as he did. It was an issue of getting that knowledge out to the crew, which was where Devious failed. He was a man of the shadows, not an officer of the quarterdeck.

Javier watched as sails were reefed, coals tossed overboard, boats, doors, and the winches reinforced, kapoks shrugged into, painters rigged between safety belts and stanchions for immediate use. The crew then disappeared below deck as their tasks were rapidly completed. The sound phone gave a tinny fart as Commander Nine's voice said, "Below decks, secure for capsizing."

Javier said to the Coxswain, "Mr. Davey, right rudder to 40 and prepare for rapid changes to helm."

Mr. Davey did, then said, "Now my mind is set on the farm I left behind. Damn it all, sweet turnips seem good today."

"Keep thinking on sweet turnips, Mr. Davey, while making damn sure that painter is tied off. I will hold the wheel with you." Javier replied.

The tack was a compromise. He needed enough wind in his sails to keep the ship making way with its rudder buried, but he also needed the sharp prow of the ship to meet the wave at the right angle to cross it without letting water pile up on her sidewall. Ironically, small sloops that could be sunk by great storms tended to weather a killer wave well. It was the larger, longer ships that could break into flinders as the force behind the water piled up on them, forcing them to climb at an angle that could break their backs. Likewise, the tall masts of a large liner, especially if still flying gallants, could catch the water as a ship was pushed over, keeping the vessel from righting itself.

The helm came around as Javier stepped up onto the edge of the cockpit to get a view of the bow. The water was calm, with waves less than a third of a meter. They were driving three-quarters into a leading wind on a starboard tack, which was his best guess on the heading they needed to stay on to survive the wave. It was a case of getting a better push from a trailing wind at the expense of taking the blow on the rear quarter or fighting upwind and across the true current to take the wave with the rudder firmly in the water, allowing them control of their destiny.

On the horizon, he spied the fire. He took a sight over the fore target, yelling, "Helm, mark this as the direction of travel."

"Sir, I mark this as the direction of travel," came the reply. Javier looked down, watching the second helm set the relative compass, locking it into position. Another sight through his rangefinder showed him that both the fires and the line of the great wave were along the same bearing. In his mind, he decided one caused the other, although the direction of causality was questionable. A wave caused a fire, a fire caused a wave, and for the second there was no clear reason to care which was which.

The real issue, Javier thought, was that no one really knew what caused a killer wave, or how to best handle one. Superstitious sailors called them the "hands of god." Sometimes one would appear in the middle of a storm, and a good sailor could almost tell that it was going to strike by feeling the small waves gather together, beat after beat until they reached a crescendo that could doom the ship like a palm kills a fly. There was no established, proven way to meet the "hand of god." Javier, who had never faced one, simply had to take all he had read and heard, then apply theory to practice.

The wave hove into view without glasses as a gathering line. It had only a small "white cap" topping it, but was kilometers long, stretching to port and starboard. It moved fast, faster than any ship, its power deceptive. In a storm, a tall wave carried enough energy to kill a ship. This one was short, maybe two meters high. The danger was that this short wave was as long as the horizon, with nothing standing between the *Remarker* and its fury. A lot of water was being disturbed by its passage. Javier climbed down into the cockpit, calling out, "Sixty count, Yeoman, mark."

"Mark, sir," replied the Yeoman.

"Helm, if we fall off, we want to fall to port," Javier said. "Starboard is death. Port up to twenty-five relative. We should make it." He took a handful of painters, tied himself in on two, then used the rest to double-tie his cockpit crew. A crew swept clean was dead, or so Javier thought. There was no succor to be had when the "hand of god" grabbed you from the deck.

The Coxswain yelled, "Sir!" He was startled by something grabbing the *Remarker* in a fist of steel, pulling and pushing it in ways that the helm was not designed to resist. He almost was tossed to the deck by the wheel, having to put his shoulder into it to keep it from flying. Javier stepped up, adding his strength. The ship must stay on course!

Then the bow of the ship started to dip down. This was where a ship went to die, Javier thought. The receding valley before the wave would cause the ship to lose its bite. Without people in the rigging to play tricks with the sheets, there would be no way to maneuver to keep the proper heading. The yeoman yelled, "Thirty," as they headed into the trough.

The Coxswain said, "Rudder's a-breach, we have no bite, Captain."

Javier felt the ship start to roll in the wave. "She will bite on the swing up. Have faith." It was nonsense, as Javier had no idea if it would bite. He said it simply to make the young farmer who wanted his turnips back feel better in what could be the last seconds of his life.

Then it bit, almost throwing the Coxswain and Javier to the deck of the cockpit again when the wheel forced itself in their hands. Recovering, they walked the wheel back, centimeter by centimeter, saving it at port twenty, riding up the wave as the ship keeled over to starboard.

It was times like these that ship captains claimed that the gods slow the speed they crank time by, as the universe crawls to near a stop. Objectively, Javier thought this was nonsense. Subjectively, it seemed as if the wheel lords were spinning the circle of time slower as the ship capsized, his own thoughts dwelling not on his last moments, but on the nature of time itself. The Coxswain, obviously religious in some manner, yelled, "And down they slid to the abyss, dreading the climb as much as the fall!" Any sailor who could quote the Heshuan in the teeth of death was one to be respected. It was a droplet of calm in a sea of fear, nothing less.

Javier watched with horror as the sea became a wall to port, the tops of the masts grabbing into the water, part of the third mast breaking free. Yet the horror was detached, almost vacant of affect. A few more meters of yaw and their world of wood, rope, and canvas would break apart to die in the middle of the sea. The splintering ship would throw them all into the water, where they would die afloat in a sea of wreckage, or dragged to the bottom tied in masts, lines, and canvas.

Then they righted. "Helm, tack port, and starboard on the line. Yeoman, call the top crew top deck. Ask the Sailing Master to the cockpit, please." The Sailing Master arrived with a bleeding forehead from being tossed around below. Javier looked her over and decided she was fit. "Get the crew into the sheets for rapid change of sail, keeping everyone ready to head for the deck to take cover for capsizing drill. I cannot say that was the last of those waves." He stopped for a second and reconsidered the Sailing Master's wound, telling her, "Alia, make sure to get the Surgeon to look at that head wound. It looks ok, though head wounds can be deceiving."

"Lots of others in line for the Surgeon, sir," she said, turning to bark out orders to her crew.

"On the starboard tack," yelled the Coxswain.

"Messenger from Supercargo, aft hold is all a-mess sir, two stack collapsed." The young apprentice was scared, battered, grimly adding, "Apprentice Eiekling was wounded taking cover and is with the Surgeon."

Javier replied, "Very well."

The Second Officer came on deck, then hobbled into the cockpit on an obviously sprained leg. "Captain, I have the watch ready to go aloft."

"Get them into the sheets, Commander Van Guerster, but in kapoks, ready to head for succor. You know the order."

Javier said. "Yes, Captain, you will shoot them off the masts if they play at the swan," the Second Officer replied.

The Steward reported, "Senior Officer says the back and ribs are solid, but cargo in the aft hold stove through, thirty minutes to repair. Do you want the fires lit?"

"No fires. Get me the Navigator and Chart Keeper to deck." Javier began to open the chart locker when the second wave hit.

It was smaller than the first, almost invisible, lacking the clear crease that the first wave had. It caught the ship on the starboard tack, making it bounce like a bobbing cork, sending everyone flying. Despite this, it was without the force of its parent, and the damage it did was limited. When it passed, the Helm yelled, "On the port tack!" The ship turned into the following wind lazily, meaning that the flooding had unbalanced the ship. Javier leaped to the wheel again, helping the struggling Coxswain bring it onto the tack, yelling for an idler to help.

The Charts Keeper reported to Javier. "Kwame," Javier pointed to the forecastle, "you and the Navigator get a read on the fire on the horizon. I think it is Stathold. Confirm that, then prepare to shape a course there, looking for a warp should we need to get away."

"Sir!" The Chart Keeper yelled while collecting the Navigator heading forward, picking up a sextant and computer.

Devious, looking dapper and collected, appeared in the cockpit, grabbing one of the stanchions to hold himself against the deck's port tilt. He said nothing until Javier was relieved by an idler in helping keep the wheel on tack. "The gods seem to have failed to sink us," he observed.

Mr. Davey yelled, "Sir, I take it back about the turnip farm."

Javier took stock of the deck. The damage was extensive topside, yet the ship was in excellent shape. He pointed out across the deck onto the dark horizon, saying, "I think that the volcano on Stathold has erupted, somehow forming a god wave. I fear what we will find at Stathold itself."

"Hell of a wave," Devious said, appearing suddenly by his side. "If there is a volcano, it will be a tough time for those people. Stathold is a small island. Where do they run?"

Javier shook his head. "Not even a tithe of what it could have been, that wave did damage from cargo shifting, also breaking a staff in one of the masts. It is the volcano I see as the likely worst of our problems. Our tolan passed twenty-odd kilometers off Stathold. We are shaping a course back to the island against the wind and tides. By dawn, we will be in full view of their harbor. I suspect we will find a disaster."

Devious stood up, looking at the fire on the horizon. "Why do we want to go to a volcano?"

"The hold is filled with food, and I think we can get a good price for it if they have a volcano disrupting things. I was worried when we were forced to take on foodstuffs, as you never make very much with them. God has cursed that island, but perhaps the food in this hold can benefit them and us," he said. "However, if things are bad there, we cannot just pass by and leave them to their fate."

"I could," Devious replied.

The captain's clerk reported in, asking, "Anything for me, sir?"

Ignoring Devious, Javier said, "Talk to the supercargo, Suela. Tell her I need the foodstuffs in the cargo holds shifted to allow easy access to them. We won't be selling hard goods or tea in this port; therefore, we may need to take on ballast."

Suela nodded. "As the captain requests." He was then off to deliver the message.

Another wave, this one tiny, struck them. Aside from a sudden sense of being in free fall, it was hardly noticeable. It did, however, cause the Navigator to stumble while entering the cockpit. Javier had to catch the officer in his arms, then lower him down into the workspace.

The Navigator and Charts Keeper spread a map on the chart table. Lieutenant Saludi clipped the computer in place, putting a table weight on the programming sheet. "Assuming, Captain, we were actually six to eight kilometers ahead of our schedule, but on the tolan, then the island is Stathold. It is populated, has plotted tolans, has a string of small water islands, and makes perfect sense as the source of the wave. Otherwise, it could only be Reaver Key, which has water and a dead volcano, but no population. For us, though, Stathold can be seen from Reaver Key, so if we hold our current course, we will either arrive at the roadstead outside of Stathold, or we will skirt Reever Key, so there is no issue either way. Wherever the problem is, we will see it."

Javier nodded, looking down to the well deck where the Senior Officer was making repairs to the battered ship. "Senior Officer, leave those repairs to the Carpenter. We are making way to Stathold with all sails bent. Curry the course as close to the wind as possible along our current line. I am going to work in my office." The Senior Officer saluted, making his way to the cockpit.

His deck under control, Javier caught Devious with his eyes, then retired to the quarterdeck cabin where his office was located. A runner was standing in the wardroom. Javier pointed out the door, saying, "My compliments to the Surgeon, when Lieutenant Durrell feels that his duties have calmed enough to permit me into his hospital, bring me a message." The apprentice lifted his cap, then hurried down the gangway.

Javier opened his office, then motioned for Devious to sit at the worktable, while he unclipped a paraffin heated kettle, setting tea water onto the flame. He pulled tins from his cupboard, asking, "Junebug or Faraway Black?"

"Should I need an anal probing, I would have an expert take care of the duty, not leave it in the hands of a cup of your horrible Junebug. Faraway Black, though, would be appreciated," Devious replied. From his jacket sleeve, he pulled a secretary's book and a grease pencil. "I am not aware of the virtues of our next port other than it appears to be on fire. Can you let me know what trade we might find there?"

Javier watched the paraffin kettle bring the water to a boil, pouring off enough for two cups when it had lifted the flag on the side of the instrument. He handed the cup of Faraway Black to Devious, taking the Junebug for himself. He then looked out the aft windows into the darkness of the night. "They are famous for their apple orchards, but we are not arriving in their season. They will have apple butter, apple brandy, and candy apples. All which will pay a small amount of coin, but nothing serious. Ten thousand islands in the expanse of the Halo, a thousand named lands with an infinite variety of plants, animals, and people, and yet there is a land where all they can boast is the best apples on Ocean. Plus, of course, as you say, some portion of their island is on fire."

A knock, then an apprentice's face. "The Surgeon is ready for you."

Devious nodded, continuing to drink his tea quietly, unnoticed by the apprentice. Javier reached into his cupboard and took a tin tea portable and a half-kilo of Cycus Superior, placing the lot into a leather backpack.

The surgery was in the forward forecastle main deck off the well that was normally crew quarters. It had the two forward heads, a large sleeping area, and crew lockers. The Surgeon met me out front in the well deck. Durrell looked minus on sleep as well as that he had gone some time without food. When Javier approached, he said, "Two dead, twelve who will be on the racks."

Javier looked at the closed surgery door. "Names of the dead?"

The surgeon replied, "Yousef al-Kastner and Ell Eiekling died in a cargo collapse in the after-hold. They were dead when they hit my table."

Javier put his hand on the surgeon's arm. "How much poppy oil do you have?"

"Down to four doses, which will be done for by the morning," Durrell responded.

Javier handed him the captain's and the quartermaine's keys, saying, "Get the Supercargo to break out 150 more doses from the sully room, then you take the next five hours to sleep. Round break of the sun, we will be sailing into a harbor of unknowns."

The surgeon nodded. "As the Captain says, my assistant will take over the dressing."

Javier watched the surgeon limp off, then turned to enter the surgery to look in on the wounded and dead.

A surgery is a grim place on a ship when there are casualties in it. A few able sailors were calmly doing the duty for the dead as other crew received medical assistance. The two dead were being wrapped in sisal cloth while a copper tag was being pounded out for each one. A pile of ballast stones was ready to weight them for their ceremonial burial, several crew were selecting stones to wrap in with their dead comrades. Javier placed his hands on the backs of the crewmates who were working on the somber task, muttering words of encouragement, which was all he could do.

He then went to the holder for the water pot. He opened the top, confirmed it was filled with hot water, then charged the tea portable with tea, enough to make a score of cups. Turning the spigot on the pot, he delivered two liters of water to his portable, letting it soak through the tea leaves in the mesh soaker, watching as the water turned from clear to misty brown.

The smell of tea seemed to perk the mood. The wounded, some under poppy, some grimacing with pain having refused the drug, sat up reaching for their personal cups. As he brought the tea around, each opened their cup to allow him to pour a measure in. He repeated the process until each sailor had tea, then looking at the two sailors wrapped in cloth, he raised his mug high. The sailors did the same.

It was a sad thing, two dying and fourteen whose injuries could end their careers on the sea, but it was also better than what could have happened. Javier looked to a sailor who had just finished the task of entombing one dead comrade, telling him, "The water in the water warmer needs replacing, and there is enough of the leaf I brought for another round. Please see to it."

"Yes, Captain," he replied and began to dismount the water warmer from its niche. Javier stood while watching him for a second, then returned to his cabin. It was still the depth of night, but he needed sleep if he was going to function when the ship reached Stathold. Javier entered his cabin and saw Devious in the corner, looking sinister and wan in the darkness, but he was too tired to converse with him. "Go to sleep," Javier commanded, going to his bunk for rest.

A few hours later, Javier woke to the major pulling his toe. "Captain, the respects of the senior officer, the island is full in our large scope."

Javier climbed out of his bunk, tidying his hair and uniform as best as he could. As he left his cabin taking the gangway up, he breached into the near dawn of the morning to hear seagulls crying and the yells of men and women tacking the great liner through the sullen sea. He made his way through the cluttered well and up the ascent into the foredeck, where Commander Nine and Mr. Bonbon, the second communicator, had set the big glasses into place. With 250mm narrow objectives, they were designed for mapping islands from the sea and rarely used for other purposes. The pair had aligned the scope with a wide object as a coach, setting the entire rig into a deck gimbal. The island was five kilometers away, visible with the naked eye, but the big glasses were needed for detailed intelligence.

Javier looked through the glasses and was shocked. According to his captain's guide, the island was roughly round, with a central mountain and a lake in the center elevation, and could be covered by fog from the number of guyots that produced steam and mineral geysers. The central mountain was supposed to be a modest bread loaf-shaped highland covered in trees, tall enough for snowfall year-round.

What he saw in the glasses though, was a terrifying stygian chaos of fire. The bread loaf had slumped on one side and climbed into the air on the other. Fires burned across the island, both in isolated spots and along a line where several lava flows were moving downhill to the sea. Rocks and cinders emitted from the volcano and could be seen majestically tumbling to earth both on land and into the water.

Moving the glasses using the micro-gears, Javier gazed at the port. A broken-masted liner sat at anchor in the roads, while dozens of sloops and bumboats were floating in complete disarray. The masts of dozens of sunken ships stood in a crazy wilderness, like trees poking above the water. They had all been destroyed by some sudden cataclysm or by human intervention.

Javier moved the glasses about, then took out his range finders, using them to estimate the distance to the roads, turning to the Senior Officer after a few quick calculations. "Message to all cadre; let them know we are shaping a course for a hostile port with the intention to take on survivors. I want all cadre to be ready to present plans for their operations in one hour. Set the crew on four watch, then have the Second Officer take her into the far anchor of the road, no less than 250 meters from the main anchorage."

An hour later, the main cadre of the ship were lining the wardroom. Javier came out of his office, then sat down at the head of the table. He was astounded when a landsman would unknowingly quote the old saw that a captain was a dictator of a ship. While he could run his wardroom as a tyrant, there simply was no way he could think about all the myriad of things that needed to be done in the next several hours. He turned to Senior Officer, Commander Nine. "Praise the sun, Ms. Nine. Would you start us off?"

Nine, a worshipper of the sun god, bowed her head, devoid of hair, with a tattoo of a stylized sun on her scalp. "There is no doubt that the island will be destroyed by the flow of lava from what appears to be a volcano that has opened in the center hill. The flow of the lava will do its work in the next five to seven days. There is mass panic on the beaches from what we can see, and many of the destroyed boats seem to have been burned by human hands rather than falling stones. My advice is we anchor at the edge of the roadstead as you ordered, but to also prepare for departure on short notice. As you have asked, we have researched, finding a tolan line to the Indigo Islands where water and food can be found, from there we can then warp to Codis Aletia, only without needing to plot through the Shoal of Clams. The tides will give an excellent boost if we leave in the span of five days, assuming the volcano cooperates."

"Very good, Commander Nine. I want you, along with the Chart Keeper and the Navigator, to maintain constant readiness to pull anchors and leave port. If god's hand hits us in the shallows, we won't survive it. I am not sure that this volcano will not get worse instead of better." Javier then looked to Devious, who nodded his agreement.

The Supercargo spoke next. "Captain al-Rasheed, *Remarker* can accommodate 800 passengers. Food will be lifted to deck, and the heavier cargo arranged as a floor in the two cargo spaces. Then all of our spare lumber will be turned into three half-decks divided along the center line by crated cargo. There will be a headline starboard for the after-hold, port for the forward hold, and we will serve simple meals from the galley house in a similar fashion. We learned a lot going to Faraway with angry castaways. We will have time to make the ship safe for an unruly human cargo." He pushed a sheaf of documents over which he had drawn out and labeled the arrangement.

There was a silence in the room when Major Standish asked, "How many people live on that island?"

Suela Fleet replied, "Fifty thousand, at least."

Standish looked like she had been hit in the stomach. "We have to understand these people have a good reason to fight over our ship. I am breaking out the 20mm serpents, as well as the 35 and 65mm cone firelocks. That is ten heavy weapons with a marine on each one with sailors ready to assist. We will default to not using the weapons. They will be available to use though, on your orders, Captain," she said.

Javier nodded. "That is it then. Now, here are my orders to you. If any of your crewmates discover a way to save more castaways, then they are to not be silent. This is Merchant's Code and every merchant's honor. History shows that disease, warfare, and natural action can kill an island, but it is not truly dead if its people live. Think of this as merely building our loyal customer base." The gallows humor brought little mirth. "Please be about your business."

Javier left the meeting and climbed up onto the quarterdeck, then into the cockpit where the Second Coxswain was working the port and starboard tacks under the charge of Second Officer Van Guerster. "Robbi," Javier asked, "how is the course shaping?"

"Sir, the wind and currents do not favor the course, yet we are staying on it true. Slow as a scudder, just as steady," he replied.

"Mr. Van Guerster, you are relieved. Get a plate and some tea, so you are ready for the ordeal," Javier said.

"As you command, sir." Van Guerster left the cockpit, then climbed down to the well deck for a visit to the galley.

Javier turned to the runner, who stood anxiously by to deliver messages. "Have the Steward make hot water so all hands may have tea." The runner soon came up with the captain's insulated copper service. Javier doled out a filter ball of Junebug into the water for his draught. The biting and acrid portion woke him as he glassed the coast, now close enough to see larger details without glasses, as his cockpit crew took turns calling the tack.

At the edge of the anchorage, Javier took over calling helm orders. He looked at the harbor plot in the atlas and considered the prevailing currents. The normal run into the harbor was south; however, it seemed easier to move in east with the wind, so he turned her to, shaping a circular plot until he was close to the steading. The *Remarker* swung easily into the roads, throwing out its anchors to position it for getaway according to the Navigator's plan.

Javier clambered up the mast, then used his range finders to look the port over. The roads and port had only one large vessel in them, a liner whose masts were broken and burned. A covey of sloops of all shapes, sizes, and conditions were cluttered around as though the water had been stirred with a large spoon. Thousands of people were on shore. The noise and smell of the port were overpowering, like some preternatural hell created by a mad person. People were in the water, with nowhere to swim. Boats were being climbed into and off of, without a single sail bent. It was a chaos of people seeking to save their own lives, with clearly no idea on how to carry this off. "Boats under flag," came a yell from the watch aloft. Javier lifted his range finders as the Marines loaded their firelocks, starting to prepare one of the 20mm serpents to take the boats under fire. The boats: three long-boats, three pinnaces, and a brace of gigs were all flying official flags at their prows instead of being naked, including distress and succor flags.

"Major Standish, use the horn and tell the boats to tie up on our starboard side, but one officer per boat on board, if they may," Javier said.

Standish took the horn, then yelled to the boats, "Tie up on our starboard, one officer per boat to the deck, please!" She then turned to the Marines along the side. "Prepare for boarding starboard side. Port side, keep a good watch!"

The dawn was breaking hard on the sea. Sailors put on their slitted eyewear to deal with the fierce brightness, however, the sky was not completely clear. A towering smudge of smoke from the volcano dominated the sky to the north, while the active nature of the eruption could be seen by flames being thrown up in lazy dollops from the top of the growing mountain.

Javier looked down at the well deck. Around thirty men and women were gathering there under the eye of the Major and Second Officer, who was sorting them out, preparing a selection of them to meet him in the wardroom. Javier caught the eye of a runner, telling them, "Message to the Steward, food, water, and tea for our guests. When they are fed, start to see to the boat crews below."

Another runner came up from below. "Captain, we have the senior officers in the wardroom."

Javier took his tea, then climbed down to the gangway and into the wardroom. Twelve men and women were sitting around the table, each had been provided with tea and stew. Major Standish said, "Sir, Captain Piker of the *Benjamin's Prize*, plus the skippers of some of the locally registered sloops." Javier looked at the liner captain, considering her demeanor. Her hands were burned and wrapped in a swaddle. She was soot-covered, yet she had a resolute visage traced across her face. The two smaller boat skippers were likewise showing signs of rough handling.

Javier sat down, addressing the liner captain. "Captain Piker, my name is Captain al-Rasheed. Can you tell me what has happened in this port concerning the volcano?"

Piker replied, "I am pleased to meet you, Captain al-Rasheed. In order to give you a full story, I must ask your permission to expand past the volcano, whose arrival was recent and was not the cause of our original problems."

"Say what you must, Captain Piker," Javier replied.

"Three weeks ago, the island of Stathold held an election. It resulted in part of the Hornisse losing most elections to the three opposition parties." She took a drink of tea, then continued. "The Hornisse were elected to shake up the island, but they proved incompetent. Their ideas led to a deteriorating water supply, multiple incidents of God Flash, erosion, damage to the apple groves, and the fleeing of traders from contact with the island. The island celebrated the end of their short rule, but they celebrated too soon."

One of the sloop masters, dressed in the brown, tan, and greens of local attire, but with a normal master's jacket, interrupted, "My name is Commander Funral. No one claimed they could predict the Hornisse would toss hundreds of years of tradition in the water. Everyone knew they had no morals, so the fault is ours. They talked about hanging the opposition. We did not know that talk was real."

"Thank you for this information, Captain Piker, Commander Funral. I cannot get involved in your politics; however, I have 800 berths to take on survivors and am ready to do so." Javier looked around the table, seeing fatigue and anger.

"You miss the point, my dear captain," Piker said. "My liner could take a thousand. The sloops could take ten thousand. The Hornisse have captured them, holding the lot captive. Many they have sunk," she said.

Javier shook his head. "Why would they do this? It sounds like political nonsense that, as a merchant, the Code says I must stay above."

Funral slammed on the table, "They claim the volcano is not erupting, that it is part of the people of the island's efforts to cheat them out of their right to rule these lands. Damn the wind of the South, they are hanging everyone who says that volcano has erupted and tries to escape. They took the fishing fleet last night to ensure no one leaves the island, and if you try to take on survivors, they will sink you as well."

Javier looked at the table of faces staring at him. "Major Standish, what are your feelings?"

"We won't get any survivors on board if they cannot leave the island. The question of the existence of the volcano seems to me to be one that is not political, but logical," Major Standish answered.

Javier said, "Major Standish, will you kindly take this group below to discuss means by which we can aid them in this time of need? Senior Officer, take the crew of the ships' boats on board, seeing to them under canvas on the forecastle." He looked at his crew, proud at what they were becoming. "Tonight, at full dark, we start the process of taking on survivors.

An hour later, as he looked over the chaos in the port, Javier was called up to the quarterdeck. The Second Officer was in charge, yelling at a pirogue filled with men that was bearing down to the *Remarker*. "Sheer off or we will fire!" the Second Officer warned.

Javier stood tall on the quarterdeck, hearing the reply from the pirogue, "I represent the Great Leader of the People of Stathold, Davos Bewq, headman of the Order of Hornisse. I demand you allow me to board."

Javier looked at the runner. "Major Standish to my office, then have the Steward prepare tea." He touched the Second Officer on the shoulder, gaining his attention. "Bring two on board, no more."

The two men from the island who arrived were dressed in the warm and comforting colors of the other islanders he had just met. Additionally, each wore a red sash that said, "Paritide Hornisse", the name of their defeated political party.

They did not introduce themselves. They just sat down uninvited, saying, "We are taking charge of your ship."

Javier laughed. "Sirs, you have no call on my ship and no ability to take it into custody. I am merely here to save as many people as I can from the oncoming menace of the volcano while leaving those that do not want succor to their fate."

"Which volcano do you refer to?" the first man asked.

Javier poured tea for each of them. "What is your name?" he asked.

"Branthwait," came the sullen reply.

Javier stepped to the windows of his office. Facing outbound from the roads, the rear of the ship looked north over the harbor and the volcano. He pointed to it with a broad stroke of his hand. "The obvious volcano exploding in the center of your island, whose lava is not five days away from overtopping this city and its harbor."

"The Hornisse live a life of free men and women, not enslaved like tea merchants are. As free people, we accept only the logic of our elders as truth. Our leader has proven through his research that there is no volcano, therefore, this is the dictate we will follow." Branthwait said.

"Research?" Javier asked. "Where was this research done?"

Branthwait's eyes shifted back and forth in the room, sweat pouring from his forehead. "You are not permitted to doubt the truth."

Javier turned from the visage of the exploding volcano. "Nonetheless, I fail to see why you have come here or what your research means."

"Great Leader of the People of Stathold, Davos Bewq, Headman of the Order of Hornisse, has designated your ship a vessel of the Stathold Navy. He warns you are to turn it over to our crews immediately!" He pounded the table as he spoke.

Javier sat down, drank some tea, and contemplated the islanders in his room. Were they insane before the volcano, or did the volcano tip them over the edge? It did not much matter. "Then we are at an impasse. If you come near my ship or interfere with my crew, I will kill you."

Turning to the silent menace of Major Standish, he said, "Major!"

Standish stepped into the light. "Yes, Captain?"

"Over the side with this lot, gentle if they allow it, hard if they force you," Javier ordered. "Do not let me delay their departure."

Standish nodded, telling the islanders, "Time to go, you lot," while she and a pair of her Marines made their desires known by grabbing up hunks of clothing while exercising their knowledge of pressure points.

Devious, who had been standing in the corner shaded by darkness, appeared into the light of the windows, watching with Javier as the lot was cleared out of his office. "That was useful for intelligence, if not very actionable," he commented. He sat down at the worktable as Javier pushed some of the tea over to him.

Devious hesitated but took a sip when Javier lifted an eyebrow, daring him to complain. Accepting the cup, he drank some down without complaint, not indicating how he felt over the matter.

"What do you think we must do?" Javier asked.

Devious leaned back, almost a reflection of how Javier was sitting. "We should send out cutting parties to take as many ships and larger boats as we can get. From what the island's legitimate rulers seem to believe, the Hornisse have a lot of weapons, but they are not organized in any meaningful manner. You can check with Standish. I believe we can muster two hundred armed men and women. Ten will come from *Remarker*, sixty from the *Benjamin's Prize*, and the rest from island sloops. At the same time, our people will take the Howling Gate, which is a fortified internment camp for people with diseases in better times, that now is crowded with people who the Hornisse see as enemies. It has a dock with no way to get from that dock to the mainland except through the fort. Take the fort, unload the people kept captive, and count that a victory." Devious said.

"No matter what happens, everything that floats leaves here in four days with whoever we can load aboard," Javier stated with finality.

Devious drank another draught of tea. "We can drop survivors off at the various uninhabited islands that have water supplies in this island group. It will not be pleasant; it will be a race getting food for them. However, if we work hard, we may be able to rescue quite a few people."

Javier nodded. He looked at Devious before saying, "Let me tell the crew this." He paused for a second, then said, "I am surprised that you are taking such a humanitarian view."

Devious shook his head sadly. "Perhaps you are infecting me with your marshmallow whimsy, Captain."

Javier shrugged. Devious was a useful ally, but he scared the captain deep inside.

When evening came, Javier dressed in his best service uniform, made sure he had his firelock and sword cleaned and on his belt, plus cleaned the objectives of his range finders. He stopped the second officer on the well deck to ask, "Any signals from our boat crews?"

The second officer replied, "Captain, I thought you would be in your quarters longer. No, there has been no word on the boat crews. The Marines still see something happening on the beach though."

Feeling sadly martial, Javier made his way to stand with the gunners on the quarterdeck. The Marines had set two 20mm serpents on pedestals, with two scopes with large objective lenses to train them with, just sitting watching the flames of the port and shore while a third marine scanned the roadstead with range finders.

Javier settled between them, asking, "How is the evening?"

One of the Marines, a whipcord-like redhead with a slouch hat on his head and an eyepatch that was pulled down around his neck, answered, "They are making noises on the beach to be about something."

Worried, Javier asked, "If they get up to no good, can you stop them?"

"Sir, they are parading around in front of a bunch of fires and carrying boats to the beach, all in plain view. You ordered me to take them if they get frisky. If they do, I could take down all of the pirogues in three minutes with these serpents. If you order it, carnage will stalk that beach," the marine replied.

"Did I say take them if they got frisky?" It sounded like something Devious would say, making Javier feel the same horrible emptiness in his stomach he had felt on his ensign cruise in the Navy when he led a gang to take a pirate. The idea that in a few minutes he would have to order the death of another human being was not something he liked. He remembered his own first blood, not thinking of it while he fought, then stopping, having carried the enemy ship, then seeing a dead pirate laying in front of him, wearing a spandrel hat and deck clogs. It was a sight that floored him, thinking that the woman had gotten up that morning and put those items on. She had made human and mundane choices, then died thousands of miles away from her home at his hand.

"In the long run," Javier said, "go easy on killing. We cannot let them on our ship. We also do not want to sink something that floats or kill someone who may survive this island's destruction."

He paused, then said, more to himself, "It's about more than the tea."

The marine said in a confused voice, "I do not understand, sir."

"You three Marines were recruited at Polyu Roads, am I correct?" Javier asked.

"Sir, my name is Gilingham, this is Benchler and Wuduck. While we signed on at Polyu Roads; we are from the Grange," he stated.

"Forest hunters?" Javier asked.

"We never saw the sea until Wuduck decided he wanted to turn over a new leaf, so we followed him to sea. It did not start out well. We were starving as stevedores until Gunner Hate signed us on." Gilingham said. He pulled some large range finders over, scoping the beach while he talked.

"Do you like the work so far?" Javier asked.

"Too early to tell, Captain. The money is promising. The ship is attractive, like having a home that moves with you. Permission to speak freely, sir?" Gilingham sat up from the large range finders, moving a paraffin-heated cooker close by. He poured four cups of tea from the cooker, handing them to Javier, Wuduck, and Benchler, keeping one for himself. All three of the new Marines were thin, with chiseled faces, searing blue eyes, and long black hair, from an insular community that lived far from the shores of mother sea.

"You may speak on the subject you wish," Javier told the marine.

"What profit can be found in saving a people who do not want to be saved?" the marine asked in a low voice.

The captain looked at the island that was experiencing its end times, tearing itself apart in lies and hatred at the very moment when coming together could see many saved. Javier finally said, "I cannot teach you of the gods or why we pay forward to honor their guidance. I can only tell you that the Merchant's Code says that if we are seeking riches from the hands of the people of Ocean, honor demands first that we give. A trader who takes without giving is a pirate. Our ship, the *Remarker*, has a name that can be tarnished by our actions, or made shiny like the best silver cup reflecting our glory. You can either accept that at times selling tea will not be our only task, or you can transfer to another ship when we reach a proper trade port."

"Hoping I did not offend, sir. It makes sense, Captain." He looked through the large range finders again while saying, "We have maybe five pirogues getting ready to take to the water, about one hundred armed people."

Javier pulled his own range finders, scoping the beach, but it was not as fine-eyed in the backlit darkness. "Are there any banners "owned by any of the pirogues?" he asked.

"They are all clean, just a rabble of armed soldiers," Gilingham replied.

It took a few seconds for Javier to screw up his nerve before he said, "Shoot into the bow of each pirogue that leaves the shore. Spare the men if you can."

The two serpents began to fire, while the third marine on the range finders gave spotting instructions. Looking through his own range finders he saw small sparks as the giant copper bullets pierced the pirogues' hulls, causing them to settle and sink, spilling their crews into the water. The crews, armed and armored heavily, struggled in the water, not all being able to gain their feet. There was massive panic as men and women drowned in the surf.

"*Benjamin's Prize* has slipped her anchors!" came a call from the sheets. "The two sloops are under oar helping kedge the *Prize.*"

Javier looked out across the roadstead watching the chaos growing all about it. He could see lighting on the decks of sloops, the *Benjamin Prize* moving slowly back to the outer port, with dozens of smaller boats flying merchant flags moving about under oar and sail. The first one, the *Remarker*'s own main pinnace which had been sent to the island earlier, came aside, then people began to climb the sides. As the people, all healers in gray uniforms came onto the ship's deck, a stout older woman whose uniform had a red sash detached herself, stating, "I am Nurse Superior Veneld of the order of Spa. Who may you be?"

Javier stepped around the crew helping the healers onto deck. "Captain Javier al-Rasheed of the tea trader *Remarker*. You are officially castaways of the land of Stathold. We plan to liberate you to a land nearby, until then you are our guests. You must first understand that we do not accept the Rules of Stathold, nor Great Leader Davos Bewq. If you are a partisan of this person, we must return you to the island."

The woman turned, saying nothing until her flock, forty-three healers who had been crammed into the pinnace which had benches for half this number, were all on board. She then bowed with the rest of her followers to Javier. "Davos Bewq can place his lips on my muff for all that I have any respect for that animal. Twenty thousand has he killed in twenty days, while he is now is preventing the people of the land from fleeing to the sea. He burned my hospital to the ground, leaving my people homeless beggars. I must give my compliments to the young men who found us, guiding us to the boats."

"We only provided boats to carry you to our ship, the people who rescued you were from your own island," Javier replied.

The Nurse Superior motioned for her people to go under deck, then said, "I think some of your crew were present."

Javier looked up to the boat captain who was preparing to shove off for a second load of survivors. No one from the *Remarker* was supposed to be on shore risking themselves. Only islanders who were untrained by the Hornisse could be taken. "Boatswain Hate, who is on shore larking about?" Javier asked.

"Captain, there were too many nurses at the hospital to take, so my brother and the one they call the Mouse clipped off, if you know my meaning, with the idea of mucking up the Hornisse a bit," he said. Then he added, "Torn white flag is what they plan to fly to let you know who is ok, begging the captain's pardon."

"Gunners," Javier yelled, "any ship's boat flying a white flag torn at the end is friendly unless found otherwise." He turned back to the Boatswain, "See if you can get those sloops out of close harbor moorage. Be careful, they may still be Hornisse!"

A jolly boat pulled up next, and hell came with it. Many of the people rescued had been burned, tortured, or shot in the melees on the various boats or docks. The skipper of the jolly leapt to deck, saying, "Captain al-Rasheed, name's Vulkrim Valdor, Skipper of the schooner *Good Looking*, now sunk in the harbor. I have a place where some people can be moved," he said.

"We plan to lead a caravan to Codis Aletia along the tolan warp," Javier replied, watching as the nurses gained their feet as they started heading below.

"Codis Usinow is a sister island, twenty kilometers off the tolan, abandoned years ago. There is a broken castle, a sweet well, and wild batata growing in the sand dunes. The Valdors used to own it," he said.

"Speak to me when this day is over when we will discuss the viability of this island. It is said islands are abandoned for a reason," Javier responded.

"As you say, Captain," then leapt for the rigging and into his ship.

Boat after boat disgorged castaways. A few fanatics drew weapons on the deck or took shots at crew, but these people were provided orange kapoks then thrown over the side to bob like bottles of rum in the water.

Several boats of children were tied up aside, all hands turning to getting the youth of the island topside then into *Remarker*'s cargo holds. It was a constant effort by most of the crew to get them water, show them places to relieve themselves, and provide a

minimum of food to slake their hunger. It let unfortunate types get aboard the ship, who had to be dealt with.

Javier saw a man cresting the edge deck of the *Remarker*'s port wearing a bright red Partide Hornisse sash. The man had a fanatical, fearsome gage. He had somehow lit two bombs which he tried to throw into the hold now filled with terrified children. Javier tackled the man, beating him with the butt of his firelock, expecting any second to hear the heart shattering sounds of an explosion in the hold. Thankfully, none came, so he turned to the marine named Wuduck and ordered, "Bind this bastard then chain him in the lazaretto."

Down into the cargo hold he clambered, seeing the two bombs smoldering and smoking, children surging away from them. Leaping on the bombs he threw one, then the other in high arcs over the side. He did not hear them land in the water, just assuming his frantic throws had worked.

A deckhand helped him out of the hold. Just as he was returning to the helm Javier saw another man cresting the edge of the deck. With a preternatural instinct Javier drew his sidearm, cocked it, then fired into the skull of the infiltrator. The man's head came apart like a pumpkin dropped from the sheets onto the deck, gore and skull pieces flying outwards. He dropped the block of the firelock, selected a ball shot from his bandolier, inserting the round paper round, closed up the handlock's action, then drew his talwar yelling, "Boarding on the port!" He felt alone for a second until twenty sailors and Marines charged the growing number of the enemy taking their side, all at his shoulder like brothers facing a bully in school.

It was carnage. The 45mm fired into the water with a roar created by the throat of an angry god, to what effect Javier could not tell, other than hearing screams and yelling, while some of the men and women climbing the side began to come over with horrible wounds. Wounds from heavy shot had broken bones, smashed skulls, and ruined the bodies of the attackers, yet they found no succor on the decks of *Remarker* where his crew was like wild sharks tearing at a sunfish. If they took the ship's deck, they would all die here today.

Turning his head, Javier saw that even as the port was being taken by Hornisse, the *Remarker*'s starboard continued to be boarded by castaways from the islands. Some of them were burned, broken, and bleeding. Many others, seeing the Hornisse, picked up bollards and planking, charging the attackers with a fury every bit as mad as his own ship's crew. Javier spotted a group of crew who seemed stunned by the sudden spark of violence roiling the ship. He rushed to them yelling, "Remarkers retake our ship!"

The men and women yelled "Remarkers!" Forming a wedge, they joined their fellows in the melee, as if all they needed was their captain's permission to tear apart the heavens and swarm the realms of the stars. There was no such return scream from the Hornisse, who seemed to wilt, despite their superior numbers, at the fierce hate they faced. Crew and castaways grabbed up arms from firelocks to boarding pikes, rushing the boarders, firing on them point blank, then using the hooks to send them over the sides. A paraffin cooker exploded on a pair of boarders, thrown by a crew member, creating a horrible sight. The burning Hornisse danced like manic candles, screaming as fire consumed them until they also were pushed over the side into the sea.

Some of the crew threw shanty hooks on heavy lines into the crowded mass of boarders, then heaved-to like they were pulling in the sheets. Men and women were dragged from their feet. Then when they were helpless, there was no quarter, just sick violence and a swift end.

Javier watched in amazement as the dour and complaining Gevin Foalix, perhaps the least man on his crew, with his dying hands pulled two boarders over the side, screaming *"Remarker"* with his last breath.

The fight ended as swiftly as it had begun, with castaways still desperately climbing the sides of *Remarker*. Hundreds of terribly wounded covered every meter of deck, while a thousand were pressed into the holds, all plans for orderly loading given up in the desperation of the minute.

At sunrise the next morning, Nine, the *Remarker*'s Senior Officer, said, "11,000 castaways estimated on everything that can float, with 240 severely injured on *Remarker*."

Javier looked at the deck. There was no way they could keep this many people on board and do anything useful for the island. As it was, there were thousands of people in small boats that had no chance if they bobbed about on the roads like so many tasty morsels for the fanatic Hornisse to feast on.

"We are going to skip best time, instead warping to Codis Aletia, Lieutenant Nine. I have spoken with a skipper who will take the wounded, the nurses, and the orphans to Codis Usinow. We will also be passing within range of five small uninhabited keys with water that could each take several dozen castaways." He looked at the fleet of five hundred boats, then said, "If half of them make land at Aletia Roads, it will be a miracle." There was no need to look back, few did. The island still had tens of thousands of people on it, people who were faced with drowning at sea or burning on land, with no other succor to be found.

A few days later, the nurses called Javier to their healing ward. Wrapped in swaddling was a man burned beyond any sense of human expression. The attending nurse said, "The man is Bastion deLand. He wishes to confess something to you."

Javier sat down next to the man. "My name is Javier, Bastion. What do you wish to confess?"

"I attacked your ship. I was a member of the Hornisse, a leader of the movement. I want you to take my life." He was wrapped around his entire body with muslin bandages, speaking through a horrible hole in his face. Javier dared not touch him, as even the large doses of poppy were bringing him no respite.

"We are not monsters. Is there anything else I can do for you besides end your life?" Javier asked.

"You can tell my story. Call me Burned-One, pretending my real name is dead under the volcano," he said, coughing.

"Burned-One, you fought my ship, but you cannot be slain for this alone. How many dead on that island? Now we fight to save each life because each life is precious," Javier replied.

"What of the men and women you captured? You will be hanging them. I heard speculation and rumors of it." He tried to wave in the direction of the other patients, but his arms instead simply flailed randomly.

Javier looked into the empty eye sockets, saying. "No one is being hanged. We are marooning some of them. That is all we can do."

"Did not one of ours try to kill children with a grenade?" the Burned One asked.

"What he intended," Javier said, "is not the point. If I could punish him, I would, but I am not interested. I have only one question for you, then your fate is in the hands of the father. How could you believe that there was no volcano?"

"The lie was better than the truth. When the truth became so bad that our lands would be destroyed, it was obvious that we could not turn back," the Burned-One said. Then there was silence, then the silence drew onward as the man seemed to struggle for a second, then died.

Javier wanted to close his eyes and forget the carnage whose sights were just now beginning to burn into his mind. He stood at the door as a marine brought him two cups of tea, then opened the lazaretto. Inside was a man in dirty clothing with a red sash, face bruised from where Javier had hit him. He left the door open, accepting a chair from the marine guard.

The man angrily said, "I demand to be returned to my government. You are kidnapping me."

"What is your name, sir?" Javier asked.

"I do not have to tell you," He replied.

Javier whistled. "That is ok. You entered my ship, a ship of trade, trying to kill numerous people and children with hand-thrown explosives. We are standing to warp and won't return to your land again. It is destroyed. There is no point in lying."

"You are kidnapping me! I demand you return me to my land! I demand you treat me as a combatant!" he shouted.

"Mister, the last 10,000 people of your land are embarked on a hundred boats and two ships. Your leaders and anyone else who did not board this fleet will not outlive the volcano." Javier said.

"Take me to see it, please?" the man asked, defeatedly.

"I am not going to take you topside to let you look. I will ask if you have family to attend to you. I have decided, with the decision maintained by a quorum of my senior officers, that you shall be marooned. I do not want you to be tortured over this. While you are on my ship, you will have access to no writing materials or books and will not be able to walk on deck. However, you will be left, with your brothers and sisters, on a small island to make your living or not, as you see fit." Javier handed him tea, watching as he gulped all of it down in one breath. "Your reality from the time of landing will be finding food to eat and water to drink. It is an honest reality."

Chapter IX

A Cup for a King

Mina begrudged the time needed to drop off the miscreants at their own private island. The Quartermaine and Supercargo had requested that she take advantage of the wealth that could be found at Codis Alethea, one of the great tea-producing lands in the Halo, which meant working rapidly through the Sublime Port to identify, bid on, acquire, test, then load the finest tea at the lowest price. After three years on a pirate, forced to merely grade tea taken from the decks of captured ships, this was her first effort at honest trade, and her nerves were making her sick to her stomach.

She stood at the rails, watching as the cranes were positioned and rafts prepared to float the fanatics from Stathold to their own private island hell, when a marine sidled up to her. It made her skin crawl to have anyone stand near her; the feeling made worse because he reeked of body order and button polish. In the front of her mind, however, she reminded herself of how this man fought like a fanatic puma saving the ship from attackers. He had a talwar at his hip as well as a firelock butt up over his shoulder, both of which she had seen in use to horrible affect. His hat read "*Remarker*" in common script, as if there was some confusion that he was one of the trader's Marines. "Corporal Hate at your service, Maudibi."

She stared at the corporal, "Call me Tea Master, please. You sound like a priest using that term."

"As the Tea Master desires. As I said, I am Corporal Hate. The captain has ordered me to escort you ashore to learn what I can about what you do so as to better protect you in your business. If that pleases the tea master." She had first met Hate on the pirate ship that kept her captive. He was not one who made trouble for her, yet it was hard to square his presence with loyalty to the ship you called home.

She looked at the rafts being lowered into the water next to a schooner that had just finished delivering a huge load of refugees to the teeming shores of Codis Alethea. "Why not hang these people?"

Corporal Hate shrugged. "You were on that pirate with me. Did all his moves make sense? Who knows why the cadre do what they do? We now serve a captain who one minute is eating beef, the next minute he is a dance master. Really, it is not worth speculating. I saw him kill forty of these animals on deck during the boarding, color me unsurprised that he then treats the rest like addled children to be marooned on some piece of island no one cares about. Are you ready to head into the port?"

She wished the captain had assigned someone else.

"Yes, can we leave before this thing gets on?" she asked. "I have no desire to see these hoodlums onto their rafts."

"The pardon of the Tea Master, we need not see them," Hate said.

"Good," Mina replied.

Hate turned to Mina. "Lads gonna get the boat over the side. You just pretend we are not with you once we hit land. In the meantime, if you can explain to me what we are about so that a child can understand, I would appreciate it. My gang is supposed to see you safe from now on, and we both know where we come from."

"Did the captain choose you because you were off the *Voyage Respite*?" she asked.

"Figured I could recognize my old bunk fellows. I will tell you this. If we see any of those crap-holes, I have a special shiv to introduce them to. You just do not run away unless I tell you. That lot and me, we have business. You do not gank a Hate then walk about. Furthermore, they got two of mine. You understand me?" he said emphatically.

"Just barely, yet enough, I think. You just hang back a little on land. I will explain how this all goes in the boat, as well as on land, if necessary," she replied.

They went over the side with a chest of silver and eight Marines, including Corporal Hate. The soldiers looked like they were from every land on Ocean; however, they all wore the red uniform with the black hat in the same manner, additionally, each was a walking armory of weapons and ammunition. Despite her fear of big, violent men, Mina felt somehow warm in the presence of the soldiers. This may have to do with the time she spent in the hold with the Hate brothers.

The trip by pinnace was twenty minutes through the busy harbor. Mina gave Corporal Hate an abridged version of what she needed to do, noting that circumstances while on land could affect her task at any time. Music played on the docks, people yelling their wares for sale. Stevedores added to the thrum with their rhythmic "hao-hay oah" chant, so mesmerizing that the metal drums and fifes sometimes fell into their rhythm, forgetting whatever song they were trying to pelt out. The pinnace stayed only long enough for Hate and his Marines to disembark, followed closely by Mina. It then expertly pushed off, shaping for the water dock to begin the process of filling the *Remarker*'s water jugs.

They walked down the dock past small traders looking to relieve silver from sailors, past a group of men and women in rags with hats laid next to them, and past a bar where a singer was trying to pull business in with a breathless basso song. He was a comely thing with strong thighs, singing with a belting voice a nonsense reel with all the air his lungs would push out.

"Them is the way that goes / See the sun by sea flows / That is how what knows / Yell to shake our wonder!"

The *Remarker*'s Marines sang a few lines with the singer, then belted out their own song.

"Let 'em blow, let 'em blow,

Let the four winds blow,

From the East to the West / They say 'Remarker' is the best / Let the four winds always blow.

Our guys dress it to the right. Our gals dress to the front,

To blow the man down

They say 'Remarker' is the best / Let the four winds always blow.

A liter of spirits each is right,

It will last half the night,

We leave the bottles for the rest / because the 'Remarker' is the best. / Let the four winds always blow."

Hate then yelled, "Port Salute!" The firelocks were off the backs of each marine in a single practiced motion. They formed a square around Mina, then started tapping their weapons rhythmically as Hate counted, "One, one, one-two." Then he ordered, "Clear the chambers," at which all six of the Marines ejected the round in their weapons with a "cling." A crowd was building up to watch, so Hate commanded, "Precision drill babies!" To the count of a cadence, they began to flip, spin, and even toss their firelocks, occasionally reaching out and grabbing another marine's weapon.

Mina was in the middle of the flying weapons, feeling for the first time since she escaped the pirate ship to be totally safe. Hate, for all of his back island dialect and dim-witted comments, was demonstrating to the port that if you wanted to get to Mina, there were eight skilled Marines you had to get through. Of course, not everyone in the crowd thought this. Most were yelling support at the free show. Mina, though, could see sideways glances and considering looks from the more sinister faces.

As fast as their drill started, it was over without a word of explanation. Hate yelled, "Two!" causing an absolute cascade of firelocks flying through the air, all of them winding up on the backs of their owner in a single motion. Hate looked at her for a second, smiling. "Gets boring in a warp, you know."

Mina pulled out her guidebook from her satchel, noting that they had to climb the Port Main to Cobble Street for their first stop, opening an account with a bandersnatch. Then they had to find a set of stairs called the Heathly Heights and proceed up them to a trader emporium called "White, Green, and Black." The bandersnatch proved easy to find, a red building with a sign that proclaimed, "Silver and Notes." They entered, finding a huge man behind the counter who proved very willing to take in a chest of silver, then hand them a surety note. While the man was pushing counting beads around while muttering to himself, Mina turned to Hate and expanded on her earlier explanation, "We always use a bandersnatch, because they have an address and don't cheat. They get our money, refusing to give it up to a merchant unless they are sure we have received the product we ordered."

Hate looked suspicious. "What if they turn-a-piker on us?"

Mina laughed. "That is why they get their fees, to not cheat us. If people do not trust the bandersnatches, they cannot get clients. They can also wind up dead. I have heard of them cheating small farms on occasion but not a big merchant."

Hate looked curious. "It does not seem perfect."

Mina shrugged. "What is?"

The trip to the tea merchant proved a harder journey. The streets on the heights were narrow and not well marked. After a few missed turns, though, they arrived at the trader, a building attached to a warehouse with a yard full of carts and drags for carrying cargo. They went inside, where they were met by a screech from a little man in a jellaba. "Only one gun-head inside!" he yelled. Mina looked at Hate, who shrugged, motioning the other seven Marines out to the front deck.

"My name is Master Mina Eversail. May I look at the trade book?" she asked the proprietor.

The man sidled over, opening a big tome of loose-leaf pages. "I do not show you. No ticket, no trades, that is the rules."

Mina pulled copies of her documents out. "Registered copies of my ticket," she said.

The trader looked it over, then called out, "Pimmy!"

A girl around ten ducked her head out from the tasting room, replying, "Yes, Saole."

"Best compliments to the Grand Master's Clerk. Please chop this if it is legitimate," he told the girl. The girl grabbed a leather document folder and stuffed the identification in, saluting before running off. The port merchant waved them into seats, otherwise ignoring them.

"What was that?" Hate asked, offering Mina a double-walled flask with hot tea in it.

Mina looked at the tea, deciding to try some, pouring herself some in one of the two cups attached to the flask. It was not bad, one of the trade teas that the *Remarker* had on board before she was hired. She explained, "The tea combine will not sell tea in bulk quantities to just anyone. Only a registered master can buy and sell tea. I have been, as you know, on a pirate ship for a number of years. The ports have to check up on me. They won't yet have me on their books." She poured a second cup of tea for Hate, then said, "Can we get the troops tea?"

"They have it. My bet is they brewed up as soon as they got outside." Hate said. He accepted his cup of tea, then asked, "So how do you prove you are a master?"

Mina sipped more of her tea. "If you want to be a master, you have to write a thesis on some type of tea, then make 100 copies of the thing. Keep in mind, it's usually pretty long, then you send it to the 100 grandmasters. Grandmasters keep libraries of all the theses ever written, tens of thousands of them stretching back a thousand years to when the practice was first started. My thesis is in the library. Attached to it are the letters from grandmasters who read it, then reported that it was supported. I just have to hand over a copy of my signature with the citation for my study, then any island with a grandmaster can check on me."

Hate looked perplexed. "Why go to all the trouble?"

Mina shrugged. "How many islands are there? Populated ones? The captain probably knows, but I've always said to myself ten thousand. A thousand of those grow tea. Some islands have one variety, some have eighty. All those varieties have to be graded by the expected versus actual quality of the tea. A tea master has to predict the value of 5,000 tea varieties and qualities on 5,000 islands, plus has to guarantee what they are selling, literally putting their reputation on the tea. That is 25 million combinations of quality and price. If you ever come with me to a grandmaster's library, there are books, monographs, drawing plates, amber samples, you name it. It is a huge amount of information. Which is why they say a master is merely an apprentice who knows how much they have to learn."

The girl came back and said, "Hokey-say Journeyman Nuvere. Grandmaster says real paper, real master." She returned the files to Mina.

Nuvere stood, saying, "My apologies, Master Eversail. The last journeyman the Master Klatch employed was lax in dealing with credentials. May I give you our listings and set up samples for testing?"

"Please," Mina replied. She turned to Hate. "Now we peruse Mr. Nuvere's inventory. I will pay a little silver for a tasting, plus to get a look at the cargo. By the rules, I can look at every cask, tasting all I want, to make sure they are not selling me garbage.

Once we make a deal, I put tags on the barrels I am purchasing, then we watch the lot until it is on the ship to make sure no one gets the monkey on us."

"This I understand," Hate said, laughing. "Where did you learn 'getting the monkey'?"

Mina shrugged. "You."

Tea tasting for merchants is an art. Mina unpacked her own paraffin burner, her own bottles of water, her own steel cups, and her own cooker. She had a light white wine palette cleanser, as well as a book to take notes in. She also invited all the Marines in to taste, not because she trusted their judgment, but because as a taster she preferred to make half-liter batches to better simulate what the average buyer would be tasting. Rather than throw out the tea, she could give it to the Marines. Being cash buying with a chest of silver, the carpet was rolled out, the objections about the armed men being in the tea merchant's shop drying up.

The trick of a tea taster is to find the least expensive tea in the largest quantity that an island broker had, which could be translated after one or two warps to an expensive and rare tea that the buyers desired. In reality, it was never cut and dried, so a tea merchant tended to cover their bets by creating a mix of products that would sell well at the next ten islands they warp to. Many small islands will pay top coin for some teas, yet be unable to buy more than twenty or thirty kilograms a month of the product. In general, a tea merchant wanted to avoid high-volume, low-profit tea. It may sound amazing to sell 2,000 kilos of tea leaves, but if the tea only nets a few points of profit, you could have simply carried keena or rice while making just as much money.

Mina took out her proposal forms, noting down the eight teas she was immediately interested in, four grown locally which were common brews though might be rare at another stop, plus four whose value and salability Mina knew would bring a good price and value to the ship and crew. She also noted a few special teas which a dozen kilograms or so could make amazing returns for the right buyer. In particular, she was excited about the King's Cup, a very rare and amazing tea blend compressed into small cubes that was sold to royal families in the Halo for amazing prices. The tea merchant's catalog had a good quantity of this rare tea, with a price lower than expected.

Tasting and balancing the first eight teas against each other, she made purchase bids on six, rejecting two. Her choices brewed well, would store and travel well, were favorite teas in the northwestern Halo, where they were headed to trade next, and they were all priced very reasonably. As she had little tea to trade, it was just a case of checking the tea merchant's inventory and paying in silver rather than having to set up a tasting of her own wares.

Once the tea was tasted, she went to the warehouse to inspect the jute-lined, double-walled, boo crates. All legitimate tea sold in big markets was shipping in these inexpensive but tough resin-coated crates. Tea merchants who handled volume like the *Remarker* preferred the standard crates because two people could shift one by hand, they had a way of inspecting the cargo and easily resealed with a tattletale, a red binder that had to be broken to open it, and finally, a pallet of four were the perfect size to move by crane. Hate watched as she inspected each crate, cutting loose the binder, pulling the top from the container, then probing the tea it contained, looking for adulterants, rot, or infestation.

All the tea proved authentic, so she had the port merchant send a runner to the docks to prepare for the delivery of the product, as well as inform the Bandersnatch to have someone dockside to transfer payment when the product arrived intact.

Once the bulk tea was purchased, it was time to look at the rare and small tea lots, looking for bargains that could turn big profits. It was the King's Cup she was most excited about, and having value left in her account, she splurged on outright purchasing an entire tea cake of 20 grams, using her last two liters of sweet water to brew it. She laid out the cups for the tea merchant's assistant, plus all the Marines, proudly watching their reactions as they tasted it.

Hate sat it down, stating, "Swill, and I have had my share."

The assistant was trying to smile while looking like she had just ingested a rat turd. Mina grabbed her cup to taste herself. It was absolutely disgusting. She banged the cup down, sternly saying, "Your merchant and his master should attend me, now."

It was ten minutes; she got not just Mr. Nuvere and his employer, Master Gamelon, but also Grandmaster Qeirk. Both the Master and the Grandmaster were dressed in fine robes, being out of their dens, in attendance at the merchant's. Gamelon had one of the boxwood containers that the King's Cup tea was shipped in, setting his personal tea maker on the counter. Mina watched as Gamelon and Qeirk each made cups of the tea, both from her remaining purchase, as well as from the newly opened box. Gamelon was a thin, older, excited man with a cockcrow of white hair. Qeirk was obese and bald, with extruding eyes and a tongue that tended to hang outside of his mouth. When all the tea was finished brewing, they each carefully sipped it, looking worried as they did. They exchanged their teacups, sipping it again. Then they drank Mina's leftover tea.

"This is quite impossible!" Qeirk said, startled. "This tea was tasted, tested, protected, and stored. This is not King's Cup. However, it was King's Cup. We were all excited about having this product in our warehouses!"

Gamelon looked at Mina, then bowed his head. "Master Eversail, two days ago, this was the finest tea on our island. We had six hundred kilograms of it, carefully stored. A tithe of this tea is worth a chest of silver. We will, of course, refund you in full for the King's Cup you had put an option on. Further, we will not charge you for this tasting. I sincerely say we are sorry for this happening."

Mina bowed, then made out the forms for the final tea transaction, riding on the carrier with the tea to the port. She could not help but think about how rare King's Cup was, and that there was half a tonne unaccounted for.

"I know what you are thinking, Tea Master," Hate said as he watched their tea purchase load into the *Remarker*.

"How could you possibly know what I am thinking?" Mina replied.

He lowered his voice, saying, "We may not have ever asked for the life of a pirate. Pressed sailors just keep their heads down. Because we lived the life, you and I both know what the shrink is, thus how once something is off the cart, it is hard to put it back on."

Mina looked at him, memory of the how the pirate worked the docks flooding back from where she kept it deeply hidden. "Do not be bashful, Hate. What are you thinking of?"

"You know we can find that tea. It existed. Now it does not, replaced by that inferior stuff. Do not tell me you cannot tell what type of tea was served us." Hate said. He looked over at the Marines under his command, larking about on the dock while they waited for the tea purchases to be loaded before going aboard the pinnace to shape a course for the ship.

"Gatonburry," she said. "It was green tea, not prepared for shipping, well on the way for the rot. It is distinctive, not something a tea merchant would normally know. That is pirate swill."

Hate nodded. "We both had that terrible stuff on the *old lady death*, did we not? Someone else pulled into port with a load of that gaff, pulling a fast one on that merchant. It means the real stuff is at large."

"We both are off for three hours after this. My guess is we get one chance to steal the King's Cup from the people who took it for themselves." Mina said.

"Let me get my brother and a few others to beg some shore leave." Hate said.

Mina nodded, scared all of a sudden. Was this piracy? Was being a pirate like a disease, something that could be caught? She did not know.

The shore leave party Corporal Banji Hate gathered was his brother, Lobar Hate, the ship's sergeant; Jeva Valdor, a transfer from the sloop *Good Looking*; Sigurmann Abrahamsson, a marine diver and castaway from Stathold; and a tiny flaxen-haired cargo hand named Jinx, along with her silent boyfriend known only as the Mouse. They walked silently into the maelstrom of noise on the docks until they were clear of the trade zone. Behind the trade dock was a series of warehouses, one of which *Remarker* had let, which Mina had keys to. They ducked into the storage room, lighting a paraffin lamp that sat in the corner.

Mina had them circle up. "This is not shore leave. We have a few hours to find a treasure in stolen tea to see if we can take ownership of it." She removed her crew jacket and hat, then said, "Leave the colors here."

Jeva, her eyes rimmed with black kohl, a scar across her cheek showing she had been in more than one scrape, asked as she removed her uniform, "Is this a wet deal?"

Corporal Hate, who Mina was learning had a trustworthy streak under his bullyrock looks, said, "We try and buy this stuff with the hard. If it gets wet, it is because they uncorked the bottle, not us, right? Trust me when I say the captain is of two minds, one of them will drill you for a side look. He does not fuck around, neither does the major."

Sergeant Hate nodded, adding, "But damn well, if the bottle gets opened, we pour it all out."

Sigurmann, built like a red-headed tank, looked like he was glowing in the night compared to the Hate brothers, like he had even more bullyrock to him. He smiled in an almost boyish fashion and offered, "I do not entertain the causation of violence, my brother Marines. If the thought turns to action, my feeling is that the ship is better for us if we leave rapidly."

Jinx clapped her hands. "What he said."

Mina took her glasses off, cleaning them, confirming, "Just so we have all the cards in our hand. Violence is the last resort."

Jeva brushed the hair from her eyes. "What is the plan, Banji?"

"My brother and I, and Mina for that matter, although they never let her off the ship, called here a few times. The captain of our pirate took in one bar for his business, the Cracked tolan. If this works in the time we have, we will find the people who have to sell what we want to buy in there. If they are smart, they will part with it at less than twenty points. We buy what we can carry, bringing it onto the ship as dunnage," he said.

Jinx questioned, "Will Supercargo make a fuss?"

Mina looked at the muscular, tiny woman. "My figure is, if we get a good deal on it, we pay guild to the Sublime Port, plus tithe the ship like. We are not pirates."

"Anymore," Banji Hate added.

Jeva screeched, "That could be thirty points!"

Sigurmann placed a huge hand on her shoulder, "Half price is an efficient use of our resources, while the original owners cannot complain we have taken advantage of them since they get twenty points instead of zero, and the ship gets its cool ten."

Lobar looked at his brother, who nodded. "I think this works for me. What is twenty points you cannot spend because you are dancing the sisal two-step on the aft crane?"

"Settled, I think," Mina said. "You-lot, let me work the bar."

The bar was the definition of a dive. Live music was being played by a wharf band singing rough dulcimer shanties with a mix-match of words. Three ball tables were in use by dock roughs who threw hard and loud, treating the game as a fight for each copper on the table. There were no crew jackets to be found. Either the clientele, like the *Remarker* crew, had removed their colors to keep from embarrassing the ship, or they were not from ships they cared to advertise. The bar served pepper mead, half-and-full beer, molasafine stout, cola nut spirits, and root-ale. The best of the drinks were acidic, the worst were one step from paint remover. There were no fountains for the drinks. The bartender dunked unclean tavern mugs into barrels which had been rudely breached. Further, there was no cleaning sink about. It was not that type of place.

Mina walked up to the bar, ignoring her shipmates who faded into corners of the establishment. She caught the attention of the bartender, stating, "Cola nut spirits with a twist."

"No lemon, bonitree," I bartender replied, looking over her as he ran his hand through his beard.

"Then what do you have?" she asked in a hard tone.

The bartender did not show any more respect. "Cranberry aspic, if your jumpers are all bound."

"Why not, I am sure you have the measure of it," she said, pushing a silver penny across the table.

The bartender caught sight of the coin; he returned quickly with the drink. There was an etiquette at bars to get information. It was a fisherman's tale that bartenders in dives were shocked or too stubborn to sell information. They made more money from what they could tell and who they could connect than they could from quarter penny bar drinks. He shoved the drink over and grabbed up the penny. "I do not deal, just direct. You have that?"

Mina laughed, then drank a sip of the cola nut and cranberry. It was disgusting. "This is not even illegal, tender-man. Five pennies for a go-to, five more if it is upside up," she replied, wincing at the dock dialect Banji had coached her with. She felt she was a fraud using the lingo, Banji explained that this would just make her seem real.

"Two if I do not know kaka, since you ask, I gotta listen," he negotiated.

"Fair enough," Mina said. "Looking for tea of the highest quality that may not have a master's name attached to it. I will buy as is, if I can taste. Nothing dock ancient or dicky, you understand, I need a quick conversion of silver into beverage."

She slid two pennies over, then positioned five more ready to respond to information.

The bartender took the pennies, then said, "Far corner, woman's name is Loot. She is quality, so you and she should have a real bow down."

"Keep that to yourself," Mina said, pushing the five additional pennies at the bartender.

The woman in question was sitting right next to the Mouse, who was drinking a tankard of something hideous, looking like a grammarian who had escaped from his headmaster. Ignoring the apprentice, Mina stepped up to the table the woman named "Loot" sat at. She was forty or so, dressed in business finery which included a parti-color gandoura with blue and red undershirts, and wide pants. Next to her was a gray-skinned woman who was at least 180 centimeters and 65 kilograms, obviously the so-called "meat." The woman had a chain shirt and gorget, probably showing what security firm she worked for in the port. Mina sat down uninvited, introducing herself by saying, "Go-to from the bartender is that you know about tea and do not get the masters upset."

The woman looked Mina over, then asked, "Who are you?" "Nona from the merchant Yerbuizness," Mina replied.

"That sort of deal. I hope if you want anonymity that you are ready to pay up front, forgetting the Bandersnatch bullies. You hand me money, I hand you tea. You pay to test, look for free, but that is it," she said.

Mina nodded, "Straight to business."

"You think I feed myself by drinking haggle, quick and to the point is how this works," the woman said. "You may call me Loot. Are you interested in anything specific, or just browsing?"

"Browsing with specific tastes. One of the royal teas or a classic blend is what I am looking for," Mina replied.

"Then come to my warehouse a few blocks down, give our inventory a look-see," the tea smuggler said.

They got up, followed by the meat, and walked a few blocks to a rickety warehouse, which was weather-beaten and leaning. Loot opened the door, then looked at Mina with a predatory grin. Mina hesitated, then saw Lobar Hate skulking in the shadows. "May I bring my guard in?" Mina asked.

"Yes," came the curt reply from Loot. "I saw the bully-rock, so it is good you gave it a straight, or else this might not have gone well."

"Daddy did not raise a stupid girl. Lobar, come here and watch my back while we make this deal," Mina said with more bravado than she felt.

Inside the warehouse, Mina discovered a tight storage room with a jumble of cases of all sizes stacked to the rockers. There were proper tea cases, along with a whole lot of small lots, dross, and bags. The whole place smelled of tea, some good, some biting, some acrid in its decay. Lobar came to her side, cautioning with a low voice, "Not good, boss."

Indeed, the powerful smell of tea was balanced by the copper and feces smell of blood and death.

Loot was looking aghast at a body of a headless man who was still leaking blood from his neck. Her bodyguard, for all her menace, started to throw up, making the room very close with competing smells of dissipation, rot, and death. Lobar ducked down, retrieved the head, turning the face so Loot could see it. "Someone you know?"

The meat started throwing up again. Loot looked sick, yet replied, "That is a journeyman tea buyer. My tea, mostly it's over aged or cannot be sourced. Scarlon, he made sure what I had was worth selling."

Lobar asked, "Any tea missing? This gentleman took the big dive just a few minutes ago."

Loot looked about. "The King's Cup." She almost slipped on the blood as she ran over to where a stack of crates had collapsed into a random pile. "Ten crates, it's obvious. They had red stripes and iron dogging. They cannot have just walked off, they must mass 700 kilograms."

Lobar grabbed Mina, telling her, "Sorry miss, dead bodies are against the rules."

"You lot stop or I will blame the body on you!" Loot said.

Lobar ignored her, rushing Mina out of the warehouse and down the street to where the rest of the group was casually holding up the wall of a building. Mina stopped before they went too far, pointing out, "Somewhere on this street is a tonne of tea, we are just a few minutes behind it."

Lobar looked skeptical, "Mina, that tea has got a body on it now. We do not have endless time to grab it before the captain starts preparing for a keel hauling."

There was a crash down the street, then the sound of a boy crying in pain. Mina and Lobar heard Jinx cry out, "That is the Mouse!"

"Stay back, let me talk," Mina said. She ran down the street, past several food stalls, a tobacco factor, and a ship's locker, to where a wagon led by two horses with a cargo hidden under canvas sat jammed up by a quick stop. Four rough characters were standing around the Mouse, who was screaming and yelling about being hit, causing customers in the roadside businesses to look outside, hoping for a free show.

Mina grabbed the shoulder of the largest of the characters, shouting, "What have you done to that boy?"

"He jumped the horses, you bent cow! Now get out of our business," the man angrily answered. He was in his thirties, with a horse-like face, a scalp knot of black hair, and a long beard. He had a small sword riding high on his hip.

Mina looked at the crowd, most of which was taking in the show but not seeming like they wanted to enter into someone else's fight, when she noticed Jinx ducking from under the tarp on the cart. She made a hand sign that meant in cargo loading 'tea.' Mina cursed under her breath, noting to herself that the Mouse and Jinx were a slick pair of scoundrels. They had found the lost tea and the murderers who had taken it.

"Look, you need to report this accident and take care of the kid," Mina said, moving to keep the thugs' attention off the cart. Mouse screamed as if on command, rolling in agony.

Sigurmann stepped into the fray. "Inquiries as to your name and what you are speeding to hit kids with cart?" The four thugs stepped back, trying to figure out what Sigurmann meant in his disjointed way of talking.

"The Port Watch!" Banji yelled, causing the people to flee for the shadows. The thugs looked at the cart, then at the wailing kid on the ground, and hoofed it. Did they realize what the cart was valued? Mina thought not, or they might have fought to keep it.

Lobar came running up. "Seems like we need to nick this cart to get back to the ship snappy." Mouse jumped up and into the driver's seat while Sigurmann and Lobar pushed the cart into motion. Jinx leaped up next to the Mouse, then gave the young apprentice a huge hug. They all then kicked the wagon and its horse team into fast action.

They arrived at the port, stopping only to collect their uniforms, then hailed a water taxi. The rowing team, a pair of women who owned a port franchise, looked astonished as crates of tea wearing sailor's jackets were thrown into the skiff, followed by a half dozen jacketless sailors. "Make time to the *Seahorse!*" Mina yelled, that being the name of a battle-liner which was laying in the roads, as they all laid on the spare oars.

"Here now, steady on," one of the taxi operators yelled as the dray lurched forward under the backs of the *Remarker* crew. They ignored her until the taxi was hidden in the mix of port traffic.

"Cancel the *Seahorse*, cabbies, we are off to *Remarker*," Mina said with a breath of relief.

Mina was up late to do her tea inventory, helping the Supercargo correct a slight list developed from uneven loading of the cargo when Captain al-Rasheed motioned her over to where he was working on a chart. He had tea on the burner in the cockpit, which he offered to Mina. She hated the Junebug he drank, knew it was stupid to antagonize the captain over bad tea. She steamed some for herself, then drank down the acrid liquid. He did the same, seeming to enjoy it. After a few minutes of uncomfortable silence, he said, "That was an impressive guild payment you made to the tea trader here in port."

"Yes, sir, legal, and airtight, as well as impressive in size," she replied.

"And dunnage divided by the entire crew, even those who did not go walkies with you last night," Captain al-Rasheed observed.

Mina smiled, "Yes, again, legal and ethical. Benefits for one, benefits for all."

"A small fracas dockside between some merchant sailors with no jackets and some thugs from a local gang," the captain added.

"That will teach the riff-raff who has the biggest bollocks, no?" Mina hazarded.

"Very well Tea Master. We warp today for Santee with a full load. I congratulate you and the rest of the cargo team for astute business deals in our favor," he said, while pulling his tolan programming sheets and instruments out of their storage containers to prepare for warp. "Do not let me keep you from your duties."

"Thank you, sir," she said, returning to getting rid of the list before they warped out of harbor.

CHAPTER X

The Hungry, Angry Sea

A cry from the watch echoed out, "Ship's Boat, forward port quarter, two kilometers adrift!"

It had been a frustrating two weeks for Javier. Following a tolan was generally the wisest move for a captain, since they predicted trailing winds and currents for a warp from one roadstead to another. The sea, though, was as fickle as the sun was reliable. The most reliable tolan could turn on a captain, blowing them far from their course, or becalming them in a sea that becomes flat as glass. For the crew, it meant forty men and women sweating six hours a day on the sculls, the long oars hanging over the side, each being walked by two crew, back and forth, forth and back, the motion seeming to wear a groove in the deck boards. Every crew person took to the sculls during the day, tempers growing thread-worn, and coping with others became more difficult as fatigue set it. Worst was the specter of a ship becalmed running out of fresh water before finding a hospitable shore.

"Anyone in the lifeboat?" Javier asked.

"One person, not moving!" came the reply from the sheets. Javier yelled for the Coxswain to bring the ship around to where it could take in the boat and passenger. Tired hands came on deck, swinging out the aft crane, while two Marines, Anala Samal and Balchandra, swarmed down the crane line to make the boat fast. Samal turned the castaway in the bottom of the boat over, then listened into his chest. She must have heard something because she gave a circular wave of her hand, the sign for "rally" or "communicate," Balchandra making the boat fast for lifting. The crane crew slowly cranked the boat in, waited for Balchandra and Samal to get the castaway out onto the deck, then upended the boat on the deck, emptying it in a rush of seawater and filth. The boat had been likely riding low due to an uncorrected leak. When it was turned on end to be landed on the deck above the water tender station, it sluiced out an acrid-smelling deluge from its bilge runnel.

Javier gathered up the Surgeon with his eyes, then leaped to the deck, rushing to the side of the stricken castaway. It was a man in a merchant's uniform, a dolphin device on his shoulders, wearing no hat or deck boots, his clothing rank and threadbare. He was semi-conscious, looking around wildly while saying, "It was sweet lassies and that they cannot vouchsafe, sweet and it filled the maw! How can this be, that the Gods who forbid us the fruits should make it sustain so well!"

Javier looked down at the man, asking him, "What is your name? What ship are you from?"

The man cackled. "I am the madman. Yes, you can call me Madman. I jump from ship-to-ship mid-warp. Death follows me, but I never cause death. Do you understand me?"

Javier reached down to shake the man's shoulders. "Get your calm, sailor. You are a merchant. Your ship cannot be far. We might save some if you can give us intelligence on their location."

"It is a damned charnel house. It has already sailed into the ether world to dwell in the lands beyond. The *Blackthorne Summit* is its name. The hell with the ship, let it remain mired, let it stay captured by the mists of midsea." the man yelled hysterically.

Javier told the Surgeon, "Take him to the lazaretto." He then yelled to the watch aloft, "sharp eyes for a ship adrift. Ten pennies to the first sight."

Only they never sighted the ship. Instead, the man raved in his bunk, his exact ailment unknown, while the crew toiled on at the sculls, making slow progress across Ocean's seas with no aid of winds.

At the cadre dinner, Igor Bosanac, Standish, Mina Eversail, Rabia Ibn Saludi, and Efen Lukas Durrell sat in the wardroom with Javier, each shaking off the wearying work of the day, trying to let it fall from their bones. The officers had taken many of the duties that the crew normally performed to allow the average sailor rest after long days at the sculls. They were, themselves, slowly losing their focus and capacity for humor. Benji Sloan, the Steward, brought in the pot of tharid, one of his best recipes, made up of potatoes, onions, salted beef, and salsify over a bed of hard toast. Igor, as head of the wardroom mess, made Black Faraway tea for the table and mint for himself and Durrell. Javier nodded to Sloan, who took that as permission to sit at the side table to have his own portion of stew in the company of the officers.

"Is this the meal for the junior wardroom?" Javier asked the Steward.

"They have already supped, sir, on the main deck. Navigator Perak fell ill," Sloan replied.

Javier turned to Durrell. "Have you looked in on Perak?"

"I did. She appears to have fatigue from the workload. It is only to be expected when we scull this long in a dolum."

"I must say, Captain, to not understand this term 'dolum,'" the Tea Master said.

"You have been on a ship in a storm, no doubt?" Javier asked.

"I have," she answered. She tasted her victuals, then nodded. "The food never fails here, at least."

Javier laughed. "No doubt. A storm is the opposite of a dolum. With a storm, the waters of the sea are blown into each other, creating waves and changing the currents. In a dolum, the winds leave us. When we warp, we use maps that predict the currents and winds, following a rhumb, which is just a straight line by star or compass, and we usually arrive where we want to go. No tolan, though, can predict perfectly what will happen, so at times the sea leaves us calm. We carry sculls that are rigged to allow oar teams to move us when there is no wind, which is not a perfect solution. A good wind bending all of our cloth can carry us at eight or nine kilometers an hour if it is at our back, the sculls can do no better than four with favorable currents, less if we are calmed."

Durrell added, "On the *Quest Venture*, our captain one time took us into a charted dolum like a fool. We almost died."

Javier nodded, sampling his tea. It made his mouth want to get a divorce from his head. "There are dolums that exist in charted form just like tolans. A tolan is a route that usually saves the energy of travel. A permanent dolum is a place where usually there blows no winds with no tides. There are even worse, of course."

"You are talking the cyclonics, Captain?" Rabia asked.

"I am" Javier replied.

Mina looked up from her stew, then removed her glasses. "What could be worse than a dolum?"

Javier said, "If you ignore the sailors' tales, the worst thing that can be proven is a cyclonic. It is a place, maybe twenty or thirty kilometers across, where the currents move quite fast in a circular direction. Garbage and filth end up packed in the center of them. If your ship gets caught in one, it can be hard to get out. They are like the worst longshore currents, but long shores called rippers eventually end, spitting you out to sea. A good captain can shape a course on a long shore to have it spit them into a tolan to get a boost of speed. In a cyclonic, you have to keep your wits and keep to your compass, moving slowly to the rim without getting mired in garbage. Only then can you make your escape. Make a mistake? You will be spinning in the middle of the 'clonic yourself."

Bosanac lifted his tea. "A dolum and God's Hand. Do not put too much metal on deck or we are sure to see God's Flash."

Javier shook his head. God's Flash was real, while it was also a superstition. No sailor dared the gods by making light of their hands on earth, the strange ways in which the Gods punished mankind. "There is no humor in all that we have faced, because the universe is like a roll of the dice. Each time you roll a die, it can be one, or it can be twelve. A die does not care if you rolled one ten times before, the next roll may be a one again. That is what all sailors understand. You do not run out of bad luck. Old sailors tell of pipes of wind lifting from the sea to the sky, which can break a ship to flinders. If you listen in the bars, they will fill your ears with floating islands of ice that appear from a fog as if driven by a captain made of snow dedicated to sinking your ship. They tell of masses of grass growing on the sea that can entangle you, dragging your ship to the bottom. There are stories of sharks 15 meters long, able to knock all the people in a pinnace into the water, then eat them up. There are lizards who swim from swampy shores to devour sailors, fixing their hulls, along with invisible beasts that can beset you in calm and beautiful waters, attacking like a swarm of bees. The lords and gods have told us to walk with a light foot on the waters of the Ocean realms, to treat our lands as lifeboats, as the ships we sail may any day be broken."

There was silence around the table. Javier looked to Devious sitting in the corner, shaking his head. Scaring a crew was not inspiring it.

That night Javier dreamed of his father, taken by the sea, and of his wife Nazira, so far from his arms, pregnant with their child. There was no rest in sleep, so he stepped on deck, hearing screaming from the lazaretto. He moved forward on the darkened deck, around their regular boats, the capstan, and the boat taken in with the survivor, then entered the forward lockers which were used as cells to hold unruly or drunk crew. The madman was inside screaming, guarded by a marine named Yas. "Does he let up?" Javier asked.

"Somewhat, sometimes, sir, yet he has no sense in him even then. He says his name is Madman, and that he served on a ghost ship traveling the ether." The marine shrugged as if to say, 'What does one expect of a crazy person?'.

"The Sea Folk believe in wytchery," Javier said. "They absolutely and totally believe it. You find one who is in the right mood and they will speak to the dead or call on winds by name. I always ignored it. If it makes them feel safe, who am I to take away their beliefs?"

Yas replied, "Captain, that makes as much sense as anything. I think if we were not calmed, this rajul-maj' would not be so disturbing to the crew."

"The crew is disturbed?" Javier asked.

"Captain, do not place me as telling qisa-fi-allay-ell. You understand, the things people say at night to blame their friends." Yas said. "I am sorry to say this, but the man is making talk."

Javier said, "I understand. You follow the old way. I know what that can mean. My father was a harsh one for the rules of the way. You are not doing wrong telling me, I am not seeking, how would you say, kabi'sha abal-alda.'"

"Yes, that is close. It means the one who is sacrificed to purify the many." Yas replied.

"Knowing the crew are disturbed, I can seek repair. Make sure your replacement on guard understands this man is to be treated with kindness. I will not make him kabi'sha abal-alda' any more than I will throw one of *Remarker*'s own into the fire, understood?" Javier said, turning to leave.

"Yes sir, understood," Yes replied.

Once out of the lazaretto Javier tracked down the crew person acting as the Oar Master for this shift, Phiab Tsu Li. Phiab was a southerner with deep amber skin, red eyes, and hair that was jet black with streaks of gray, who wore a prelab to show her faith. "How is the work?" Javier asked.

"People are tired, sir, like they are wearing thin. Someone said we were making four or five kilometers an hour," Phiab answered. "Around that. Nine more days if we can keep up with this rate." Javier admitted.

Phiab said, "We might. How do oared ships make this work?"

"A reme or skeld has 50 or 100 oars in one or two banks. Four crew per oar means the smallest reme has more people at the sculls than we have on our entire ship. The limit to them is feeding all those people. A person eats up one or two kilograms of food when at the sculls each day, drinking up to three liters of water, without, they start getting sick. On a reme, everyone sits on the cargo. Mostly, they do not go more than a few days from shore. They never sail tolans." Javier said. He noticed one of the sailors pulling a skull. "Who is the one with all the jewelry?"

Phiab said, "Terk, he is not normally apostolic, superstitious really, but the calming has him spooked."

Javier lowered his voice. "Ask him, on my behalf, for now, if he keep an even keel. Just as a favor to me, leave the metal below deck. I do not want a sudden rush of superstition no matter what direction it goes."

"Yes sir," Phiab said.

Merchants were so much nicer than naval ships. No naval ship would ever see an officer taking a minute to talk with a deckhand. It was just not heard of. On a merchant, you could run the crew easier, let them work more at their own pace. It meant you did not need threats of harsh punishments to keep their backs bent. Merchant crews on profitable ships generally knew their lash was a good one, not too far from the Code. Being stranded at a strange port without a letter to recommend you was the fear of every merchant sailor.

Javier went to the helm station, falling asleep in the back of the cockpit. He must have slept six hours because the sun was breasting the sky and Nine, his Senior Officer, was praying on the forecastle top. As he started to wake, he found the Surgeon, wearing a worried look, was standing in front of him, holding a cup of tea. "My apologies, Captain al-Rasheed. We have an issue." He handed Javier the tea, who drank it down, disappointed that it was a fine brew whose origins he could not place. Certainly, some of the new trade goods they took on.

"What issue could be such a worry, cutter?" Javier asked. "Sickness," the Surgeon answered.

Javier blanched and felt his stomach break. He looked at his log on the navigation desk, then asked, "How many are sick, Efen?"

The Surgeon answered, "Thirty-two, all isolated now in the forward hold. I have no idea what is doing it, it is moving very fast. It seems to be a disease, but none that I have ever heard of. I looked at their blood under a glass. Nothing stood out. I took seaweed cultures and saw no obvious contagion. I have to admit to being out of my depth."

"How did it happen this fast, do you believe? Is a guess better than no answer?" Javier looked to the rowing crew, noting it was full Staff. That would not last long.

The Surgeon took out a notebook and opened it up. "Perak fell ill before dinner, then it was Siva Hussain, both ill with shivering. An hour later, Salene Hazar collapsed like a rag doll standing to take a drink, followed an hour later by Hujja el-Nawaz, who also suffered a nasty gash tripping down the after gangway. Beef Malley, one of our strongest crew suffered a sweat, working on until he also fell insensible. The crew was rushing Beef to his bunk when Yahsin fell into the doldrums. Since then, it has been a few an hour, with no time to wake you."

Devious, sitting almost unnoticed in the corner of the cockpit, said, "Have him make a matrix."

Javier nodded. "Can you make a matrix to see if there is a correlation between the sick and what they do or who they are?"

"What is a matrix sir?" the Surgeon asked in response.

"Why are we all not sick? How come the madman is not sick? Do the sick crew have something in common? Restarchus of Quorna wrote, 'A sickness that does not infect everyone speaks more from its absence than its presence.' What are the common characteristics of this disease?" Devious asked in his dull, forceful voice. Javier repeated it to the Surgeon.

"Captain, the common characteristics are weakness, blue ears and lips, blue fingers, with unconsciousness or lunacy on the edge of unconsciousness. Occasionally there is regurgitation," the Surgeon replied.

Devious stood, took a large chart out from the cockpit chart case, turning it to its back, then grabbed for tacks to fix it to the back of the cockpit. Next, he wrote the symptoms listed by the doctor. When finished, he asked, "What have you treated the sick with?"

Javier waited for the Surgeon to answer but he stood mute. He looked at Devious, shrugged, then repeated the question. "What are you treating the sick with?"

"Blankets, water, tincture of yew taken internally, tincture of feverfew. If the heart grows faint or irregular, they are given a small doze of foxglove. This either is very effective or has to be discontinued due to the negative effects. Most of my cures are either palliative only, or have the effect of slowing the sickness, not leading to recovery," the Surgeon explained remorsefully.

Javier shook his head, stepping up in front of Devious. "Keep good records. That is all I can ask. Let me know if you make any progress."

"Yes, Captain," the Surgeon said as he left the office.

Javier looked at Devious, saying, "You really need to keep on with the crew better."

"Not my fault the Surgeon has selective hearing," Devious replied.

Javier smirked. "You think it is my fault?"

"I did not say that, Captain." He walked over to the chart where the information about the sickness had been written. "Captain, do you remember when we first served with each other?"

"The war," Javier replied.

Devious made a few notes about crew available for rowing, along with the amount of water and food on board. "You were a scared kid. A scared kid from a broken fisher's home, charged with carrying the deck of a war frigate with twenty other scared kids. Then the Boatswain, do you remember what he said?"

"He said that horror is best handled by having someone else do the stabbing," Javier replied.

Devious turned, then settled into an office chair. "So it is. You have to be strong, decisive to command. When that Bosun died after eleven steps on the enemy deck, it was all you. That is why I decided to help you, so you did not have to wield the sword yourself. So you did not have to look at the face of another kid, the same age as you, as you disemboweled him on the deck of that ship, hear him scream for his mother, know that he was no more guilty, no more worthy of a horrible death than you were."

Javier questioned, "Why say this now?"

"You pretend not to hear or understand, yet you know what people thought of you before this voyage. A drunk, a spendthrift, a gambler, a man who blew like a cockle on the waves from one bit of dishonor to the next. Scared to go to sea and face the fate of your father, unwilling to wield another sword that could end the life of another child dressed up and playing soldier. Nazira saw something in you, and it was not just the shadow of my own protection of you. She saw a person who could find a way to live selling tea." Devious looked seriously into Javier's own soul, as if to be a reflection of him, opposite in many ways, yet noticeably the same.

"It is not about the tea," Javier said.

"Everything is about the tea," Devious replied. He stood again, approached Javier, looked him right in the eye. "Everything is about the tea. You keep nattering on about connecting society through trade, of doing kind things to help your fellow human navigate through the world, seeking redemption in standing on other shores. However, the thing that drives this is the money we make, the tea we sell. The problem you have is being half a man, having discarded the other half a long time ago. Your bride, Nazira, has bet her fortunes that you can become whole."

Javier looked out the window at the flat sea, so much like green glass that washed up on the short of his home when he was a child, polished into little stones by the water and the waves. "If I am half a man, what are you?"

Devious laughed. "The one telling you that you need to solve this problem. Your men are sick. Your food and water are dwindling. Maybe you need to throw one passenger overboard to save the rest. You know in your heart this, before the crew has even figured it out. Further, I cannot do it for you.

"No," Javier shook his head. "I am tired. Leave me alone while I get some sleep."

A few hours later Javier woke, deciding to do some climbing to look at the situation from the vantage of the topgallants. He dressed for climbing, then left his cabin, taking to the sheets, enjoying the freedom of scarring upon the ropes and stays, moving ever upwards until he found himself clinging to the highest point on mast number three that a climber could reach. The idea that a ghost ship was at large in the seas of the Halo that they may have passed troubled him. He was also troubled by the workload of his crew. In an emergency, he could hang sails with two dozen healthy crew to get the ship to a port. Alta Pelinore was a large roadstead where they could sit off the main port in quarantine while the disease worked itself through the crew while getting water and food from shore. There were four islands used by ships' crews available to water their ships, and the bumboats in harbor would feed them.

Also, he was worried about Devious. The man was his second-in-command, but his aggression was starting to scare him. As Javier clung to the sheets, Devious was tearing about the ship, looking for the hidden cause of the outbreak of disease. Javier knew that Devious felt they had been poisoned by the man in the lazaretto, the screaming man who had lost his mind as he lost his ship.

Yelling on deck disturbed his thoughts. He looked down, a scuffle forward of the first hold, one which had brought out firelocks that were being held in hand in a threatening manner. No one was using them, at least yet; however, the situation was dire.

Devious looked up at him, doing nothing. He just shrugged as if to say, "This is your business, not mine."

"Damn, Devious," Javier thought. This was exactly what he was supposed to handle. Javier hated turning on a crew member, a person who he called friend, who sailed by his side and faced death from the harsh waters of the Halo. So he forced himself to think, *what would Devious do?* How could he face the sailors like Devious did, without selling his own soul?

Javier was tied in with a painter attached to a seat with a D-ring, so it was easy to hook in to rope walk down to the deck. He stepped into the melee, grabbed a firelock from a marine named Manik, fired it into the air, then grabbed a round from the marine's cross belts, loading the firelock again.

"What is happening?!" he yelled. "Speak quick before someone visits the yards."

There was silence. Lobar Hate said, "There was a misunderstanding about cleaning the decks, which is solved now, sir."

Javier looked over the scene. Hate, along with a dozen Marines, were apparently in some sort of argument with several gangs of apprentice and ordinary sailors. He scanned the sailors, spotting Winston al-Luis, an opinionated, profane sailor who was part of the first crew. The way the sailors stood around him, he was the ringleader.

"Al-Luis, state your complaint. You have the deck with no punishment." Javier said. He knew Devious would have scoffed. Devious would have seen the ringleader over the side in the midst of a dark watch if he felt that the man was a danger. Yet no matter how much he lobbied for it to be so, he knew he could not be Devious.

The sailor addressed looked around, guilty as charged yet surprised to be called out. "Captain, it is that madman in the lazaretto. He brought sickness here. If too many of us get sick, we won't be making Alta Pelinore."

The man was completely correct. As the crew sickened, it grew harder and harder to make way on just the sculls. Without wind, their more than ample crew became tight for labor as more fell ill. They were not a REME with a hundred to staff the oars. Further, no REME would have made it this far into the waters between the lands.

Javier noted that Nine was on the Quarterdeck with a fire-lock, while Standish was standing in the gangway descent, half-dressed, a brace of handlocks around her shoulders. He handed the firelock back to the marine he had taken it from, then walked up to al-Luis. "You are from Wadi al'Aghnam correct? The Luis clan?" Javier asked.

"Yessir," he said.

"Your family raises Kharufiut Abayadi, the silver sheep?" Javier asked.

"My family, yes, but I was not a shepherd," al-Luis said.

"You know about sheep though. You are proud of 'kanai-alab,' the heritage of your father and mother?" Javier asked. The man was an individual even as he was part of a crew. What Devious did not understand was that while levers of pain and fear were effective in a quick way, there were other levels that were much more subtle to work.

"Sir, we do not follow the old ways, yet it is true that I have pride for the works of my parents and family, just as they have pride in my work." His faced showed that while he might scoff at the rigid forms of honor his family and his people followed, he still clung to them deep in the core of his being. It also reminded him of the logic of the shepherd.

"Then explain to me, pretending that he is a sheep, how that the madman could bring this disease onto our ship? Pretend he is a stray from another flock, then give me the reasons and methods he is sickening your own flock." Javier waved at the lazaretto, then cut off al-Luis before he could speak again. "You cannot because it makes no sense. No herder with a herd of fat Kharufiut Abayadi would consider a disease from a stray they immediately locked away as the the cause of forty of the number falling ill. It makes no sense."

"Same with kennel hounds, Captain," came an anony-mous voice from the back of the crowd. Enough of his crew had quit the world of farming that this line of thought held meaning to them. Their crew may not have the sheer ability of a group of lifetime sailors; however, they had the logic of people who lived by a code that allowed them to survive year after year on the bounty of a fickle land.

Javier said, "I agree we are growing ill, further that our port fall at Alta Pelinore is not as assured as it once was. However, mutiny sees the fall of this ship. Do your sheep survive if they break the paddocks to flee for the sandy shores? If an ewe slips the protection of the ram, can it fight the wolves? Did you hear the madman talking about the ghost ship, the *Blackthorne Summit*, the dead who are forever forced to stand at their stations, never reaching port? There is no way that I will allow the *Remarker* to sail off into the ether as a vessel for wytchery and dwimmer. Now I understand you are scared. There is reason to be scared. I am also. Therefore, I will hang no man or woman for fear or for a little breakdown. If you go off the ends though, I will give you a cockle and an oar, then send you to whatever fate you find."

There was silence as Javier looked in each eye of each sailor. "Mr. Hate, rack the firelocks, we do not need them. Mr. Raffi, as senior able sailor, on deck at this minute, you are responsible for getting the sculls back in action, the old crew to a meal, the new crew making way. When you feel this is accomplished, hand the task to the next senior able. From this point, the senior able hand is the one who I will speak to if those sculls are not propelling us through the water, understand?"

Hate and Raffi saluted. The deck was cleared, some to a meal, some to the sculls, and some to the hold where the sick grew sicker.

Javier turned, then walked up to the bridge deck. On the top of the cockpit, Devious stopped Javier. "There needs to be new eyes on this. The crew is right. At this rate, we will not make port.

We will die out here, the crew too sick to row. Or … we will finally get our wind after the last crew is too sick to take to the sheet."

"I know you are correct, but I cannot throw someone into the sea because they brought a disease to us. It is no cure." Javier replied. "We need a cure, not a spasm of idiocy in the face of a dark killer."

Salvador Lingongo, the Captain's Clerk interrupted them. "Captain, the Surgeon has this personal report for your log. Also, here are the cargo records for your review."

Javier took the papers from the young man, who had signed on at the Cape of Darts. Ignoring Devious, who stepped back into the edge of the deck, he said, "Have the Mouse and Fiddler come up to the quarterdeck."

"Immediately, sir," Lingongo said. Javier looked at Devious, telling him, "I will have fresh eyes on this, use Fiddler and the Mouse. You think they are the keenest eyes on the ship. Let us see if you are right."

A crew temporary steward delivered a pot of Cycus Black tea, obviously not knowing that Javier preferred Junebug, as he sat down in at the cockpit chart table. Mouse arrived first, dressed in his crew uniform, bright and respectable, with his shy demeanor on full display. He was a constant source of quiet information to Devious, who shared it all with Javier, yet he had the admirable habit of never putting a fellow sailor in the hack. Information that was reliable but not vindictive was an important commodity.

Fiddler arrived next. She had wispy long platinum hair plaited tight, curled under a mitten cap. In a crew that tended to swarthy or darker skin, she looked like she glowed with her pale, ghost-like skin. Devious told Javier he had seen her singing on a dock in the sugar islands, unable, or so people thought, to work because she had cleft hands like crab claws. After Devious spoke to her, he discovered that she was amazing in other ways no one had apparently ever noticed. She could do math in her head like a computer wheel and could tell the difference between voices she heard with her eyes closed. He discovered she could imitate sounds with eerie precision, additionally she could hear sounds so soft that no one else could tell they existed.

Javier broke out the mugs Devious had made specially for Fiddler and the Mouse to use, Mouse's smaller because he had small hands, Fiddler's with a mug handle that her hands could better deal with, then poured them all a draught of the Cycus Black.

After Javier served the tea, he pulled a small bag of silver out, telling the two, "I need information, and I have silver. You need silver and can get information. So here is the question. Five days ago, a man came on our ship who acted delusional. Shortly afterward, people started getting sick. Assume that is all we know. I want you both to scour this ship asking the questions, one, how is his arrival related to the sickness, and two, is there a reason why he might be a madman other than some mythical sickness?"

"That it, Mr. Devious?" Mouse asked.

Javier laughed, "Do not call me Devious, even as a joke." Mouse looked confused, nodding ascent. "Now, get it done today or we are all dead," Javier said in a soft voice. "You won't get any silver if we are all dead."

"Might get it all, sir," Fiddler said with a twinkle in her eye.

Javier turned his eyes, looking at Devious, who was hanging in the shadows behind the cockpit. Devious nodded. It was usually his duty to deal with the more subtle and unusual of the crew who he had recruited. When the pair scampered off, Javier stepped back into the shadows, then braced Devious. "I did not agree with bringing those two on board. I thought Mouse would never find a place in the crew, and that people would be cruel to Fiddler."

Devious reached, took the captain's tea mug, then took a long draw. "Javier, some of the most innocent and seemingly weak people have skills you can never imagine. How odd that you love and trust so easily, while I see the true darkness in people, yet you could not see what a cunning tool those two are."

Javier drank from his tea mug, replying, "Humans are not tools."

Devious laughed quietly. "Are they not tools? How do you get a sail sewed?"

"I use sail thread and a canvas needle," Javier said.

"No, you do not," Devious scolded. "You call the sail maker and say 'fix this sail.'"

Javier shrugged. "I just hope they come up with something."

An hour later, Javier was looking over the scull crews walking back and forth in their rhythmic flow when the Mouse and the Fiddler returned. Fiddler's cheeks glowed red, while the Mouse had a big grin. "What do you have for me?" Javier asked.

"A riddle, sir," I Fiddler replied.

Javier looked at her, instructing her, "Then tell me."

"The madman came on board with something, and in that something, he hid the answers. What is that something?" Fiddler asked with relish.

"His clothing was not worth keeping, so my guess is he had nothing when he came on board," Javier replied.

The Mouse smiled, gave a little skip, then pointed to the deck. Javier allowed his eyes to flow along the small sailor's arm. It was pointed at the ship's boats. The *Remarker* carried two pinnaces, a launch, a captain's cutter, and four cockles. There were two winches and the first windlass in the well deck.

There was also another boat, one more than usual.

"When the madman had come on board, he had his own boat," Javier said to himself. "You do not waste a ship's boat. You store it away until you can sell it on. They are usually well made and valuable." Javier turned to Devious, staying out of sight in the shadow of the cockpit, who nodded that he agreed.

Javier jumped down the quarterdeck gang ascent to the well deck. He grabbed an apprentice and told them, "Sergeant Hate and the major, get them on deck with a boat team." The young hand nodded with weariness in her eyes, moving off quickly.

The boat was a medium-sized pinnace, tumbled onto the deck, just tied down in their emergency. Its hull was painted an unusual brown-gray, in some places bare wood showed through.

Major Standish came up on deck with a crew of sleepy Marines, and asked, "Flip boat, sir?"

"Winch into the air so I can look all over it," Javier replied.

The crew ran the lines for the winch into the eye-bolts, then hoisted the ship off the deck. Javier looked at the boat as it came off, wrinkling his nose. "Major Standish, have the Carpenter report."

A moment later Bright Day Fifteen reported in front of Javier. "Sorry Sir," he said, "Carpenter's down, but I can do, I suppose."

Javier looked over the sun worshiper with his shorn hair. "Inspect this boat and tell me what you think of it," he said.

"Captain, I do not really have to inspect it over. You can smell it once it is off the deck. This thing is bent laurel, which is ok if you keep her painted. Only this one is all coddly." Bright Day spat on the deck to emphasize.

"What is bent laurel?" Javier asked.

"Captain, it's used in some boats that have to work in places where you get ship lice and lickkers. Like near swamps, where they come out, doing a lot more damage than normal borers. The wood is pure poison. Boat makers who use the stuff get sick real quick unless it is treated well." Bright Day said, not realizing the importance of what he was describing.

"It could make a whole ship sick?" Javier asked.

Bright Day stood still for a second, then said, "I think unless we all got down on all fours and licked the thing, we would be safe. Making them is the dangerous part, followed by repairing them. Otherwise, there is no reason why anyone should be sick off it," he answered.

Javier walked around the boat suspended off the deck, then said, "Sergeant Hate, get me a painter, your bayonet, and some red cloth."

The Sergeant was quick at it. Javier took the items he requested, tied the cloth to the painter, then looked at the deck, then shoved the painter through a hole that the falling boat had made. He then looked at the major, ordering, "Everyone else stay topside." They went below, finding the painter with the red rag tied to it directly over the port water storage. Javier moved the barrels a bit, then looked at the major.

Standish said, "They look sealed." She ran her hands around the edge of several of the barrels, her eyes considering them carefully.

Javier pulled her hand away. "Obviously they are not. Pass word for the Surgeon."

The Surgeon, looking dazed and tired, arrived in a minute to where the barrels were stored. "Reporting, sir," he said.

"Efren," Javier asked, "Have you ever heard of bent laurel?"

"Sure, shore parties get sick when they use it for firewood, sir," the Surgeon replied.

Javier prayed for a second, then queried, "Is there any way to cure it?"

"Easy, you boil canyon spruce with a few slugs of copper in it. Plus, do not let them have any more poi," the Surgeon replied.

Three days later, the crew was mostly on the mend, no worse off than a light flu or cowpox outbreak, which were common travelers on ships. On the next day after, the rains fell, and there turned a wind in their sail fair for Alta Pelinore. The offending boat and the barrels of contaminated water were tipped over the side and lit afire with a staff.

On the night their destination was sighted, Major Standish came up to Javier as he sat on the forecastle above the protective roof of the cockpit. Javier was taking sights, noting them down, then programming their location on programming sheets, unneeded since the lights of Alta Pelinore were on the horizon where any sailor could not fail to miss landfall.

"Do you need to do that?" Standish asked.

Javier looked up. "It is good practice. If the voyage had been ordinary, there would be a dozen cadre and crew up here plotting the rhumb as a training exercise. Easy to check your work when you know the answer."

Standish walked up to the railing, asking, "Captain, may I speak freely?"

"You may," Javier replied, fixing his sextant on its staff to take a few comparison sights.

"I have known you for a number of years as you and the Princess carried out your affair, during which time I was of the mind the King was, that you were not a useful being. Or perhaps you were useful for one thing, that being only as a cockade in the henhouse," she said. Moving to the edge of the deck, she added, "Your insanity and lack of responsibility met with my disapproval. I felt you were not good enough for the Princess."

"You are forgiven," Javier said, as he looked through the sights of his sextant.

"Oh, Captain, I am not asking you to forgive me. I was correct in all of this," Standish commented, looking at the waters. "You were a feather in a hat back then. If the wind blew you away, you would still have a hat."

"Perhaps an accurate assessment still, and still forgiven my dear Justicar," Javier said.

Standish turned to him. "My compliments are for who you have become on this voyage, specifically your kindness to the madman, and how you give purpose to those two who most would find useless, the Mouse and Fiddler. Many would have never brought those two on board, as many would have tossed the madman to the sea."

"I had little to do with their success. The crew serves best where they each can find their human spark and unique talents. They are present on this ship because of that practice, not because I brought them on board. As for the madman..." Javier pulled a leather tome from a pouch by his feet, handing it to the major.

"What is this?" she asked.

"It was in the boat, hidden under the bench work. I have had it since the madman came on board," he replied, scribbling on a programming sheet.

Standish held the book to the wax burners behind in the cockpit door. "The Log of the *Blackthorne Summit*," she read from its cover.

Javier said, "There is no need to read it unless you want. The *Blackthorne Summit* was blown from its tolan by a storm, then was caught in the sea of reeds. When they were able to bring themselves from this, they fought the currents around the sea, then ran out of food. Finally, they were desperate, sailing a course they hoped would cause them to cross the island of Wimbway, whose tall peak allows it to be seen for many miles, when they became becalmed like us. They placed their boats in the water to haul their ship forward, but starvation, then cannibalism, took them."

There was a silence for a minute with Standish looking at the logbook and Javier peering through his scope. When the weight of the quiet broke, Standish asked, "Did he?"

Javier turned, nodding. "He admits it in the log. He even lifted his hand to take a life rather than just make do with the dead, who quickly became too tainted to eat. He was far from the first to do this."

"Thus, his madness?" Standish asked.

Javier stood up, walking to the edge of the quarterdeck to stand with Standish. "Sanity is a frail thing, Major Standish. I liken it to scar tissue. Our bodies form that tissue when we are harmed as if to say to the universe that, 'you can never harm us again in this manner.' Somewhere inside him there is a realization of what had been done, why it was done, and how it was accomplished. There is a visual memory of what happened, the steps he took, the guilty pleasure he felt as the gnawing hunger was sated. The realization afterward that he had indeed eaten human flesh. Can you imagine how that can affect a mind?"

Standish looked at him somberly, asking, "What about finding your way back to sanity? Is there a way back for him as well?"

Javier shrugged. "Maybe once broken, the mind cannot be so easily mended, yet maybe a truce in the mind can be had that allows the person to move on from the horrors they experienced. I would liken it to work. Making the scar tissue on the human mind requires work, I think, is an answer; you cannot just let it form as it wants." He reached for the logbook. "It would be a sin to destroy this account of all those lost people on the ghost ship *Blackthorne Summit*, but also it would be a crime against our nameless madman to let the world know what he did in the extremity of life. Alta Pelinore has a sailor's house. We will pass the hat to see him set by there to heal, if ever he can. The log will go with my other books in my collection, where people can someday learn the fate of that ship. We can inform her home port she was lost at sea. That should be enough."

Standish looked doubtful. "Your desires are good, but perhaps the story of the *Blackthorne Summit* is more difficult than you think to quash. For many, there will always be a ghost ship of the dead plying the waters of the Halo, looking to claim its next victim."

Chapter XI

Devious Games

Devious heeled the horse to wait for the Marines and the tea grower to catch up. Many people claimed that Devious was just a shadow of Captain al-Rasheed who skulked in the corners of the ship, coming out only to carry out some horrible intrigue. But Devious knew his value, including when he was better sent than the captain. Devious knew that most of the crew ignored him, or worse, feared him. To him, this was all to the good. Javier was simply not built for taking the dark actions. He was always the playboy, the child who loved numbers and books. It was the duty of Devious to put iron into the silk gauntlet of the captain.

Besides, Javier could not ride horses, while Devious had ridden well since he first teamed up with the captain as a young man. There was no way this deal could be worked out on foot. "Sergeant, is everything ok?" Devious asked. He had a hard time remembering the names of the Marines. They all had a sinister simian proclivity to overt physicality, mostly lacking characteristics which Devious considered essential to individuality. They were useful mobile furniture.

"Sir, just a bit of a difficulty with the horses. Not like many of us have had time to ride in the past year." This reply by their lead hand was unsatisfactory to Devious.

"Sergeant, is this what I was asking?" Devious questioned. In fact, the answer was accurate, what he was asking in a technical sense, but the real answer had escaped the marine. He was indeed used to Javier and his whimsy.

One of the Marines farther back said, "Does he have his noodle bent?"

The Sergeant, in a harsh low tone, replied, "You put that back, Wearn. He has his commander hat on." He then yelled out to Devious, "No excuse, Commander. We are on it."

Devious nodded. The men could bitch; however, they needed to fear him worse than the unknown darkness that made the world. "Send the tea grower forward to me, then take a few minutes to get your horses adjusted. You are slow because their harness is sloppy."

"At once, Commander," came the reply.

The tea farmer was a slight man, red-faced with shocking orange hair, as was common of Kaelinese. He was a native speaker of Kalendi, also having a sufficient grasp of the common tongue of the Halo to communicate. Unlike the Marines, he had perfectly adjusted the tack on his horse, riding with an easy seat. He moved competently through the Marines, who had started to dismount to adjust their tack.

"The marine say you, Captain?" the farmer asked.

Devious sniffed. "Of course not. You cut a deal with the captain. However, it is my duty to honor it."

The farmer, who was known as Kilby Kay, pulled around a skin, offering it to Devious. Devious took it, drinking a generous portion. It was a grape wine of an unpleasant, sweet type, cut with something like vinegar, maybe even a little turpentine. It was an obvious test by the tea farmer; drink my swill to prove you are my equal. If anyone else had handed Devious such utter, poisonous garbage, he would have thrashed the man at the first chance he could find to do it secretly, but Kay was a master at growing tea. That tea was why they were here on this fetid trail, heading to the camp of the local warlord.

Pretending like the swill was ambrosia, Devious handed it back, then spat on the ground to show his contempt. The man missed the gesture, and spit as well. "You like the drink of the Cape?"

Devious considered the question. "It is piss," he replied.

"I know you like it man. So the deal, it stands?" The farmer asked, drinking deeply from the skin.

Devious nodded. "We get your children from Basher Kk-Riki. You provide us tea at a suitable rate." The rate that Devious considered suitable was highway robbery, no less; however, the man did not know what his tea was worth when it was placed into a market in a major market center controlled by the Sublime Port. That was the way to profit, after all. Find the goods others could not find, pay as little as possible for them, then sell them for a high profit. It was how a tea merchant paid for all the Marines, ship expenses, salaries, and even sometimes death benefits, and still turned a profit.

The tea grower spat again. "Basher Kk-Riki was paid guild. He took my children anyway. My wife, she cries."

Far as Devious saw it, the farmer had no one other than himself to blame. The Kaelinese lived in a small archipelago in the south of the Halo that consisted of one large island and a series of smaller ones. The people of the main island had, in generations past, a stable and relatively benign social kleptocracy where pretenders who wanted to rule would hire mercenaries from the smaller islands to fight bloody wars that never really affected the life of the rural areas. Then the mercenaries decided that instead of fighting for the Kaelinese, they would simply move as a group to the main island to become warlords themselves. They called themselves bashers, which was a direct translation of their word which meant "to break." This told Devious all he needed to know about their tender mercies and fondness for war. The twenty or so Bashers basically turned occasional political grudge matches into a never-ending war to control the island that none could win, only they no longer used people from the smaller islands to fight it out, they conscripted the people from the lands they controlled.

Which is where Javier, Captain of the *Remarker*, had found a way to do what he considered good, plus make a profit on tea. The finest grower of the island had lost his son and daughter to this Kk-Riki fellow, of course, wanting them back. He could not grow more tea without them, nor would he sell what he had without them. His tea was about the only thing Devious thought worth trading here, at least for a tea merchant. Let the slow traders lug mugs, loom ware, knitting, and bags of keena. The tea was where the silver came out by the chest.

"Tell me of this fight that Kk-Riki is in." Devious said.

The tea grower keened a low wail. "It is as it ever is. Kk-Riki says that Basher RoviKaw insulted his heir, who is known for being addle-minded, a lad named Kovi-Gan. Kk-Riki, he cannot see that his son is useless. RoviKaw says that Kk-Riki threatened his daughter, three young ones which live in strict purdah, which is why he made guild Kovi-Gan. That is the reason for the war. It is as is, you see," the grower said.

Devious set the pace again, motioning the grower to keep up with him. "So your children have nothing to do with the war itself?"

"They are not henchmen. They just carry the wood, the food, get the water, and if it comes to a fight, they die like the rest," he replied.

"They live in Kk-Riki's Dominion, do they not?" Devious asked.

The tea grower considered this, taking a deep pull from his wineskin. "This is not how it goes. I feel perhaps things are different in other lands, but here there are no lands. The Bashers each have a camp. They have henchmen. They take boys and girls as they need them from where they wish, when they become expensive to feed, let them go. I pay through the temple of the Bashers guild, which is kept by all the Bashers. My children should not be taken. You understand trader?"

Indeed, Devious understood. What a lovely land, he thought. The thugs thought that the whip and the sword ruled. They would never feel their pockets for the hand of a skilled master.

The camps of Kk-Riki and RoviKaw were a mere kilometer apart, each on the bank of a different oxbow of a rather fast racing, intimidating river. The camps themselves were loud with raucous laughter from a center cluster of tents, with hundreds of rude tents made from scraps of wood and canvas spreading out. They reeked of bad cooking and human odors; they also were not particularly tactically sophisticated. Devious reined up his horse, yelling out, "Sergeant, come forward!"

The Sergeant came forward. "Yes, sir," he said.

Devious pulled out his big range finders from his saddlebag, handing them over. It was getting late in the day. The shadows were drawing deep, yet there was plenty of light left to see. "Give me your assessment."

The sergeant took the range finders, spied through them, then returned them. "'Bout five hundred in each camp. Only fifty are professionals, with another fifty camp followers of the professionals. They are not well positioned, they are all drunk, they have no guards in suitable locations, they just look bad. The only advantage is both camps are the same."

Devious took the range finders back, scoped the camps, saying to the marine, "Sergeant, I am going into the camp of Kk-Riki. Given two days, do you think you can arrange to have a few people attend me?"

The Sergeant looked curious. "What do you mean?"

"Come with me. Let me explain," Devious said, putting his range finders back into their leather case.

The night had fallen dark when the tea grower and Devious arrived at the heart of the war camp of Kk-Riki. The camp was raucous, at least in the expensive tents of the professional warriors. Devious said sternly to Kilby Kay, "If your children speak to you, shut them down, and you keep your own mouth shut. I did not work all day to build these possibilities that will keep your children from armed service."

"I am aware, Mr. Devious. I am your silent shadow. Myself, I am not sure how you have done anything to get my children. You have mostly worked to secure my tea. If my children are not returned, then your arrangements for the tea are forfeit, and you will have no tea from my fields," the farmer said.

"That is fine by me," Devious replied.

They rode around a bend, coming to the camp of Kk-Riki. A pair of guards of the upper class stood in the way of their progress. They were obviously leery, yet clearly not prepared for much trouble. Guard duty seemed to be the last thing they wanted to do. Devious assessed them as thugs, deciding to treat them as such.

"Take me to Kk-Riki, now," Devious said in a laconic voice.

"How about you kiss my ass, farmer, and dismount?" The guard put a flagon of mead down on a nearby table.

Devious in one move dismounted from his horse, while drawing his talwar. He kicked out the guard's legs, pommel punched the second guard, then stuck the sharp point of his weapon to the neck of the first one. "Listen 'Ankle-break.' 'Nose-punch' there is going to get one of the Warlord Kk-Riki's Fanes, then we will be escorted in to see the man. Now, you will bow your head in my presence." Devious turned, pointing his talwar at the second guard. "Off with you. Get a Fane," he said, poking the guard in the ass as he ran into the tent area.

A few minutes later, a well-dressed man surrounded by an entourage of warriors approached. "What is this!?" he yelled.

Devious said, "I am Commander Sederick Devious of the tea merchant *Remarker*. I have been employed to transact business with Warlord Kk-Riki, to communicate with him concerning an issue. Who are you, my dear Fane?"

"You are the rich cat. Captain al-Rasheed?" he asked.

Devious laughed. "I am much better looking than the captain. As I said, my name is Commander Sederick Devious."

"Never heard of you. Do you have silver?" the Fane replied.

"If you have silver, I am Fane Rkansas. I am fine with seeing you to the tent then introducing you to the great Warlord Kk-Riki."

"This is excellent. Should I apologize to your guards?" Devious asked.

"Which ones?" the Fane laughingly asked.

"'Ankle-break' and 'Nose-punch' here wanted to shake me down for some silver before I could get to you and the Warlord," Devious said, pointing to the injured guards.

"Why do you call them this?" the Fane asked, looking questioningly at the two manhandled guards.

"Because I broke that one's nose and that one's ankle..." Devious replied, letting the joke set in with a pause.

The Fane laughed. "The little bastards! Well, Haughtman Kk-Riki, have these two crucified with my name around their necks."

A well-appointed officer collected a few men with his eyes, who fell on the unfortunate guards. The guards screamed, the soldiers showing no remorse or bad feelings over torturing their own to death. The Fane licked his lips, nodded, then said, "Come to the tent now, unless you want to watch. Crucifying is quite the show, of course. Helps morale to no end. Usually, you string up a few conscripts in a ten or twenty day, but it is useful to take out some of the apprentice warriors when guard duty goes slack."

Devious bowed. "You are a scholar of leadership, Fane Rkansas."

The warriors in their gold cloth and fine silks turned, then returned to the great tents, while Kilby Kay held onto Devious's shoulder. "They are going to crucify those men!"

"They would crucify your children. Did you not see the crucifixion posts in the parade ground they set up? Who builds poles for torture in a temporary war camp? Better two of them slaking the lust of these so-called warriors, instead of two conscripts that could be two of your children. Captain al-Rasheed will, of course, be angry, however, he is not the boss right this second. Now keep your mouth shut farmer Kay, let me make this work," Devious said. Kay nodded, falling silent.

Screams started behind them as they entered the tent of Warlord Kk-Riki. The tent was huge, with fifty or more people sitting on cushions around a fire pit where several butchered animals were being spun by servants. A cluster of Fanes were listening to Rkansas tell Kk-Riki of the new arrivals to the party. They all wore gold and red "uniforms" that were in no way uniform, more merely suggesting that they had been produced by the members of a tea club to resemble each other. They all seemed to favor axes and were usually bearded, some carrying five or six in leather holdalls around their bodies.

Kk-Riki was a big man, both because he had an expansive body that was well fed on piles of butter-roasted meats, plus he was the center of all attention in the tent. Each time he spoke, his Fanes leaned forward to hear. If it seemed he had made a joke, they laughed, no matter how lame his japes were. His anecdotes were met with rapt wonder, even when improbable to the extreme, with his factual discourse, despite being inaccurate and narrow-minded, was seen as the philosophy of the first water.

Devious, ignored by the barbarians, ate his awful food as if it was the best scones with the clearest dandelion butter from a cart on the Oxbow of the capital of Cycus. After hours of this, Kay could take no more. "When will you do something about my children?"

With a wave, Devious dismissed him. "I already have done what is needed. Now we simply wait for our turn to speak our lines. This is a play, and we are but players, farmer. Do you not see how each in this party is saying lines, that our own words have been inserted into the script?"

A new coming, dirty and bleeding, wearing the garb of a junior soldier, causing a commotion at the main table. Devious looked at the farmer, telling him, "Say nothing." He stood, walked to the arguing Fanes around Kk-Riki, then said with a piercing voice, "Your greatness, I must be going as it seems you cannot transact business tonight."

Kk-Riki looked over from his huddle, asking, "You are here why?"

Devious bowed. "I am a person who finds things that must be found, who arranges for things that must be done. I am here to make an arrangement with you about the delivery of farm products to the port each six months, as well as to purchase two of your lesser soldiers to aid in the farming of this tea, but I understand if you are busy."

"Wait, foreigner. You find things?" Kk-Riki asked.

"For a price I do," Devious replied.

"My son and heir is missing. If you find him, there are many boxes of silver for you," the hulking war chief stated.

"I have already found him. A warlord called RoviKaw has been bragging to many that he would have the ultimate revenge on you. It is obvious that this is what he meant," Devious said, reaching over to a tankard that had just been filled with wine, taking it for himself. After drinking a portion, he said, "I can get him back."

Fane Rkansas said, "My chief, this makes sense. The heir was taken from a strong guard in a hidden place. Who else would know of the place or have enough men to carry out the attack?"

Kk-Riki nodded as his Fanes made noises of general agreement. "These are two chests of silver for his return," he said, while motioning to the chests with his hand.

"What about the tea?" Devious asked. "I need the boys you have impressed to work the farm, plus your soldiers to deliver the tea each season to the port."

Kk-Riki waved his hands. "A small thing. You tithe us, the tea will come. Two foolish farmers are hardly a loss.

Kk-Riki, see that this is done. I warn you though, if my heir dies, you die, and hard."

Devious bowed with a flourish. "I will return before dawn."

Being reunited with his son and daughter was emotional for the farmer, Kilby Kay. Devious sent him to the small camp where he could be guarded by the two Marines which had remained behind to tend the fire. He did not need either a marine or a farmer for this next bit, but he took the farmer's horse with him for good luck. He took his horse, leading the farmer's, riding down a wizened old path that, according to his map, lead to a series of highland caves. As luck would have it, someone had marked the path with foxfire, which glowed dimly in the inky-dark. Foxfire only lasted a few hours when expressed from the sack of the fox bulb plant, so his find of the markers was an amazing coincidence. Soon the glowing markers left the trail, so Devious decided he would also leave it, following the signs into the tangled forest, up a hillside, where he eventually spied a tiny fire with three small figures huddled around it. As he approached, it turned out not to be the heir of KK-Riki, Kovi-Gan, but three scared girls looking to be five-to nine-years-old. They were tied both to a tree and each other; although they could get the water and food that had been left for them, as well as feed the fire, they could not escape.

Devious stepped down from his horse, wishing sometimes he could call on the compassion of Captain al-Rasheed. What did one say to a scared little girl? "Are you safe?" he finally asked.

The oldest one stood up imperiously, stating firmly, "You shall untie us, foreigner, then return us to our father, RoviKaw, at once."

"Little girl, I am looking for the heir to Kk-Riki. It may be that your father took the heir. That is my duty," Devious explained.

The girl stepped up to him fearlessly, as far as her ropes would stretch, replying, "If my father took the idiot child Kovi-Gan, then he did it because men in the colors of Kk-Riki took us. However, if you return us, then you will get Kovi-Gan, if my father has him."

Devious nodded, taking a knife from his horse. Each girl, in turn, he cut from her bonds, then sat each on the horses. With each secured to a horse, the two youngest on his animal, the older on the animal owned by Kilby Kay, he walked them down the hill. After an hour, he could hear and see the camp of RoviKaw and his army. He approached cautiously, in vain. As the first guard the girls saw, they screamed out. It might have ended too badly, especially when several of the angry men tried to manhandle Devious, until the oldest girl screamed, "Stop, he has my protection!" to which the warriors immediately followed orders.

RoviKaw was older than Kk-Riki, otherwise could have been his brother or uncle. Both men were large, boisterous, profane, violent, cunning, and ignorant. Devious was about to speak when the oldest girl walked up to the warlord, saying, "Hello Father, this man saved us and wants guild in return. He wants Kovi-Gan as payment."

The warlord got to his knees as his warriors pretended to not notice, replying, "My daughter, I do not have the boy. We just discovered you had been taken by Kk-Riki's men."

"Then reward him, as he is my special friend," she said, kissing her father on the cheek.

The warlord stood. "What do you want, foreigner?"

"Only Kovi-Gan. I merely stumbled on your daughters and would return them for free. I am in this land to arrange a deal with Kk-Riki to protect a farmer of tea in order to ensure I get shipments each season of his product, in exchange for a tithe of the payments." Devious looked a bit sourly at the little girl looking up at him. "I did not seek any recompense for your daughters."

"In truth, Father," the girl said, her young voice lisping but her words adult-like in her clarity, "Kk-Riki may have harmed your dragomen, yet he did not harm us. The warriors that took us did so with a silk glove on their hands. Give this man though, what he asks of Kk-Riki to make me happy, even if you cannot give him the warlord's idiot son."

RoviKaw stood. "Then I will do what you propose of Kk-Riki. Your tea will arrive, the farmer protected by my hand, as long as you pay the tithe you promise."

"In truth, I offered to Kk-Riki the deal," Devious replied, shrugging his shoulders.

RoviKaw looked at his daughter, then at Devious. "I will share with Kk-Riki this duty. I must demand the whole tithe though." Devious considered. "You each take a tithe, the farmer the rest, correct?"

There was a second of silence from RoviKaw, then he nodded.

"The deal is acceptable and accepted. If Kk-Riki agrees, then we will both deliver the tea, with each receiving a tithe of the money paid the farmer. Each of us will pledge to protect the farmer if only to assure our profits."

Devious bowed. "Then I must find Kovi-Gan. If you do not have him, I fear this may all collapse before me. Kk-Riki was most demanding I return Kovi-Gan."

RoviKaw made a dismissing gesture, spitting on the ground. "I will tell you Kovi-Gan is not worth the effort, yet I understand you need to do what you must do, foreigner. "

Devious left the camp, again riding his horse while leading the other. He looked at the moon, judging it was just past midnight. It was no longer quite as dark, however. Now the roadstead lacked the markings of foxfire. It was a wide road, though easy to follow. Still, it was an hour later when he saw that someone had tied a long, white cloth to a tree by the left lane of the road. Devious swung his horse across a field, finding another fluttering rag. He took a flinder from his pocket, struck it, then applied the burning stick to the rag, which flared into bright fire. Someone had soaked it with tar. In the distance, he could see another rag, so he started to follow their trail, lighting each rag, which burned brightly for a few minutes, its light showing the next one a hundred meters away.

After twenty rags had been burned, Devious saw a ramshackle herder's hut built from waddle and daub. Its furnace was blazing white with light. He rode up and saw that the furnace was being tended by a boy of thirteen who had been chained to the cement and stone structure. Devious climbed down from his horse, then walked up to the child. "Are you ok?" Devious asked.

The boy looked at him. "I am free, stranger, even with this chain on my ankle."

"Are you Kovi-Gan, son of Kk-Riki?" Devious asked. The child was odd, just like the eldest daughter of RoviKaw. An old soul in a child's body, a voice of youth saying words of maturity. "I am tired of being a warrior. I do not like it. I do not want to follow my father, nor lead the clan. It is not what I want at all."

Devious sat down by the youth. "I cannot help you, Kovi-Gan. I have been hired to return you to Kk-Riki, who seems very concerned for you."

Kovi-Gan shrugged. "If you must, just know this has been the best time of my life, tending this fire. Not being the son of Kk-Riki."

Devious had no desire to deal with the angst of a child, yet he could feel something inside of his own being, knowing that he could not simply return the child. Not that he would let the child abscond, but that he could plant the seed in Kovi-Gan's mind that had once been planted in his, that there was a way that his elders did not contemplate. "Listen to me Kovi-Gan. I would not want to follow your father either. For now, though, use the power that the gods hand you. Imagine what you want while you follow your father, craft it. Start laying the bricks today, then in twenty years you will have something that is not the senseless killing and fighting that the war chiefs do now."

Kovi-Gan looked at Devious, eyes burning in the light of the fire, asking, "How can I tell if you are truth-saying?"

Devious shrugged. "You cannot, child. You are going back to your father. I merely offer you the wisdom that the path of the father is not automatically that of the son. Take the tea my people would be buying. You are, in the eyes of your people, almost a man. So be a man. One tea farmer is to sell us tea, so why not start more tea farms, protect those farms with warriors, then sell more tea to fatten your purses. Then look to RoviKaw, marry his eldest, then you and she will control both bands. Your father and RoviKaw war for nothing, no gain. They just take umbrage on issues that do not matter so they can fight. True power is in building."

Kovi-Gan reached down, unlocking the lock that held his chains in place. He had obviously removed it earlier. He then put on his sandals, then walked to the spare horse. "Take me to my father. We will have the same deal as RoviKaw. You will get your tea. I will assure you of that."

Two days later, the Marines were breaking camp where they had set it the night before in a back field at the farm of Kilby Kay, Devious standing while watching the process with the farmer.

"I am confused, Mr. Devious. You act like finding two sets of kidnapped heirs, then arranging a mutual deal between two warlords to protect my farm was just happenstance. Is this what you are saying?" Kay asked.

Devious shrugged. "You see those wrappings, each with forty kilos of tea leaf?" He motioned to the back stock that Kay had cozened into one of his storage barns.

Kay nodded. "Of course, you came for the tea."

"You are correct, I came for the tea. Our captain has a great, huge heart. He thinks that this trading business is all about building some great, peaceful society. He has seen the same horrors as I have and should know better. Children tied to trees in the woods, warlords with their sabers drawn, even your own children, are beside the point. The point is the tea," Devious said.

"How can you suggest that tea is the most important thing of all that has happened here?" Kay squawked.

Devious shrugged. "Then we can have the tea without paying you?"

"Come now, Devious, you cannot simply take my tea," Kaby replied.

"See! It is always about the tea. Never forget that." Devious said, even if under his own bluster he wondered that perhaps al-Rasheed was right and he was wrong.

Chapter XII

An Account of My Travels

It is with no small trepidation that I have undertaken, at the advice of my Captain Javier al-Rasheed of the merchant liner *Remarker*, to record some small aspects of my travels. Ironically, the occasion for my taking up the pen comes as a result of a threatened book burning, along with my personal discovery that words written on common scap, then sewn between two covers of heath wood, could be valuable to a person, who might pay for a copy for the pleasure of reading thoughts that came from someone who has stood on what my captain calls other shores, plus has had the luck to learn how to entertain people with ink and pen.

I should reveal my name at this point. Although I write this missive as an aspirant, which is to say a very junior officer of a merchant ship where I have found employment as the Captain's Clerk, in fact my journey starts in a land called Lingongo, located in the south reaches of the sea, fairly isolated from the people of the Halo. The island I come from is a wonderful paradise where I was blessed to be born into the family of my village's Tempters, which are the warriors of my people. Of all the Tempters in the Village of Irontree, my father Neymar was the most powerful, bringing praise from not only the village but also the Staff-Holder Mayor, who ruled us all in great wisdom. I say this because when I was born it was agreed to allow me to take one of the silent names, those names of our famed relations long past. Thus, I was the first Salvador in anyone's memory. My mother Alandra, a magician of no small powers herself, along with my father, were a cause of pride to me growing up. I feel I made them proud as well.

This missive is not to be about Lingongo. I just feel certain facts must be placed before my loyal reader in order to understand how my path started, as it was unusual for a sailor. As the eldest of my parents' children, it was forbidden to me to take on the honor of becoming a Tempter. My sister, just eleven months younger than me, could become one. However, I, as the oldest, was bound by traditions that could not be ignored while I lived in Lingongo.

When I was barely eight, I was introduced into the world of tree herding. If that sounds boring, it is because tree herding simply meant that I made maps of the forest. Also helping decide when a tree could be cut for our use, as well as which tree to cut.

Do not get me wrong, many would have loved to have been a tree herder. I did not enjoy it simply because trees rarely move, never say anything worth noting. While making maps was amazing, those maps did not lead to exciting places, just to trees.

After I was introduced to my job, it took only a few weeks to decide that I would run away to another village to become a pearl diver, which I guess says more about the sensibility of an eight-year-old than their grasp on reality, when the village had a once-in-a-lifetime experience. A wanderer from the Halo showed up on our beach in a funny little boat, just him with his strange ways.

He had made the impossible journey from a land that was more myth than reality to us, undertaking this amazing task alone in a boat that looked dangerous, even for a pearl diver. I was entranced, begging my parents to meet the man, which they accomplished quite easily. If not for that meeting, my life would have been a pointless journey across time. That was because the man, he called himself Rafael, could do an amazing trick. He could read.

That is correct. No one on the island Lingongo even knew what a letter was. Sentences were fairy dust, the idea that I could communicate to a person through time and space with a piece of paper marked up with inked figures was nonsense. Yet it was true! Not only was fact proven over and over by curious people of my village who made poor Raphael transmit various phrases like, "I farted on a duck," from one person to another to prove the validity of his claim, Raphael offered to teach the young folk of our village to read and write if we would feed him and provide shelter for a season.

I was able to wheedle my parents into having this man teach me to read and write.

It was like opening a new world to me, although it was also difficult. As Rafael taught me to read, he also told me stories of the Halo, of thousands of islands, the people of a hundred different gens who could travel, if they wanted, simply by working for a tolerable amount of time to afford the price of a ticket. It was then and there I knew I had to travel. I loved my village. My parents were the best, most honorable parents a boy could have. My island was the most beautiful I could imagine, possibly because it was the only one I had ever seen. Yet I knew in my heart I had to see what the Halo was.

I was older, and maybe wiser, when Rafael left, equipped with a good knowledge of letters and words, an understanding of how the people of the Halo sailed across the seas, and a firm belief that what I had to do was create my own boat. When I brought the idea to my father, he was sad, because he felt that I would die alone on the open water away from the arms of my loved ones, yet he agreed to help. In fact, every person in the village participated.

My boat had to be small enough for me to manage by myself in an open sea. It also had to be large enough that it could carry food and water for many days. It had to handle the great waves Raphael told me to expect, and it had to be buildable by what I could scrounge for myself.

Oddly enough, my work with trees helped me immediately, as an ironwood, after which our village was named, had fallen in the forest, with various people planning to disassemble it for its valuable lumber. The village agreed I would have four lengths of its strong interior to form the all-important four frame points for a traditional mayee boat, something our fish catchers had been building for generations. In addition, several lots of scrap were gifted to me. Scrap is wood of varying lengths left over after a tree is used for building. It is less useful to crafts people, usually shared out for personal projects and decoration, so it was not really against any covenant for me to use these items in a boat. This gave me a wide range of small lumber pieces to choose from for my boat.

I selected boo-wood and elder to weave into a tight basket, then attached it with wood plugs to the four frame points. More boo-wood strips were used to fix twenty water and twenty food casks permanently to the boat. The casks were all older, each required work to repair, but were also freely donated to me.

I had access to jute scraps enough to turn into many useful things. Two sails, one square and one triangular, would give my boat good push, while oars of the appropriate length to stay within the out-rigging would allow me to use muscle to propel the boat when needed. A farmer who had built a new shed gave me her old one. This gave my boat a deck house just big enough for me to escape the weather in. Onto the house I installed a set of fishermen's friends to wake me if the boat drifted off course, a sanitary, canvas water catchers, trot poles, and a beeswax burner for cooking.

It took me six years to make that boat, starting when I was eleven, finishing it when I was seventeen. It was then that my father had "the talk." He was proud of me and my boat, knew I could make the voyage, adding I could, without dishonor, stay on with the village for a few seasons as I prepared my body and heart for the trip.

At my coming-of-age ceremony, my parents proved even further their quality and heart. My dad came, dressed in his woven strapped armor, his great ironwood club proudly holstered to his chest, and his spiked palm helm resplendent with newly picked loft ivy. My mother wore her best samshu with a spree of matching loft ivy, while my brothers and sisters each carried boo-wood fans. They then did the "dance-of-centuries" for me, in the last steps revealing a flag of boo-wood fiber dyed with the deep dark red that I had chosen for my boat's standard. Even more touching, they had written my name on the standard in the alphabet of the people of the Halo. To quell any talk among the village, to assure that I was seen as properly filial, that I was not challenging the father-kin right of my dad, he stood in front of the mass of people who I had known from birth, five-hundred-and-eighty-three souls, and announced that he and his wife, my mother, as parents, and the village elder, as leader of us all, accepted my new work to be that of adventurer, in the manner of that glorious visitor to our village. Thus, my journey was vouchsafed as my life task. The ship I had built stood as a testament to my ability to make the journey.

My mother and sisters cried because they knew that I would be gone twenty or more years. I would leave knowing that none of my family may still be living when I returned to the shores of my home. My great day, the greatest of my short life up until then, was in some ways bittersweet. Yet my father addressed this. Bittersweet though it may be, it was my task and destiny, and not a soul in the land could or would speak against it.

Yet each great day must be followed by many normal days, where a normal day for me was preparing for my trip. While I could not be a soldier like my father, he insisted that I learn the way of soldiers. The great club I was taught could be swung, and it could also be used to trip, be thrown, or block attacks. An old fighter named Danao showed me to make and use hand-darts, tossing them under hand so they plummeted from the sky. The village weaver taught me how to weave the same armor my father made so resplendently, turning strips of boo-wood into breastplates, paldrons, and gegits, more flexible than just a basket around your body, as was done in other villages.

My brother Tao, apprenticed to the fish takers, taught me how to make a fish stand from a tree-pole that you could sit on in order to take fish without having to expose your feet in the water all day risking ray-sting. He showed me how to clean a fish, dry them on a drying rack, brine pack them, and prepare them to eat using only a single beeswax candle. He also warned me candle-fried fish was addictive, but salty, so if I had limited water that it might not be the best food to consume, to instead eat porridge.

My sister Allendia, who was learning to grow and prepare sacred kallo, was given permission to show me the secrets of this amazing plant. Raphael, the only Halo person I had known to the point, assured me he had never heard of kallo, was amazed by this food. A kallo is a bush of blue-colored leaves and purple flowers that is deadly poisonous. It grows from a huge corm that is half underground and half above, which is also poisonous if consumed directly. To make it edible, the root is quartered using a flint adze, then it is crushed by a rolling rock driven by a moot or sallow cow. Once crushed, a sugary sap compound is poured on top in a boxwood barrel hooped with boo-wood, then allowed to sit for not less than twenty days. This is followed by adding sauce from crushed soybean, then the product is dried in the sun for two weeks, finally rolled flat on drying mats.

In a way, making kallo was my most important training, because I learned that it was one of the few foods we ate on Lingongo that could be stored for future use. Raphael had explained to me years ago that sea travelers ate dried or heavily salted food when they left the security of shore, encouraging me to watch as he had prepared these foods for his trip. He found, though, that a dish from my own village was his favorite. It was made with only dried fish, crushed tubers, and powdered soy, which was then mixed with water, then stirred until thick. This would be a dish I would carry, preparing it for my journey. I also discovered from Allendia that the reason the priestesses of the silent god considered kallo sacred was not from some subtle hint given in the heavens. It was because when enclosed in a boxwood cask, kallo could be stored buried in the sand for 25 years! While it was rare that the people of Lingongo suffered crop failures and the loss of fishing at the same time, when it did, the priestesses fed the island off the stocks of kallo they kept in their chantries.

That solved most of my need for traveling food. I would help the priestesses make kallo, withdrawing their oldest casks from the ground. Further, they would crush and cask me limes for lime juice, which I was to mix with water to fight mouth blight. They also provided dried bean and jungle leaf pastes to protect against many other diseases. The priestesses soon had completely taken over my food planning, breaking me of the idea that the answer was solely quantity, but instead a question of quality and healthfulness. They declared their goal for my trip was to arrive fat as a hamster and shiny as a seal.

Soon the food was ready, the water safely in its casks, the boat checked and provisioned in every way possible. It was the start of the windy season, but five weeks from the time of storms. It would be the next day I would set out. As honor and practice approved, I would do so alone without an audience, my last image not being of leaving, but of having my last meal with my family cooked by my father, served to me by my siblings as if I was an honored guest.

After the meal, my father came to me as I retreated to the tent they had erected, from which I could leave quietly the next morning, to give me the "abrakar," which is our term for the hug a leader gives his follower before the follower performs a task of honor. In a small leather bag, he handed me duplicates of the family gods and a boo-wood carving of the silent god. He then said, "I, Neymar, and your mother, Allandra, bid you luck on the waters of Ocean, declaring that, return or not, you are as treasured as each of our other children, and will always have a place at our table and theirs. I also tell you that the village elder is waiting to meet you, our wisest and most noble, the Staff-Holder Mayor and Chief of our Order of Tempters. You may have played at her feet when you were born. Despite that, I ask that you give her all of the deference as if as she was the personification of the silent god for the few minutes of time she asks to share with you."

I genuflected to my father as deserved a senior Tempter, replying, "Neymar, my parent, please give these words to the illustrious Allandra, who brought me to life as well, if I make a good sight to the gods and the silent god, if my visage is fair and my honor strong, I will see you again. If I exist with any credit, it is merely because I am a reflection of the parents who raised me, and they the shining glory of not just our village, but also the island Lingongo. I will be known in the eyes of the gods as Salvador de Neymar'Allandre d'terras Lingongo. When I pass from this life, the silent god will have the chanter of the ethers call out my story as but an extension of yours and my mother's."

Neymar, the stolid warrior, who had stood in the broken times without fear, who had fought the fires of the autumn yallends to save many souls, who had the respect of one-hundred staff-holders, who had received the bow of high priestess Queno' Falo-palavra before the Cohorts Mienchas, let slip a single tear from his eyes. All the honors given to me were nothing to this expression of real emotion from a loving father.

Turning away from the man who I might not see for a sheaf of years, I walked down the trail to the ceremonial clearing, to the tent that had been set up for me to sleep. In front of the tent was Bisa Jovanao, the Staff-Holder Mayor of the Village of Ironwood. She motioned to me to sit as she prepared tea and a savory smelt stew over a small fire of sandalwood. Her tea service was beautiful, made from a blackened copper plate that had been pounded and forged, with a flat bottom, an ironwood handle and top, with a tea filter of boo-wood straps. The stew was simmering in one of the smaller soup tureens created from black-stone that was kept permanently in the ceremonial clearing. When the tea and stew were finished, she divided the meal into equal portions, placing it on two sets of carved and tanned wood bowls, which she subsequently placed on two applewood trays, along with boxwood spoons for them to use. Mayor Jovanao was natural in her observations of the great way, never using metal of any sort outside of her lodgings, except occasionally at night, always washing her hands, bowls, trays, and utensils in soy soap and boiled water at the ablutions trencher, always serving herself first, tasting both food and drink before expecting others to partake. In some ways it was her effortless piety, I believe, that had made her the staff-holder of my village when others had perhaps greater claim to the title. I knew my mother worshipped her, as did many of the Tempters and seniors craft makers, even though others outside of the Village of Ironwood might not see the quality of her quiet leadership.

We drank tea and ate stew in silence. When we finished, I carefully cleaned all the utensils, setting them to dry on a rack at the edge of the clearing. When the cleaning was done, I returned to the staff-holder mayor, who had removed a small, wax-sealed gourd from a small box of banded ironwood. She looked at me intensely while handing me the gourd.

"Salvador, son of Allandra'Neymar, what I hand you is the final honor. We call it thus because there is an end, when the fight has been fought, when you wish an opportunity to escape to the ethers. It is our most forbidden act, that of self-harm, yet is also our most cherished right for a person whose time has in all other ways come to an end, when they face nothing but senseless suffering. You are allowed this bottle and its contents for this journey to the Halo only. You must destroy it when you see new land. You must only use it after having no water for two days, or no food for twenty," she instructed.

"What is in the bottle, Staff-Holder?" I asked.

"Sleep," she replied. "Final rest and a quiet pathway to the end of life, with no way to return." She put the gourd back in the box, then handed the box to me. "Your boat has been loaded for you. I note that you named it *Neymar's Heart*. The chanters will add it and your adventure to the books. My personal feeling is you will never be seen again, though my prayer is that you will ride the horizon into our memories, while someday my daughters and their daughters will greet your return to these lands. Do not get up, I must have my sleep. I will not see you tomorrow. The tide breaks with favor in the first light of dawn."

There is a natural alarm to wake on Lingongo in the form of birds, jays, and caws, who begin to serenade the island with their cacophonous laughter about forty minutes before the sun peaks its head over the sea's horizon. Few heed the alarm; it is better to wake with dawn when there is light to work by. This time, for me, this oddity of my home island brought me awake with time to catch the tide.

I set out in *Neymar's Heart* into the bosom of boredom. It is true that there was the tinge of boredom, even a little terror, as I sailed in the direction and manner the Halo traveler Raphael had shared with me so many years before, heading to his homeland of Dartia. For months he had told me of his home, a little farm on the southern coast of the island, where he had built his own boat, traveling to the reaches of the south and west, before returning to take his last trip to a land that he knew only through rumor. His planned route home was the route that I would travel in my attempt to find land. It proved to be day-after-day the sail filled with wind, with nothing to do but wait for the next day.

At night I slipped my leg into a fish catcher's friend. If you have never seen this rig, they are comical contraptions which, if the ship tiller falls off the true course set by the ship's fixed compass, causes the sailor's leg to be lifted in the air in a crazy way, while also recording in wrapped twine how far and what direction the boat has moved away from the intended direction of travel. While I cannot say the device was perfect, it served my purposes quite well. Further, I had the advantage of no one being present to see my anterior regions exposed to the eyes of the silent god as my leg was dragged skyward.

I had expected storms. None came. It rained almost daily, often at the same time in the afternoon. The routine of sailing soon became maddening. There was no one, for the first time in my life, to speak to. With the sun I would wake, sighting where it rose compared to the prow of my ship. At night when Ferris first rose, I would note where it rose, again compared to my prow. I had two carved sticks as a sight, with a slider to show how far off true I was from my intended direction of north-by-northeast. I knew that the techniques used by Raphael when he arrived at Lingongo were far more sophisticated than I could ever master, so I also knew that my quest was similar to throwing myself off the cliff at the "End of Land" while hoping I had timed my leap with the incoming wave, else I would be dashed on the rocks of time below.

I can honestly say I was not scared. At night, the silent god looked down on me. During the long days, the gods of my ancestors smiled. I had water fill my barrels three times over. I had fish nearly jumping into the boat. Then, through providence, I saw land, but was it the right land?

Raphael had drawn me his island as it looked from the endless sea, including where his house sat on the promontory of one of Dartia's great rivers, overlooking a cliff. I took this old document from my notebook, examining the island before me against the image he drew.

It was an exact match! I had survived to see the Halo. It was with great pride I unlocked the oars to make for the rocky alcove of a beach he had described launching from himself, finding it a forgiving landing with bollard made from some concrete made of shells pierced with a metal ring-tie. I made a force extender from a pair of hand-carved six-wheeled hubbards, with great effort bringing the *Neymar's Heart* above the surf-line, safe from the vagaries of an angry sea. I pulled my small pack, a water bottle, and a straight stick for walking out of the boat, then started up the steep ascent.

Now here is a trick to remember when on a boat, which I now take to heart. Jog in place if you can as the boat permits it. The problem you will face when you first reach land is that the land is not itself stable, at least to your mind. It rocks back and forth like it is free on the sea's tides, which makes walking hard. I found after all that time at sea my legs were sore in a few minutes, the strength and wind I called my own by nature fleet, eluding my grasp. I barely made it to the house. A person who wants to be a sailor must still use their legs.

At the house, itself made of cement blocks formed from seashells and sand, Raphael sat looking out to sea. As I walked up he startled, then it struck him that I was known, in a minute, connecting my face with the year he spent teaching me to write.

As he stood, though, he did not rush to embrace me as men do on my island, and as we had done when we parted ways. If a man could be wounded without a blow from a weapon, he was thus harmed. He was joyed to see me, I could see the blossom of his heart lift into the air, yet the blossom was weighed down.

"Salvador, my friend, you are a man? Shall I serve us tea on my veranda?" he asked in greeting.

I nodded with graveness, "My friend, that would give me pleasure."

He motioned to a pair of chairs on the veranda, and I sat. Soon he arrived with tea and a plate of leafy plants with oil poured on, which was just what I had dreamed of. I drank his excellent tea, ate the leafy plants, feeling contentment, yet it was not shared by my silent friend.

"Raphael, has time soured the mentorship you gave me?" I asked.

He looked at the sky, saying, "No, it has brought to me what I lost in my adventures. I returned to this house, as you know, found that my wife and children had left, my business was closed, my hidden treasure stolen, the house was occupied. I fought to regain it, and in the end I did, but like a child playing stones on a grid, my heart stone was soon confined to a nest. My house falls in around me, with even my stories of living on other shores considered lies," he said sadly.

"You never see your wife or your child anymore?" I asked, incredulously.

He stroked his beard, saying, "No, they live in an apartment in the town. I see them often, but they cannot see me, as I am invisible. Still, you are welcome to stay for what good it does you. How did you reach this shore? By merchant?"

"No," I said, "I did as you did, building my own boat."

Raphael laughed deeply. "That is wonderful, and surprising. My long-lost boat was the one true saving grace of my travels. I sold it for a good price. The money has allowed me to keep the house, even if I wish that I had kept it, traveling the world more, given how things turned out."

"I will stay with you," I told him. "At least for a few days. I would love to explore this island even if I see no other land."

Raphael nodded, smiling. "Then I am happy to oblige your adventure."

As a stranger to the shores of the Halo, I immediately noted what was different and what was the same. Raphael looked over my boat, taking the overstock of dried fish I had, claiming he could save money eating the supply, handing me a small bag of silver coins each with the number 2-1/2 embossed on them. A coin with a "1" on it is called a "zot." A coin with "2-1/2" is called a "half-penny." A coin with a "5" on it is called a "silver penny."

That says a lot about the people of the Halo. They are serious about weights, measures, and time. In my land, a fish catcher brings in a set of ten salmon, then engages to trade them for baskets of kallo, scoops of salt, or a day's work on your house. Fish, scoops, baskets of kallo, and work days come in all sizes. Everyone knows this. So you do what we call "the fiddle." The biggest fish and the smallest fish equal a medium fish. Their basket poured into your basket either fills it to the top or does not fill it at all. You will do business with this person or village all your life, so you compromise. The salt maker knows their scoops are big or small. You know your scoop containers are big or small. The salt maker assures you are happy, you assure the salt maker is happy with the fish. It all works out.

This is not how it is done in the Halo. I went to the village with a small purse of silver, expecting to hand it over for some food and a trinket, finding out that silver is actually quite valuable, with the vendors writing how much silver buys how much product right over their heads if they are honest. (I should say they have what they call dark trade, that explanation is for another time.)

I found in my first visit to town an older man who, for a cup of tea, explained the practice to me.

Many years ago, he explained, when the people of the Halo first invented the square sail and discovered the tolan, a god walked among them called al-Metrikus. This was the God of the North Wind, and s/he, his gender is not known today, demanded that order be put to the chaos of boats sailing across the waters of Ocean without leave by the gods. So he outlined this order should be an agreed manner of measure. When I say measure, I mean everything is measured. For you and me, a basket of grain and a bottle of water do not seem related. Al-Metrikus and the people of the Halo disagree, not letting you forget it. S/he declared that the length of his step was a meter, they measured this out. S/he said if you took that space then formed a box with six sides, the water it contained was 1,000 kilograms in weight. This would be called 1,000 liters; the liter could then be divided smaller and smaller so that a gram of water was 1/1,000th of a liter. A zot, it turned out, displaced one gram of water.

I am not joking that they have a device in any town worth its name where a coin can be measured to determine if it really is silver, plus how much silver is in it. You take the coin, which must be round, then load it in a gate. The coin tumbles down, and if it comes out in one particular box, it contains silver. It then is deposited into water, which spills off into a cylinder of a clear material they call glass, with the amount of water displaced indicating how much silver the coin has in it.

My half-penny is accepted because it is minute in a land known for the quality of the coinage, as well as because it conforms to some tricks that allow it to be quickly judged for what they call a forgery, which is a term for any half-penny that does not have two and one-half grams of silver in it.

I never thought about it, the old sailor explaining that you did not weigh a ship. You estimated how much water it displaced using wooden models. How could you otherwise figure out how much a ship weighed? I had not previously understood ships had a weight or that it might matter until I designed one that had to be pulled out of the water by my own muscles.

The temperature is measured in degrees. This is figured out by how much fresh water expands in a closed tube. I asked if the system works everywhere, as I knew math from a perspective of ten numbers, taught to me by none-other than Raphael. He said no, because a different god demanded that time and angles be related to allow the worship of the sun and the locations of stars to be plotted. A circle, he informed me, has 360 degrees, although he does not know why. An hour is a measure of time. There are 24 of them in a day. Each hour, the world of Ocean turns 15 degrees. A minute is the division of an hour by thinking that during this time the world turned one-fourth of a degree. It was there his knowledge fled because he had no idea how this was worked out, except the bell in the tower rang each half-hour.

Which it did. Forty-eight precisely divided times each day, most Halo towns who have a "bell tower" ring the bell. It is soft 32 times a day, louder 8 times a day, then even louder 8 more times. It works. You can believe me even if all of this sounds crazy. When the bell rings, someone may put down his tools because he has earned his penny, as they say (even if he earns more than a penny, it is just a saying).

For example, you order a fish; you are brought a fish that the fishmonger weighs on a scale. "Two zots," they say. I wonder why the woman does not take some fish off, then wonder would happen if she was to take all the meat, leaving me just the heads? I tell her, "I have only this coin that says two-and-one-half zots."

"Why is that a problem, sonny?" she asks. "By the way, you have a beautiful way of speaking." Then she bags the fish in a rough muslin, pushing me a coin across the counter. A coin made of copper called a "half-zot." One-tenth of a silver penny in buying power, yet twice the size of a penny at least.

This gave me a theory. I asked, "Those crystals in the tureen, what are their cost?"

The lady smiles, saying, "What it says on the sign, sonny. A penny gets you seventy-grams. They are called sugar rocks. I would advise going easy on them because they are addictive. To tell you the truth, most adults just use them to sweeten bitter tea."

I did the math in my head, "Could I have three-and-a-half grams?" I asked.

She nodded, using tiny weights while carefully adding rocks of sugar to her scale, coming to somewhere under four grams, but above three-and-a-half. These she slipped into a little leaf, then did up in twine. I passed her the copper coin, and she took it without blinking, giving me the "rocks-of-sugar." I hesitated, then asked, "Do I not owe you five-six-teenths of a zot?"

"Oh, honey, times are not so hard that we bend coppers here. You get what you pay for, sometimes more," she said. I found out later "bending a copper" was the practice of cutting a copper one-tenth zot into fractional pieces. It was considered rude or miserly since small copper coins were created when there was a need for them.

Then I asked her my real question. "Do you know Raphael, who lives on the headland?" It was a risk to ask, as I had already figured that the people of these lands were not as close to each other as where I came from. They could walk by each other, never saying as much as a greeting. Sitting at a teahouse, they formed little clusters of fish folk, farmers, sailors, merchants, as well as other people whose occupations were mysterious to me. It was very possible I would ask fifty people, with none knowing Raphael.

"Yes, I do, sweetie. He was our forge-hand before he took off on a boat. Do not go round to bother him. He has a reputation," she answered.

"What reputation?" I asked.

"He tells tall tales when in reality he was a drunk who abandoned his family. I see his poor wife and children at the beggary being given scraps each week. Who does that to their own?" she asked.

I asked, "Where does she live?"

"The pastoralist cares for them, although he is not a man of fitness, or of honor. He takes the charity money, working the inmates of that place for his own gain. If the Clive of O-town let us, we would toss him in the ravine, then have those poor committals let free," she said.

I nodded, leaving the store.

Now understand this, my readers, I am not criticizing the people of the Halo, but right here I began to see where my own land, for all its faults, was very different. Raphael lived alone and sad when his former wife and child were only a short walk away from him. His business had fallen, he had been stolen from, so now he lived a life of quiet desperation. Where was the staff-holder to arrange for people to visit him each day? Why were the Tempters not tracking down those who stole from him?

His family? If a family split apart in my land, the community moved in to assure that both were cared for, the Staff holder calling the leading members of the guilds to say there is no falsehood in the vagaries of the world of life, that we must respect the choice of each person. I walked to the middle of the village, then looked at the tower with the bell.

It was shockingly, to me, made of metal.

There was so much wealth in this land, along with so much hubris. In my land, a tea brewer made from a small amount of copper is taken out only on a cloudy night under the shade of trees least it causes the gods to chastise us. Here, a giant bell of metal rings out the day and night in the sight of the gods without the slightest worry of retribution.

I only wish the silent one was a god that would tell me what to do. Here I stood on Raphael's "other shores" where they built houses of plaster, the town square made of masonry stone. Where water was piped into their town, then into fountains, even houses could have as much as they wanted. Where even the smallest town in the smallest island, such as this one, was attached to a network of merchant ships that spanned a thousand unique peoples, where reaching all that diversity and variety could be had for anyone with the will to work the lines of one of those ships, or even to build one's own as Raphael and I had.

Then I realized my own error. The priestesses said the silent god did not speak because it was our job to make the best of what we faced. Yet they said we could also take counsel in our ancestors by looking to the words they passed us in history, the words of their deeds, not the written ones of the people of the Halo. In reflection, I thought those words could also be the words of my mother and father, people whose least deeds shook the world in a way I never would. What would the most honored Tempter of my village do when he saw misery? What would my quiet mother, working through her network of crafters, work at to solve the conflicts which existed around her?

A man leading a small horse they called a "donk-ee" was passing by the tiled fountain in the cobblestone-lined courtyard that was the town center. He had a slouch hat, pants wide at the legs that narrowed to show his hips and buttocks in an odd way, a little half jacket, and a bundle of fine carrots on a stick that he used to move the animal he was leading forward. "Master," I said to him.

"I am not a master," he replied. "I am just old Bluju, the refuse hauler. A silver lets you pitch your kitchen waste and night soil in my hauler for my strong donkey to carry outward."

I whistled in appreciation. "You say you are not a master, but unless it is digging the water ways in or tending the children in the day, I cannot image what is more important."

He laughed, saying, "Well, I am the king of this land, but it is a good disguise to rule from the mouth of a donkey with a dung cart."

"May I ask you for directions?" I asked him.

He came to the fountain, taking from his side pouch a little cup of copper. People of the Halo, you will learn, carried small pouches at their waist. One carried coins. Another carried a little book to write in if they were literate. A third carries a spoon, a fork, a clasp knife, and a cup, often made of metal. The drover took his cup, filled it with water, then drank it down. "You may certainly ask me for directions, 'deena.'"

"There is in this town a place where a priest cares for men or women who have become homeless. Where may I find this pastoralist and his charges?" I asked.

The drover's face grew darker. "Young son, aside from running with the cliques, there is no worse idea than to beard Bevan Vibard at the chantry of Graven Oaks. You seem a clean young man filled with vigor ... and polite. What that man would do with you marks no goodness to your body or soul. Walk clear from him."

"I must see him, sadly," I said.

"Look to the mountain range that divides the island. On the far side is O-Town, there you will find the Capes of Dartia, which the foreign call the Cape of Darts. There is a path out of town that you will see past the granaries and the brew master that leads over hard trails to O-Town. However, you need not go anywhere that far. The chantry is an hour walk from this fountain, clearly marked with a sign. Yet I must again say, you are not the first to travel that path for revenge or to serve his evil designs, but if you return, you will be the first to do that. I again say, do not go there," the man said, putting his cup away, then taking up his bundle of carrots on a stick. He then left with his cart on his business.

I brought back food from the markets to Raphael, which we ate that evening. It was a nice meal of fish and tubers called battatas, both cooked in the coals of the fire. People on Dartia make fires from a wood that looks like boo-wood, with its hollow center filled with the dust from log cutting. The wood burns with little smoke, makes satisfying coals, plus is easy to light. As we ate in silence, I thought of how complex the process of preparing a fire following the rules of my people and the wood that the tree herders, which

I almost became, allowed us to use. "This wood," I asked Raphael, "do many islands use it for fires?"

He nodded. "I never really thought of it, but in my travels a lot do. It grows fast. A lot of towns and small islands will have planted lots where they grow fire trees in order to distribute them to the people to protect their woods from being burned. Your land is naturally filled with trees, but on some of our islands, if you cut the trees, they only return with great difficulty."

"Who makes that choice to grow this wood?" The issue seemed to point to my consideration of what to do here on the island of darts.

"The church does; it is their sacred business. To tell the truth though, I do not know much of how this came about. I am sad to say that I know more of your lands than I do of my own." Raphael looked into the growing sunset, slipping the sun behind the spinal mountain, while adding, "Knowledge is a wonderful thing, but not always a common thing."

"How do you mean?" I asked.

"You ask wonderful questions about subjects that, honestly, do not get discussed or considered. Little things on how our world works. The fire trees burn so well it is almost like the gods designed them on a drawing rack just to be fuel for our fires, but they do not grow in your lands. Yet boo-wood, in all of its splendid varieties and types, grows on nearly every island to my knowledge. At least a person who studied it says that the hot sands of the farthest north and the frozen wastes of the southern Extents have their own kinds of boo-wood, all interrelated. Yet he said there was a secret to this. Fire trees cannot float, neither can their seeds, they also do not grow unless a human plants and tends to them, at which time they grow like garden weeds. Boo-wood floats. A shot landing on a distant shore becomes a tree. No human need intervene. Thus boo-wood goes where the gods' hands go, whereas fire trees just go where our hands point." He picked up a piece of fire tree, putting it on the fire.

"Would you want your wife and daughter to again take root on the shores of this home you have made?" I asked.

"I wish life made us human boo-wood. Unfortunately, they are held by both their own choice and by the laws of the land. They are fire trees, burning bright, something I should have considered. I would like nothing better than to see them again, yet that will not be." He stared at the fire, then asked, "May I make you some tea?"

Dear Raphael,

I have thought upon this for days, now having decided there is no other route for me but that which honors my father and mother. To do that honor, and to follow the silent god in my path I will work to return your wife and daughter to you, if they are willing to go of their free will

By the time you read this, the deed will either be done, or I will be. You cannot stop this. My boat, I have discovered, is worth a great deal of silver. It is yours to do as you wish. Its name is "Neymar's Heart." Treat her well, as she has carried me far in a short time.

Salvador.

I walked through the strange land in darkness, following the notes I had made in my mind on how to make to reach the over-mountain road. In my pack was my fishing gear, my brushes, some ink, a small package of sugar candy, two bottles of water, changes of clothing, a tarp borrowed from Raphael to sleep under if ever again I needed to sleep, and the small container my father had made me of the gods. Then I remembered one item. I reached into the pack side-pocket then pulled the box given me by the village Staff-Holder Mayor. I opened the box, dumped the gourd filled with the bitter liquid to the ground, then stepped on it, which released the potion. There would be no need of that route. What I had to face, I would face as my father would.

It was the turning of the night when dawn and dusk are balanced when I swung onto the trail into and over the mountains, finding a man sitting by a fire. He had set up a herder's tent. There was water boiling on the fire in a stew pot. Next to him were two wood mugs, a wanderer's cup, and a small tea chest open and ready for selecting tea. Moving closer to the man, it appeared to be Bluju, the trash drover, who asked, "I have a chest of tea, with no one to share it. Will you sit with me and have a drink?"

I thought about it. "I can only sit for a short while. Did you come here to catch me?"

"Oh," Bluju considered. "I am a drover. I can sleep any-where I like. I just felt there was a chance I might see you here. What tea would you like?"

I sat down, setting my pack by my side. "I do not know."

"Well, I am not the Clive who can tell the tastes of fifty teas plus the money to buy from the furthest reach. My chest is merely to be shared with my fellow laborers when the nights grow cold. Yet what I have is a useful variety of tea that is undistinguished, yet fitting and tasty. I have Cycus Light and Black, the Trangoone of our own Dartia, Quorna trade tea, and an unnamed but respectable tea from the sugar islands. What would you like tonight during your short visit with me?" the drover asked.

"May I please have what you are having?" I replied, having tasted none of these teas.

"Let us taste the Trangoone, which is grown by a single farm on the west tip of our island, and not exported to my knowledge. It is a local secret." He took two measures of tea, charged the wanderer's cup, then unclipped the deep bowled wood ladle to pour the steaming water into the device. When the tea had steeped, he twisted the device one way, then the next, then took the bottom off of it, dividing the contents into two cups. One he handed me, the other he claimed for himself.

I tried the tea, immediately happy I had stopped to sit with the man. My duty was dark. I did not really know if I could carry out what I had to do with honor. The friendly laborer and his hot tea were just the break I needed before I hardened by heart to the task at hand.

After the first cup and a second round, Bluju leaned back, telling me, "I have to say sorry, lad. I was thinking all day of what I said to you, eventually realizing I was addressing you as a child."

I understood why he would say that, so replied, "I doubt my own existence in the world of adults. It seems it could be argued that I am a child at play in the islands of the sea, not yet ready for the responsibilities of honor that my father or mother would handle with calm precision."

"You sell yourself short," Bluju said to me. "I, too, stood on the end of a great mountain when I was young. I, too, when the thinking was over, had two routes to take. I could climb the mountain, see what was to be seen, then return to consideration on further steps. Or I could climb the mountain, take steps that would damn me but release me from my honor-bound duty, then flee to the other side of the mountain, eventually out to sea, turning my back for a sheaf of years on the land I once called home. You faced these two choices."

I nodded. It was a tidy summation of my choices, even though I did not see how, if the deed was done, I would not be caught and punished. I looked into the fire, feeling for the first time in my life that tears may be needed to clear my soul of the clutter of childhood so that I could carry out what honor demanded of me. When I felt Bluju touch my shoulder, I understood there was a beat to be taken in this dance. "I need a father who cannot be by me for advice."

Bluju said, "Can you accept a vagabond and a garbage man in that role?"

I looked at him, replying, "In my land, the people who deal in the soil-of-the-night are wealthy and wise patrons of the art of reuse. They are held in great honor."

"Then you have learned your first lesson," Bluju said. "People here in this village of Nedartus, as well as those in the greater Ocean City, dismiss what I do. A penny and I take your buckets of night soil. The wooden house you tear down costs twelve pennies for me to carry away. The soil you give me is piled up, then, in two years, is sold to the church for a penny a bucket to use as a top dressing on the fire trees. The wood is cut down into clean usable lots, the nails salvaged and sold to metal workers, the wood sold to wood workers who use it again. You pay me to take your waste. You pay me to buy it back. I make a good living while looking like it is poor. I camp out by a fire when I want, visit my family and my children when I want. I leave no grudges or hatred behind me when I am called away. Not many men or women can say that."

I nodded, looking into the kind man's honest face. "Then guide me, please. How do you suggest I proceed?"

Bluju took a stick, then pointed up the mountain. "You can go up there, speak with the poor people under the thumb of Bevan Vibard at the Chantry, then come back down here. I will find work for you. You can then pursue a recognition of the plight of the family of Raphael in a way that they can find peace in this world. I know the Clive, he is a man who cares only for himself and the church he leads. He does recognize that public opinion matters, and we can sway that public opinion. Two or three years, with luck, we will succeed." He then stirred the fire with the stick. "In this case I will see you in the first eaves of light on the morrow when you will start a new journey."

"The second way?" I asked.

"You can march up the mountain, rescue a woman and her daughter, send them back to me here, then continue on over to O-Town, ending up at the gate to the ports-karidde by the roadstead of the Cape of Darts, meeting the man with the lamplighter who douses the lamps at dawn. Tell him my name, that you want to take the first ship that needs crew away from this island, and do not return until that same man gets word to your ship that it is safe to do so. You may by then be hunted, unable to stay here." The night soil driver placed some wood on the fire, appearing to lose interest in the conversation. I looked at him for a few minutes, then left up the mountain.

I will keep the ivy curtain around what happened next, of the details of what is either my moment of honor or shame. I will say what you could discover yourself by finding the night soil drover named Bluju, in the town of Nedartu, then asking him because this much I know he will tell you. The next morning after he and I shared tea, two women approached him with tales of escaping the evil chantry where they had been forced to work in demeaning and horrible conditions. The Master of the Chantry, a pastoralist man of low repute named Bevan Vibard, was found having fallen from the side of a steep ascent, likely taken low by his habit of drinking to excess paw-paw brandy. Meanwhile, he would tell you that the next day, one Luis al-Shrute, the lamplighter of O-Town, informed him that a child of the outer sea had signed onto a merchant ship named *Remarker* as the Captain's Clerk. There the story would end, as I and the escape of the loves of a man named Raphael was never something I was ever part of. It happened. I was close by, my role having never been discussed.

Now the beginning of my missive meets the end. Captain Javier al-Rasheed and I stood above the cockpit on the quarterdeck of the merchant liner *Remarker*, watching as the Port Master of Squalus Acanthia left the deck. The man was a polite soul, having come to apologize that the island was in turmoil due to the plan to burn all of their books in two weeks' time. With an apology accompanied by much genuflection, he said that we, as traders, were welcome to trade, that we would be held in the highest honor. However, we were not to criticize their God-Emperor-King Travail II, nor bring a book to the island. In fact, he said, only one book was to survive the burning, specifically the one written by the God-Emperor-King and his daughter Brunella, Princess-Queen of Acanthia Minor.

The captain watched the man go with a twinkle in his eyes. I could sense he wanted to speak, so as I had done before, I asked a question. "Why would one burn a book?"

Captain al-Rasheed replied, "Because it tells a lie, or it tells the truth. Always remember the Merchant's Code. If a person cares so little for something they discard it without thought, and burning a book I feel shows little care, then perhaps that merchant can buy the uncared-for object at a very reasonable price, later to sell what they have bought cheaply to great profit."

"Can you make money from a book?" I asked.

He smiled a deep smile again, seeming distracted for a second, then told me, "Mr. Lingongo, let me tell you that, as a person from, let's say, the Cape of Darts, you may think your story is boring or without value. However, to a person from the far north, say the Weather Islands, a body who grew up on the beaches of the far south, such as you, is an exotic thing. Take your story, write it, have it copied for others. Read it to them, then, after they listen, sell them a copy to keep for their own."

I looked at my captain, thinking that despite his quirks (he muttered a lot and argued with shadows, he could stand still without action, suddenly barking orders) that he was fair as well as tough. I decided right then that my life story would be written as well. Now I write it.

Chapter XIII

The Mysteries of Canus Cragia

Captain Javier al-Rasheed watched his breath roll from his mouth into the cold mountain-side air. His own birth-place could get cold. This land was extreme, as it could see snow in the depths of winter even by the seaside, and the steep, heavily forested glades above the capital city were nippy even on the verges of summer. It was a bit much, Javier thought. "Mr. Sandals," he said, at which a sailor appeared by his side.

"Captain, sir," Sandals said. He was a lithe man, part of the monkey crew that swarmed the masts, taking in and letting out the sails, keeping the rigs flying well.

"Do you understand your business, Mr. Sandals?" Javier asked.

"Chaten, Fleet, and Wuduck are to wait for a man who will trade books for silver. The books are to go to the ship for crating, the silver to go into the man's pockets only when the books are safe and away in the launch," Sandals replied, then asking, "May I speak, Captain?"

"You may," Javier replied.

Sandals took off his hat, revealing his tightly plaited and bangled corn rows. Many of the sailors, at least those with enough hair to ruck, were adopting the fashion. "The librarians are a harsh lot. I have no wish to get in the way of their union. They make the lamplighters look like a group of toads."

Chaten, a sailor apprentice, along with Pua Fleet and Wuduck, a pair of Marines, stopped making camp to listen. They had been collecting wood, cutting brush for concealment, and setting up a canvas shelter, all the tasks to make the camp comfortable. Now their attention was caught by the issue of the Librarians., As well it should, thought Javier. "You do not want to catch a librarian in a bar fight, do you lot?" Javier asked.

Collectively, there was a shiver among the crew. Javier could understand completely that there were guilds no one wanted to get afoul of. You could talk your way out of the bad graces of the Barristers, the Printers, the Surgeons, or the Butchers, but the Librarians had no sense of humor. They had long arms, not scared to show their power if wronged. "Apply some logic, my jacks, and fear not. The God-Emperor of this land is burning books each night. We are not acting as the Librarians, instead, we are acting as the Librarians would wish us to act. Buy the books while feeling safe in doing so. We will make a profit, at the same time saving some of the knowledge that keeps the lands of the Halo from barbarism."

"It is like the docks, boys and girls, the captain always has our backs. No need to fear the darkness in a Librarian's heart." Mr. Sandals said. "Captain, you do what you have to do, we will save the books."

Javier nodded. The crew had done all he asked of them, every time it was asked. The Steward had prepared him a leather pack on a wooden frame filled with camping gear, envelopes of cracker, flint and steel, three liters of water in gut bags, a copper hanging pot, fire stand irons, a canvas shelter half, and a lantern with paraffin oil. Everything he needed for a week away from the ship alone.

Mr. Sandals helped him into the pack, strapped a talwar and a short bow onto him, set a pair of knives at his wrist and shoulder, finally stringing a pair of new water bags on his belt and over the shoulder. "About thirty kilograms, sir, is that ok?" he asked.

"Thank you, Mr. Sandals, it is fine. Take care of the crew, remembering, no matter what, the books are not worth your life. They are worth everything short though," Javier said.

"Captain, you be on about it and worry not. The first and major are keeping *Remarker* safe, and the Marines are doing the loading with firelocks on their back. If this Overlord kicks up a fuss, he will find his fingers get burned," Mr. Sandals said.

Javier nodded, looked at his crew for a second, then turned into the woods.

The cold woods, all strange greens and browns, folded in around Javier as he hiked away from camp. He had miles to go, with only a vague idea of where to go. When his wife had set him on this mission, she had emphasized several points. One of them was to contact a great moderator, only five of which remained alive and living in the Halo. Of the five, only one was near their route, which is what drove them to this blighted island with its horrid rulers. The trade itself was not worth the hassle. Only a cargo load of banned books, taken on in the dead of night, would make the trip profitable in either a financial sense or as a social mission. Javier could have skipped a dozen better ports, and this port would have, according to his wife, paid for a quarter of the journey.

It was only an hour before Javier felt his muscles, unused to the rhythm of walking in a mountainous land, begin to burn. He had left the trackless woods for a trail of sorts that followed a brook, switching back and forth up the mountain. At first, he saw the constant weave of the trail as a useless contrivance, designed to make the path steady for horses, so he cut the corners of each switchback. That lasted only a short while. He soon realized that the switchbacks were not there for horses at all, but to allow people on foot with heavy packs to safely navigate the steep hillside.

Rain started to fall—cold, horrible, drizzly rain that fell past the leaves of the trees, soaking Javier's oilcloth, great cloak, as well as his clothing underneath. He started to stumble, making a new discovery. There was a reason old men used staves. He stopped, cut himself a sturdy piece of pole-wood, shaving off part of the bark, giving himself a strong purchase for his hands. So equipped, he found his going easier.

Yet as he climbed into the clouds, he made a whole new discovery. There was no way he could walk more than ten or fifteen switchbacks without stopping. He just could not keep his climb. It was like there was not enough air in the tall mountain. He could walk five kilometers an hour on level ground, discovering he would be lucky to make two in the higher mountains. No wonder some of the mountaineers had such huge legs and big lungs. They needed them to just get around.

If you dove deep enough in the water, it became difficult to hold on to breath, something Javier knew from personal experience. As he climbed the mountain, he reflected on the premise that perhaps the same was somehow true when climbing a great mountain. He observed the further you climbed into the clouds, the more labor it took to fill your lungs with air. There was science somewhere in there, science that could be explained with numbers and measures. It would take him a dozen lifetimes to make any headway in knowing how it all worked together.

Javier thought of his Clerk who wanted to tell of his homelands in a book. If Javier had his choice, he would write of his discoveries of weather, air, rain, temperature, and fire. It would be a book of nature, describing the science of things. Why did the barometer drop when the weather was turning foul? Could one reverse the barometer using some force of humankind, thus controlling the weather?

Eight hours in, his mind was numb, yet he was less than a dozen kilometers from the valley floor. He had started shivering uncontrollably in the past ten minutes, further, he was no longer able to see clearly. Finally, it was all too much. He collapsed into the mud and rocks.

He thought it was laughable. A rainy day and a short hike were causing him to fade, possibly even taking his life. He turned over, looking into the trees and the gray sky. He did not remember doing it, but the heavy pack and the walking stick he had been carrying were sitting in a runnel of water, barely in his vision. He must have dropped them.

"What is a trader doing on the mountain?" asked a deep, sultry voice. Javier tried to swing his head, unable to see the woman speaking to him. All he could see was mud, rocks, and the blurred universe as he shivered uncontrollably. Yet, as he felt his soul was fading, he caught a life hold in the sound of the woman. She had a deep, basso voice that spoke slowly, almost pedantically, yet with a definite warmth that someone had dragged him back into the living. He tried to answer, unable to as the shivering nearly broke his teeth.

"Do not try to answer, ship-trader. The shaking you are feeling is the next-to-last stage of weather consumption. If you do not get warm, you will stop shaking, feel much better, then die," the woman explained as she was rifling his pockets. She came out with the document folder, waterproof and untampered with, that Nazira had given him ages ago, before his journey across the sea as a tea merchant had commenced. He tried to grab them away from the woman. She batted his feeble hands away with a gentle, dismissive cuff.

"Your weapons stay with me until you leave us. These documents, along with the innocent items in your pack, will be waiting for you when you recover from weather consumption." She said this with no hint of it being a request, but rather the command of a person used to being obeyed.

"Liena, you and Amina take him into the cabin, so we can save his life," the woman said.

"Yes, ma'am," came a lilting response. Javier felt hands grab, then manhandle him into what must have been a cart, which was used to take him to a stacked stone hut set into the side of the mountain. The hut itself was boiling inside, being lit by both a fire and a series of oil lamps. Unable to resist, or even to see the who was giving him aid, his coat, uniform, boots, and other clothing were taken off without ceremony, then several bags of what must have been hot water were hung about his body. He was then placed in a stuffed armchair by the roaring fire, after first being wrapped in a large wool blanket.

A wisp of a young girl then brought in a gnarl-wood mug, filled with what turned out to be water and honey. She first looked at him, selected a second woolen blanket, wrapping it around the first, then handed him the mug.

"Can I have tea?" he asked.

The girl looked at him solemnly, her white hair and pale skin ghostlike in the orange glow of the cabin. "No," she said without emotion.

Another young woman entered the room, older than the other girl, not yet a woman. She was holding a tray with some sort of stew in a wooden bowl. "Forgive Liena, she is a clear-reader. While they do not have much in the way of empathy for strangers, she is nice as can be." The dark-haired girl handed the wooden bowl to him.

The bowl turned out to have a thick beet-and-onion stew in it, with carrots, salsify, and burdock cooked soft. He was provided a wooden spoon, discovering he was unable to hold it. The dark-haired girl gently took the mug and spoon from him, then fed him alternate servings from each until he was able to see to his own feeding.

"Liena did not say it, but tea can kill someone who is dying from weather consumption. I have seen it. Tricky, the consumption is. Someone has it, then they keel over. The mistress wants us to keep you from taking the last trip, so honey water and stew is what you get." The girl smiled as if everyone should know the process of freezing to death. She had a slightly bent nose, along with a way at looking the person they were talking to with an intense stare, almost the opposite of the girl called Liena, who showed little desire to make eye contact.

When he had eaten his stew and drank two mugs of honey water, Javier felt more able to express himself. "I am seeking the Moderator said to live in the mountains of Acanthia Minor. I must leave as soon as I am able." Javier explained.

The dark-haired girl said, "You almost died making it to the Canus Cragia, Mr. Stranger. Only the sheep herds go further into the weather this time of year. Instead, perhaps you can get busy not dying, so I can tell the Mistress my duty is fulfilled."

"My name is Captain Javier al-Rasheed. It is imperative that I see the Moderator. You have my deepest gratitude, however I must be going." Javier tried to stand, instead falling back down.

The deep voice he originally heard came from behind him, softly saying, "Captain, you cannot go further. Happily, you have arrived at the Moderator, for I am she."

Javier let himself slump back into the armchair he had been sitting in. He tried to respond, finding the words caught in his mouth, making him seem the imbecile in front of the woman who his wife had commanded him to see. "Then, thank you?" He was not sure he meant thanks, as his language skills seemed to have failed him.

"Your body is warming, but your blood still runs cold. No need to offer thanks you do not really mean, despite our timely intervention in your life story. My name is Irula, the Mistress of Canus Cragia. I suggest you rest the night, letting us defrost and mend your frozen clothing. Tomorrow, you can tell me why you would do such a foolish thing as take the pass in a storm just to see me." The woman was gray-haired, with strong legs and arms, her dark complexion making her look of the same family or hereditary sect as the older of the two girls who had worked to feed him. He tried to speak, the woman cutting him off, saying in an adamant tone, "No more discussion. Tomorrow, you can join me on the verge to tell me what you have to say." Before Javier could say more, she turned and left.

The pale girl watched as her mistress left, then said, while looking at the ground, "That stings a bit for you, Mr. Man."

Javier laughed mirthlessly. "She reminds me of my wife."

"Then you are a lucky person, trader. The Mistress is a great scholar." She opened a chest, then pulled bedding from it. "I am Liena, and I am an orphan."

"I am sorry," Javier said.

The girl spun, her hands filled with bedding, asking sharply, "Are you sorry that my name is Liena, that I am an orphan, or for some other thing?"

Before he could answer, the dark-haired girl said, "Liena, he was making a polite noise." She walked over, took the bedding, making a pallet by the fire. Liena watched the other work, who said, "My name is Amina, Mister. Liena, as I said is not rude, merely direct."

Javier nodded, pulling the blankets around him for greater warmth. "What do you do here?" He was indeed making polite conversation while he studied the room he was in. The main feature of the space was a fireplace, which was helping, albeit slowly, to drive the shivers from him. The fire was stoked and drawing well while making little smoke, nor casting any sparks past its hearth. The room was otherwise some sort of library, with leather-bound codex books lining each wall. The books were cleverly marked in silver filigree with their titles. They were also free of dust or rot. In fact, unlike most libraries where the decaying missives would take on a smell of dying animals and detritus, this room was free of almost all taint, as if it were religiously cleaned with a vinegar and lemon mixture, or some other cleaning product. The stone flags were well set into the floor, free of rushes or sand; the staff lamps were properly trimmed, with no hint of foul oil; and the furniture was either new or well cared for. Javier turned his attention back to Liena, telling her, "I am sorry. I missed what you said."

Liena nodded, "I said that I am an auditor. Does that mean anything to you?"

Javier shook his head. The warmth of the stone cabin and the effects of the food were having an amazing effect on his sense of reality. If he was in danger of dying earlier, his health was rapidly returning. "Should it?" Javier asked.

The girl shrugged, questioning, "You likely have never heard of Canus Cragia or the Moderators?"

Amina laughed as she worked on his pallet, "He is a trader. Why would he have heard of us?"

"Liena, you perhaps should wait for the mistress before you educate strange visitors from god knows where in the Halo," Amina said in a deadpan.

"My dear youngsters," Javier interjected. "I am not here to start a war. I am simply making 'polite noises.' I do have business with your mistress, and truly no wish to intrude on secrets and understandings that are not my own."

Liena waved him off in an imperious gesture. "She will see you tomorrow, or so she claims. She can be unreliable at tasks she does not want to see finished. In any case, an auditor checks facts written in history books. Certain individuals set silver aside for us to examine books written by the scholars, that are offered to us as the true past. These books are often filled with false assertions and outright lies. Auditors like me, we look for the truth... Moderators edit them, based on the Auditors' findings."

Amina added, "Liena is not telling you she is not a finished auditor. She is an apprentice."

"You be silent, Amina." Liena said, her voice raising an octave with a hint of anger.

"Why? It is the truth, Liena." Amina said. "Mister, should we always tell the truth?" Amina asked Javier.

Javier saw two young women, with intelligence, well-taught, hungry for intellectual discussions, therefore showing off for a rare stranger who had entered their cloistered world. He felt it was not his place to father, although he could offer advice. "The truth is important to understand. I recently learned a great deal of truth, truth that hurt me, which also could have hurt others. I had to learn the truth or face oblivion. However, consider the role truth plays in your own relations. Liena, am I to understand you are a clear-reader?"

"I am," she replied. She reached her hand into her straw-colored hair, playing with a stubborn curl of it. It was obviously her tell that she was nervous.

"Tell me what that means," Javier enjoined.

Liena had a fierce, uncomfortable look on her face. She balled her fist, then said, "It means I read, that from what I read, I can tell what the writer meant."

Javier adjusted his wrapping, trying to get smaller on the chair he was sitting in, so as to be more the girl's own size. "That is a powerful skill for one your age. Yet, there is a silent truth you are not saying. Tell me, what is that silent truth," he gently pried.

The girl hesitated, then said, "It is the stories, the things that are meaningful, yet not true. They do not affect me. When I listen to a skald or a skellie, yet even when in a room full of people that are crying or laughing while singing one, I cannot feel what they feel."

Amina gasped. Javier turned to her. "You are shocked she told me this secret, for I imagine it is a secret that the two of you keep under a sister's bond. Yet you have your own secret. You love the mistress, even as you dismiss her, even fear her. Love is strange when it lands on one who has a mission. I love a woman who has a mission. A powerful soul, much more powerful than I am, so we share the same silent truth. We love people who may love us back, but can never hold us the way we want to be held."

Amina gasped again. "If you displayed these tricks to a shepherd, they might throw you from the Casus Overlook."

Javier grinned. "Many would cheer. Yet all I said was the truth. Does this answer your questions?"

Both of the girls nodded, yet their faces were unsure. "I must be asleep. Thank you for preparing the room," Javier said pointedly, so the two girls left without more discussion.

Javier opened his eyes after a time, seeing that a small window, high in the room, was letting a wan light into the space. He had slept poorly, having nightmares all night that something terrible was happening to his wife and he could do nothing to stop it. He sat up to find his clothing folded at his feet. They were dry and warm, but not well pressed. Likely, they had simply been hung by a fire rather than being laundered.

"That is my fault." It was Liena, standing in the corner of the room. Javier did not have the chance to notice much detail the night before. Now, he saw the room was adjacent to the entrance, having one wall carved from granite. The hut apparently was an improved cave system.

"What is your fault?" Javier asked the girl.

"None of us knew how to properly press your uniform. It is wrinkled," she said.

He looked down at his blue, worsted-serge uniform jacket, seeing that indeed it was disreputable and shaggy from abuse. His undershirt was clean, but it also looked like it had spent time crumpled on a cabin floor. He did not appreciate having a yeoman care for his uniform until the service was absent. It would never do to appear in court looking like a legan vagabond. Here though, he could see how it was simply a humble wear. The girl herself was in a linen dress with woolen stockings like any schoolboy or schoolgirl in the Halo might wear. Next to her was a long dun soutane, a ridsy-hood, fisher's gloves, and amber brooks with strong cleats. Her clothing was likewise a bit wrinkled, although clearly well cared for and clean. Apparently, here there was no instruction for young people on the finer points of caring for their clothes; however, in consideration, Javier realized his own instruction had been lacking, such is the wont of a fisher family.

Amina entered the room with both a wool bassock and Javier's oilcloth in her hands. "How is the captain doing, Liena?" she queried. Amina was a bit older than Liena, maybe fifteen years, starting to fill out to maturity. It was too early to call her beautiful, as you would a woman. Despite being a petite child, she had wide, athletic hips, as well as wide shoulders, with athletic arms and legs. Her head carried a fountain of blue-black hair, her amber eyes ever searching.

"He seems willful. Amina," Liena observed.

"You are used to goatherds and shepherds. This is a sailor captain, dear. I am told they are different," Amina replied. She then turned to Javier. "Captain, I am to bring you to the Mistress. She is at the instrument shelter."

"I thank you, Amina. You may call me Javier," he replied.

She tossed him the warm clothing she was holding, saying in return, "I think Captain is enough."

The wool bassock was like a sweater that wrapped around your chest, being held in place by wooden toggles. It was thin enough to be worn under his oilcloth and serge jacket, as both were admittedly more about protecting from rain than keeping warm. Amina was wearing several layers of wool herself, having the same ridsy-hood, fisher's gloves, and amber brooks style cleats Liena had stacked next to her. The three of them dressed warmly in all of their woolens, borrowed or owned. When they left the shelter, Javier immediately knew it was a good choice. The rain had been replaced with bitter cold, clear skies. He could see a rime of frost on the morning ground, while not a cloud blurred the sky. "The clouds keep us warmer here, Captain. You should see us in the winter, a mug of water can be thrown into the air, freezing before it lands on the ground."

Javier was doubtful. Even if it was true, he did not want to find out. They walked into a small field, finding a shepherd with a flock of sheep. Amina asked her loudly, "Ready to head for the lower eighty, Mitchie?"

The shepherd, an older woman dressed in red homespun, cupped her hands, and responded in the same volume, "Coming up after turnover feast!"

"Lots of wool this season!" Amina noted. Turning to Javier, in a more normal voice, said, "Not that she will get a price from it, what with the God-Emperor running the port."

Javier speculated, "Things cannot be well for trade, given that the Sublime Port was given the shove-off."

Amina kept walking, sighing. "The Sublime Port was a problem itself. They chose old Commander Clack to be the cure. He then turned himself into God-Emperor-King, with his disgusting daughter, Brunella, as Princess-Queen. You know all about tyrants, I would assume, being from Cycus."

Javier shrugged. "I am on the bad side of the Dominar right now, however I would not call him a tyrant."

Amina laughed, "Then you do not really know the man."

"I have met him, in fact," Javier said, recalling that the last time was strapped to a gelding rack. "Have you?"

Amina stopped on the verge of the field to say, "I do not have to meet him to know the man. I know him through his acts, including his harm to me and mine."

Javier did not know what to say at her intensity, the way she stood still with her arms drawn in and legs spread, like she was a mountain. Liena scoffed, saying, "Amina, he is just a man of the Halo. You expect too much of him."

Javier bowed. "I am sorry to cause you pain, as I have my own reasons to hate the Dominar of Cycus, but mission supersedes hate. I have been tasked to meet your Mistress."

Amina turned. saying loudly, "Mistress and mother, you can have them both."

Indeed, as they broke out of the verge to a cliffside where a wood structure stood, he could see that the woman who called herself Irula, the Mistress of Canus Cragia, Moderator of Acanthia Minor, looked very much like her self-professed daughter. She also looked a bit like his wife, only around six-ty-years old, her blue-black mane of hair shot through with iron gray. She was hale, athletic looking, wearing immacu-late sheep's wool clothing or serge with a weft halt weave.

Next to her was something even more amazing, so amazing it took Javier's breath from his chest. In a wooden cradle was an immense structure of beaten copper, faced with silver leaf, catching the light like a fireball. The device was able to be finely directed like a master sextant, with a half-dozen wheels corresponding to different input calcu-lations, moving the coarse and fine controls of a toothed pan-tilt. "Is this a helioscope?" Javier asked incredulously.

Irula turned at his voice, looking first at Javier, then at the scope. "Many years ago, a king in a foreign land com-peted for my hand in marriage. This was the gift he gave my father. My father studied the skies. This was intended to allow him to communicate with the heavens. It is more useful for contacting ships at sea, not that we do much of that with it," she replied.

"How does it work?" Javier asked, enthralled.

"It has two functions. It allows you to look at a star, or even the sun indirectly, by gathering and filtering or reinforcing the light. Alternatively, on clear days with good sun, it can be used to signal to ships at sea a kilometer away." Irula looked at her pouting daughter, instructing her, "Amina, you make tea. I already have a wax burner going in the shed."

"Should you be left alone with this man?" Amina asked.

Irula replied, "We shall see." Amina seemed not to like this answer as she turned to make the tea in the shed.

Turning back to the helioscope, Irula continued, "There are six wheels, each with sixty teeth, three for vertical training and three for horizontal training. The first pair trains the date, the second pair trains the time of day, the third pair trains the target. There are tables in the shed that allow you to locate objects in the sky or on the sea. When used to signal, the device catches the sun, which allows you to send light messages. When used to read, the device can be set to gather or filter light." Her voice sounded bored.

"It is amazing, Mistress. Absolutely amazing!" Javier exclaimed.

"It was bought at too high a price," Irula cryptically replied. She turned and looked out into the sea. "I see your ship in the harbor. You cannot find business with the current God-Emperor to be all that useful or profitable."

"It won't be," Javier admitted.

"Then why are you here?" Irula sternly asked. "Why risk your life to climb into these mountains in the middle of a cold blow? If you had not been found wallowing in the mud, you would be dead. You can freeze to death when the water falling from the sky is not yet frozen!"

Javier bowed, as it was all he could do. "My wife, Nazira, gave me a message to bring to you."

Irula turned to him, shocked. "Tell me the truth, merchant, and tell me now. You are married to Nazira, the Princess of Cycus?"

"She has sent you a message," Javier replied. From inside of his pocket he pulled the leather, waterproof packet that Nazira had given him almost eight months before, which had been returned to him. Irula walked up, took the envelope, opened it, revealing several more envelopes along with a long hand-written missive. Her eyes became soft as she read the papers, looking over the small envelopes as she finished a portion of the message. She looked up at Javier, asking quietly, "You are al-Rasheed?"

"I am," he answered.

"You are husband to Nazira, daughter of the Dominar of Cycus, the Princess?" she asked again.

Javier was suddenly afraid, as the woman's eyes had gone cold as the day, and dark as night. "I am her husband, yes, though the marriage is not recognized by the Dominar."

"I suspect not. Do you believe what is written in this missive?" she asked.

Javier shrugged his shoulders. "I do not know. I have not read it."

"People make pilgrimages to Canus Cragia looking for gnosis. Do you know what that is?" Irula asked.

Javier looked at his feet. "I do not, Mistress."

The woman swept her hands across the horizon. "It is nonsense,

The woman swept her hands across the horizon. "It is nonsense, the idea that there is secret knowledge that can be tapped for personal benefit. The concept that the Moderators know secrets so can thus predict the future. Down in the city below us, that fool of a God-Emperor is murdering people and burning books because he fears this gnosis. Yet he also fears to reach his hand out and pluck me from my mountain, scared that I may indeed have some secret hold on the future through my understanding of the past. It is all nonsense."

Javier felt the weight of the world pressing on his mind in the presence of the Moderator's intensity, even if he did not clearly understand her meaning. "Guide me, Mistress," he said.

"The streets burn. Fools ask me what I see. They come to me with their hands cut off or their eyes plucked out, asking me, 'What secrets does the Mistress know, guide me.' They do not come to study, only to take a spin of the wheel, hoping the huckster hands them a prize of silver." The Moderator hugged herself, seeming to shiver with vision. "I will guide you, Captain Javier al-Rasheed, who has married Nazira of the Cycus Dominion. Listen to me closely. There is an island you fear, one that you do not remember, but which remembers you. Return to where you broke. Find the puppet master in her lair of skulls. Tell her that Irula of Canus Cragia demands her to act. Tell her that her debts will never be forgotten, but will be paid."

Javier said, "I do not understand, Mistress."

"Debts, tea merchant," Irula said, her eyes tearing. "The daughter lost to the hands of the giant. The broken children deeded rest. The flames in the streets taken into the heart, held there for twenty-years." She grabbed his shoulders, then shook him. "You will take Amina with you. I will bind her to duty. As you face the 'Lady of the Lost Children,' have Amina stand to the side of Nazira. I name you, the broken waif who lost his mind. I call you collector of the damned. I grant you the title of father to the ship of misfits, and I tell you do your duty. Do what I could not."

Javier stood like he had been struck by a wave of a ten thousand liters dropped from the sky, knowing he was supposed to understand the words, but finding a wall in his mind that he could not cross, that resisted all attempts to climb. Irula turned from him, shouting, "Amina!"

Amina appeared, carrying three cups of tea. Javier could see that she had merely sketched a look of calm on her face; the girl was clearly frightened. "Mother?" she asked timidly.

"Be silent. We talked of the break in time, did we not?" Irula asked forcefully.

"I want to stay in Canus Cragia, Mother," was her reply.

Irula nodded, responding in a gentler tone, "I know, daughter. Yet, you are the butterfly, and you cannot stay." Javier turned as Irula embraced her daughter. "I told you, Amina, that the God-Emperor of our tiny land becomes bold, that other lands grow unsure and blind. You were never intended to perch in my hiding nest, instead to spread your wings, seeking the sky. Do you understand, daughter?"

Amina started to cry. "We can fight. The mountaineers would fight."

"Daughter, they will fight. However, there is another fight in a land you know only from my stories. I was taken there against my will, in the silence of my youth. I left something there that only rivals you in value to me. Perhaps, years from now, you will return to Canus Cragia finding me still Mistress, our tears long dried. Right now, all of my art says that this time cannot be hidden from. You know this. You and I have spoken of it." Irula looked at the copper heliograph for a second.

"It is amazing, Captain, in many ways," she said to Javier. "What is, Mistress?" Javier asked.

"This was the wage for my destruction, yet never once have the heavens called god-fire down upon it. From the verge here, I have seen god-fire ravage the conceited, tearing down their towers and burning their toys, yet never once did it burn this thing. How I wished it would." She pondered the device with its obscene amount of metal and its intricate gears. Without looking back at Amina, she told her, "You will take Liena with you, protecting her, remembering that she has the touched. Protect her without shadowing her, you know what I mean."

Amina replied, "I do, Mother."

"Captain, do you remember your task, the response that I set you on?" Irula asked.

Javier responded truthfully, while quashing his confusion, "I do."

"There is one more thing before you go. Know that you are a father of a son," Irula said.

CHAPTER XIV

Misfits

Javier al-Rasheed tossed his oars, then leapt from the cockle as it crashed into the soft sand of the shore. Amina sat in the boat until it lodged on the beach, then stepped into the sand. There was a minute of vertigo as he looked at the black sand and bent trees of their landing place. It was like a bad dream was haunting him. He kept feeling a sense of otherness, a queer thought that his brain was an island, and there was a storm brewing somewhere in the darkness of the world's seas, casting forth great waves that crashed into the beach of his thoughts, carrying away the sands of his soul. Liena, although fair, appeared dark, silent, a shadow that was cast over him. He did not understand her, nor why she was here.

"My mother sent us here?" Amina asked, walking up onto the dark beach, looking into the deep, black forest.

Javier did not respond. His task had been burning him since it was given. He walked up to stand next to Amina, then turned to look out to the sea, the sound of the breakers creating a rich synoptic fandango of sound with glows of light. "My father died off this island when I was very small," Javier mused.

Amina sniffed. She had never said a good word about her mother, having nothing but silence on her father.

A noise from the forest startled them. A woman in a white robe walked out to the beach, making a clicking sound with her tongue. A second woman held her arm. "It was said a child of the silence had returned," the second woman said as the pair stopped.

Javier looked at Amina, then said, "We have never been to this island."

"Not accurate," the woman said. "At least not accurate for you, Captain Javier al-Rasheed. I do not know this second person who stands by your side."

Javier noticed the women's eyes. One had milky white orbs with no iris, the other simply had no eyes; they had been ripped from her head sometime in the past. "You are both blind?" Javier asked in horror.

"Not accurate again," the second woman with the ripped-out eyes said. "Clicker cannot see or speak. I cannot see. Neither of us is blind," she replied.

Javier was thrown back mentally. "I understand."

"You do not. It is polite to say you do. Clicker knows more about you from her own ways than you know yourself. She can stand in the dark forest, seeing a chinook hanging in a tree. She can tell if the tide is ebbing or swelling. She knows if ice on a lake can hold a human as easily as she can tell the mood of a human hiding behind a tree. Is that, I ask, blindness?" The woman seemed proud of her companion.

Amina laughed, "What of you, eyeless one?"

"I am Deziree. I can understand and speak with Clicker. That is my power that makes me 'unblind.' Yet, I name Javier of the Rasheeds, I do not name you. You are a sound not heard on the Island of Silence. You are whom?" Her tone was commanding, like a schoolteacher, speaking in clipped, rapid chirps of language.

"You may call me Amina aibna Irula. I am an auditor for the Moderator of Canus Cragia, woman," she responded, putting all of her teenage pride into her self-name.

The one named Deziree gasped. In a lower voice she said, "Follow me and Clicker." Javier immediately obeyed, not looking to see if Amina followed. He could feel a cold shiver as he left the beach as the forest enfolded them, although it was not from the loneliness that he felt the claws of time rend into his soul. It was the presence of others. As he followed the pair of women with their snapping tongue clicks, he began to see the woods come alive with creatures stepping forth from the dusky glades. They were scarred, horrible things, with cropped ears, bulging muscles, crossed eyes. Some had burning painful tattoos, horrid body piercings, and/or cavernous and poorly healed wounds. Amina closed in with him, grabbing his hands. "Captain, who are these things?"

Javier closed his eyes, hearing the soft murmur of voices, the footfall of tiny noises, and the scuffle as clothing passed through brush. He thought he could tell what they were. "They are the silent, the lost."

"They named you. How do they know you?" Amina asked, fear in her voice.

Javier grasped her hand tightly, gently saying, "Amina, they named you as well."

"They did no such thing," she replied.

Javier groaned softly as a pain shot through his heart. "They did, just not so you could hear it."

"How did they name me?" she asked in a spooked, hushed voice.

"They reflected your name back to you. Amina aibna Irula, could you not hear the screams when you said that?" he questioned.

"No one screamed," she answered.

"My girl, that is the loudest type of scream, one that cannot be heard," Javier said as they entered a clearing with a great fire burning in the middle.

Hundreds of people in rough jute loom cloaks, with branches and vines woven through them, were around the fire. An uncomfortable man Javier knew stood next to an impossibly tall woman who he did not. The man, Regnal Bish al-Beijus, a courtier of the Dominar, stepped forward. "You did as your mistress bid?" He was unarmed, except for a kirpan, and wore a particolor swallowtail coat in drab shades of brown and gray.

Javier dropped Amina's hand, saying, "I did."

Bish was an assassin of the great order, yet here in this clearing he looked like a child in a grammar gymnasium. "You did. Now you must explain it to the Mistress Silence."

Javier noted that Bish was not alone. A very small woman and a huge man stood behind him, each holding a wicked ken-jee loosely at their sides. However, it was not the two islanders that Bish referred to. It was a silent woman who sat on a cut log; plain, dowdy, dressed in sackcloth, surrounded by sinister faces fixed with growling open mouths whispering putter-putters of angry discussion over the arrival of Amina and Javier. It was a test; if could he tell their leader and liege hidden in the midst of the horrid flesh.

Yet he knew her, which disturbed him. As he approached, the crowd broke open like a jar of flour dropped on a flagstone floor, sudden and violent, pushing and shoving against him. As he approached, she slowly turned her face to him, until she was almost, but not quite, meeting his gaze.

"I knew my Devious-child would recognize me," she said. It was like a serpent ball shot into his heart, a comment that made no sense, yet crashed home with a final surety of truth.

"Mistress Silence," Javier said, solemnly.

Amina broke through the shards of the crowd, taken aback that instead of pushing and shoving her as they did Javier, they melted away without contact, leaving her protected from their touch as if she was armored by a blanket of clinging oil. "You know this woman?" she asked, grabbing his shoulder.

The touch almost woke him from the dream. Before he could fully wake, four men wrenched him away from her. Harshly they spun him, forced him onto his knees, then one drew a glowing silverback sword, putting the weapon on his neck. It bit Javier's skin, drawing blood with only the slightest touch. A sneeze would decapitate him. Mistress Silence stood, then walked to Javier. "The brave captain knows me from when he was neither brave nor a captain." She placed her hand on Javier's face, a gentle, almost loving act, then turned to Amina. "Memory is a strange thing, Lady Amina aibna Irula aihtilal-mudaqiq hisabat min-jabal Canus Cragia. He has lived, yet has no memory. I have lived, having memory of you, even though I have never met you. You have lived, yet have no memory at all. The captain ... his memory was a mirror shattered in the surf. My memory is that of a dream contemplated on waking. Your memory is considering a dark and dangerous shore which you have not visited before."

"Riddles and nonsense," Amina said. "My mother tasked us to come here, vouchsafing this merchant with her protection and employment to see a person saved, and a Dominion righted. You are the tools she placed in our hands. Further, she declared you were oath-sworn to her service. Speak straight."

"Little girl demands I speak straight with a sword to this man's neck? Spend his coin, prove your mastery!" the woman exclaimed. She stood, which allowed her long, straight gray hair to fall to her sides. A horrible, bent man handed her a cane, which she used it to unfold herself to her full height, at least 190, towering over Amina's head by 30 centimeters or more.

Amina threw back her shoulders, saying, "His is not my coin to spend." A second later, she added, "He is the husband of my half-sister. Guild..."

"Now I have more to work with," the woman interrupted. She turned to Javier, then said, "Open up the vault hero, my warrior child, and remember." She turned her back on Amina, adding, "Do the math if that works better for you. It always was math with you."

Amina watched amazed as Javier al-Rasheed transformed before her eyes. Nothing physical changed about him; however, the manner in which he stood, his affect, his facial features, even how he held his hands and turned his head indicated the spirit of the dashing, kindly, dedicated, captain was no longer present, having somehow been replaced by something else.

"You remember?" Mistress Silence asked, pulling a fagot from the fire, holding it in 'Javier's' face as he rose from his crouch.

"I am of two minds, Mistress," said the spirit who had taken Javier's body.

Mistress Silence smirked. "That much has always been true. Are you husband to the Princess Nazira?"

The man pushed away the blade at his neck with a shrug, replying, "I, Devious, am not. It is Captain Javier al-Rasheed who wedded the child of the Dominar, your enemy sworn. His wife is also the daughter of your savior, the Moderator Irula, whom you knew when she was a scared child. This minor child at my side is her second child, Amina. Javier is yet unaware of what else Irula prepared, the ghost who followed us through the woods." He stopped, shouting into the crowded night, "Apparat Liena, whom I name Lost One."

Mistress Silence sketched a look of anger on her face until she saw the white glow of a young girl walking through the edges of the glade. As one, it seemed, the crowd of the damned turned, seeing her as well, and the murmurs silenced. Devious said, "Mistress Silence, your daughter."

Mistress Silence shed her dignity, running for the girl. There was no suspicion in her mind. This was indeed her own child returned.

Amina grabbed Devious, who apparently was, in another guise, Javier al-Rasheed, asking, "What witchyness is this?"

Devious turned to her, then in a confidential voice said, "There are some who say great beings write our stories out, making us move like puppets at their whims, but the truth is never so simple. The gods, in fact, hide truth from us ... conceal the story. Only around campfires does a tale ever flow neatly, with all of its details laid out in logical order for the listener to inspect. Imagine a nervous Dominar, on the throne new, with a young son to protect while the nobles of the land are looking to relieve him of his heir. He takes captives from the greater families, as well as the yeoman of the fish and field. They are consigned to an island, into the hands of a madman, a person the Dominar trusted, a person of the day, who turned into a terrible creature, doing horrible things to his charges."

"Then the Dominar finds a wife for his son, a woman from a far island, and they marry. They have a child, your sister Nazira, and as the laws say, that child is the designated heir. When the old Dominar dies, the new Dominar replaces him, which is when his wife finds out about the horrible secret of his father, this, the Island of Silence. The children of the high-born were not merely detained and deported, they were sent here and damaged beyond repair. Irula demanded that the master of the island be deposed, that conditions made better for the inhabitants." He motioned at Mistress Silence cuddling her lost child. "Where a child could be saved, they were rescued."

"My mother must have demanded that," Amina said. "Yet, how do you know this?"

"A second story? How tiring, little girl." He stood silent for a few moments, then the force of silence caused him to talk again. "Not myself. It was Javier with his father when their boat sank. Javier washed up on this island, living here until he was ten, during the last years of the torture, right before Irula briefly stopped at the island and saved them from the horrors. Your step-sister is an example of what that torture did. It made the children break, then lose themselves. The old Dominar was killed by one of the children, which was how the current Dominar reached the throne," Devious explained.

"But why the horror?" Amina asked.

"I do not know. Javier may. The Mistress Silence almost certainly does, as does your mother," Devious replied.

"It was sadism, nothing more, and it created a special group of children, who now are adults." Mistress Silence interjected. "Devious, give me the request from Irula," she commanded.

"I was never told, only Javier, who is not speaking to me. I fear his return here has caused him to be lost," Devious stated in a grim tone.

"Nonsense," Mistress Silence said. "He was the first. You, Devious, are just a shadow of the real man."

"Oh Mistress, there is no precedence to consider. I am stronger. Returning to the Islands was more than Javier, with his tea trading, his history books, and his petty games could handle. There are some scars that should never be removed. They protect the body from oblivion." Devious shrugged like it was no worry of his if Javier never returned from the dark.

Amina slapped Devious, who stumbled back under the assault, then repaired his dignity. "I assure you, Amina, daughter of Irula, that you cannot lay hands on me to get Javier back. We lived, two as one, under a compact, knowing that someday the balance had to break one way or the other. Mistress Silence, the secrets Javier al-Rasheed carried with him, to you are dead. If the letter does not have them, then I cannot produce them for you."

"Yes, you can," came a little voice next to him. It was the slight girl. Liena, named Lost One.

"What is this?" Devious questioned.

Liena walked up to Devious, who seemed lost as the attention of hundreds of souls turned their apparitions to face him. The girl was serious, unable to tell witticism from truth, lacking in soft curves, instead turned into a being of sharp edges from horrors that even her young mind could never remember, or even describe. She reached her hand out and grasped Devious, who tried to resist but found he was unable to. "Let go of me, girl!" he commanded. She ignored him.

Suddenly Javier was there, a shadow on the ground, unseen by any except Liena and Devious. The shadow broke loose, then welled up into a form that looked like a doughy cookie made to appear vaguely like the captain. He keened loudly, a sound heard only by two, saying, "The streets are dark."

"Tell me," Liena said, forcing Devious into silence.

"The master said it would not be this way. He said the light from the stores would guide me, but he lied," the shadow said, sounding like a young boy. "I know you Liena, *Remarker.*"

"Think back, Javier. I was very young," Liena replied.

"Yes. Not yet real. A decade before you would form," Javier said in a wail of pain. "The dark woman would take you from your mother, who was dying like we all were."

"What about the street?" Liena asked.

"I do not want to go back there," he said in a frightened voice. Liena let Devious go, frozen in place, gathering up the Soul of Javier al-Rasheed. "One more task, brave child," she said. Suddenly, she was older, much older. Her child form was an illusion, a piece of dwimmer held in check by the great evils of the island where children were turned into beasts for the entertainment of a man now long dead. "Forget what you did. Remember what you were told to do."

"I believe I am close to rest. Let me fall into dreamness," he said, in both spirit and body, while Devious was pushed back into the darkness.

What Amina saw was a flash. Liena had grabbed the hand of Devious, then Devious had keened, his voice slowly being replaced by the more mellow sounds of Javier al-Rasheed. The captain collapsed, yelling, "Dreamness!" Then he turned to the Mistress of Silence to say, "Put Nazira on the throne and save her child from the grip of the man whose father tortured the inhabitants of this island for so many years. That is all the repayment that she demands for the guild you own."

Mistress Silence swept forward, taking the captain's head in her hands, his face having gone taut and clammy. His eyes stared into the heavens, while his mouth slacked as the animus of his spirt faded into the ether, no longer held in check by the dwimmer of Liena.

"What has happened, Mistress?" Amina asked.

Mistress Silence looked at Liena, then into the faces of her closest followers. Clicker did not click, instead she bowed her head, as did the rest of those in the clearing. It was as it happened, sometimes one of them would find the task of living too hard, finally laying down after pronouncing their requiem. It was all they could do from then on. They called it "dreamness," while it was actually death in a few days as the body did not do anything to support it.

"Princess Amina, you are now the second daughter of the Dominar, and Liena, you are the third. There is secession and continuity, if not yet the strength to vouchsafe you the dream of Nazira." She stood, taking Liena's hand. "Liena, my dear, you are the daughter I had with the brother of the Dominar. The lines have returned to the island. All who could oppose the Dominar are now in one place and must not be separated."

"This is all logic, my newly found mother." Liena hesitated, then said, "My face is heavy."

Amina said, crying, "It is the weight of the world, as well as the sadness for the dead and those who will soon be dying, that pulls at your heart."

Mistress Silence said, "Quite." Then she motioned to Bish to approach and sit at her knee. "I know what the Princess asks, and I agree that the people you have chosen are to a needle point, the ones who young Nazira needs. Bish, I want you, Kylde, and Reggira to go to the Dominar's chambers, joining the side of the Princess. This relieves you of your second vow. Go now! Protect the Princess!" The three nodded, running into the glades like hunting cats, which was in some ways that is what they were.

"Amina. The people of the hidden island, the Island of Silence, vowed to live our lives out and away from the world, to protect the people we love from what we had become. You and Liena are of us, so we ask that tonight as we explode forth, you take your places by our sides." Mistress Silence looked at Amina, so adult, yet still a child in a strange land.

Amina responded, "People ruin beautiful things," as she looked at Javier.

Mistress Silence replied, "Yet we live a true love story." She kneeled by the comatose al-Rasheed, whose mind was currently unable to handle the revelation of the tragedy that hid inside of his broken spirit, which was now sailing into the sunset to the greater life. "We will protect him while he prepares for the journey to the land where only dreams fall from the sky."

She turned to Delindest, the old healer who tended them each through their journey. "He has a wife and a child. Keep him with us until they can chant the ritual of life to him. We owe our brother for his painful crossing, as we owe those he fought to save, a minute by his side before the twilight reaches for him."

Delindest lowered his spectacles, scratching the metal plate that had long ago replaced part of his skull. "It will be done Mistress."

The Mistress then levered herself back up to her full height and said, "Life is precious, do not take it when it can be spared. Pray to the leaving star, because the dice will be cast and tallied before we see it return."

CHAPTER XV

The Puppeteer of Cycus

Standish climbed the stairs of the to the Queen's room on its very pinnacle. Nazira was sitting alone on a settee admiring the port view out her southern window. She had a wistful look on her face, a letter of scap along with a leather envelope in her hand. She turned, saw her old friend, smiled, rising from the chair while putting the papers in her bodice. Oban-Bey, the old eunuch that has raised Nazira and Standish to adulthood, stood in the corner of the presence chamber, rummaging through a chest that lay open, filled with books. He affected not to see the muscular sandy-haired warrior, instead moving a candle set over for him to see his work more clearly.

Instead of words, they fell together in passionate kissing, giving physical practice to their long affair, an affair that had lasted since they were bashful teenagers attending the noble's "normal" school at Baelsh. There was no law against their love, nor its expression save one. Nazira, the Princess, must have children with a man that was designated the prince. Standish was forbidden her as she was forbidden Standish by the simple fact that Standish could not father a child of the line of the Dominars' of Cycus.

The veranda, 60 meters above the port, allowed one to see the Navy docks where *Remarker* was allowed to make fast. They both could see the crew of the trader unloading the treasures and chests of silver onto the docks, under the guard of soldiers of the Dominar. Standish saw that her own Marines were lending a hand in the work, worried for them, lest this be a night of blood.

She turned back, saying in close confidence, "My first question, of course," Standish asked, "is for the safety of the child."

Nazira beamed with an inner fire that Standish always loved, the fire of pride. "My father passed a decree naming him Jamil al-Youseffi d'Tariq, the Prince of Telemark. I had no say in the matter, of course, but it shows the child will not be exposed."

"What of the matter of Javier?" Standish asked, putting her hand on Nazira's shoulder.

Nazira reached up to hold hands with Standish. "Is this a question of us, or of the Dominar?" She then pushed herself away from the major.

"Is there a way to separate these questions?" Standish asked.

Nazira replied, "Of course, not in our hearts, but in practice. We said this a year and more ago. We cannot be together, no matter how much we want. It is for my life I fight now."

"My dearest Nazira, nothing of what you say means a thing about your heart, your happiness," Standish said pointedly. "There is a ship out there, a whole world. My Marines could take young Jamil and be done with this place.

The Dominar's soldiers are flat-footed and fat. My Marines are mean and deadly."

Nazira shook her head. "It cannot be so, my love."

"Javier is missing. He fled the ship when the navy took us in tow. If they catch him, he will not survive the night. They will likely take me as well. The Dominar cannot be over my betrayal." Standish said with a pressing voice.

"This is where, Standish, I cannot understand you. Do you know I actually love Javier? He dedicated himself to me when I needed someone to do exactly that. He risked his life, gave up his foolish ways, took on a task that may yet see me free of my father, although he cannot know it's full import. You always talk about your duty and your need to follow your calling, yet you forget there is a calling for me, one that I have prepared all my life for, which is Dominar. This last year I have seen clearly that my father is not just a silly man who fears time. There is an evil in his ways, he is actively destroying the Dominion. My Dominion!" she cried.

Standish stepped away. "Does this mean you have come to your father's way of thinking about grabbing the throne and holding it?"

Nazira reached out her hand, holding it forth until Standish took it. She said, "I have always been of my father's way of thinking, in some aspects. Cycus needs a strong leader to face the future. Did you know Javier visited a Moderator?"

"Why would he see a Moderator? When did he have time?" Standish questioned, taken aback.

"Oh he has foolish hobbies, all men do, but in the hobby, there is an element of deception. It was at my instructions he went. The Moderator he saw is my mother. I have been told he was returned with my sister to the Island of Silence," Nazira said with great passion. "Javier did not flee. He went with my sister to the Island to recruit the denizens. The ones who owe my mother that their crooked lives were spared."

"That is madness!" Standish cried. "The denizens of that island are cursed!"

"Not cursed," came a quiet entreaty from Oban Bey, who was met with a wave of the hand by Nazira.

Standish stood, tears absurdly in her eyes. *The great warrior cries*, Nazira thought, making her sad. She turned to her work desk, removing a clutch of scap sewn into a book. From her bodice, she took the letter that had been sent to her, placed it into the book with the only other communication she had ever received from her mother. "Will you follow me Standish, see me through this night of nights?"

"I will," Standish said.

Nazira flipped through the book. If the wrong eyes saw what was written inside, understood the nature of the communications contained between the soft leather covers, her father would execute her on a spike before a howling crowd. She took a small sliver of scap from the book, presenting it to Standish.

"This is what I am to do?" the marine asked.

She stepped forward, speaking quietly to Standish, her head bent to Standish's ear. "Your Marines are to finish the unloading, then take to the streets. Tell each the word is 'madrigal.' A person who uses that word is assured to be a friend. If they hear it, they are to say 'dolor' in return. The list is of two groups. One which is told the word. The other shall not be able to respond to any words ever again. Do you understand?"

"I will do it, my Princess. I will do as you ask," Standish said, her hands on her heart.

"I know you will. Now be off," Nazira replied. She watched as Standish left, then said softly, "Oban."

"Güzel çiçek speaks and I hear," he said in the strange tongue he spoke.

"Bring in Bish and his assistants," she requested.

Oban put down his work and nodded. He left from the same exit Standish did, then returned a few minutes later. Bish was not alone, but was, as expected, followed by a huge man and a very small woman. "Princess, you are ready?" Bish asked.

"Are these two to be trusted?" she asked.

Bish al-Beijus was an odd man, with eyes that did not track right, bearing an expression of being lost; however, this was not even remotely true. He was one of the smartest people Nazira had ever met, for five-years had been a closely held confident and unpaid agent. "They are the Dominar's things," Bish said. "They have met with al-Rasheed." With this, Oban stiffened. Oban was of the Island, not immediately recognizing the people with Bish, which made him uncomfortable.

"Oban, do not fear," Nazira said gently.

"Princess, the future is darkness. The Island is cracking open, the people of chains flow out," Oban said.

Nazira looked at Bish, her eyes flaring. "Why would Oban fear this night?"

Bish stepped forward, looking down at the floor with his eyes. He was never able to make eye contact with people he was speaking to. Nazira knew that if the man appeared to be looking at you, he was actually gazing elsewhere. It was a strange disability that did not seem to hurt the man one bit, except to make others who dealt with him uncomfortable. "Oban is quoting the Prophecy. The island has broken open, so all the toys of the Dominar are rushing to the aid of the daughter of the blessed one. She foretold it before my Princess was born. Now it has happened."

Oban nodded, saying, "The changed are loose. The cork will not go back in the bottle."

Nazira nodded her assent in return. "Indeed, it will not."

"Yes, Princess," Bish agreed. "Al-Rasheed delivered a letter from your mother and your younger sister, begging on his knees, knife to his throat, for the misfits and the forsaken to aid in your cause. He would have been killed, that he was known saved him. Did you understand who he was when you married him?"

Oban gasped. "It is not possible. I know the look. I see Bish as one of my brethren, though he is not truly of the island. These two, this woman and this man who stand silent here, blood dripping from their souls, are two of the most hard of the island's hidden folk. Javier al-Rasheed?"

Nazira replied, "Is one of you." She turned back to Bish. "Where is my husband now?"

"He was taken by the dreamness. He breathes, nothing else," Bish replied, falling to his knees, followed by the silent man and woman who had come in with him.

Nazira grew worried. "What is this 'dreamness?'"

Oban reached out for his mistress's hands. "Your Grandfather saw the island as a place to make his followers fanatics, able to carry his will to the Halo, and make him a great king. The orphans who lost their parents, the stolen children, the hidden ones, and the waifs of the surf, they were taken there and ... horrible things were done to them."

"I know this, tell me of Javier!" Nazira snapped.

Oban bowed, then rose again. "I am making this effort. It is hard to speak as I speak of myself as well. Sometimes, what was done to make us ... special ... it shatters a person. You can see the other children break, like a glass of crystal dropped from the castle wall. Then they may glue themselves together, never whole, always a construct rather than a natural thing. A very special construct, with very special powers. Their memory can also be altered. Sometimes, they form personalities that compete with each other. No one knows why. Javier returned to the place where he was shattered, and it was too much. He left us for dreamness when he understood his mission was completed."

"Again, what is 'dreamness?'" Nazira asked sharply. She began to dress in her black leathers, then plait her dark, black hair.

Oban said, "It is sleep, sometimes waking, sometimes with closed eyes, but a deep and endless sleep. Dreamness is a sleep that lasts until…"

Nazira stepped up to him, grabbing his shoulders. "Until what, old friend?"

"Death. They waste away and die without food and drink. It is to die in a dream that is a better world than the one we live in." Oban said sadly.

Nazira looked at Bish. "These both, they are who I asked for?"

"They volunteered after Captain al-Rasheed succumbed. They are as close as we can find to your body servants, but they are … much more dangerous." Bish replied. "They are changed, but loyal to the daughter of their savior, who also married one of the lost. You mean a great deal to the changed of the Hidden Island."

Nazira motioned them over to her. "Do you each accept me?" she asked the two 'changed.' "I cannot guarantee any of us see the night through."

The two nodded. Neither said a word.

"They are not speakers, my Princess," Bish said. "They understand you though. Do you wish them to write their assent?"

"No need," she said, then thought of something. She pointed to each, then awkwardly signed, "Accept-service-question, take-money-and flee-if-not-statement." It was the best she could do, but she preferred to see their response from her own hand.

The large man had long hair and sad eyes. He turned to his petite companion. They then apparently communicated through shrugs and nods. Then the small woman tapped her face. It meant, "To serve." Then she rubbed her thumb in her hand, following it with a circular motion. "No money," it meant.

Bish said, "There are many changed here, changed whose lives have been stolen. They see you as a hope for them."

Oban looked worried, stating, "On the wings of kindness, love flows. On the wind of power, only hate."

Nazira laughed. That Oban could recite the Heshuan like he had memorized every passage was just a new bit of knowledge in the massive tidewater of information she was learning tonight. "What are they called?" she asked Bish

"Kylde and Reggira," Bish replied.

Nazira bowed deeply to the two, then signed, "You hold success in your hearts. Dress as my servants. Also, prepare for our summons by the Dominar, my father." They nodded, retreating to the side room.

When they had left, Nazira asked, "What did you observe about Standish as she left?"

"Princess, she was, and has been, closely followed by a man of the Dominar. She seemed determined though. I am afraid the messages you sent with her may be intercepted, with her being jailed."

"No, she will get through. If they think they can take her down, they will find that she has the heart of a jaguar, and more than one tail at that."

"As you say, Princess," Bish said.

A man in a green guard's uniform appeared at the door without knocking. "Princess Nazira..." he started to say.

"You have been ordered to take me against my will before my father," Nazira told him.

"Just so, and all of your people," the guard replied.

"Then we must obey," Nazira acknowledged with all the haughty dignity she could muster.

The Dominar's Presence Room always disgusted Nazira. Her grandfather had low tastes, with burning braziers dressed in horrid, twisted visages, spewing terrible acrid smoke; suits of ancient armor dressed with iron cod pieces, holding crooked pikestaffs; with gold and red washed recliners for the nobles. The Life Guards were assembled in strength, resplendent in their yellow and green uniforms, a clear sign that the Dominar was worried over this meeting. At their head was Chief Justicar Colonel Abrams Taffez, standing with his talwar drawn, looking strangely detached, his eyes glancing to the genuflection bench, where Petrovson and al-Cinci, two of the Dominar's murderous dungeon masters, stood. Nazira and her entourage were pushed into the center of the Presence Chamber to stand at the genuflection bench, pikes at their backs.

Domingus bar Calad, one of the priests of the Dominion, stood then struck his Staff on the ground, causing a loud crack that silenced the room. "Dominar Abelard 'Arba'a 'Aashar', King of the Cyclonidees, Lord Cycus, Admiral of the Camellia Fleet, may the gods have mercy on each of you," he announced.

The Dominar of Cycus marched in with a coterie of Life Guards, then stood, looking first at Chief Justicar Abrams Taffez, then at the crowded room. He ignored his daughter and her entourage in the middle of the great throne room.

He instead walked slowly along the spectator's gallery where the power brokers of the Dominion were present. There was a frisson of rage in his walk, causing the spectators to be fearful while trying to maintain the required partial eye contact. Look the Dominar in the eyes, you could end up in the gelding rack. Look too far away, a Life Guard could take it as dismissal, striking the hapless audience member a butt stroke to the face with their firelocks in reply.

He turned at the end of the audience line, looking over his Life Guards. They always looked like delicate candies, the three regiments of them, the first in silvery yellow-and-green satin uniforms with greened breast plates, while the second regiment wore orange-and-yellow striped particolored swallow-tail coats with green and yellow pants. His own current bodyguard was from the third regiment, dressed in satin-black with a green-and-yellow stripe. Only twelve stood with him, the other ninety-one were preparing for the putsch. "Taffez," he said.

Taffez struck to attention, while his battalion sergeant yelled, "Brigades!"

The Dominar walked up to Chief Justicar, commanding him, "Extended order if you please, Abrams."

Taffez nodded, as his sergeant barked the follow-up to his first yell, "Attend the monarch, extended order left and right."

It was an impressive display, the Dominar thought. While the third regiment were only a body detail, not participating in the pomp of court, the two main regiments, which were called the Life Battalion when together, extended out to the edges of the room aggressively, with icy precision, taking up the ordered positions. It was not lost on the audience that the soldiers did this with precision without further talk except for turn and wheel commands from the regiments' corporals. The candy-wrapper soldiers took on a sinister visage in the hall as they moved into stiff poses of attention, their firelocks held at extended presentation. As the last of the soldiers hit their appointed mark, Taffez yelled, "Order for detail, odds and evens." The regiment sergeants drew silver whistles and played two dissonant wails, causing half the soldiers to shoulder arms, then take up talwars with flashing waves, while the other half-checked their arms. Then, as if each man and woman was an automaton, the fury of death steel ended with odd rankers at order arms with their firelocks, the even rankers holding their talwars on their shoulders.

The silence was deafening.

"Is my daughter here, Abrams?" the Dominar asked.

"You know I am, Father," Nazira replied defiantly, but was ignored.

Taffez stepped forward, stating, "Your daughter and her liege folk are present."

"Have the dungeon masters secure her before me," the Dominar said with a wave, pointing to the open area in the middle of the Presence Chamber.

Petrovson and al-Cinci, dressed in black, hung with chains and small knives, prepared to carry out their trade even in the Presence Chamber, stood from their seats on the genuflecting bench, then approached Nazira. Bish and Oban tried to push their bodies in front of the Princess, Oban clumsily while Bish was smooth and deadly to purpose; however, Nazira put her hands on their shoulders. "Stay with Kylde and Reggira. They are young and must understand."

Oban turned, looking confused, while Bish nodded. "We obey, Princess. Even in this."

Oban looked at Petrovson and al-Cinci, looking about to resist, finally wilting. Petrovson laughed at him, "Fat men with no balls should not pretend to have a hand in things." Then the dungeon masters grabbed up Nazira, roughly dragging her to a point where the floor concealed eye hooks. Into the hooks she was chained, a small lock set into place.

The Dominar watched the shackling of his daughter, finally feeling safe enough to walk to the throne which was towering over her. He climbed to his dais, falling into his seat, waving his hands, accepting a demitasse of tea. He drank the absurdly small cup with his big clumsy hands, swordsman hands, the hands of a bully who knew nothing but how to swing and defile. His daughter, he thought, was cut from such wrong cloth. He laughed out loud. "If only you had been male rather than silk, you could have ruled by my side, daughter."

Nazira tugged at her chains, then looked up at her father. She said nothing, but her hate suddenly slipped from wherever she kept it, blazing bright under her dark brows and curly hair.

"No matter, daughter, you did what you were destined to do. You gave me an heir that the priest Domingus says is vouchsafed to reach adulthood. Your role in the court has become extraneous, to use a word that the priest says is appropriate." He drank his tea in one gulp, then threw the fragile glass at Nazira, striking her in the forehead. She made no effort to duck it, receiving a nasty gash just below her hairline.

"What is the form priest?" the Dominar asked.

Domingus bar Calad removed his fez, then used a satin rag to wipe perspiration from his head. He then stepped to the center of the room next to where Nazira was chained. "Dominar, she is of royal blood. The Code is clear that you must announce her crime and her attainder, then there has to be assent from the council."

The Dominar looked at the crowd of cowed nobles. "Do we have enough members of the Quorna? Be right about this, I want to have her done, and not attacking me from the afterlife because some umlaut was dropped from a word."

Domingus bowed. "There are only a few passages on the matter of executing an heir. It is actually quite simple. You announce the charge, she responds, the council votes in Quorna through objection. Then the sentence is carried out. There will be no objections."

Nazira looked at the cluster of court followers, the richest, most powerful men and women in the Dominion, standing dutifully in their assigned spot where they would congregate during important sessions, saying, "The ones who would object are dead or hiding."

The priest walked quietly to her, glanced at the crowd in the viewing stands, then at the two dungeon masters looming over Nazira. He bent down to the Dominar's daughter, whispering, "You should be silent dear. You really should think not of the length of your life, but of the quality remaining to you. You can die rapidly, walk into the deep night, or you could end screaming, a spectacle. No?"

There was a second as Nazira looked at the priest, feeling his heart, knowing the man was scared; what was more, he saw that she knew. She looked back at her father, then to the crowd, then to the dungeon masters. Staring at Petrovson, sire of her grandfather's insane and murderous master of torture, she acknowledged to herself that indeed the man was just as cold, just as horrible as his father or hers, for that matter. She absolutely knew Domingus was telling nothing less than the truth he saw. Her gaze went back to her father, ignoring his puppet Domingus, telling him, "Then have your show and be done. I am not scared of you, father. If the rule of law is your whim and not a stout shield covering us all, then what use to have a daughter once you have my child?"

Domingus stepped away from Nazira, then walked over to her coterie, standing in a group with a dozen soldiers at their shoulders. He looked at Oban, then at Bish, asking Bish, "Regnal Bish al-Beijus, as a master of the guild, you are in the wrong crowd, are you not?"

Bish looked off into the distance. With his eyes, it was difficult to say if he was being aloof, or if that was where he needed to look in order to center his vision on Domingus. Instead of answering, he made a small gesture with his hand, a dismissive movement of his arm that was a little like shooing a fly. Domingus looked vexed, saying in a stout and penetrating voice, "Your guild cannot intimidate the court, Regnal. If you stand here with the servants of the Princess, you will die with the Princess. You will be long dead before the Masters are able to protest."

Bish stepped forward, flicking his hand suddenly. The soldiers around him tensed, even unarmed and in the middle of a group of old men and children, they knew the assassin was deadly, but he merely took a small red square of cloth out then slowly, infuriatingly, moved it to the priest's head, rubbing the perspiration that was running down his cheek from under his fez. The action was cold and calculated. The Domingus seemed riveted in place, unable to protest the invasion of his personal space by the deadly killer.

Retrieving his wits, the Domingus grabbed the cloth square from Bish's hands, pulled his sweat-soaked fez from his head, then used the small rag to wipe clear his perspiration again in savage wipes. Finished, he threw the red cloth to the ground, then said, "So be it, assassin. Your guild cannot cry that you were given no chance to separate yourself from the Princess. You will stand and fall with her."

With preternatural care, Bish let a silky smile sketch his face, replying, "I accept that I stand or fall with the heir of the Dominion."

Domingus shrugged. He turned, walked to the side of the Dominar, then announced, "Dominar Abelard 'Arba'a 'Aashar', myself as magistrate, priest of the Byronia Faith, second priest of the Dominion, declare that before you is Nazira al-Youseffi, designated 'am alshaeb', who has pretended to be muta-Rasheed. With neither consent nor permission, she vouchsafed a contract to a man of ill repute. Then, with said man, broke the laws and the world of the Dominar of this land." He paused, then asked, "Dominar, do you accept these charges?"

The Dominar replied, "These charges are just and right to publish here."

Domingus turned to Nazira to say, "You may respond."

Nazira stood tall, letting her chains settle in her hands. "I am a free woman of the Dominion, and may marry whom I chose. That is what I say."

"Dominar, it is your response," Domingus stated, turning to the scowling dictator. Domingus was no longer sweating, though he had turned a cherry red with his exertions of speech.

Dominar Abelard stood from his throne-chair. "Everyone in my court is to listen to this. This is my testimony before I take the life of my daughter. I have made mistakes. I took Nazira's mother on advice of council but against my own judgement; she left me and the child five years later. I looked to the child, and I loved her. Her mother, though, demanded that my father change some of his acts, acts that we now call inhuman, but which then saved our reign and our nation. We may not speak of it, but it happened. The products of this horror were kept to an island, left to be or do as they may."

"My daughter did not just marry a commoner. She did not just marry a person forbidden her, but against my orders she married one of the secret folk, the broken ones who must be kept from us. Those who I wrongly agreed, in my love for my wife and my daughter, to permit to live their lives away from us once the use of the island was at an end. How he escaped the island, how he made it into polite society, and how he became a child of the Rasheed clan, we do not know." The Dominar stopped, looked for a second at Nazira, then continued. "When I found out, I told her that. She would end the affair, and I would return the man safely to the island for him to live as he would without harm. She refused, he refused, and they had a child."

The Dominar swept down off his throne, thundering in anger. "The fact al-Rasheed was a drunk, a liar, a killer, and a thief, that was only part of the ban on marriage! He is a changed one, therefore, he cannot be the father of the heir to my Dominion. Yet the child came. I named him Jamil al-Youseffi d'Tariq and styled him the Prince of Telemark, and embraced the youth as my true heir, the one who will someday follow after me as the ruler of this land."

The Dominar's speech was distracted by shooting in the distance. "Hear that, Nazira, it need not have happened." The Dominar strode to the windows in the Presence Chamber, then said, "Four-thousand will die tonight. Your partisans Nazira, they die. Your followers, they die. The scholar who you spoke with on the fall of the Guisarmes, he dies. All of the hidden ones on that damn island will die. The crew of that merchant you forced on me, and the bankers who loaned you the money against your inheritance, they will all die. It is you who killed them, Nazira. You touched this off as if you have your fingers in each trigger well of all of the fire-locks that are triggered tonight. Each dagger plunged into a pleading heart, each person who dies begging for another minute of life, dies with your hands on the blade that opens their bodies. The gods curse you, my daughter, and prove my love was weakness, not strength." His voice slurred the words, and he hesitated often, but he knew that no one would point it out. Or they would die as well.

Domingus seemed to be getting more excited as the Dominar spoke, then, as the dictator paused, he clutched his throat and yelled, pitching over forward, whimpering and kicking as if possessed by some strange miasma. The Dominar looked down at the priest, then at the Life Guard. He saw two people streaking from the cluster of Nazira's followers detained by guardsmen. Two of the guardsmen were down, while another was being broken by the rapid attack of the assassin Bish. However, it was the two rapidly moving figures, a small girl and a large obese man, that carried the Dominar's attention. The obese man reached Nazira, then, with his bare hands and oblivious of pain, broke her chains, then wrapped his immense body around her. The small girl he saw kept running right at him. He returned quickly to his throne, pulled out the knife he kept hidden in the arm, pushing it forward, it feeling as he connected with the small child. She looked at him with vacant eyes, then he felt a splash of liquid, and then he could feel no more. Not for a long time, at least.

If the crowd was curious at the yell from the priest, interested in the fat man who enfolded the Princess, unaware that a small girl had splashed some sort of liquid on the Dominar having been stabbed in doing so, then the next second resolved themselves as terror came to them in the form of gunfire. From the three main doors into the Presence Chamber, sailors in uniform with firelocks drove in as a group. Instead of lighting them, the Life Battalion divided itself, then started battling each other. Many of the Battalion had donned red and blue sashes, turning on their brethren in all three regiments, leading to a massive blood-letting. Struggling men and women were taking and giving lives in a mass of chaotic and uncontrolled struggles. In the midst of the sailors, a huge woman in silvered armor fired from matching short firelocks. When she could not reload, she treated them each like clubs. Fighters yelled, "Dominar, Dominar!" Others screamed, "Princess, Princess!" The sailors yelled, "*Remarker!*"

It was into this scrum that another force entered. A dozen ghostly pale beings in green and gray ragged cloth nets, wearing them as if they were fish who had broken from a fishing ground, taking the tools which have taken them captive as clothing, entered. These pale beings took aim at Life Guards who were not wearing the sashes. The new fighters darted about like blurs, stabbing and killing, or else they used their sheer bulk to overwhelm profes-sional soldiers, pulling their firelocks from their hands, then smashing them about like clubs.

Then it was over. A crowd of defeated soldiers stood in a tightly packed circle, while the nobles of the Dominion stood in their corral, facing the gray faces of horrible beings whose scars, swollen muscles, and bent shapes seemed to be an image from hell. Nazira emerged from the grasp of the man who held her, looking sadly at the giant. He was dead, as was Oban, who had embraced the giant as if brothers, defending her from the shots of snipers ordered to kill her if anything happened. She stood in the carnage, starting to cry, stopping only when Bish came to her side. "Kylde, Oban, and Reggira knew what they sacrificed," Bish reminded her.

Major Standish approached, as did one of the Marine officers and a number of the loyal Life Guard. Nazira soon realized she was the center of a widely growing circle of fol-lowers. Major Standish said, "We have carried all before us. You are the Dominar now."

Nazira nodded. "My father is dead?" she asked.

Bish placed his hand on her shoulder. "No, he lives. He will awake blind, mute, and for some days will have terrible dreams. He yet lives though."

Nazira rose up, feeling tiny in stature, although strong in authority. "Summon Mistress Silence to take my father. He is hers now. She is to have the island she was exiled to, and all who were interned there may, as my mother wished, remain their entire lives. However, they may also enter our Dominion and live free. This is my first order."

There was a shuffling of feet, to which Standish said loudly, "Yes, Dominar!" When no one else said it, she repeated the acknowledgment, with more than half the people in the room picking up the words this time.

Nazira said, "My second order, bring peace to the streets. My third order, bring all who need to the healers. There will be no revenge, not until those who are accused are brought before me."

She turned, looking right at Bish. "Jamil is safe?"

Bish said, "Your child is in hiding with your husband, who remains without movement or mentation."

"Then take me to them," Nazira said.

Chapter XVI

Setting Sail on the Sunset Tide

Javier was as if asleep, except his eyes were open and he blinked as if conscious. Mistress Silence sat next to him with a small, wiry boy and an equally young girl. The girl was silent as Nazira walked into the room. However, the boy said, "My Dominar, I am Mouse. Can I serve you?"

"Young Mouse, your captain has written of you. Why are you here?" she asked.

Mouse stood. "The crew, we won't leave the captain alone. No one knows what is happening or how this affects us all, yet we all agree that the captain deserves better than to be killed in his bed. Not when any of us live."

Nazira walked up and touched Mouse and the silent girl who sat next to him each on the cheek. They were both dressed in crew uniforms. "You need not fear, yet need not drop your guard. May I have the room with my husband and Mistress Silence?"

Mouse looked at his compatriot, nodded, and they left quietly.

Nazira sat down in the vacated chair, looking at Javier. His face was normally so mobile that it was a shock to see it gone waxy, plastic, dead. The blinking eyes did not help matters, as there was nothing behind them. "You have secrets to tell, Mistress Silence. Shall I ask as the daughter of my mother, or ask as the ruler of this realm?"

"You may ask as either, Dominar, the answer will be the same. There are no secrets, you can know all I know," Mistress Silence replied, taking the other seat, pulling her long, gray hair in front of her.

"I am not Dominar," Nazira said.

"Abdication?" Mistress Silence asked, shocked.

"Renewal," Nazira corrected her. "My concern for Javier is not simply to put a piece on the game board again. He and I fell in love over a dream. A dream of a world where law and knowledge connected the islands. Where we were not as straw thrown onto a tile floor, vulnerable to the broom of a servant, but were clustered, each reed separate, yet bound as one."

Mistress Silence sat back with the enormity of the concept. She looked over at the comatose man, saying, "I knew your mother and her high mind. I know you are more her daughter than you could imagine."

"My mother is a person who I remember only in dreams. She left me. I now have my sisters, the two women she sent with Javier to serve in my court, even to supplant me if needed, yet I do not know if the move was hostile or kindness." Nazira looked at Javier again. "Does he drink, or will he die from want?"

"He drinks. He may take food. My healer will tend him as long as can be done. If he keeps taking water and food, he may live years looking at that same spot in the ceiling," Mistress Silence replied. "As for your mother, do not judge her too harshly. I knew her, met her as I fled for my life from your grandfather's pogrom. My mother before me, as well as my aunt, were Silence, both died for it. Perhaps I was lucky..."

"Continue," Nazira said.

"When your grandfather took the throne from the Guisarmes, he declared that the Kingdom was subsumed into the Dominion, demanding that all of the priests bend their knees. My mother and aunt, I will never know why they would not. I was born in hiding, fleeing from village to village, hid by followers. Your grandfather killed my aunt and my mother. I was too young to understand why they resisted him. Then I was caught and sent to the island." She paused, then looked with watery eyes at Nazira.

"What does the island really mean? I now have my mother's accounts. They are confused, bitter, filled with hateful rhetoric instead of what I want to know. My husband is from the island. I know you know what that means." Nazira looked about her, seeing a delicate crystal cup with water in it on a stand by Javier's bed. She picked it up and carefully cradled his head in her arms, which allowed her to give him a portion. He drank without expression. "Make gruel from fruit, barley flour, ground beans, dried brassica, and lemon. That is thick enough to be valuable, yet thin enough to be fed to him."

"You have a good sense, my princess," Mistress Silence said.

"It is what they feed sailors who are brought to shore starving. Now tell me of the island and my husband."

Mistress Silence bent her head. "The Island was where captives of the families who had opposed Abelard's father were taken, where they were subjected to ... experiments imply they were looking to learn something. Cruelties, indignation, horrors, tortures all describe it better. The master of the prison, for that was what it was, had only two orders. Make each suffer and keep each alive. Their purpose was terrible enough, very simple. Each of the families who opposed the dominars and the new Dominion knew that their loved ones were in hell and that they could themselves go there. They obeyed."

She looked at a painting on the wall, one of a deer in a glen. Then she locked eyes with Nazira. "Javier. He was fishing with his father when they landed on the island after days at sea, lost to a great storm. The guards killed his father, but Javier ran into the woods, saved by myself and others. He was raised by us, but we could not shield him from the horror, the torture, the mind games. Do you take food or give it to someone else? Do you scream? How soon? Do you feed the blinded ones, or protect those whose bodies have been ravaged by abuse, or do you retreat to the caves and hide from the world?" Mistress Silence sighed, then said, "What luck was it that Javier was not on the list? The guards did not know he was on the island. They passed him each day, never even caring that he might be an innocent."

Nazira nodded, asking, "So he escaped and became a Rasheed?"

"Yes, his dead father was a Rasheed. He knew the family. Further, he was broken but broken in a way that was hard to tell in the early days," Mistress Silence explained.

"Devious," Nazira stated. She did not need to guess.

Lady Silence nodded grimly. "His alter ego. He was kind, gave to everyone. He lived to serve, even as a child he was a leader. Devious was different. Devious was his way of staying alive. Devious was not evil, not cruel, just not bothered by the ideals that Javier held. As far as I know, it was only the past year or two that he was troubled by the two sides of his being competing with each other."

"It was marrying me, as he could not be Devious in front of me. It must have led to his breaking in the end," Nazira postulated.

Mistress Silence stood, embraced Nazira, Dominar in all but name of a great nation. Nazira teared up, but Mistress Silence reminded her, "He was broken before he met you, and it was destroying him then. The drinking and dissoluteness were not him. It was medication. Someday he had to heal or break for good. This may be how he was always meant to die, having retreated from this world into his own head."

Nazira nodded; her head buried in the older woman's arms. "My mother?" she asked.

"The story of your mother comes before that," Silence replied. "The island was worse before … when the old man lived. Your father married a woman from an exotic land, out of love, I believe. At some point, he must have told her about the island. That was the end for her. She demanded that the island be cleaned up. She threatened Abelard, insisting that he persuade your grandfather to free the captives. Abelard made a deal with her. When he took power, the tortures would stop, and they would be freed. Yet your grandfather banished your mother. Your caretaker Oban was brought from the island to satisfy your father. When your grandfather died in your thirteenth year, the torture stopped, yet Abelard would not release the captives. A few escaped over time; Javier was one. What stopped your father was his belief that the islanders were dangerous. Deadly even."

"Thus, the island is today as it is?" Nazira asked. "A guilty secret, my father's legacy of pain."

Mistress Silence did not respond. Nazira stood, shrugging herself from Mistress Silence's embrace. Mistress Silence was wise. Unfortunately, she was also narrow-minded. She had been in a play living a part for so long, she could not flip the script to see the world in any way other than she now did. That was why she had to leave. "Mistress Silence, you are deeded the island. You are the leader of the people. My intention is to allow all of them to live with us in the new world we are building. We will discuss these matters later. Now leave me and my husband."

Mistress Silence gazed long at Javier, then turned to take a pillow from a small stack. "I have thought long about this. I feel I am too weak. I know what you want to do. This pillow is all you will need. Know that you cannot stop until four minutes after he quits struggling. You cannot. If he resumes breathing, he will not just be a lost soul, he will also be a vessel that no longer thinks. I will tell everyone that he was fading as we spoke, that his death was expected." Mistress Silence handed the soft pillow to Nazira and left the room.

Nazira held the pillow as she looked at the face of her husband and friend. "Oh, Mistress Silence, how little you know." She dropped the pillow, moving closer to Javier.

"Javier," she said softly into his ear. "I married you, not knowing of your brother hidden inside of you. If you want to be him, then this is who I married. If you want to be Javier, then that is who I married. If you want to be someone else, anyone else, speak to me, knowing we will be married as partners to save this world. I swear."

Javier started to move. He blinked a few times, rolled onto his side, then stared into her eyes. "I want to be a tea merchant, a captain."

Nazira nodded. "You can be all that, as well as a father and a friend."

Javier sat up and embraced his princess.

Book Club Questions

1. How does Nazira see her husband, Javier?

2. Why did she send Standish with Javier?

3. How do the characters of Devious and Javier compare and contrast?

4. How does Mouse integrate with the crew?

5. How does the crew of the *Remarker* handle bullies?

6. How does tea serve as a social lubricant?

7. Why do you think the crew fears metal?

8. What is an apostolical person saying to their community

9. What is an el dari person saying to their community?

10. Why does the crew support Nazira in the revolution?

11. What is the Island of Silence and how does Mistress Silence fit into the story?

12. What do you think the nature of Javier's ailment is?

About the Author

Nelson McKeeby is a native of Iowa, born near Spirit Lake to a Navy Officer and his teacher wife. Placed in classes for slow learners at a young age, he was never able to make education work and left school by age sixteen. He immediately landed a job as one of the country's youngest live-air television directors and professional television writers, a career he has maintained since then. Nelson is neurodiverse with both autism and severe epilepsy. A long-time hitchhiker who often uses his experiences in his writing, he has also served with the Department of Justice and as a deputy sheriff.

Nelson is known for non-fiction writing about insider politics, law enforcement, the entertainment industry, and the Quaker faith. He splits his time between La Habra, California and Iowa, living with a Brazilian doctor of biology and nurse, and four cats in a multilingual household.